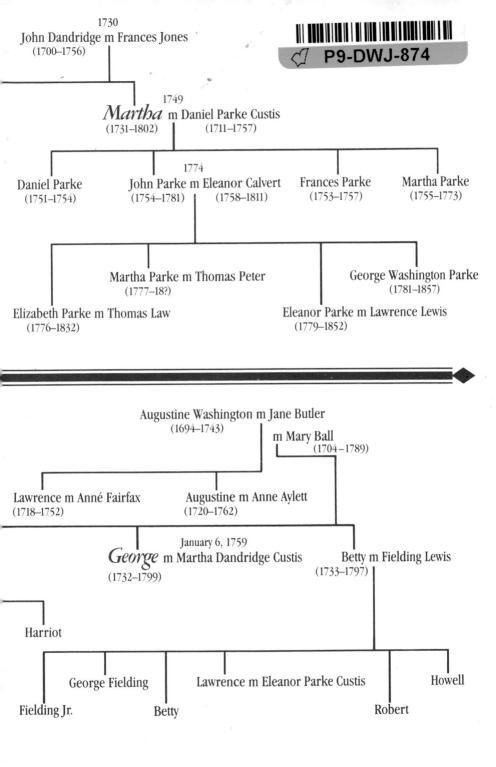

1730
John Dandridge m Frances Jones
(1700–1756)

1749
Martha m Daniel Parke Custis
(1731–1802)   (1711–1757)

Daniel Parke
(1751–1754)

1774
John Parke m Eleanor Calvert
(1754–1781)   (1758–1811)

Frances Parke
(1753–1757)

Martha Parke
(1755–1773)

Martha Parke m Thomas Peter
(1777–18?)

George Washington Parke
(1781–1857)

Elizabeth Parke m Thomas Law
(1776–1832)

Eleanor Parke m Lawrence Lewis
(1779–1852)

Augustine Washington m Jane Butler
(1694–1743)

m Mary Ball
(1704–1789)

Lawrence m Anné Fairfax
(1718–1752)

Augustine m Anne Aylett
(1720–1762)

January 6, 1759
George m Martha Dandridge Custis
(1732–1799)

Betty m Fielding Lewis
(1733–1797)

Harriot

George Fielding

Lawrence m Eleanor Parke Custis

Howell

Fielding Jr.

Betty

Robert

Lady Washington

Books by Dorothy Clarke Wilson

LADY WASHINGTON

I WILL BE A DOCTOR

LINCOLN'S MOTHERS

APOSTLE OF SIGHT

GRANNY BRAND

CLIMB EVERY MOUNTAIN

STRANGER AND TRAVELER

BRIGHT EYES

HILARY

THE BIG-LITTLE WORLD OF DOC PRITHAM

LONE WOMAN

PALACE OF HEALING

HANDICAP RACE

TEN FINGERS FOR GOD

THE THREE GIFTS

TAKE MY HANDS

THE JOURNEY

DR. IDA

THE GIFTS

JEZEBEL

HOUSE OF EARTH

PRINCE OF EGYPT

THE HERDSMAN

THE BROTHER

Lady
Washington

Dorothy Clarke Wilson

DOUBLEDAY & COMPANY, INC.
GARDEN CITY, NEW YORK
1984

Library of Congress Cataloging in Publication Data
Wilson, Dorothy Clarke
    Lady Washington: the story of America's first First Lady.
    Bibliography: p. 373
    1. Washington, Martha, 1731–1802—Fiction. I. Title
PS3545.I6235L3   1984   813'.52
ISBN 0-385-18033-0
Library of Congress Catalog Card Number 82–45342

ACKNOWLEDGMENTS

The author wishes to make grateful acknowledgment:

To the Mount Vernon Ladies' Association of the Union for generously providing entertainment on the estate during a period of intensive research;

To the Mount Vernon Librarian, Mrs. Ellen McAllister Clark, the archivist, Mr. John Rodehamel, and other members of the Mount Vernon staff for making all their facilities and materials available for study;

To the Library of the University of Maine for making possible the use of their extensive Washington collection for long weeks at a time and for securing innumerable books and publications from other parts of the country.

Lady Washington

1

"Stand still, child! How can Miss Nancy fit your gown if you prance about like a skittish horse?"

"I'm sorry, Mama. But—I feel like I'm bursting! You've laced me so tight I can hardly breathe."

"I know, dear. You'll get used to it in time. It's the price we have to pay for being women."

"But I'm not a woman—not yet. Didn't you just call me *child?*"

"You're almost fifteen, child—I mean, Patsy, dear. Many young women are already married, and mothers, at your age. Now please hold still, just a few minutes longer."

Martha Dandridge, usually called "Patsy" by her family, gritted her teeth and strained her muscles taut. A skittish horse? That was exactly what she felt like, a wild colt suddenly burdened with bit and saddle. Grimly she applied a tight rein to her restlessness and managed to stand still.

The ordeal was over at last. Miss Nancy West, the traveling seamstress who was at Chestnut Grove for a week's work, put in her last pin. Frances Dandridge stepped back and regarded her oldest daughter with critical appraisal, her eyes lighting with surprised approval. Just so the fabled mother duck might have looked on discovering that her ugly duckling had turned into a swan.

"Good! I shouldn't say it, Patsy, it might make you vain, but you're really beautiful. Come and look at yourself."

Reluctantly, impatient for release, Martha let Mama lead her to the long gilt-framed mirror which had come with the last shipment of luxuries from London. Then she stood staring. This must be some stranger, not plain little Martha Dandridge, short of stature, inclined to plumpness, despair of mother, aunts, disapproving female cousins—all adults but Papa—for being such a tomboy! This creature, swathed in billowing clouds of pink silk and brocade, incredibly slender of waist, stiff bodice molded to the roundness of budding breasts, even the ordinary brown hair and hazel eyes ashimmer with highlights—why, she looked actually tall, yes, even beautiful, with all the poise and dignity of a woman! But she didn't want to be a woman, not yet. Swiftly she turned away from the mirror, and the vision faded.

"You'll be one of the prettiest debutantes at the Assembly Ball," said Frances Dandridge with satisfaction. "Papa and I will be proud of you."

Back in everyday garments—full homespun skirt but no hoops, only a stiff petticoat, pack-thread stays under the bodice but not tightly laced, a mobcap of net pulled over her fine light-brown hair—she drew a long breath of relief. At least she could breathe deeply again! But she could not feel really free indoors. If only Mama would not call her for her morning stint of stitchery and her hour of practicing on the spinet, she might steal an hour of riding. That was what she needed most after the stifling prison of hoops and tight lacings and brocades, to move faster than her feet could run, spring scents of new flowers and running sap and wet earth in her nostrils, the April wind warm on her cheeks.

But she could not get out of the house unobserved. "Patsy! Where you going? Can we come too?" It was seven-year-old Anna Maria, usually called Nancy, with their younger sister, Frances, one and a half, holding tightly to her long ruffled skirt.

Martha tried not to show her annoyance. She put a warning finger to her lips. "Shh! Not this time, pet. I'm going riding. But—please, don't let anybody know I'm gone. I promise, we'll take a run down to the wharf later."

There! Release at last. As she ran past the outbuildings and the slave cabins toward the stables, the path took her by the small garden plot which Papa had given her for her own to plant and care for. If there was one thing she took pleasure in more than riding, it was in growing flowers. Were her tulips yet in full bloom? Had her scarlet larkspur budded? She almost stopped to see. But no, not this morning. Now she needed *motion*.

Near the stables three figures came catapulting from the small outbuilding which had been made into a schoolhouse, her brothers joyously released from their morning lessons with the newest tutor, a young man from England whom Papa had recently employed. Before this Martha had always been a part of the school session, Papa insisting that his daughters must be educated in the essentials as well as his sons, but now that she was turning fifteen Mama had other ideas.

"Of course she must know how to read and write and figure. She is quick to learn and knows all those things. But for a woman there are other things more important, Colonel Dandridge. She must know how to run a household, train her servants in skills of spinning, weaving, sewing, cooking; entertain guests with dignity and poise; take her place in society with credit to her family heritage and upbringing."

"In other words," Papa had responded with tongue-in-cheek gravity, "prepare herself for an early and advantageous marriage."

Mama had not been amused. She took her maternal responsibilities seriously and with a strong sense of obligation to her by no means insignificant forebears. Her grandfather, the Reverend Roland Jones, son of another divine of the same name, had graduated from Oxford and, coming to Virginia in 1633, had for fourteen years been rector of the important Bruton Parish in Williamsburg. Her father, Orlando, had been burgess from this county of New Kent, and he had married Martha Macon, daughter of the secretary to Sir William Berkeley, the grandmother for whom Martha had been named.

Also, it had been impressed on Martha, she could be proud of being a Dandridge. Though neither the Joneses nor the Dandridges could be classed among the *very* first families of Virginia, like the Lees, the Masons, the Carys, the Fairfaxes, they at least deserved the appellative of *first*. Colonel John, her father, was not only a planter with a large estate but also clerk of New Kent County, an honorable and lucrative position. With his brother William, who had married a great-great niece of the third Lord Delaware and been on the King's Council, he had a right to display the lion's-head coat of arms of the Dandridges of Great Malvern, Worcestershire, in their native England.

Mama had her way. Martha spent her days now in long hours of sewing, cross, tent, and satin stitch, hem, fell, and overseam; in playing popular tunes on the spinet; in learning all the minuets, quadrilles, and country dances taught by the master who visited many of the plantations in turn, intricate steps with queer names—High Betty Martin, Leather-the-Strap, Allemand Vally's, Priest's House, Innocent Maid. They were no problem for Martha, for she was light of step, pulsing with inner rhythms, though it had taken practice to keep her silk-clad foot so firm, so straight that not a crease or wrinkle would appear in her quilted petticoat.

The boys came hurtling toward her, twelve-year-old William, always the most eager to end the study period, in the lead.

"Lucky for you!" he greeted Martha with boisterous glee. "What do you s'pose the master made us do today? Spelling!"

Martha made a wry face. That old "Dilworth Speller"! How she had hated it! And the Primer too, with its alphabet all set in rhymes from A ("In Adam's fall,/We sinned all") to Z ("Zacchaeus he/Did climb a tree/His Lord to see"). The rhymes had been easy to remember, like the prayers for morning and evening. "Now I lay me down to sleep . . ." Every night for years she had repeated it. But, oh, those five- and six-syllable words! She could pronounce them glibly by rote—abomination, edification, humiliation, mortification, purification, and all the rest. But when it came to spelling them! Spelling had always been her nemesis. She was bound to put an "e" on such words as "do," "no," "go." And why on earth should you write "been" instead of "bin," or "they" instead of "tha"?

"I've begun to learn Latin," announced Bartholomew, who, though only nine, gave promise of becoming the student of the family. "I can already decline five nouns, Patsy. Want to hear me?"

"No!" John, the oldest of the three and at fourteen the most assertive, nipped this scholarly enthusiasm in the bud. "We're going riding. Want to come, Patsy?"

Martha certainly did. Riding was the one thing she needed most, together with the comforting assurance that she still belonged to this world of her childhood. "Race you to the stables!" She and John arrived neck and neck, the other two not far behind.

It was only then she remembered that her own horse, Graylegs, had lamed a foreleg a few days before and must not be ridden. True, there were others available. Papa kept a well-stocked stable. But none of them seemed to fit her present mood, satisfy her desire for bold, per-

haps even a bit reckless motion. Unless . . . Her eyes gleamed. There
was that new young roan that Papa had just bought, so new that he had
not even been given a name. No one on the plantation had ridden him
as yet, but it was time someone did.

"I dunno, child." Joshua, the head groom, wagged his head, his
round black face troubled. "Massa, I feared he might not like it, and he
ain't here to ask, gone to far fields. Thet thar hoss he terrible proud of,
and he's not been rid yet. Mebbe yo pa wants to try him fust."

"Nonsense, Joshua. You know I'm a good rider, and Papa knows it
too. I'm sure he wouldn't mind."

She smiled to herself, remembering a certain incident of a few years
before. The family had been visiting Uncle William, Papa's fascinating
brother, whose plantation had been just across the Pamunkey River.
They had crossed at Williams's Ferry, taking both the carriage and
several horses. Martha, as usual, had ridden Graylegs. Uncle William's
mansion had wide shallow steps leading to a broad veranda. On arriving
Martha had found the long flight of steps too tempting. Flicking her
little whip smartly on Graylegs's flank, she had ridden her little horse
straight up the steps and onto the porch, prancing its full length several
times before riding him down again.

"Patsy Dandridge!" Mama had been shocked almost speechless.
"You—you—How dare you do such an unladylike thing! You must be
punished!"

Papa had only laughed. "No, no, let her alone. She hasn't hurt William's steps, or his veranda. And, by heaven, how she can ride!"

Now she had her way. Joshua, like most of the servants, was more
indulgent even than Papa. Her new silk-plush riding saddle was
brought from the stable and put on the roan's back. Deftly she swung
herself up, disdaining Joshua's outstretched hand. What a nuisance,
she thought, that she could not ride astride, like her brothers, their
tightly breeched limbs unconfined by billowing skirts! But there was
one consolation. It must take greater skill to jump fences, leap ditches,
ford streams, and all the rest, when riding side-saddle!

"Where shall we go?" Even John, just a year younger, was used to
deferring to her superior age—or was it to her more imaginative talents? "Down to the river?"

It was one of their favorite haunts, the shore of the Pamunkey,
which was a virtual thoroughfare for the plantations along this branch

of the York River. Here to Papa's landing came the crafts of visiting neighbors or of tobacco freighters, or, far more exciting, an occasional ship from London bringing merchandise which Papa had ordered, furniture, clothing, books for the boys, saddles, bridles, such luxuries as perfumed powder, hairpins, pickles, salt, raisins, tea. But one such ship had just come up the river, bringing in its largesse the silks and brocades and ribbons and laces and other doodads which Mama and Miss Nancy were fussing over. No, not the river. Nothing to do there but sit and watch fishing boats or barge-loads of tobacco, for it was too early in the day for pleasure craft from the many plantations. Besides, she wanted *motion*. Though there were miles of bridle paths traversing the thousand and more acres of Papa's plantation, at the moment they held no attraction. Was she a bit wary of meeting Papa on one of them, suspicious that he might not look with indulgence on this appropriation of his new prize horse?

"Let's ride on the road," she suggested recklessly.

"Yes, let's!" This from William, the most adventurous of the three boys.

"Should we?" John, always the most cautious, looked doubtful. "You know Papa likes to be with us when we go outside the grounds."

Again Martha had her way. Papa, she knew, might frown at first, but his displeasure was always short-lived, especially with her, his firstborn. Mama was the disciplinarian. Besides, if they just took a short run on the road, he might never know. They would be back long before three o'clock dinner.

She felt immediate rapport with the roan. Like herself, the horse was rebelling against confinement and keyed to seek freedom in motion. She had to keep a tight curb on the rein to hold him in check. Resting her free hand against the smooth tawny flank, she could feel the quivering urgency, and once out on the road she relaxed her tight grip. They shot ahead, and the boys had to apply their short whips to keep up.

"Not so fast!" shouted John. "That's a new mount you've got, remember? He's not your old Graylegs."

Reluctantly Martha slowed the roan to a canter, the letdown somewhat assuaged by the swiftness with which he responded to her touch. Perhaps Papa would give her this wonderful horse for her own if she could show him how well they were matched. Graylegs was indeed getting old. What would she name this beauty if he were hers? Lightning? No. Something steadier than a brief flash. Smoothness. Redness. Foxglove. That was it! He was red like a fox and smooth like a velvet glove.

Lessening speed had been wise, for the road in this spring season was a shambles of stony hummocks, ruts, and mud. The main thoroughfare for the planters on this south side of the Pamunkey was the river, but once the land had dried and the road been dragged fairly smooth, wagons, carriages, and even fancy chariots would be vying with the river craft.

"We'd better go back," urged John when they reached New Kent Court House and Martha showed no sign of stopping. She might not have heard. Once the settlement was passed the road plunged into woods, revealing at every turn a fresh vista of riotous blossoming trees and shrubs, pink and white dogwood, redbuds bursting into great masses of rosy pink, creamy white magnolias. It was a world of new life and running sap, akin to the warm flow of blood through her own youthful veins. She yielded herself to its magic, forgetting even to hold a firm grip on the reins. Wanting to feel more a part of it, she undid the strings of her cap and pushed it back, letting her soft brown hair flow loose about her shoulders.

Suddenly there was a sound of pounding hoofs, and a horseman rounded a curve in the road. Martha felt a swift tensing in the horse-flesh beneath her as the roan stopped short, then upreared in quivering terror. Unprepared for such an emergency and accustomed to Graylegs's sturdy acceptance of unforeseen action, she tried too late to curb his fright. Off she went, flying through the air and landing, fortunately, not on hard earth or rocks, but in a mud puddle.

The three boys riding behind, shocked and horrified, spurred toward her, but the horseman who had caused the mishap was there first.

"I say, I'm so sorry. I was riding too fast and frightened your horse. Are you hurt, child?"

Martha looked up into a strange face, dark eyes alight with kindliness and concern. She felt strong arms lifting her, setting her on her feet.

"No, thank you. I'm not hurt." She tried to sound grown-up and dignified, a difficult business with clothes bedraggled, face mud-streaked, hair, which should have been neatly imprisoned in a cap, flying in all directions. She was hurt, yes, but in pride, not body. She, the expert horsewoman, permitting herself to be thrown, even though by an animal with unsuspected nervous tremors! The roan was pliant enough now, standing meekly while William held his halter and Bartholomew soothingly stroked his neck. Martha felt shamed in the presence of her brothers and this stranger.

But—was he a stranger? On more careful scrutiny she thought he looked vaguely familiar. Yet she knew all the members of the families whose plantations skirted the south shore of the Pamunkey—Symes, Webbs, Chamberlaynes, Macons, Daingerfields, Bassetts, Rootes, Gooches, and others. Their boats were often docked at the Dandridge wharf, bringing visitors to hunt in Dandridge fields, feast at the Dandridge table, even sleep in Dandridge beds. Who was he? A mature man, probably in his thirties, not exactly handsome, rather full of figure, but with a kindly, open countenance, the severity of heavy dark brows belied by twinkling eyes and generous smiling lips. Taking a clean silk handkerchief from his waistcoat pocket, he gently wiped the mud from her face.

"Your horse seems to be quieted now. Is your home near here, child?"

"Just a few miles back," volunteered John. "We're Dandridges, Colonel John Dandridge's children."

The man nodded, a sudden gleam in his eyes. "Fine. I know your father well. We'll take your sister home, shall we not? I'll ride along beside her, just to be sure she has no further trouble with her horse."

"But—I'm quite capable—"

Before Martha could protest further, she felt herself being lifted again by the same strong arms and placed in the saddle. Dismayed, she saw that mud from her full skirt had stained the man's spotless white embroidered waistcoat.

"No matter," he insisted, smiling, noting her agonized glance. "After all, child, it was my clumsy horse that caused all the damage. And—it isn't the first time I've run the risk of your soiling my clothes."

Martha gasped. She stared at him, wide-eyed. "What—who—"

"You don't remember me, do you, child? No wonder! You were not much more than a baby when I used to dandle you on my knee. And a very sweet little cherub you were, Patsy."

"You—you know my name?"

He smiled mischievously. "I ought to. At least I should know the name Martha. I was there when it was given you."

"You—you were?" Martha was completely bewildered.

But he did not explain further. Mounting his horse, he rode by her side, the three boys bringing up the rear. When they arrived at Chestnut Grove, he made no move to go on but turned in with them at the gate.

Papa had returned. He was standing at the stables waiting. Martha's heart sank. His usually good-natured features were dark with anger, portentous as a thundercloud. The head groom, beside him, looked miserably apprehensive.

"At least," thought Martha, "I must make it plain that it was my idea and that Joshua tried to stop me." Words of contrite apology on her lips, she slipped from the saddle. "Papa, it was all my fault, I know I shouldn't have—"

But she saw to her amazement that he was not listening. The anger had left his face. Smiling broadly, he was approaching the stranger, both hands outstretched. "Daniel! Daniel Parke Custis! Welcome back to Chestnut Grove. I'd heard you were coming. Wonderful to know that there are Custises once again at the White House!"

Martha stared at the newcomer with sudden understanding. So that was why he had looked vaguely familiar. He was Daniel Parke Custis, her godfather, so of course he had been present at her christening. And he probably had dandled her on his knee when she was no bigger than Little Frannie. At that time he had been living at the White House, some five miles up the road, one of the Custis family's many plantations, but he had been away for many years, and the place had been rented. She had probably been five or six when she saw him last.

In the excitement her misbehavior was apparently forgotten. If punishment was to come, it would at least be postponed. While Papa was extending even more voluble greetings and persuading the guest to stay for dinner, she managed to slip away to the house and fortunately encountered no members of the family before reaching her room. Her maid Sally was there waiting, eyes widening to white circles in her black face. "Miss Patsy, what you done to yo-sef? All that mud—!" Sally was as much confidante and playmate as servant, for they had grown up together.

"No matter, Sally. Just help me get washed and changed. There's company for dinner."

Instead of another homespun outfit, she chose a hooped petticoat with an overskirt of flowered calico, a basque of bombazine with lace-edged sleeves, and a mobcap with pink ribbons. "Lace me a little tighter, will you please, Sally."

When she slipped into her place at the long oak table, the guest smiled appreciatively. "So—the beautiful little cherub I used to dandle on my knee has turned into a beautiful child!"

Martha felt herself flushing, but more from irritation than embarrassment. Child, indeed! That was at least the fifth time he had used the word. One would think she was no older than Nancy, dimpling and chattering away with a total disregard of the solemn rule for children, "never to speak in the presence of elders except to reply to a question." At least she could show this undiscerning newcomer that she had been reared with manners proper to a lady, even if his first impression had been of a hoyden dumped in a mud puddle. She took her salt with a clean knife, broke her bread before eating it, kept her knife in a sloping position and laid it beside her plate when not in use, was careful to make no sound with her tongue, mouth, or lips while eating or drinking. And though ravenously hungry as usual, she helped herself sparingly from the huge platters of fish, smoked ham, duck, venison, stewed pumpkin, even her favorite cakes and puddings.

"What's the matter, Patsy, child?" Papa demanded with concern. "Where's your good healthy appetite? Not worrying about taking my new horse without permission, I hope? That was unwise, of course, but I can't blame you." He turned with pride to the guest. "Our little Patsy is a wonderful horsewoman, Colonel."

William snickered, eliciting a stern rebuke from Mama. Martha looked up, flushing again painfully, her glance drawn as by a magnet to a pair of kindly, twinkling eyes, whimsically smiling lips. "Our secret," they assured her silently.

"Yes," said Daniel Custis. "I could see that she is."

She was glad when conversation shifted, as it usually did when men were present, to lands and crops, the fluctuating price of tobacco as a medium of exchange for British goods, the difficulty of securing honest factors in London, the coming Assembly in Williamsburg. Daniel was faced with the task of restoring his father's plantation at the White House to its former prosperity, for it had been leased to indifferent proprietors while he had been away. He would welcome advice.

"Nothing the trouble with your ability as a planter," John Dandridge assured him heartily. He chuckled. "Seems to me I remember reading in the *Virginia Gazette* years ago about a monster cucumber you raised. How did they put it? 'A yard in length and nearly fourteen inches around the thickest part, grown in the garden of Mr. Daniel Parke Custis in New Kent County.'"

Daniel grinned wryly. "Cucumbers, yes. But it will take more than a big cucumber to impress my father."

Much later, after the guest had gone, Martha sat busied with her daily stint of embroidery, only half-listening to her parents' discussion of the day's activities. Suddenly she pricked up her ears.

"At last," Papa was saying with a burst of laughter, "old John Custis may be coming to his senses. Queer old codger! Imagine, keeping his only son on tenterhooks all these years, not even trusting him to manage one of his numerous plantations! Sheer nonsense, and worse, meanness, I call it, not lack of trust. He never did get over the boy's refusal to marry the girl of *his* choice."

Frances Dandridge's knitting needles fell momentarily idle. "Let's see, it was that beautiful Evelyn Byrd he was set on his son's marrying, wasn't it? His cousin. Daniel's father threatened to disinherit him if he didn't."

John Dandridge chuckled. "Right. And he was doubtless more interested in uniting the Byrds' big fortune with his own than in acquiring the beautiful Evelyn as a daughter. But the boy showed gumption in refusing. Ever since then his father has punished him by keeping him subject to his whims and threats. Daniel must be at least thirty-five and still unmarried. Most of his contemporaries have sons old enough to be thinking of marriage, but the old Colonel doesn't think any girl good enough, or wealthy enough, for his precious son. And of course the boy is as helpless as one of the old man's slaves, not a penny of his own, though heir to one of the biggest fortunes in Virginia."

Frances Dandridge's hands remained idle. "It was all so romantic," she mused, dreamily reminiscent. "The beautiful Evelyn was in love with a young nobleman in England, but he was a Catholic, and William Byrd, her father, was a staunch churchman. He brought her to Virginia, to their estate at Westover, and she died, they say, of a broken heart."

Her husband scoffed. "Consumption, more likely. People don't die of broken hearts. Anyway," he continued, "Daniel is still alive, a victim of the whole sorry mess." He chuckled. "I guess the old man has reason enough, though, to fear the vagaries of marriage for his son."

"Why? What do you mean?"

"Haven't you women heard the rumors? You spend plenty of time gossiping at Assembly Week! Well, according to the story, Frances Parke Custis was a regular hellion. She was the daughter of old Colonel Daniel Parke, famous in England for bringing Queen Anne the news of Marlborough's victory, but murdered in a riot while he was Governor of the Leeward Islands. Deserved it, too, I guess, for he was a lecherous, arrogant fellow. John Custis, they say, was so much in love with the beautiful Frances Parke that he wrote her impassioned love letters. Imagine, the crusty old codger! But he soon became disillusioned. The beautiful Frances had as hot a temper as her father. Along with the huge Parke fortune she brought him a wedded life of constant bickering and strife. It's said they used to go for weeks without speaking to each other, only through servants. Like this. 'Pompey,' she would say, 'ask your master if he will have coffee or tea, and sugar and cream,' to which Custis would reply, 'Tell your mistress I will have coffee as usual, with no cream.' But there's an even better story than that, one that's hard to believe. Want to hear it?"

"If it's fit for a lady's ears," his wife replied primly but with obvious eagerness. She had apparently forgotten the presence of Martha.

Gleefully Papa told the story. Once John Custis had surprised his wife by inviting her to go for a drive. To his amazement she had accepted the invitation. It had been too good an opportunity to miss. He had headed the horses straight into Chesapeake Bay.

"Where are you going, Mr. Custis?" she had demanded.

"To hell, madam," he had replied.

"Drive on," she had said acidly. "Any place is better than your house."

When her feet were drawn up on the seat and the horse was forced to swim, he had finally headed for the shore, saying, "I believe you would as lief meet the devil himself, if I should drive you to hell."

"Quite true, sir," she had retorted. "I know you so well I would not be afraid to go anywhere you would go."

"They finally signed an agreement to keep the peace," John Dandridge finished when they were through laughing. "She lived only a few years longer before dying of smallpox."

Martha did not feel like laughing, Poor Daniel Custis, she was thinking, to have had a mother and father who quarreled like that! How lonely he must be, with no wife, like Mama, to manage his household, tend him when he was sick, teach his slaves to spin and weave and sew and knit and cook properly, the way Mama did, to—she blushed at the sheer thought of the unmentionable subject—to bear his children and bring them up properly. All the rest of the day, even as she lay in bed that night chastely swathed in a high-necked gown of unbleached muslin, nightcap of fine gauze tied beneath her chin, she kept thinking about him.

Her godfather! Old, at least thirty-five, Papa had said, yet he had not seemed old. She drifted off to sleep, still remembering the kindly twinkle in his eyes, the strength of his arms lifting her out of the mud, his silent assurance to keep the secret of her misadventure, the way he had kept his outer coat tightly buttoned to hide the smudge on his waistcoat.

It did not occur to her to wonder why she had been pleased when Mama called her "child" but annoyed by the same word on the lips of Daniel Parke Custis.

2

Williamsburg! All her life Martha had heard tales of its magnificence, but the reality far exceeded her expectations. So many houses—mansions—all crowded together in one place, as if all the plantations on the Pamunkey had been compressed into a single unit! Riding in the family carriage along the Duke of Gloucester Street, she gazed wide-eyed at rows of pretentious brick houses, less imposing but attractive white cottages neatly enclosed within picket fences, taverns with queer names, shops displaying the signs of apothecaries, blacksmiths, barbers, wigmakers, woodworkers, and other craftsmen.

The thirty-mile, two-day journey from Chestnut Grove had not been easy. The four horses drawing the carriage had forded streams, wallowed through sand, plowed through mud, only the skill of black Joshua, who served as coachman as well as head groom, keeping them from foundering. Papa, riding his horse alongside, was muddied to the waist, and even Martha and Mama, inside the closed carriage, had felt bedraggled and dusty. Unlike many of the planters who came to Williamsburg for the spring and fall Assemblies, Papa owned no house in town, but he had reserved rooms at the Raleigh, Williamsburg's most prestigious tavern.

"Look there, child!" Mama pointed eagerly. "That's Bruton Church, where your great-grandfather, the Reverend Roland Jones, was rector for fourteen years, the very first one the church had. Its plans were drawn by Governor Spotswood himself, and all the royal governors have worshiped there. You should be very proud. Yes, and your grandfather, Orlando Jones, was burgess here from Kent County. You'll see people here who are much richer and may look down their noses at families like ours from what they call the back country, but you can hold up your head with any of them."

Martha glanced obediently at the ivy-covered brick building surrounded by a stone wall and spreading trees, but she was more interested in the other carriages and coaches moving like theirs along the wide sandy street. Many bore crests and were escorted by uniformed attendants. As drivers whipped their more spirited horses past the slower-moving Joshua, she caught glimpses of women and young girls in silks and velvets, already as powdered and embellished on arrival as if outfitted for the Governor's Ball. Yes, and, as Mama had said, obviously "looking down their noses" at the mud-spattered coach from "back country." Well—let them! She'd like to see one of them perched on a good horse trying to race her across a field! She tilted her chin and, as Mama had urged, held her head high—but not because her great-grandfather had once preached to governors from his pulpit.

The entrance room of the Raleigh was crowded, noisy, for the tavern was not only a social center of the town and a gathering place for the hundreds of Assembly visitors from all over Tidewater Virginia, but also a marketplace for the exchange of both ideas and merchandise. Here and in the adjoining bar land was changing hands by the thousands of acres. Factors from London were negotiating purchases of tons of tobacco. Burgesses were arguing heatedly over subjects to be hotly debated in the coming Assembly. Martha was glad when they could escape from the confusion and go to their rooms.

"Now, Patsy," said Papa after she had washed at a luxurious marble basin and changed her dusty travel gown for a frock of flowered pink calico, "I'm going to show you a heritage a Virginia maiden should be proud of."

"Be sure and take her into Bruton Church," reminded Mama, "and show her the canopied pew where the Governor always sits. And, remember, your great-grandfather once stood in the high pulpit."

Dutifully, when they entered the dim interior of the church close by, Martha remembered. But she felt no great stirring of pride. Great-grandfather Roland Jones was long dead, while the world outside was teeming with life. In spite of the canopied pew, the high pulpit, the chancel floor and aisles of polished English stone, she was not impressed. She felt far more worshipful in their own St. Peter's Church in New Kent County.

But she was intrigued by the streets laid out in the form of a "W" and an "M", in honor of King William and Queen Mary, the town's patrons, and when they entered the great hall of William and Mary College, designed over fifty years ago by Sir Christopher Wren, she felt like treading softly as if on holy ground. A school where people could come and learn, instead of just having a tutor who would come for a few weeks and then go somewhere else to teach others!

"Will my brothers come here?" she asked eagerly.

"Perhaps," said Papa. "It depends on what they want to make of themselves. We're not rich, like many Virginians who think they have to send their sons off to England to get educated. Your brothers will have to work for a living. And you don't have to know Latin and Greek to grow tobacco."

Martha, always curious, persisted. "Could a girl come here to learn things? Could I?"

Papa laughed. Appreciatively his glance encompassed the lithe young figure, hazel eyes alert with intelligence, vigorous young body just budding to maturity. "Hardly, my pet. What use would you have for the knowledge found in books, even if the college would let you in, which of course it would not. If I'm not mistaken, after the ball tonight you'll have a dozen young swains anxious to let you use the knowledge you've acquired in running their plantations."

"But," thought Martha, "what if I don't want to just run a plantation all my life, teach slaves how to sew, cook, spin, weave, and entertain guests with senseless prattle?" Not that she had any other ideas. Certainly she had no desire to learn Latin and Greek. She was no student, like Bartholomew. But neither was obstreperous William, nor was John very fond of study. Why, then, should they have a chance to learn more if they wanted to, become planters or lawyers or merchants or whatever they chose, while her life was all mapped out for her, just because she was a girl? She sighed. Life was perplexing.

But out in the street again, caught in the medley of wagons and carriages and chariots and riding chairs and jostling pedestrians, trying to keep her voluminous pink skirts free from the dust raised by prancing horses, it was all she could do to keep her attention on the landmarks Papa was pointing out with so much pride—the Court House, the Powder Horn with its peaked roof, where the colony stored its munitions, the Public Gaol with its pillory and stocks, where debtors and other offenders were confined. There were some there now with their hands and feet thrust through the holes while passersby stopped to pelt them with stones, and the sight made her shudder.

She was glad when they turned off into a quieter street where there were no public buildings, only imposing brick houses.

"Oh!" Suddenly she exclaimed in delight. "How beautiful!"

"You think so?" Papa sounded dubious. "You know what that house is called? The House of the Six Chimneys. You can see why." He chuckled. "They say you can tell how much wealth a man has by the number of his chimneys. No wonder this one has a lot. You know who this house belongs to, pet?"

"No, Papa, of course I don't."

"It's the property of old John Custis, father of your godfather Daniel —*one* of his properties. He spends most of his time at Arlington, across the bay, though he may be here in town now, being a member of the Governor's Council. Personally I think it's rather ugly, like its owner. Old John boasts that it's 'as strong and high a house as any in the government.'"

"Oh, I didn't mean the house," Martha hastened to correct him. "I was looking at the garden."

Indeed, she had not even noticed the big brick building almost hidden within a thick growth of cedars. Her eyes were all for the masses of riotous color, beds and beds of blossoms interspersed with rare shrubs and bushes, many in full bloom. Never had she seen such a display of rare and varied plants.

"Oh, yes, Custis and his garden!" John Dandridge scoffed. "He's as proud of that as most of us are of a good field of tobacco. Claims he's imported varieties from almost every place on earth."

Martha gazed ecstatically, wishing she could fly over the low wall like the birds, tanagers, cardinals, orioles, whose gay colors were vying with the bright hues of the exotic blooms. She wished she could know all their names, perhaps get seeds or shoots to plant in her own garden. She could not guess that two hundred years later people would be pointing out a yew tree in this same yard, declaring that it had been planted by her own hand!

"If John Parke Custis had been as tenderly attentive to his wife as to his precious flowers," observed Papa acidly, "perhaps she wouldn't have been such a shrew. I reckon the old curmudgeon had a temper to match hers any day."

Martha was curious. She would like to meet this "old curmudgeon" who was the kindly Daniel's father. Anybody this fond of growing things must have a soft spot in his hard crust. "Did I ever see this Mr. John Custis?" she asked.

"John *Parke* Custis," corrected Papa with ironic emphasis. "Never forget the *Parke*. His father-in-law, Colonel Daniel Parke, who had only two daughters, stipulated that all his descendants, on pain of forfeiting their fortune, include the 'Parke' in the names of all their offspring."

Martha laughed. How very funny! She visioned a vast succession of infants christened "something-Parke-this," "something-Parke-that" stretching away ad infinitum!

They returned to the Raleigh, where Papa insisted on showing her the main features of the tavern. Peering into the paneled parlor, she felt suddenly self-conscious, for the room was filled with women, some seated around the open fire or about the gateleg table, some standing, but all chattering in gossipy intimacy and all elaborately gowned in silks, brocades, laces. Hastily she drew back, hoping no one had noticed her ordinary calico dress and homespun shawl. She felt equally shy when Papa showed her the Apollo Room at the rear of the tavern, where the chief dinners and balls were held, for it was overflowing with men resplendent in crimson velvet and ruffles, all bewigged or powdered. The fact that admiring glances were cast in her direction did not relieve her shyness. Yet in spite of her embarrassment she curiously noted every detail of the big luxurious room, little realizing that events would take place within its walls which would profoundly shape her own future. The ordeal was over at last, and she was back in her little room under the eaves.

Not to relax, however. As the time approached for the Assembly Ball, she grew more and more nervous. This was a different world. Could she ever belong in it? Could even the beautiful new silk ball gown make her into one of those gaudily bedecked creatures in the parlor who, she was sure, had regarded her with disdain? She ran to the little mirror over the marble washbasin. No, she didn't look at all like them. Her cheeks were too browned from the sun, her hair, though shining and lustrous, was plainly dressed, not fluffed into a high pompadour and powdered. And her hands! She lifted them ruefully. No lily-whiteness there! She had dug too often in her garden. She belonged back there, with her flowers and horses.

But when she was laced tightly into the new gown, holding her breath until she thought she would burst, her short shapely body molded into hourglass perfection, Mama seemed satisfied, though as usual she dispensed advice rather than compliments. "Remember—low curtsy to the Governor, half curtsy to his lady—when you dance, eyes down, never look your partner in the face—not more than two dances with the same partner—in the minuet keep your foot pointed and straight so there is not a wrinkle in your quilted petticoat—and, need I say, always conduct yourself like a lady."

But Papa, when he handed her into the carriage, was all pride and compliments. "Beautiful, my pet! But—what became of the little girl I used to have? I'll wager the young men will be fighting each other for your first dance!"

"Nonsense, Papa!" But his approval helped allay her nervousness and the fear that nobody would ask her for a dance.

Caught in the congestion of a dozen other carriages, they inched up the long catalpa-lined drive to the Governor's Palace. Torches blazing at the entrance and along the walk illumined the figures of the British lion and unicorn atop the narrow iron-grilled gate and cast a lurid glow on the square high brick building beyond. Symbol of the regal dominance of the mother country, though elegantly simple in architecture, the Palace exuded an aura of British pomp and majesty.

So did its present occupant, Governor William Gooch, large and imposing in white wig and crimson velvet. Martha managed the deep curtsy with aplomb but teetered precariously on the lesser obeisance to the haughty Lady Rebecca and would have fallen but for the stiff supporting hoops of her expansive skirt.

The next hour passed in a blur of impressions and emotions. Moving with other silk-laden figures up and down a huge staircase to lay aside her velvet wrap. ("Like angels on Jacob's ladder," she thought wryly, wondering if wings were as unwieldy as skirts.) Noticing with sudden dismay that almost every other woman, even the youngest like herself, had powdered hair, many with intricately puffed coiffures, none like her own, brushed smoothly back and topped with a simple triangle of ruffled lace. Sitting with other debutantes in a row along one side of the big candlelit ballroom and waiting . . . waiting . . .

She hoped Papa was not watching, that he was away in some parlor discussing tobacco prices with his cronies. Young men fighting for her first dance, indeed! Moments that seemed hours passed. For dance after dance bewigged and bedizened young gentlemen bowed low before gorgeously bedecked young ladies, some obviously debutantes like herself, and led them through the stately measures of minuets or the livelier rhythms of rigadoons and contra dances. Under her flowered skirt her silk-clad foot tapped anxiously to the cadences of violins and harps. Mama of course would be looking, worrying. Martha forced her stiff lips to curve into what she hoped was a carefree smile, but her whole body felt compressed in a tenseness far more oppressive than her tightly laced stays. The evening was still young, hours yet to go. And she was sure it would continue like this, interminably. And why not? Why should any one of those gay young blades in white wigs and velvet breeches and brocaded coats pick her out of the galaxy of faultlessly attired and powdered beauties?

One young woman in particular was like a bright star in the galaxy, and Martha's eyes kept following her through dance after dance, for she was never without a partner. In fact, the moment one dance was over, she was immediately surrounded by eager applicants for the next. She was tall, slender, supple, yet dignified in motion, moving through the most complicated figures of the dances with consummate ease and grace. And, unlike any of the other young women, she was dressed very simply, all in white with no jewels, her powdered hair and fair skin so blending into the silks and laces of her low-cut gown that she seemed like a marble statue, except that there was nothing hard or cold about her. She was virulently, vibrantly alive.

"She doesn't need color," thought Martha, "nor jewels. She herself sparkles. And, after all, white is all colors combined into one."

She was so busy watching the fascinating figure that she did not notice the young man who approached her chair.

"Well—Cousin Patsy! I couldn't believe it was you. The last time I saw you, you were riding your old Graylegs to the hounds, and certainly not looking like this!"

"Nat!" She gazed up in relief at the merry, familiar face of Nathanael Dandridge, her Uncle William's oldest son. Though a few years older than she, he had good-naturedly accepted her as a playmate, and they had shared many childhood adventures both at Chestnut Grove and at Elsing Green, Uncle William's plantation across the river. Now, since the death of his father, Nathanael had become the proprietor of the estate.

"This is my—er—my young friend, Dorothea Spotswood," the young man continued. "Dorothea, may I introduce my cousin Martha Dandridge, usually known as Patsy?"

The two greeted each other cordially. So this was the daughter of ex-Governor Spotswood with whom Nat was supposed to be in love! She approved his choice. Though older than herself by some years, Dorothea with her frank friendliness of manner put Martha instantly at ease.

"I'll leave her here to rest," said Nat, "that is, if you will permit me to have this dance with you, Patsy."

Would she! "Certainly," replied Martha, hoping she sounded more dignified than relieved.

It was a contra dance, one of the more complicated called "The Orange Tree," and Martha was unfamiliar with its intricate steps. She felt awkward and wooden and knew she was making many mistakes. "Take it easy," urged Nathanael when they met in a whirling turn during which she almost stumbled. "You're not jumping a fence with Graylegs."

As he returned her to her seat she felt hot, breathless almost to strangulation, disgraced. Nat would never ask her again, and she hoped no one else would. Not that she needed to worry!

"I'm going to leave you and Dorothea to get acquainted," said Nathanael, "while I find your father and talk with him about selling my tobacco."

"I've been wanting to know you," said Dorothea. "Nat has told me so much about you. You're his favorite cousin, you know."

"Am I? He's mine, too."

Martha warmed eagerly to this new friend. Suddenly she did not mind if she was not asked to dance. She was no longer an outsider, an awkward stranger from the "back country." Just by becoming her friend this girl who was the ex-Governor's daughter and had lived much of her life in this very palace had given Martha a sense of belonging to her world. Dorothea pointed out some of the prominent young women on the dancing floor and commented on them briefly. But one she did not mention.

"Who," asked Martha at last, "is the beautiful girl all in white?"

Dorothea gave her an understanding smile. "You noticed her? No wonder. Everybody does. And she is beautiful, isn't she? And I probably should add"—was there a slight hesitation in Dorothea's voice?—"she's as good as she is beautiful. That is Sally Cary. She's the oldest of four Cary sisters, and by far the most clever and fascinating. Ever since she came of age at fifteen—was it two years ago?—she has been the belle of the Assembly. Her family is one of the most important in Virginia. Their plantation is Ceelys on the James River. As you can see, she is surrounded by admirers anxious to be her dancing partners, and I imagine at least half of them are would-be suitors."

"She—she sparkles," said Martha, unable to take her eyes from the graceful white-clad figure. "She stands out like—like a white rose in a bouquet of dandelions."

"Yes," agreed Dorothea. "Clever, wasn't it, wearing white when she probably knew every other girl here would be decked out like a peacock?" There was no malice in her voice, only amusement. "There's a funny little story told about her. Once, they say, she was riding in her carriage and came to a military line. She was stopped by a sentry, who demanded the password. She was confused and stammered her own name, and the sentry let her pass. Oddly enough, she was right, for the officer of the day, who was one of her admirers, had given her name as the password. Of course it's just a story and probably isn't true, but it shows how popular she is."

Martha laughed gaily. "Looking at her, I could well believe it."

"But she's not only beautiful to look at," conceded Dorothea. "She has a mind most of us girls could well envy. They say she has read most of the books in her father's library, Greek, Latin, philosophy. And she speaks and writes French almost as well as English."

Even after Cousin Nat had come back and claimed Dorothea for another dance, Martha continued to follow the motions of the tall slender figure in white. It must be wonderful to be tall instead of short and, yes, dumpy like herself! So slender was she that perhaps she had no need to be encased in whalebone prisons so tight one could scarcely breathe. As she dipped and swirled, her graceful, lissome body seemed to move in perfect freedom. Martha was so engrossed in watching that she was hardly aware of an approaching figure.

"Patsy, my dear chi—" Startled, she looked up into the kindly, whimsical gaze of familiar eyes. "No, not child. I'll never call you that again. What happened? Did you grow up overnight?"

"Why, I—" Martha was confused. Why under the scrutiny of those eyes did she feel herself blushing?

"How fortunate for me that the most beautiful girl in the room is unclaimed for this next dance! May I?"

Taking both her hands, Daniel Custis raised her to her feet, gently but firmly, just as he had recently lifted her from a mud puddle. Almost without her volition she made the proper curtsy, took the proffered arm, and was led into the midst of the couples preparing for the next dance. To her delight she recognized the melody the moment it started. It was the Lady Coventry minuet, a favorite in England during these years of King George II's reign and already popular in Virginia. Martha knew the steps well from the long hours of tutoring by the traveling dance master. Daniel was an excellent partner, graceful on his feet, meticulous in every movement.

Martha yielded herself to the stately rhythms with an ease and grace she had not known she possessed. Gone was the feeling of tight imprisonment. She curtsied easily to the floor, pirouetted, hands on hips, with a swirl of silken skirts, bowed to her partner with finesse, accepted his neatly turned compliments with a proper gay smile and seductive upturned eye, approached, receded, whirled, dipped, all with a sense of perfect dignity and confidence. Then came the gavotte which followed the slow and stately minuet.

Perhaps it was the feeling of release from the long, anxious moments on the sidelines, perhaps the smiling encouragement in her partner's eyes, or merely the exuberance of youth, but she flung herself into the faster rhythms with pure abandon. It was joyous, intoxicating motion, like racing her brothers to meet a ship at the landing, or riding Graylegs at full speed.

When the music came to an end and she made her final sweeping curtsy and heard the sound of clapping, she was amazed and disconcerted to see that other couples were turning admiring glances toward her and her partner.

"You were superb!" complimented Daniel as he led her back to the sidelines. "Lucky for me you were free to give me this dance, because after this I won't have a chance."

He was right. The rest of the evening there was no dearth of partners for the "back country" newcomer with the homemade gown and the unpowdered hair. As they drove back to the tavern Mama was voluble with pride and satisfaction.

"You should have spent more time watching the dancing, Colonel Dandridge," she chided, "instead of hiding away somewhere chewing over crops and politics. You ought to have witnessed the triumph of our little girl. I'll confess I was worried at first, but not for long. Our Patsy was the belle of the Assembly Ball!"

Oh, no! Martha silently protested. Compared with that other one, all in white and sparkling, she had been but a candle beside a flaming torch. Except for one person, she would probably have sat with her back to the wall most of the evening.

In her little room under the eaves her young servant Sally was curled up on her mat fast asleep. Martha hated to wake her, but it was impossible to get out of her much-hooked and buttoned and laced gown and petticoat and stays and other unmentionable items without her expert help. Awake, the little slave girl wanted to hear all about the evening's adventures. Tired though she was, Martha obediently described the Palace, the ballroom with its shining woodwork and pale blue walls, the dances, the magnificent gowns, while the little servant's eyes gleamed round and white in her black face.

"O-oh, missy! And I jest knows you was the most be-eautiful crittur there!"

"Oh, no—no, I wasn't. You should have seen—" She stopped. Some things were just impossible to describe. "Thank you, Sally, dear. Now go back to sleep."

But lying in the dark swathed in high-necked bedgown and nightcap, Martha herself remained wide-awake. Her mind whirled in a kaleidoscopic medley of swirling skirts, crimson waistcoats, sparkling jewels, flickering candles, and beneath the long coarse gown her foot moved in rhythm with remembered cadences. She tried to recall the faces of some of the men who had asked her to dance, but they were all a blur. All except one. She finally went to sleep feeling safe and protected in the memory of its gentle smile and whimsical kindly eyes.

3

It was three years later, 1749, and Martha was almost eighteen. She had increased in wisdom if not in stature. (She would never be taller than five feet one or two.) The new wisdom had taught her to conform, at least outwardly, to the accepted models of decorum prescribed by Mama and society.

No longer did she tear down the path toward the river in pursuit of her brothers. "A young lady does not run," said Mama sternly. Except on the hunt with Papa she seldom spurred Graylegs to reckless speed in order to relieve her pent-up frustrations. "A *lady* is always dignified and in control of her emotions." But one provision of the accepted credo Martha refused to obey. "A *lady* does not dig in the earth with her hands. She directs her servants in the correct performance of such labors." Martha could no more relinquish the satisfaction of nurturing with her own grubby hands the plants in her beloved garden than a mother could consign to a nurse all the intimate handling of her new baby.

She was in her garden now on this spring morning, down on her knees, weeding a bed of poppies that would soon be coming into bloom. Today the labor was therapy as well as pleasure, release from an excitement that was half worry, half expectation. For she knew that at the moment Daniel Parke Custis was in the house asking her parents' permission to seek her hand in marriage.

All the happenings of the three years had been leading to this climax

—the gala Assembly Balls each spring and fall, with Daniel always in the background ready to become her dancing partner if the usual coterie of aspirants failed to materialize; his increasingly frequent visits to Chestnut Grove and invitations to the family for hunts and dinners at the White House; their rides together; finally his tender avoval of love and confession that he wanted to make her his wife.

"Patsy!" It was ten-year-old Anna Maria, bounding from the house with the same disregard for decorum which had once characterized Martha. "Mama and Papa say you're to come. They want to talk with you."

Martha rose hastily from her knees, brushing the soil from her hands. She forced her voice to remain calm. "Is—is Colonel Custis still here?"

"No," said Anna Maria, "he's gone. He rode away on his horse fast, like a fox with the dogs at his heels."

Martha was confused. Daniel had expected to come to her after his interview, whether her parents were favorable to his proposal or not. What had happened? Could Papa have sent him away, forbidden him any further association with the family? No, impossible. Colonel Custis and Papa were friends, neighbors. Then what—? She hurried to the house and, without stopping to wash her hands or freshen her clothes, went straight to the breakfast room where morning guests were usually received. Outside she stopped short, hearing the sound of voices.

"But," Papa was saying, "he's old enough to be her father, she not yet eighteen and he all of thirty-seven! I was only a lad of twelve when he was born!"

"Yes, but remember, Colonel Dandridge," Mama's voice was less vehement but equally firm, "Daniel Custis is a fine, dependable young man—yes, I do say *young*. He's good-looking and kind and even-tempered—"

Papa jeered. "Ha! How can you be sure of that? Like father, like son."

"And," continued Mama as if there had been no interruption, "he is the heir to one of the biggest fortunes in Virginia."

"You're sure of that?" scoffed Papa. "I'm not. The way old John changes his mind he's likely to leave his only son with no more fortune than his slaves. Less, in fact. You know what I've heard, and on good authority? He's taken a fancy to a little slave boy named Jack, set him free and made him a household favorite. Some people say that after one of his outbursts of temper against Daniel he actually made a will in which he left nothing to his son or daughter and everything to the little Negro. Of course I've heard too that with great difficulty he was persuaded to revoke the will, but who can tell? Even if he did, who knows what he might do again?"

Martha decided it was time to make her presence known. Pretending she had just come from the garden, she entered quickly. "Here I am. Nancy said you wished to see me."

Mama regarded her earth-stained hands disapprovingly. "Ladies don't—" she began, but at a warning glance from her husband she fell dutifully silent.

"Colonel Custis has been here," said Papa, "as you perhaps know."

"Yes," said Martha.

"He has asked permission to pursue his courtship. In other words, he seeks your hand in marriage."

"Yes," said Martha. "I know."

"I assumed you did," observed Papa dryly. While Mama sat quietly and continued to ply her usual tiny even stitches along the hem of an embroidered pillow sham, he walked restlessly up and down, thumbs thrust under the lapels of his silk waistcoat. Suddenly he stopped, came close to her and stood, feet wide apart, his troubled eyes probing into hers.

"Are you in love with him?" he asked abruptly.

Mama gasped. She looked shocked, for the question came close to violating the tabu on certain unmentionable subjects in conversation between the sexes. She opened her mouth to protest, then closed it.

Martha looked back at him, giving no indication of the uncertainty aroused by his question. Her mind whirled. *Am I in love?* And what does that mean? They said Cousin Nathanael and his Dorothea were "in love" before they married. Isn't that the same as loving? Not the way I love my parents and brothers and sisters, I know that. It's different with a man and a woman. But if liking to be with him, feeling warmly excited when he asks me to dance or to ride, happy in the thought of spending the rest of my life in his company, enjoying his sympathy and kindly protection, if all that is being *in love* . . .

"Yes," she said, almost defiantly.

Papa nodded. "Very well," he conceded. "I shall send a message to

Daniel saying his suit is approved. Then"—he smiled grimly—"all that remains will be for him to get the permission of that old curmudgeon his father."

"But why"—Martha felt suddenly rebellious—"why does he have to ask his father's permission to get married? He's a man grown, not underage like me."

"You'd better believe he needs his father's permission," retorted John Dandridge. "How would you like to be married to a man without a British pound to his name and no prospect of getting one?"

Days passed. Martha waited impatiently. There was no word from Daniel. Had he gone to visit his father and, if so, would he have gone by horse or by boat? Probably the latter, since Colonel John spent most of his time at Arlington, his plantation on the other side of the bay. It would be a long trip from the White House, down the Pamunkey and into York River, down past Williamsburg and Yorktown and across the wide expanse of the Chesapeake. But if his mission was successful, surely he would hurry back. Dozens of times a day she would find an excuse to leave her sewing or weaving or gardening or practicing on the spinet to glance down the path toward the docks or up the lane where a horseman would come from the road.

Then all at once he was there, sitting with her parents in the morning room, his face revealing not merely disappointment, but desperation. He had seen his father, asked his blessing on marriage with Martha. He had been refused. In fact, they had engaged in another bitter quarrel. He was too kind to give them all the details.

"Marry one of those New Kent Dandridges!" John Custis had exploded, his heavy jowls vying with his red wig in color. "I know John Dandridge. He's nothing but a county clerk, one of the four sons of an immigrant merchant. A good enough man of his class but surely no equal of the Parkes and Custises." The ruddy face had turned a mottled purple. "If you marry that girl, I'll disown you. I'll—I'll"—once more he threatened—"I'll leave all my money—everything—to my Negro boy Jack!"

But Daniel, it developed, had not given up all hope. He had gone to his good friend James Power, a burgess from New Kent and the Custis family attorney, who promised to use his influence in getting John Custis to change his mind. Power was hopeful, knowing that John Custis was a man of shifting emotions, his bursts of temper often as evanescent as summer fogs. He had even suggested that Daniel might marry Martha and take his chances that his father would accept a *fait accompli.*

"Yes," said Martha instantly. "Why don't we do just that?"

John Dandridge's lips twisted sardonically. "And suppose he didn't change. Suppose he made good his threat. What then?"

"We could go west," said Martha, eyes blazing with defiance, "and homestead. Other people are doing it."

"Oh—no!" Mama moaned in horror. "Not that awful wilderness!"

"Don't worry," Daniel hastened to assure her, but his eyes on Martha were soft with gratitude. "I wouldn't marry her without the means to care for her properly. We'll just have to wait and see, that's all."

So it was left, and the waiting began. Daniel continued to come sometimes to Chestnut Grove, and they took rides together, but there was little gaiety in their meetings. As the time of the spring Assembly approached, Martha's usual anticipation ebbed, for Daniel was not going.

"Then I'll stay at home too," she said once, impulsively.

No, he would not hear of it. She must go and be the belle of the ball, as usual. She would not be lacking partners, some as eager, and worthier, to pay court to her. And, he did not add, she might soon have to choose among them.

This year Mama was unable to go to Williamsburg, for she was expecting another child in May. Cousin Nathanael, now married to Dorothea Spotswood, had rented a house in Francis Street, and Martha had been invited to visit them during the week of the Assembly. To her surprise, in spite of Daniel's absence, it was the most enjoyable gala she had ever attended. Dorothea was an ideal companion. She knew Williamsburg as Martha knew the fields and woods of Chestnut Grove, and the two roamed the streets, explored the three pink-brick buildings of the College of William and Mary, marveling at the beauty of the Great Hall and Chapel, bought perfumes and powders in Dr. Archibald Blair's Apothecary Shop, stared fascinated at the pillory and stocks in front of the red brick public gaol. Together they attended all the races, fairs, and entertainments which were features of the Assembly week.

The Governor's Ball should have been for Martha the crowning delight. She had a new gown, far more modish than the flowered silk of her first appearance, embodying the latest quirks in style from England —a lace apron worn long to barely show the silk petticoat beneath the open-fronted robe, pocket hoops worn on the hips to spread out the paniers, a whalebone stomacher to make an even slenderer waist, wide edging of real Brussels lace around the extremely low neck and fluffing about the wrists. Her hair under its triangle of frothy lace was fashionably coiffed and powdered.

Tonight it was Martha Dandridge of New Kent, not Sally Cary of Ceelys, about whom the aspiring partners flocked before each dance. Sally was there, yes, as beautiful and scintillating as ever, all in black and silver instead of white, but she was a matron now, not a debutante, having married just the previous year George William Fairfax, heir to the sumptuous estate of Belvoir up in the Northern Neck on the Potomac. While she still had her admirers eager for partnership in dance, they were no longer aspirants for her hand.

But for Martha the gaiety of the evening was flawed. Her partners seemed painfully young and unexciting, as immature and ignorant as her three brothers. Unconsciously she kept searching beyond the circle of would-be partners for a figure in plainer but faultlessly correct garb, older and a bit stockier, watching the scene with twinkling eyes and an indulgent smile, always ready to come to her rescue at the slightest signal. She was almost glad when the ball was over and she was in the family carriage.

"Did you have a good time, Patsy? You seemed to have plenty of partners."

"Yes, Papa, but—"

"But you missed one partner in particular. Is that it?" Papa cleared his throat. "You'd better be thinking, daughter, about another of those young swains who seem so attentive. There are some just as worthy and desirable as your Daniel, and with fathers who would be glad enough to relate themselves to the Dandridges."

The gala week dragged on—teas, shopping, afternoon calls, races, puppet shows, fairs, while the burgesses transacted the business of the colony in the ballroom of the Governor's Palace, the beautiful pink-brick Capitol having burned two years before in 1747. Martha longed to be home again, where at least she would be within a few miles of Daniel, even though he had visited Chestnut Grove less often since his father's refusal to bless their marriage. On their daily walks she and Dorothea often passed the House of the Six Chimneys, and always Martha's steps lagged at this point, her eyes drawn not to the ornate mansion but to the garden and magnificent grounds surrounding it. There were trees, flowers, shrubs which she had never seen before, did not even know their names.

"It's a pity," said Dorothea, regarding Martha's flushed eager face on one such occasion, "that old Colonel Custis can't see you right now, so pretty you are! If he were here, I'd be tempted to take you in and introduce you. I know him a little; he used to come often to the Palace when my father was Governor. But he didn't come to the Assembly this time. I hear he's still at Arlington, recovering from some kind of illness."

"Perhaps caused by his son's wanting to marry me," thought Martha ruefully.

Suddenly she clutched Dorothea's arm. "Look! The gate's open! I just have to look at some of those plants close to. They're so beautiful!"

Before her companion could protest she had hurried along the street to the open gate and slipped inside. The garden was even more wonderful than she had expected, the flora more rare and beautiful. She moved among the beds in sheer delight, hands stroking a queer-shaped leaf or cupped about an exotic blossom, nose absorbing sweet and tangy fragrances, eyes reveling in the medley of new shapes and designs and colors, every sense alert except hearing, or she would have been conscious of the scuff of heavy feet on a gravel walk leading from one of the outbuildings.

"Egad! Who are you, pray, and what are you doing here?"

Startled, Martha turned to face a strange-looking figure in homespun breeches and earth-stained waistcoat, a scowl on his beetling brows, cheeks an angry mottled crimson, red wig slipped to one side revealing an untidy fringe of white hair.

"Oh, sir, I'm sorry," she said meekly. "I didn't mean to trespass."

"I asked—who are you?"

"My name is Martha Dandridge. And I do ask your forgiveness. I know I shouldn't have come in."

The eyes under the heavy protruding brows bored into hers. "But you did. Why?"

"Because of the plants and flowers. They were so beautiful I felt I just had to look at them, near to."

"You like flowers, do you?"

"Oh—yes, very much!" In her enthusiasm Martha almost forgot her embarrassment. Her face became radiant. "Better than almost anything. I have a garden of my own, up in New Kent County. Are you the gardener here?"

If the eyes had not been so deepset under the lowering brows, she might have detected in them a slight twinkle. "Yes, you might call me that. I work here in Colonel Custis's garden."

"Is he hard to work for?" asked Martha. "I've heard that he has a terrible temper, is a real curmudgeon."

The gardener succumbed to a sudden fit of choking. It lasted so long and seemed so severe that Martha, alarmed, went and pounded him on the back. "Are you all right, sir?" she asked anxiously when the fit had somewhat subsided.

"Yes, thank you." The choking ended, he wiped his eyes on his coat sleeve. "To answer your question. No, I don't find him hard to work for. In fact, he and I get along together very well."

Martha nodded. "I'm glad. He can't be as difficult as people say he is," she admitted reluctantly, "to care about having a beautiful garden like this."

The gardener almost choked again, but the sound turned into a chuckle. "Huh! Good! I'll tell the—the old curmudgeon what you said."

Martha gasped. "Oh, no, please don't! He'd know then what people think of him, and that wouldn't be kind."

He nodded. "That's true. All right, I won't tell him. But—you really like his garden, don't you?"

"Oh, yes, I do! It's not only beautiful but different. A lot of the plants and shrubs and trees I don't even know the names of."

"No wonder! These plants come from all over the world. I—er—the Colonel imports them. He takes more satisfaction in this pretty little garden than in almost anything else in the world, and he has a tolerably good collection. Shall I show you some of them?"

"Oh, yes, please do!"

The gardener took her on a tour, pointing out various shrubs and flowers—Arabian jessamine, arbutus, carnations, globe thistle, India pinks, Jerusalem cowslips, Persian lilacs, passion flowers, and a dozen others.

"The long voyage often ruins plants and even seeds," he said regretfully. "Any roots that are bulbous will come safe if the ships come in early, but ship's captains are careless and ignorant. Sometimes the only ones that survive are those that neither ignorance nor carelessness can destroy."

He showed her varieties of trees, also imported, fringe trees, Siberian cedar, strawberry, yew, holly of many varieties, gilded, silver, and striped. Martha listened, admired, glowed when he picked some rare blossoms and put them in her hands. "Oh, thank you! But you shouldn't. The Colonel might not like it."

The gardener cackled slyly. "Then we won't tell him."

Suddenly Martha looked conscience-stricken. "Oh, I must go! All this time my friend has been waiting. I was so interested in the garden that I forgot."

She hurried to the gate. Dorothea was still standing outside. There was a mischievous smile on her face. "Well! I see you had quite a conversation with the old Colonel. What did you find to talk about? Your marriage to his son?"

Martha turned pale. She gasped. "You—you mean—that was—? Oh —how terrible! I—I thought he was just the—the gardener!"

What had she said? One word stood out in her memory from all the rest. *Curmudgeon!* She had called him an old curmudgeon. Now, of course, he would never agree to their marriage, even if before there had been hope. She had spoiled everything. She could never forgive herself. The rest of the week passed, for her all its gaiety turned into gloom. Finally it was over. The thirty miles of grueling travel back to Chestnut Grove—splashing through mud, grinding over stones and ruts, fording streams, absorbing dust through one's clothes and into one's flesh and bones—seemed like a foretaste of the rest of her life. She settled into the routine of housekeeping, sewing, weaving, superintending the slaves' activities, caring for four-year-old Frances while Mama awaited the arrival of her seventh child. There was no time now to watch the boat landing or the road for a visitor from the White House, nor was there any pleasurable anticipation of his coming. She did not want to see him. She had ruined all hope of their dream being fulfilled. He would not blame her, he was too kind for that, but even greater than her own self-reproach was the fear of causing him further pain.

Then suddenly he was there. She recognized the sound of his horse's hooves as they pounded along the drive, and her heart quickened with apprehension. Should she tell him of the thoughtless mistake she had made? But even before she could decide, he was in the house, calling her name, waving a paper over his head. When she appeared, still confused and apprehensive, he swept her into his arms, lifted her off her feet, swung her with a strength born of sheer exuberance.

"It's all right, Patsy, we've won! Go get your parents. I've a letter I want you all to hear."

But Anna Maria, always alert to excitement, had already gone to fetch her mother, and John Dandridge, summoned by Bartholomew, who had witnessed the horseman's precipitate arrival, soon followed. When all were assembled and seated, Daniel read the letter he had been triumphantly waving.

"Listen to this. It's from my friend, Mr. Power, whom I requested to plead with my father. 'Dear Sir, This comes at last to bring you the news that I believe will be most agreeable to you of any you have ever heard—that you may not be long in suspense I shall tell you at once—I am empowered by your father to let you know that he heartily and willingly consents to your marriage with Miss Dandridge, that he has so good a character of her, that he had rather you should have her than any lady in Virginia. Nay, if possible, he is as much enamoured with her character as you are with her person, and this is owing chiefly to a prudent speech of her own. Hurry down immediately for fear he should change the strong inclination he has to your marrying directly. I stayed with him all night, and presented Jack with my little Jack's horse, bridle, and saddle, in your name, which was taken as a singular favor. I shall say no more, as I expect to see you soon, tomorrow, but conclude what I really am, Your most obliged and affectionate servant, J. Power.' "

Martha's head whirled. While the rest of the family was surrounding Daniel, congratulating him, certain words of the letter were coursing crazily through her mind. Something she had said? What could it have been? Certainly not her impertinent defamation of his character! Had he liked her in spite of it, or—impossible but tantalizing idea!—because of it? Was he so independent, so arrogant, perhaps, that he might welcome a bit of brazen candor in someone else? Or was it because he had discovered a kindred spirit in her love of his garden? She would never know. Enough that he had given his consent.

Much of the credit, Daniel assured them, belonged to his friend James Power. And what a stroke of genius, pleasing the old Colonel by giving his favorite slave a present in Daniel's name, though he wondered how Power's own "little Jack" had reacted to the loss! Daniel must give the boy a better horse in its place and the best saddle and bridle he could purchase. Now he was on his way to Williamsburg, as his friend had advised, to make sure his father had not changed his mind. And he hoped the wedding could take place as soon as possible, in June at the latest.

"June!" gasped Martha. It was only two months away.

"Yes," said Mama cheerfully, apparently oblivious of the fact that she would be mothering her seventh within a month. "June will be fine."

Daniel returned in record time bearing a signed statement in his father's handwriting. "I give my free consent to the union of my son Daniel with Miss Martha Dandridge."

Chestnut Grove sprang into a frenzy of activity. Miss Nancy, the traveling seamstress, was summoned for not one week but two of frantic sewing.

"But my new ball gown will do very well for a wedding dress," protested Martha.

Calmly Mama produced yards and yards of brocade silk, quilted satin, silvered ribbons, gold laces of the finest Brussels weaving, which she had apparently ordered from London in preparation for this very occasion. "The Custises will find the Dandridges not wholly lacking in proper manners and decencies, I hope." Out in the slave quarters spinning wheels hummed, looms thumped and clattered. The kitchens were busy from morning to night, their vast stone chimneys smoking in preparation for the hundreds of expected guests. And Mama managed to supervise all these activities with her usual calm but thorough efficiency. Even the arrival of little Elizabeth Dandridge on May twenty-fifth did not end, just briefly interrupted, her personal involvement in every phase of the preparation. She was able to direct operations almost as effectively during the period of her lying-in.

As Martha's arms closed about the soft bundle which held the red, squirming mite, she was stirred with new, poignant emotion. At thirteen she had regarded baby Frances with indifference if not distaste. Would she soon be holding a sweet bundle like this, all her own—and, of course, Daniel's? The apprehension she had begun to feel about the unmentionable mysteries of the coming relationship dissolved. Whatever resulted in a blessing like this must be good.

The wedding was solemnized in what would later be called St. Peter's Church, not quite ten miles from Chestnut Grove, where John Dandridge owned a pew and the family worshiped whenever possible. Now it was known simply as the Brick Church. It had been built nearly fifty years before at a cost of 146 pounds of tobacco. Martha loved the church with its arched windows, its huge tower, its pyramidal steeple which she had seen erected in her childhood and which had always seemed like a Jacob's ladder leading to heaven. Each morning before her hour of devotions she closed her eyes and imagined that she was climbing it, up, up, into a blue tranquility. As she entered the walled churchyard now, she stopped for a moment and lifted her eyes. How wonderful to be starting a new life in June, with the sky so blue and the air redolent with the fragrance of roses and laurel and honeysuckle!

The Reverend David Mossum, who was the parish rector, officiated. Martha knew him well, for he had come to the church four years before her birth, and she liked him in spite of his bursts of temper, sometimes even in the pulpit. Perhaps he had reason to be irritable, for his fourth wife had the reputation of being a shrew.

John Dandridge gave his daughter away, but it was Colonel John Custis who reached the couple first after the Church of England ceremony and planted a resounding kiss on both her cheeks. He was faultlessly garbed now, as became a King's Councilor, in satin breeches, purple velvet waistcoat, shirt ruffles, buckled stock, and pumps. But his carefully curled wig was once more awry.

"Salute from the gardener, my dear," he said in a conspiratorial whisper, "or, should we say, from the old curmudgeon?"

Impulsively Martha put her arms about his neck and kissed him back.

From the church the wedding party rode to the White House in a coach drawn by four white horses, accompanied by six young black outriders all dressed in white. There a sumptuous banquet awaited them. The plantation now was Daniel's property, a wedding gift from his father.

The White House. Was its name an omen of events far in the future, as some fancymonger long afterward would be sure to speculate, even though Martha herself would never occupy its successor? Certainly as she was lifted in strong arms and carried over the threshold, she had no desire or expectation of ever being anything but Daniel Custis's "first lady."

4

Happiness and sorrow, must they always go hand in hand? Martha had been married only a month when news came of the death of her brother John at age seventeen, nearest to her in age and lifelong playfellow, comrade, fellow adventurer. Poor Mama, to have given birth to a beautiful new babe only to lose her firstborn son! Martha was glad she had moved only five miles from home so she could be of comfort to the family in their grief.

She was glad of Mama's closeness for other reasons. She was a novice not only at marriage but at all the manifold duties which a huge plantation like that of the White House entailed. She must run the house—a mansion many would call it—efficiently. She must direct the activities of dozens of slaves assigned to such duties as spinning, weaving, dyeing, wool carding, cooking, preserving, churning, soapmaking, the preparing and smoking of meats, and a bewildering array of other tasks. She must always be ready for an influx of guests—relatives from Chestnut Grove or Elsing Green, neighbors from the estates along the Pamunkey, Chamberlaynes, Bassetts, Webbs, Rootes, and others, travelers from other parts arriving to transact business.

"Thank you for teaching me so many household skills!" she often told Mama fervently.

But even Mama could not have prepared her for some of her new problems. Daniel had been an undemanding and easygoing master. His slaves, accustomed to proceeding at their own pace and lack of thoroughness, resented her intrusion. The washing came back dingy and wrinkled. Wool, left ungreased, was sometimes too stiff to card. Corn pones came to the table mixed with flakes from the hot ashes. How win the respect and loyalty of these servants, many so much older and more experienced than herself?

One morning she entered the washhouse to find the women assigned to laundry duties seated crosslegged on the floor, her sudden entrance obviously interrupting a bout of gossip, but they made no move to rise.

"Washing done?" she inquired pleasantly.

"No, missy," one of them whined, "but we's tired. Such hard work."

"Yes," said Martha, "I know it is. Perhaps I can help you."

Smiling brightly, she approached the huge wooden tub, added hot water and soft soap to the tepid contents topped by a congealed scum, and began scrubbing. "It's such a satisfaction, don't you think, to see sheets and towels become white and gleaming? It makes one so proud to have done one's job well, to please one's self as well as other people."

The women were soon working with her, unwilling respect mingled with a hint of shame on their black faces.

Slowly, quietly, by such gentle tactics she brought order into the household. The oak floors and mahogany furniture gleamed. The silver bearing the Custis crest, a griffin's head, was always polished. Daniel gratefully donned neckstocks which fell in smooth stiff folds and waistcoats with ruffles frothy and white as snow. But it would be many months before Martha could produce a garden containing all her favorite herbs and flowers, and by that time it would be too late to share it with the person to whom she owed all her present happiness.

For in November of that year of her marriage, 1749, old Colonel Custis died. Martha was genuinely grieved, for she had come to love her irascible, unpredictable father-in-law. And unpredictable he had remained to the end, making another will on November 14, this time in favor of his son and obligingly dying only eight days later before changing his mind again. His favorite slave boy Jack had not been forgotten, however. He was to have built for him a "handsome, strong convenient dwelling house," furnished with two dozen Russian leather chairs, a couch, "good and strong" feather beds, a black walnut table. Daniel was to be his guardian, with liberal provision provided. The boy presumably had been Custis's illegitimate son by his slave Alice.

Another provision in the will drew from Daniel an amused but anguished reaction: "Patsy! You'll never believe this!"

John Custis had enjoined his son to erect his tombstone with an inscription in the precise language he indicated. Failure to do this would result in forfeiture of the estate.

"Age 71 years," it must read in part, "and yet lived but seven years, which was the space of time he kept a bachelor's home at Arlington on the Eastern Shore of Virginia." On the rear panel of the monument was to be inscribed: "This inscription put on his tomb was by his own positive orders."

"Oh!" exclaimed Martha. Poor Daniel, obliged to execute this order with its ugly stigma on his mother's name! How cruel of the old man to advertise both to present and to future generations his marriage to a shrew—and yet, how clever! She could almost hear him chuckling. He had managed at last to get the better of their eternal arguments.

Daniel Custis had suddenly become one of the most wealthy men in Virginia. He now owned nearly eighteen thousand acres of good land. He was raising superior tobacco, operating fisheries, draining his marshes, leasing his swampland. Though he was never to become a county burgess, he was made a warden of the parish, a distinctive honor with great responsibility. When they attended the Assemblies, he in clothes fashioned by the best Williamsburg tailor, Martha pridefully considered him one of the handsomest men there, and she herself at his insistence was able to purchase the finest ribbons and laces and silks and velvets and stomachers. Life would have been perfect except for one major lack. A year of their marriage passed, eighteen months, and they still had no expectancy of children.

Then in 1751 her happiness became complete. That summer every burgeoning blossom in her garden seemed an archetype of the growing life within her. It was November when their son was born.

"Daniel," she insisted. And, of course, the proud father explained somewhat ruefully, he must also be named "Parke," as must all his children. So it had been decreed in the will of Daniel Parke the Second, his mother's father, who had made the name both famous and notorious, the latter by his scandalous life and murder as Governor of the Leeward Islands. So the mite was christened Daniel Parke Custis the Second. To Martha's deep satisfaction the same service was performed a little more than a year later for Frances Parke Custis, born in

April 1753. The name Frances, fortunately, honored both grandmothers.

Daniel was a doting father. Forty when his namesake was born, perhaps he cherished the joy of family more than most men, having waited so long for its fulfillment. When he came from his fields, his first act usually was to call for his son, hoist him to his shoulders, and cavort with him, shrieking with glee, about the house. After the child turned two, he often could be seen perched on the horse in front of his father, a diminutive replica in red riding coat and breeches, already being initiated into management of the vast acreage he would someday inherit. But if Daniel took pleasure in his son, he fairly idolized his baby daughter, namesake of the beautiful mother enshrined in his memory despite her unfortunate disposition. He could not do enough for his children, sending off orders for fineries, toys, trinkets with every ship that went with his loads of fine tobacco to London.

"But it's as if he had three children instead of two," Martha thought ruefully. For he often seemed to regard her as another child, to be petted, protected from all worries, lavished with every luxury obtainable.

The watch, for instance. Martha had once admired the timepiece their neighbor Burwell Bassett had bought for his wife Anne. So what did Daniel do but dispatch a letter posthaste to his agent, Robert Carey, in London!

"I desire a handsome watch for my wife, a pattern like the one you bought for Mrs. Burwell Bassett, with her name around the dial. There are just twelve letters in her name—Martha Custis—a letter for each hour marked on the dial plate."

When it arrived Martha was speechless with admiration. It had a gold case with a circle of white enamel, all inlaid with gold, and over each numeral on the dial was a letter of her name. But it was an unnecessary luxury. Few men of the time and almost no women owned watches. Dutifully of course she thanked him and wore it with pride—and a bit of embarrassment. She did not enjoy arousing envy in other women.

Baby Frances was only ten months old, little Daniel Parke two and a half when tragedy came. It was February. The month had been extremely mild. Daniel took his son on a long ride over the farm, the boy perched delightedly in front of him on the saddle. While they were gone the weather turned suddenly cold and when they returned it was snowing hard. Afraid that the child might have contracted one of his frequent colds, Martha wrapped him in a blanket and set him by the fire, then hurried to prepare the remedy long in use by her family for coughs and colds, taking a half pint of flaxseed, adding a quart of water and boiling the mixture until it was reduced to a pint, straining it, then adding some pieces of sugar candy and licorice, and stewing all together. A little lemon juice and a tablespoon of French brandy completed the mixture. She fed it to him all that day in small doses, and when she put him to bed that evening he seemed no worse for the adventure. But she was wakened in the night by the familiar rasping cough.

"Should we send for the doctor?" asked Daniel anxiously.

"Not yet." She tried to sound assuring. "It's probably just the usual croup." Daniel held him while she prepared her croup medicine, equal parts of camphor, spirits of wine and hartshorn, well mixed together. The rasping cough subsided, but she did not go back to bed again. Daniel summoned one of the servants to build up the fire in their bedroom, and she sat beside it holding the child all the rest of the night.

In the morning he was hot with fever. Still she did not want to send for the doctor. He would insist on bloodletting, blistering, and she hated the very idea. Little Daniel was already so pale. They ought to be giving him more blood, it seemed, instead of taking it. And the thought of putting those ugly leeches on that delicate skin or burning it with a corroding mustard plaster made her almost sick herself. But when he became worse, finding it hard to breathe, the doctor was summoned. It was no use. Putrid sore throat, he called it. And all his remedies, bleedings, purgings, blisterings, were of no avail.

"If only I hadn't taken him out riding that day!" despaired Daniel after it was all over and they had returned from the little service of burial.

"It wasn't your fault," comforted Martha. "It was so warm and he was so happy to go with you!" Perhaps, she thought in agony, if she had been willing to call the doctor sooner!

Her grief was deep and devastating, but her sympathy for Daniel was even more profound. He seemed to have aged overnight. His devotion to baby Frances became now all-consuming. He would return to the house a dozen times a day just to assure himself, apparently, that the child was well and happy. Martha's one consolation was that she was soon to bear another child, and she dared to hope that its coming would bring back buoyancy to his step and laughter to his eyes. "Let it be another boy!" she prayed.

It was. John Parke Custis came into the world with promise of all the vigor, possibly also the temper, of his redoubtable grandfather, for whom he was named. Daniel seemed almost his old self. Once more the White House became a center for gala neighborhood activities, as families assembled for sumptuous three-o'clock dinners, the table loaded with venison, oysters, crabs, turkey, pork, mutton, sweet potatoes, pies, jellies, fruits, then adjourned to the parlor for games and dancing. Martha's spinet, which had remained silent during the months of mourning, again woke to tinkling life, and the plantation fiddler was kept busy with the rollicking tunes of "Hunting the Squirrel," "High Betty Martin," or "Leather-the-Strap."

Time passed, marked by the sowing and harvesting of crops, the ebbing and flowing of the river, the growth of children, visits to Chestnut Grove and the homes of other neighbors. Life once more began to seem complete, especially after Martha found herself once more with child. Would it be a boy or a girl? Watching Daniel's delighted rompings with little Frances, she hoped it would be another girl. Then, seeing him cavort about the house and grounds with John Parke hoisted, crowing, astride his shoulders, or perched before him on a horse . . . Of course a man wanted sons! Fortunately she did not have to choose. The baby came early in 1755, and it was a girl, delicate as a bit of china and indescribably beautiful.

"This time we must name her Martha," said Daniel, his fond smile more for his wife than for his new daughter. "But of course we'll call her Patsy."

In August 1755 they were in Williamsburg for the Assembly, traveling with the family in the fine coach Daniel had ordered from London, settling into the House of the Six Chimneys, as was usual on such occasions. Strange to be mistress of the imposing mansion at which she had once peered in awe, even stranger to call its exotic garden her own, though there was a little yew tree there now which she had planted. As always, she made a tour of the garden before entering the house, to make sure the gardener was taking good care of the old Colonel's precious acquisitions. She could easily imagine a grotesque figure following her among the flowers, coattails flapping, wig awry, watching with eagle eye to see if she missed anything.

"See?" She almost spoke the words aloud. "It's still thriving, our garden. And did you see my yew tree? I had it brought from England. But come into the house and I'll show you an even better memento of your life, John Parke Custis the Fifth."

The Six-Chimney House was always full during Assembly weeks. Martha exulted in its size, for under its many gables were rooms to accommodate any number of guests, Cousin Nathanael and Dorothea with their children, as well as her own family. Papa had been ailing and had not come, but Mama was here, also brother William, now with the King's navy and home on furlough; Anna Maria (Nancy), a lovely debutante, eighteen-year-old Bartholomew, still the sober scholar of the family; Frances, now twelve; and Elizabeth, a bouncing seven-year-old.

It was Nancy now over whom the women fussed. Sixteen, beautiful, and of course ready for marriage. So much depended on a girl's popularity at the Assembly Balls! Martha hoped she would attract as fine a man as Daniel, not necessarily as wealthy but as kind and loving. Nancy must have not just one new gown, as Martha had had at her first Assembly Ball, but several. Fashion decreed a long, pointed bodice, full-bosomed, narrow-waisted to the point of near suffocation, a very low neck, lace-edged, broad lace cuffs under full silken sleeves, hoops stiffer and wider than ever. As the wife of Daniel Custis, mistress of the luxurious Six-Chimney mansion, Martha was welcome in every one of the ornate houses lining the Duke of Gloucester Street and in the Palace of the present Governor, Robert Dinwiddie. That season, for Nancy's sake, she accepted every invitation, which meant a ball or a dinner or a tea almost every day, sometimes events both afternoon and evening.

But in this year of 1755 Williamsburg was concerned with more crucial matters than such gala festivities. At dinners and dances the men withdrew into small knots for hot political discussion unrelated to the price of tobacco. Even the women, usually protected from participation in and even knowledge of more serious issues than fashion, food, furbelows, and romantic gossip, knew that momentous events were happening beyond the bounds of the colony.

These were the years of what was to be known in history as the

French and Indian War. Possession of land to the west of the Alleghe-
nies was in dispute between the French and the English. Both sides
had endeavored to purchase the allegiance of the Indians inhabiting
the area with gifts and promises, but the French, who did not seize the
land, only traded, had been more successful, inciting Indian raids on
the English border settlements, resulting in massacres, terror, and agonized appeals for help.

In 1753 Governor Dinwiddie had sent a scouting expedition into the
west to challenge the encroaching French on the far frontier. The
leader of the group had been a young Virginian, an adjutant in the
colony's militia, who had had much experience in surveying western
lands. It was a thousand-mile journey of incredible hardship and difficulty through almost impenetrable forests, frozen waterways, Indian
ambushes, attempted assassinations, and the answer they brought back
was threatening. The French considered the territory theirs. They declared that they would build all the forts they chose, and that no
Englishman had a right to trade or settle on the waters of the Ohio
River or its tributaries.

The following year, 1754, the same young Virginian, promoted to
lieutenant colonel, had been ordered again by Governor Dinwiddie to
the Ohio in command of a military expedition to build forts and defend the possessions of His Majesty against the hostilities of the
French. The expedition was a failure, but it marked the beginning of a
war which would spread not only through the Ohio Valley but also all
over Europe and would last for sixty years.

Now, in the summer of 1755, three names dominated much of the
conversation in Williamsburg: *Braddock. Monongahela. Washington.*

England, aroused to the fact of crisis in her colonies, had dispatched
a competent general named Braddock to take an army of Redcoats into
the wilderness to conquer the encroaching French. Braddock had taken
the young Virginian along as his aide. Attempting to conquer the
French Fort Duquesne on the banks of the Monongahela River, he
arrived close to his objective without apparent opposition. Then tragedy struck. Insisting on deploying his regiments in English fashion,
marching in perfect formation, ignorant of wilderness travel and Indian
fighting tactics and refusing to take advice, Braddock encountered a
band of French and Indians, unseen, crawling through the grass, hiding
behind trees, firing with devastating accuracy. Their orderly ranks flung

into confusion by the barrage of shells and the hair-raising whoops, their red coats perfect targets for the invisible guns, the British suffered ignominious defeat. Braddock himself, after five bullets had struck one or another of the horses he had bravely ridden, received his own death missile through his lungs. It had been a crushing defeat, almost a massacre. But out of it his aide, the young Virginian named George Washington, had emerged a hero. As Martha caught snatches of the conversation among guests, on the streets, at the dinner table, a picture of his part in the debacle took shape.

". . . sick with severe fever, left behind the lines . . . insisted on rejoining Braddock and his army, rode on his back in a jolting baggage cart for miles, racked with pain . . ."

". . . dashed about on his horse through the battle's crisis, tried to rally the troops . . . nothing could stop him, not even a bullet . . . horse shot from under him, fell, too weak to rise, but Braddock's man helped him up to mount another . . . reckless, daring . . . twice thrown from mortally wounded mounts . . . half sick . . . four times escaped death from bullets which pierced his clothing . . . two holes through his hat . . ."

". . . rode all night in the rain to bring succor . . . still sick and weak, rode on a pillow fastened to the saddle . . . wet, chilled, desperate . . ."

". . . saw to it that Braddock, mortally wounded, was put in a wagon and taken to the supply camp . . . fourth day after the battle the end came . . . read the funeral service of the Church of England by light of flickering torches . . ."

The Assembly, still in session, spent hours in hot criticism of Braddock. At the same time it hastened to thank and commend the gallant young Virginian, and Governor Dinwiddie appointed him commander of the Virginia forces that must be raised to protect settlers on the western boundaries of the colony, now beginning to be molested anew by marauding bands of Indians.

The town buzzed with rumors. Colonel Washington was in town! No, he was not coming but had gone to his home up north on the Potomac to recuperate from sickness. He was refusing the Governor's commission, he was accepting it, he had not decided whether to accept it or not. Then, suddenly, the wildest rumor of all—*he was dead!* The words of his dying speech were reported verbatim. The report was soon corrected, but not until much later would the young Colonel's personal reaction to this false rumor be publicized for posterity, quoted from a letter he wrote to his brother Jack:

"As I have heard . . . a circumstantial report of my death and dying speech, I take this early opportunity of contradicting the first, and of assuring you that I have not as yet composed the latter . . ."

Martha listened, but more with curiosity than with genuine interest or concern. The western lands were far removed from the comfort and luxury of the Virginia tidewaters. It would be fascinating, of course, to see this paragon of courage and bravado, but with all this adulation he would undoubtedly be either unbearably stuffy or hopelessly arrogant. Her chief concern during the Assembly days was to see that Nancy enjoyed every opportunity for enhancing her chances for a happy and successful marriage, but as time passed she saw little evidence that her beautiful young sister was impressed with any of the prospects.

"You had partners aplenty," Martha would observe after one of the exciting parties. "Did you find any one of them especially—er—appealing?"

Nancy would shrug. Oh, they had all been friendly, but—well, they seemed so young and so—uninteresting.

Martha could only nod. The words sounded strangely familiar. Gently she began prodding. Was there any—well, older man whom Nancy especially admired, just as a sort of model, of course?

The girl's cheeks flamed. Barriers suddenly down, she confided that she could think of no person more worthy of admiration than—she stopped, embarrassed, then rushed on—than their neighbor Burwell Bassett.

Concealing her surprise, Martha calmly agreed. Burwell Bassett was indeed a most admirable person. But her mind raced. Bassett, their neighbor at Eltham, about six miles downriver from Chestnut Grove had been a playmate of her brothers, perhaps three years younger than herself. Not long ago he had lost his young wife Anne, who had been a Chamberlayne, the owner of the watch like hers. So Nancy was in love with Burwell! Well, why not? His family was honored in Virginia. Immediately Martha began planning. As soon as she returned home she would arrange dinners, parties, teas, various events to which the neighbors at both Chestnut Grove and Eltham would be invited. The young widower would have every opportunity to observe that the hoydenish child with whose brothers he used to play had grown into a charming and wholly desirable young woman. Martha was glad the Assembly festivities were nearly over. She could not wait to get home.

But one excitement was yet to come. On the morning of August 27 William rushed into the house with momentous news. Colonel Washington was in Williamsburg. He had actually seen him sitting in the chair of the French barber on the Duke of Gloucester Street. A whole crowd was gathered out front. If she hurried, she could probably see him as he went along the street.

Martha sniffed. A barber! Just as she had thought. A prig, getting his hair curled and powdered and no one knew what else for his first appearance in the capital after his triumphant exhibition of bravery! Nevertheless, she hurried to accompany William, stopping to summon Nancy and to pick up her most becoming lace shawl as an adornment for her calico morning gown. Silly woman! As if she needed to bedeck herself with finery just to see a stranger passing, even one supposed to be a hero! He was certainly nothing to her but a curiosity, and she would likely never see him again.

They joined the crowds moving along the Duke of Gloucester Street toward the restored Capitol at the far end where the Assembly would be meeting. Presumably the young Colonel would be appearing before the session. As a group of burgesses approached, looking very important in their official garb, velvet-coated, wigged, and powdered, Martha and other mere pedestrians moved aside to let them pass.

"There he is!" William suddenly clutched her arm. "The tall one!"

Tall, yes. There was no mistaking the description. He towered above the surrounding burgesses. Walking with the flabbily corpulent and bedizened Governor Dinwiddie, with his moon face, double chin, and frizzled wig, he was like a giant tree beside a scrubby but flamboyant bush. Straight as an Indian, he walked like one, as if treading lightly along a forest path. His plain blue uniform with red facings of the Virginia militia, contrasting oddly with the crimsons and purples of the elaborately garbed burgesses, seemed to enhance rather than belittle his dignity. Whatever his business in the barbershop, it had not been for a complicated coiffure, for the hair under the cocked hat was only slightly powdered and plainly dressed. But all these details Martha absorbed in a brief glance, for she was far more interested in his face. The crowd cheered and clapped. Not Martha. She was too busy looking. The man's features were clean-cut, regular, if a bit heavy, nose prominent, lips tightly compressed, eyes . . . She wished he would turn in their direction so she could see what they were like. Eyes told so much about a person. And then suddenly he did. They were rather pale in color, she thought, a gray-blue, and so penetrating that they seemed to look right through a person.

"He's still sick," she realized, "and terribly tired."

"Oh!" breathed Nancy when the group had passed. "Isn't he handsome! I think he's the handsomest man I've ever seen."

Martha suddenly had a wild idea. There would be parties while the Colonel was here. Surely the Governor would give a ball, and of course they would be invited. Certainly Nancy was one of the prettiest of the season's debutantes, and the Colonel was rumored to have an eye for female beauty. Suppose . . . "How would you like to be married to him?" she asked half-jokingly.

"No!" The answer was prompt and decisive. "He looks too stern. Did you see his lips? I'd be willing to wager he never smiles, to say nothing of laughing."

Stern? Martha had not thought so. To her the compressed lips had been a mark of tension, worry, weariness, perhaps even of pain.

There were no social events honoring the young Colonel, for he left almost immediately to assume his new duties as Commander of the Virginia forces. Not long after the close of the Assembly the Custises and Dandridges returned to their homes on the Pamunkey.

Border trouble seemed even farther from the White House than from the House of the Six Chimneys. The household measured the passing of time by its own hourglass of change: the planting and growing and harvesting of a crop, with its final loading in great bales on the vessel bound for England; the metamorphosis of little John Parke Custis from crawler into toddler into lusty two-year-old, leading his nurse Molly a merry chase; the emergence of little Frances out of linen baby dresses into her first party outfit of ruffled petticoat, lace-trimmed bodice stiffened with light pack-thread stays, silk coat and shoes, cap with blue ribbons; little Patsy learning to creep, then to walk; the burgeoning of romance as Burwell Bassett slowly awoke to the adult charms of his playmates' teasing little sister; the rising and falling of the river as it meandered around the jutting prongs of shoreline; the inexorable ticking away of minutes and hours by the beautiful watch bearing her name.

Must life always go hand in hand with death? One day in August 1756 she was summoned to Chestnut Grove. Papa, who had long been ailing, was suddenly very ill. The doctor feared he had only a few hours to live. Daniel went with her in the chariot, and they arrived just in time. Papa's eyes lighted at sight of her, and, kneeling by the bed, she felt his hand reach out to stroke her cheek. It was almost his last gesture. With Daniel's comforting arms around her she let her tears flow unrestrained, and not only for this most recent loss. So much death? First her beloved brother, then her own baby, and now Papa, the gay, gentle, wise mentor and guardian through all her growing years. Yet here also there was life in the midst of death, for Mama had a new baby, Mary, at her breast, born in April, and Papa had at least been able to enjoy her a little while. The hourglass seemed always to empty only to be refilled.

Even death interrupted its normal flow only briefly. They attended the fall Assembly in Williamsburg as usual, and Martha laid aside her mourning dresses long enough to sit for a portrait by the eminent John Wollaston. It was the fashion to patronize him that season. She was not too pleased with the result although most people considered it an excellent likeness and very beautiful.

"I look too self-satisfied and smug," was her private opinion, "and he made my eyes look queer. But they say he makes all his eyes like that, small and sort of slanted like an Oriental's. At least he's managed to make me look tall and dignified."

She had left her hair unpowdered, smoothed straight back and bound with pearls. Her silk gown was cut low, laces at the sleeves to reveal her round white arms, one of them outstretched to pluck a rose. Beneath the silk sacque drawn in at the breast by a large bow, the bodice came to a point in tight smoothness.

Daniel looked handsome in his portrait, though stiff and unsmiling with his hand resting on a table. But the expanse of his bright yellow waistcoat was not exactly flattering, since it gave full evidence of his increasing girth. But, then, Daniel was almost forty-five, and at twenty-five she herself was beginning to develop a bit more plumpness.

Another spring came. The willows along the riverbank dripped gold. Trees burst into pale, shimmering greens. Everywhere there was the promise of new life. Martha was radiant with expectation. Frances would be four on the twelfth of April. She must have a birthday party. In May, Anna Maria, her beloved Nancy, was to marry Burwell Bassett.

"Come in like a lion, go out like a lamb." March was living up to the old adage. She had arrived amid driving winds and rains. Now at her farewell appearance the sun was shining with almost summer warmth, breezes were soft and balmy, the redbuds and dogwoods were beginning to bloom, and out in her garden, Martha knew, there would be daffodils and tulips in blossom. She could hardly wait to see them.

"Would my little lady like to ride with Papa this morning?" Daniel asked at breakfast.

"Oh—yes, Papa!" Frances joyfully laid down her spoon. "May I, Mama?"

Martha regarded her daughter anxiously. The child, delicate from birth, had seemed unwell during the past month, pale and without appetite. But her eyes were bright now, and there were roses in her cheeks. "Yes," she said, "I think it would be good for you." And for Daniel too, she thought, for he also had been ailing, tiring quickly and unable to rid himself of a racking cough. "But eat your porridge first, darling."

"Jacky go too?" inquired little John Parke hopefully.

"Not this time, son. Later, perhaps." Daniel's voice was kindly but abrupt, with none of the caressing tenderness it always held for his little daughter. Martha sighed. Sometimes it was almost as if he resented the presence of this second son who had taken the place of his beloved firstborn.

"You and I will go to the garden later and see all the pretty flowers," she consoled him.

After breakfast, as usual, she went to her room, closed the door against all interruptions, and spent her hour in devotions. Psalms it must be this morning, she decided, songs of thanksgiving. The growing world outside, her contented family—all demanded thanks.

"Sing praises unto the Lord, O ye saints of his;
And give thanks unto him, for a remembrance of his holiness . . .
Heaviness may endure for a night,
But joy cometh in the morning . . ."

Yes. This was morning, and her whole world resounded with psalms of joy and thanksgiving.

Daniel came in from their ride carrying little Frances. "She complained of being tired, and of hurting. I—I hope there's nothing wrong."

Alarmed, Martha took the child from him. The small body trembled in her arms, as if shivering with cold. But the flesh against her hands was unnaturally hot. Those bright eyes and red cheeks! Had they been signs of fever instead of increasing health? Oh, she should have been more careful!

"She's ill," she told Daniel. "We must send for the doctor."

The next hours were a nightmare. The child grew steadily worse. Martha applied all the remedies she knew for fever—calomel, lobelia, quinine, bathing with cool, wet cloths. The doctor, who lived many miles away, summoned by one of the servants riding on the fastest horse, finally arrived and performed the bleedings which were the stock treatments for all such sicknesses, while Martha cringed, feeling the pain as if it were her own vein being cut open. Did it really help, she wondered, making the child's suffering so much greater and taking the blood that she must need? Frances's cheeks were now so pale.

It was just as it had been with little Daniel, the end coming very quickly. Early on the morning of April 1, with the birds caroling outside the bedroom window, the tortured little body became still. Wordlessly they closed the bright eyes, and Martha gently drew up the embroidered sheet to cover the face, drained of all its deceptive color.

She dared not yield wholly to grief because of Daniel. Once more he seemed to be blaming himself. It had been so much a repetition of the other disaster—his taking the child to ride, the sudden, almost inexplicable illness, the frantic efforts to save, the swift end. No, she tried to reassure him, the ride could not have hastened the onset of fever. It had been a beautiful warm day, and, indeed, he had given her a last happy experience of his loving care and of the world's springtime beauty. But he would not be consoled. Once more he seemed to have aged, this time by at least ten years.

Of course they did not go to Nancy's wedding on May 7. A wedding should be a happy occasion, and a woman in black mourning garb and a man with tight lips and tortured eyes would not have added to its gaiety. But Martha rode over to Chestnut Grove before the day to help with preparations and to take gifts, one of them the yards and yards of rose velvet and silk brocade she had been saving for the next Assembly.

"Oh, but you shouldn't!" Nancy's protest was belied by the radiant delight in her eyes. "You'll soon be wearing colors again."

Martha smiled. "Not for a while. And I can always send for more." She little suspected that it would be many months before she laid aside her mourning.

She worried about Daniel. She knew it was not wholly grief which had changed him, though that had taken a severe toll. The troublesome cough persisted. He had developed an unhealthy color and had lost weight. Though he doggedly continued to ride over the plantation each morning, checking his fields and directing his overseers, he was so weary and out of breath when he returned that he had to rest.

Grief, overwork, feelings of guilt—or some mysterious malady? Martha tried every resource at her command—foods to tempt his appetite, herb concoctions, persuasion to take more rest, and, in spite of her own deep despondency, persistent expressions of bright encouragement. Finally she persuaded him to go to Williamsburg to consult Dr. James Carter, one of the best-known physicians and apothecaries in Virginia. Reluctantly he went.

"It's all right," he told her cheerfully on his return. "The doctor says I have no trouble that time won't take care of." It was not really a deception, for time *would* resolve his problems but not in the way he implied. The doctor had told him that he might not have long to live.

Martha's relief was short-lived. On July 4 Daniel fell really ill and took to his bed. Frantically she sent a messenger to Williamsburg to summon Dr. Carter, and he arrived at the White House on the fifth. To her relief he promised to stay as long as he was needed, until— what? Until color came back into those ashen cheeks and strength into the weakened arms which seemed unable even to reach out toward his small son who came to bid Papa good night? Or until the numerous bleedings drained the wasted body of all life? The next days seemed endless. Martha did not leave the room except for necessities. What little sleep she got was taken in a chair. Though Daniel kept begging her in his weakening voice to go and rest, she could tell by the look in his eyes that he liked having her near. It had been Monday when he fell sick. Though days passed, Tuesday, Wednesday, Thursday, she lost all consciousness of time. It became only a succession of darkness, light, sunshine slanting through the windows, candlelighting, going to the bedside, holding his limp hand until someone gently took her away, led her back to the chair. This could not be happening—again! Surely she had already drunk the bitter cup to its dregs—brother, father, son, daughter—not another, not her gentle, loving, protecting, fun-loving husband!

She would always be glad that she was with him, kneeling by the bed holding his hand, feeling its faint pressure, then its slow final relaxation, before someone—Dr. Carter?—lifted her, turned her away, led her firmly from the room. It was Friday, July 8, 1757, when Daniel Parke Custis died at the age of forty-five years and nine months.

Numbly but with surprising efficiency Martha set about the necessary tasks. She hired Charles Crump to provide a black walnut coffin and made sure when he brought it to the White House that it was properly lined with the best silk. She had the plantation seamstress remove all the trimmings from another of her best black gowns and alter it for mourning. She called the rector of St. Peter's Church to perform the funeral service with relatives, friends, and servants in attendance. And at last it was over. Now there were three fairly new mounds in the little cemetery on the hill overlooking the river. Too late to plant flowers on the newest one to bloom this year, but another year was coming . . . another and another. They seemed to stretch ahead, all empty and without an ending, into a bleak and lonely future.

For never had she felt so alone. It was Daniel who had given her assurance, protection, security. Sometimes she had resented his treating her like a child, but she had been one. Now suddenly she must grow up, become a woman, overnight.

It was to Frances Dandridge that she turned, not for comfort, no one could give her that, but for understanding. They had both suffered the same loss, and both were mothers of little girls who would never remember their fathers.

"How can I go on?" she sobbed. "I have nothing left to live for."

"Of course you have." Mama was practical even in sorrow and adversity. "You have your children, and you are young, only twenty-six. Wait a year, Patsy, as I have. Time will heal."

Martha did not believe her. In her morning devotions now she did not look for psalms of thanksgiving. Once, however, the Psalter opened to familiar words. Could she have read them so joyously just a short time ago?

"Sing praises unto the Lord, O ye saints of his;
And give thanks unto him, for a remembrance of his holiness . . .
Heaviness may endure for a night . . ."

Ah, here were words that fitted her mood! Yes, it was night. But— "joy cometh in the morning"? Impossible!

Life seemed to have ended. She could not know that it was just beginning.

5

Not only must she grow suddenly into a woman, alone, unprotected, independent. She must also assume the responsibilities of a competent and self-sufficient man. The latter was by choice, not necessity.

"You are the inheritor of a very large estate, Mrs. Custis," said Robert Carter Nicholas, who had come from his home in James City soon after Daniel's death to advise her about legal matters. He had been Daniel's good friend as well as one of his attorneys. "I would suggest that you hire an able administrator to conduct its management. If you wish, I shall be glad to make inquiries and locate a competent person for you. In fact, I have in mind—"

"Thank you, sir," Martha interposed quietly, "but I do not want an administrator. I shall direct the business of my husband's estate myself."

"But, my dear Mrs. Custis"—the visitor looked more amused than amazed—"forgive me, but I'm sure you have no idea what such a responsibility entails. Your courage is commendable, and I admire you for it, but it's no job for a"—he cleared his throat—"for an inexperienced person."

Martha lifted her chin. For a woman, she knew he had been about to say, and she suspected that in his lexicon the word was interchangeable with "child." She had been a child long enough. "Nevertheless," she replied firmly, "I intend to acquire the necessary experience, if possible, and I shall not hesitate to consult competent and trustworthy lawyers like yourself."

Robert Nicholas continued to protest, but his manner ceased to be that of an indulgent parent toward an unreasonable child. At age twenty-six Martha had become one of the wealthiest widows in Virginia. There would be innumerable opportunists trying to take advantage of her position. There were accumulated obligations on the estate, the question of the guardianship of her children, with the protection of their shares in the property. There would be the sales and shipments of the tobacco crops, the bargaining with shrewd factors certain to exploit the weakness of a—another throat clearing—of inexperience, rentals or sales of the various properties, the management of slaves, servants, overseers, livestock, to say nothing of a large acreage of land.

Martha listened, hoping her composed features gave no indication of her mounting fear and uncertainty. She remained adamant. Yielding now, she sensed, would be a retreat into the old entity of childlike impotence and dependence. Robert Carter Nicholas left, still amazed but no longer amused, his indulgent manner replaced by an attitude of admiration and respect.

Daniel Custis had died without a will, leaving an estate worth over twenty-three thousand British pounds, to be apportioned in equal shares among Martha and her two children. There were fifteen thousand acres of land near Williamsburg, plus other acres in various areas, lots in the city, the two homes, the White House and Six Chimneys, and perhaps two hundred Negro slaves.

Robert Nicholas was right. Management of such an estate was a job for a man, one with competence and experience. But slowly, as the months passed, she acquired some of both. On matters of law she consulted her attorneys. Painstakingly she wrote letters, using the same forms Daniel had employed for his transactions with London merchants, hoping that her poor spelling would not indicate ignorance in business details. (After all, *male* planters were not distinguished for their ability to spell!) She was careful to take receipts even for small sums paid out by the estate. John Robinson, speaker of the Assembly, assumed the legal guardianship of the children. Many details of the plantation she could entrust to Daniel's manager, Joseph Valentine, whom he had found trustworthy.

But, try as she would, efficient as she was able to become in management, she could not compensate for the liability of being a woman. When she rode out each day, as Daniel had, to check on work in the fields, the laborers regarded her with indifference, if not actual insolence. Since her first difficulties she had never had trouble with her house servants, but they were accustomed to taking orders from a woman. Not the field hands. When she issued a sharp reproof for idleness or incompetence, the response would be shrugged shoulders, vacant stares, indulgent smiles, whining excuses: "Yes, missy . . . No, missy . . . Such hard work, missy . . . We's so tired, missy . . . Better nex' time, missy." Even her manager, Joseph Valentine, seemed to have slackened his pace. Certainly the fields were not yielding their usual profitable abundance.

Nor were her London factors and other agents as cooperative— scrupulous?—as formerly. She was sure they quoted her a lesser price for tobacco than Daniel had received. The goods she ordered with such painstaking care were shoddy, of cheaper grade than specified, poorly packed so that they came badly damaged. What to do?

"Don't worry," consoled Mama on one of her hurried and infrequent visits to Chestnut Grove. "A young widow will not long remain unsought in marriage, especially one with a fortune. Suitors will soon come flocking, if they haven't already. Just be wise, my dear, in your choice."

Martha was shocked, dismayed. Daniel had not been gone a year. He was still her husband. She loved him, missed him, thought about him constantly. The very idea of another man in his place was both startling and distasteful, yet she knew that prompt marriage after the death of a spouse was the accepted norm of a prudent and thrifty society. A widow needed male guidance and security. A widower needed female oversight of his household and children. Mama had been fortunate in having sons who could assume responsibility, but even without them, Martha thought wryly, she would have continued to be self-sufficient.

"Suitors will soon come flocking—*if they haven't already!*" Startled by the idea, Martha flushed, remembering speculative glances cast in her direction by young males after church service at St. Peter's, neighbors—yes, and strangers—who had come to the house on business, stayed longer than necessary, returned to discuss matters which seemed already settled. There was one such visitor in particular, a neighbor who had recently lost his wife and was known to be in financial difficulties.

She returned home, angry that she had been so blind and resolved that nothing, certainly no *man*, would turn her from her avowed purpose. She *would* prove that she was capable of managing her own affairs.

She plunged into the business of the plantation with even more obstinate diligence, spending more hours at Daniel's desk painstakingly penning letters and trying to balance accounts, giving sharper orders to her overseer Valentine and checking to see that they were carried out, taking longer rides into the fields in an attempt to awe delinquent laborers into increased activity. Up at sunrise or earlier, punctiliously loyal to her hour of devotions, she was often at the desk straining her eyes by candlelight far into the night. Grudgingly she entrusted more and more of the care of Jacky and Patsy to their faithful nurse Molly. She grew pale, lost weight, so that she had less need of the tight, confining stays to keep her black mourning gowns in proper trimness. Since Daniel's death she had hardly left the plantation except for occasional visits to Chestnut Grove and church attendance, and during the cold months of winter there had been few services in the unheated and drafty St. Peter's.

Then suddenly it was spring. Through the open window beside her desk stole aromas of moist earth, cherry blossoms, the honeysuckle bush just coming into bloom. Her ears quickened to sounds of gaiety: the high-pitched laughter of children, Jacky playing hide-and-seek with some of the servants' children; Molly's lilting voice as she swung Patsy round and round to the tune of "Here we go round the mulberry bush"; the joyous whinnying of a horse being led to pasture; the throaty "ka ka ka" of a cuckoo and the answering call of its mate.

She could not resist. She must see as well as smell and hear. Springing up, she went to the door and flung it open, eyes reveling in the clear sky, the tender green of new grass, the loveliness of an early blooming redbud, and, far below, the lively spring turbulence of the river. For the first time in months she felt a stirring of excitement, anticipation. Life was good, to be savored and enjoyed, not buried in the past. It had been winter, but now it was spring.

Returning to the desk, she picked up the letter she had been about to answer, an invitation from her near neighbors, the Richard Chamberlaynes, to a dinner at their house the following day. "Please come, Patsy. It's so long since you have visited us. It will be just a small party. Plan to stay overnight and bring the children."

There had been many such invitations in the last eight months. She had refused them all, as she had intended to do with this. But—why not accept? She could not imprison herself in mourning forever. Daniel would not want her to. The winter was past. Picking up her quill pen, she hastily scribbled an acceptance and sent Cully, her personal servant, to take it to the Chamberlaynes.

The household sprang into activity. Even the servants felt the excitement. Missy was going somewhere. For weeks, months, she had hardly set foot off the grounds. Jacky was overjoyed. Could he ride his pony to the Chamberlaynes, the one Mama had promised him could be his very own? Reluctantly Martha shook her head, for he was only four. Not this time, darling. He must still be content with riding around the paddock, with the groom leading. But perhaps when he was five . . .

She herself was charged with anticipation. No more struggling with accounts, debits, credits, letters, for at least three days! And such a lot to do to get ready! So much had been neglected in these months, her clothes, her hair, her complexion! At least her hands were now as soft and white as Mama could wish, for she had had no time for grubby digging in her garden.

She regarded the mourning gowns in her wardrobe with distaste. Most were of bombazine, a combination of silk and cotton, heavy and unattractive. One was of fine silk, with quilted petticoat and brocaded sacque, its embroidered pattern all in black, somber. But with a ruffle of lace at throat and sleeves, black lace, of course . . . She called Betty, her plantation seamstress.

The vision in her mirror surprised her. The soft ruff of lace accentuated the whiteness of throat and arms. The freshly washed and simply coiffed brown hair held glints of gold. Powder? No, Daniel liked it smooth and natural. Impossible to forget that there was no longer need to cater to his wishes! Excitement had restored color to her cheeks. Excitement? Over a simple dinner with a neighbor? Equally impossible! Yet it seemed like escape from a long sentence in prison.

Poplar Grove, the Chamberlayne estate, was only about a mile away, but it might have been Williamsburg, so extensive were preparations for the journey. The chariot, unused for months, was refurbished, horses groomed. Molly, the nurse, and her own servant, Sally, would accompany Martha and the ecstatic children.

She was no stranger to the big two-story L-shaped Chamberlayne house, built before her birth by Colonel William, father of Richard. She and her brothers had danced there, played forfeits, London Bridge, and other noisy games with the Chamberlayne children, attended their weddings, ridden over their fields, fished off their dock. Now Richard and his wife greeted her like a long-absent relative, and indeed there was a slight family connection, for Anne Chamberlayne had been Burwell Bassett's first wife. There were only a few other guests, all of them near neighbors, some of Martha's intimate friends.

"They planned this just for me," she thought gratefully. "They knew it was time for me to start to live again."

But there was to be another guest, one wholly unexpected. As the three-o'clock dinner hour approached, a servant came running to Colonel Richard with the announcement that the ferryboat had been sighted crossing the river. Richard immediately left for the landing, within sight of Poplar Grove, for every traveler, friend, acquaintance, or stranger must be accorded the traditional hospitality of the Virginia plantation household. Dinner must wait. Proximity to the public dock of Williams's Ferry, one of the main crossings on the route from Fredericksburg to Williamsburg, made unexpected guests at the Chamberlayne table the rule rather than the exception.

While the men of the party hurried after Richard, the women flocked curiously to the windows overlooking the river. They saw the ferryboat dock, discharge its passengers, two men with two horses, then, after what seemed to be a long parley, the group of men with the two newcomers moved up the lawn toward the house.

As they came closer Martha felt a sudden surge of excitement. That tall figure, towering above the others . . . surely she had seen it before! A day in Williamsburg, a crowded street, people cheering, a blue uniform, oddly impressive in contrast with flamboyant crimsons and purples, a face with tightly compressed lips and penetrating gray-blue eyes.

Richard's wife gasped. "It—it's Colonel Washington!" she exclaimed. "Oh—I must change the arrangements at table!" She rushed away.

One of the newcomers, obviously a servant, took the horses to the rear of the house. Richard brought the guest inside and introduced him to the waiting women.

"Colonel George Washington—Mrs. Daniel Custis," Martha heard him say. She made a slight curtsy, and the Colonel bowed low, and, as he had done with the other women guests, took her hand and brushed his lips against it. There was no reason for her to feel flustered, for her pulses to quicken to a strange warmth coursing suddenly through her veins. She was no callow adolescent, susceptible to the attraction of handsome features and broad shoulders, or to the fervor of youthful hero-worship. And, looked at more closely, the handsome face had its flaws. The nose was too large, eyes too deep-set under heavy brows, skin definitely pockmarked. And as for his being such a hero, perhaps that was exaggerated. There were rumors that he was sometimes at odds with Governor Dinwiddie, and, after all, what had he accomplished except assist a defeated general to retreat from the battlefield?

Colonel Washington, she learned, was on his way to Williamsburg to consult with the Governor. He had spent the previous night at the home of John Robinson, Speaker of the Assembly, at Pleasant Hill. Intending to cross the river by the nearest route, at Eltham, he had found the ferry laid up for repairs, so had come up the river to Williams's. But it had been a happy alteration in plans, enabling him to renew acquaintance with his old friend Richard Chamberlayne, who had been with him in one of his western campaigns.

"But I had hard work persuading him to stay for dinner," explained Richard. "He intended to push on immediately for the capital, even traveling through the night. But I had to agree it would be only for dinner. He ordered his servant to have his horse saddled and ready to leave by four at the latest."

Richard did not add that he had held out a further inducement, half-jokingly, for the acceptance of his invitation, promising the Colonel an introduction to the prettiest and wealthiest widow in all Virginia!

Dinner was served immediately. Seated at the right of the host, Martha found herself diagonally across the table from the guest of honor, seated at the right of Mrs. Chamberlayne. Good! She could observe him without becoming involved in conversation. What could she possibly find to say to a man whose exploits were bruited with such admiration, whose exciting life was as far removed from her simple plantation existence as was London society from its humble replica in Virginia? But doubtless once Richard's leading questions got him started on a recital of his heroic achievements, he would monopolize the conversation.

She was wrong. It was Richard who did most of the talking, unable to elicit more than an occasional acquiescence or remonstrance from his guest. He recounted the familiar details of Washington's heroic actions at Monongahela, how he had tried to rally the scattered troops, had had one after another horse shot from under him, received bullets through his hat, yet had escaped unscathed as by a miracle.

"Is it true, Colonel," Richard inquired finally, "that story Dr. Craik tells about the prophecy of the Indian chief?" He turned to the other guests, punctuating the tale with dramatic gestures. "When every bullet seemed to miss the young warrior, this old chief is said to have remarked with admiration, 'He's not of the red-coat tribe, for he has an Indian's wisdom in fighting.' Then he added, 'The Great Spirit protects that man and guides him. He will become the chief of nations. He cannot die in battle.' "

The young Colonel's lips tightened still further and his cheeks flushed. "Craik usually knows better than to talk such foolishness," he said briefly.

"Why," thought Martha, "I believe he's embarrassed by all that laudation, and perhaps even a bit shy!" She studied his face less critically, wondering how she could have decided that it was not handsome. There was beauty in strength and dignity. Eyes less deep-set would have been less keen and penetrating. The pockmarks . . . who cared about such little imperfections? They were marks of having suffered and survived. The lips . . . Again she ascribed their tight compression not to harshness but to pain and worry. "He's still suffering," she decided. "He's ill, the way Daniel was. I wish I could do something to help."

As if her concern had acted as a magnet, suddenly he turned his head and their eyes met. The same warmth coursed through her as when his lips had brushed her hand. Confused, feeling herself flushing, she hastily turned her attention to her plate.

"This bread and butter pudding," she said to Richard's wife, "you make it better than anyone I know. I like the flavor of lemon and cinnamon. I must have your recipe."

After dinner all adjourned to the parlor. If the Colonel was in a hurry to be gone, he gave no sign. "Good manners," thought Martha. "It would not be polite to leave too soon after the meal." Four o'clock came and went. She pictured the servant waiting outside, the horse saddled and ready. The man, Richard had explained earlier, was Thomas Bishop, who had been Braddock's body servant, and the horse, a fine English charger, had also been Braddock's. He had bequeathed both of them to Washington at the time of his death.

One by one, or family by family, the other guests left until only Washington remained. Still he made no move to leave. When the Chamberlaynes, exchanging significant glances, excused themselves for necessary duties, Martha suddenly found herself alone with the Colonel. There was a silence which threatened to be embarrassing while she worked busily on a bit of sewing she had brought and searched her mind desperately for something to say.

He cleared his throat. "I was sorry to hear of your husband's death," he said with stiff courtesy. "I'm not sure I ever met him in Williamsburg, but I know his family and have heard excellent reports of his character. I hope he did not suffer."

"Not for long," replied Martha, "and he bore his suffering and illness with fortitude," she lifted her eyes to his, "as you are doing, Colonel."

"How—how did you guess?" he stammered.

It was as if her kindly concern had unlocked a gate of reticence. Presently he had drawn his chair nearer to hers by the open fire and, as if relieved to unburden himself to someone who had offered unexpected understanding, he began to tell her of his problems. It was true. For months he had been struggling with pain and illness, trying to carry on the direction of his Virginia regiment against almost impossible odds, forced finally to retreat to his home on the Potomac for recuperation. He was going to Williamsburg to see the Governor, yes, but also to consult with a physician. He had started for the capital in January, two months ago, but had been obliged to turn back because of pain and renewed symptoms of his illness. He feared, in fact was almost sure, that these symptoms . . .

"Yes?" encouraged Martha as he hesitated. This was not the first time she had found herself the confidante of a man's difficulties. For some reason her brothers had always come to her with their problems, not because she could solve them, but because she was gifted with the ability to listen. She listened now, her bit of sewing lying untouched in her lap, the light from the fire kindling soft glints of sympathetic understanding in her eyes. Somehow it did not seem at all strange that this man, famed for physical strength and heroic courage, should find solace in sharing his difficulties with a woman he had met only a few hours before.

As he continued, his own eyes became soft with reminiscence. He had had a brother named Lawrence, a half brother to be exact, but the bond between them had been very strong. Whatever he had accomplished and become he owed to this brother and—again he hesitated—perhaps to one other person. Lawrence had been his hero. He had gone to England to school, then distinguished himself under Admiral Edward Vernon in the expedition against the Spanish seaport of Cartagena in the Caribbean. In fact, he had named his estate up on the Potomac Mount Vernon in honor of the Admiral. Lawrence, it seemed, had had everything to make life worth living, a beautiful wife, a fine estate, a promising career—everything except good health. He had somewhere, perhaps on an island riddled with swamps and fever, picked up a fatal disease. Washington had gone with his brother to Barbados in the hope of restoring him to health. It was there that he himself had fallen victim to the smallpox which had left its marks on his face. But the climate had done little for Lawrence; he had returned home only to die the following year, in 1752. Now—the voice which had momentarily betrayed the stress of emotion became crisply matter-of-fact—he suspected that his symptoms were the same as his brother's. He was probably also a victim of "decay," as the disease of consumption was usually called. He was on his way to Williamsburg to find out.

Martha felt like crying out in horror. Instead, she picked up her sewing and began plying small even stitches in the manner that Mama would approve. "You may be wrong," she said with as much cheerfulness as she could muster. "The doctors in Williamsburg are very good. Sometimes one worries all for nothing."

"Yes," he said. He would consult Dr. John Amson, who was supposed to be an authority on the ailment known as "bloody flux." And he knew he shouldn't have bothered her with such personal problems. He really didn't know what had possessed him.

He was embarrassed, Martha knew, at having shared such intimate confidences with a comparative stranger, especially a woman. Somehow she must put him at ease. But how? Suppose he had been one of her brothers. "You and I must have similar problems," she suggested on an impulse, "you with your estate on the Potomac, I with mine here on the Pamunkey. Perhaps you can give me some advice."

They were soon discussing the difficulties of keeping a plantation profitable. It was Martha now who acknowledged worry and weakness. "I try so hard," she confessed, "but somehow accounts never seem to come right. I have no trouble keeping my house servants busy and apparently happy, but my field workers are often idle and—yes, even impudent to their overseers." She sighed. "I suppose it's because I'm a woman."

He nodded sympathetically. He also had difficulties being an absentee owner. Perhaps she would do well to take her lawyers' advice and hire a competent administrator.

Richard Chamberlayne looked into the room, smiled as he saw them in earnest conversation, and quietly withdrew. He went outside to where Bishop, Washington's servant, had been waiting for some two hours, the horses saddled and ready to leave. Already the sun was sinking behind the thick grove of poplar trees which gave the plantation its name.

"The Colonel seems to be a bit late," said Richard, smiling sympathetically.

Bishop shook his head, puzzled. "It's strange, passing strange," he replied. "He's never a single minute behind in keeping his appointments. I never knew a man more punctual."

"You might as well take the horses back to the stables," advised Richard. "I doubt if he will be moving on tonight."

"No." The servant was stubborn. "I couldn't do that. He told me to be ready, and I always do what he says."

Richard was waiting when, sometime after sunset, Washington emerged from the house looking crestfallen. "What have I been thinking of! I should have been gone two hours ago. Now we'll have to ride all night."

No, his host would not hear of his leaving now. No guest ever left his house after sunset. And it would be much easier traveling by daylight. Washington was not hard to persuade. Giving the surprised Bishop an order to return the horses to the stable and have a good night's rest in the servants' quarters, he returned with Richard to the house.

There was more conversation as the Chamberlaynes and their guests gathered in the firelit parlor. As evening approached candles were lighted. Though Washington seemed reluctant to talk about his military exploits or the new western campaign, when at Richard's urging he launched into a description of his house and lands at Mount Vernon he became a different person. Martha, amazed, could actually see broad expanses of fields, lawns sloping to a swift, sparkling river, a house—no mansion, he insisted, but, oh, the plans he had for it, if only he was given the opportunity to carry them out! "Why," she thought, "he's not really a soldier at heart, he's a—" She sought for the right word. Farmer? No, that didn't suffice. In fact, there seemed to be no word to encompass such an obsessive love of land, of animals, of one cherished spot of earth called home.

"You sound as if you're planning to settle down," said Richard in surprise, "and perhaps become a genuine country squire!"

His guest became suddenly grave, again almost taciturn. Well, he admitted finally, he was thinking of retiring after this western campaign, depending on certain developments. "On what the doctor in Williamsburg has to say," thought Martha, and, meeting his swift glance, she gave an encouraging smile. In fact, he admitted with a touch of whimsy, in his last order to London, along with almonds, raisins, currants, and other luxuries, he had included six dozen plates and told his agent, "pray let them to be neat and fashionable or send none."

For some reason Richard and his wife kept finding business to attend to in other parts of the house and grounds. Alone with the other guest, Martha did not force conversation. She sensed that in his worry and uncertainty, silence in this quiet, softly lighted sanctuary might be more welcome than meaningless chatter. She had no idea that, seated by the fire and rocking gently back and forth, head bent over her sewing, face softly illumined, she created for the man watching in the shadows a picture of both arresting beauty and quiet, serene domesticity, as different from another picture he carried in his mind as was soft candlelight from a vivid lightning flash. Martha would have scoffed at the idea of serenity and domesticity.

It was during one of these interludes that Molly came in with the children to bid their mother good night. Instantly the mood of quietness changed to one of charged activity. "My children, Jacky and Patsy," said Martha to Washington after they had rushed to her embrace. "Children, this is Colonel Washington."

He rose to his feet and bowed as courteously as if they had been adults worthy of honor. "Good manners," thought Martha. "Someone taught him well." Patsy gave a proper curtsy, but Jacky was less conventional. Spreading his legs wide apart, he thrust back his head and looked up, up into the man's face. "My, but you're tall!" he exclaimed admiringly.

Washington laughed. "Six feet two," he agreed. "But I can make you even taller." Stooping, he lifted the stocky youngster high above his head, then, settling him on his shoulders, made several circuits of the room before setting him down.

"My father used to do that," said Jacky, his delight tempered by soberness. "He used to ride me in front of him on his horse, too. But I've got a pony," he added with a return to gaiety. "You ought to see me ride him, all by myself."

"Perhaps I can," said Washington. "Suppose I stop on my way back from Williamsburg—that is, if your mother doesn't mind." He turned to her questioningly, their eyes meeting over the boy's head.

"Guests are always welcome at the White House," she said, her voice carefully casual.

"Promise?" demanded Jacky.

"I promise," was the reply.

Patsy, much shyer, clung to Molly's hand, but after Washington had again seated himself, Jacky hovering at his side, she approached timidly and let him lift her to his knee. Martha added two favorable deductions to her appraisal of this unpredictable and disturbingly complex new acquaintance. "He can laugh, and he likes children."

Washington seemed in no hurry to leave the next morning. The sun was high when Bishop was ordered to bring the horses. All assembled in the yard to see them leave. After he had swung himself into the saddle, he leaned over and spoke to his servant. Smiling, Bishop lifted Jacky and Washington leaned down, hoisted the child to a seat in front of him on the huge charger, and rode with him several times around the yard, once urging the steed to an exciting canter, then delivered the enraptured child into Bishop's waiting arms. Martha's eyes filled with tears. Kind, she added to her growing list, and thoughtful.

As they stood looking after the galloping horsemen, Richard's wife seized her arm. "Patsy! Did you notice how splendidly he rides his horse, as if—as if—Oh, I can't describe it!"

Yes, Martha had noticed. As if, she finished silently, a perfect equestrian statue had come to life.

She wondered if she would ever see him again.

6

"But he promised!" wailed Jacky.

It was three days after their return to the White House, and the boy had spent most of his waking hours close to the lane leading to the main road.

"I know," comforted Martha, "but it wouldn't be time for him to come yet. It's a long ride to Williamsburg from Poplar Grove, and he had many things to attend to in the city. And you mustn't set your heart on his coming, son. He is a very busy and important man, and it isn't likely that he can spend time visiting people on the way back to his regiment."

"But he promised," insisted the child stoutly.

Jacky was not the only one who kept watch of the plantation workers and frequent visitors who came along the lane. Just so, Martha recalled, she had once run to the doors and windows in expectation of the coming of Daniel Custis, and the memory brought a disconcerting flush to her cheeks. As if a few hours of conversation with a stranger and the exchange of a sympathetic glance or two had meant more than a mere chance encounter! After all, she was a widow of nearly twenty-seven, presumably no longer susceptible to youthful emotions. If he should take time to visit the White House on his way back from Williamsburg—and it would take him several miles out of his way—of course it would be because he had promised Jacky.

Nevertheless, she rose each dawn with a feeling of inexplicable excitement, making sure that the house was spotless, that special food was prepared in case of guests, and that there were vases of new spring flowers in every room in the house. She even dispatched her faithful servant Cully to keep watch on the river side of the estate, just in case a visitor she was half-expecting might come that way. All this was normal preparation for any chance traveler. Not so a final change of habit. When she rose now in the morning, instead of donning one of the heavy black bombazines, so uncomfortable now it was spring—yes, and so homely—she put on one of her calico gowns, sober in color but delicately printed with flowers. It was not being disloyal to Daniel, she decided. He had always hated to see her in black.

Days passed. Comforting the disconsolate Jacky, she smiled brightly, but it was a forced, mechanical smile. Impossible not to feel disappointed herself, though she knew she should not have expected him to come. What had happened, she wondered, in Williamsburg? What had the doctor told him? And why should it matter so much to her if this comparative stranger had been given a death sentence, especially since it was likely she would never see him again?

And then in the last week of March, nearly a fortnight after their return from the Chamberlaynes, he was there, striding up the path from the river, with Jacky clinging to his hand. "Ma! Look, he's here!"

She was out in the garden down on her knees weeding a bed of tulips when the cry brought her swiftly to her feet. Yes, there he was, and the spring day became suddenly imbued with all the warmth and luxuriant bloom of summer.

Cully, watching as bidden by the dock, had seen the two horsemen on the other side of the river, apparently wishing to cross. He had taken the rowboat and gone over. The conversation which then ensued would be preserved for posterity, due no doubt to the frequent renditions by Cully himself.

"Is your mistress at home?"

"Yes, sah, I reckon you'se the man what's expected."

Martha watched him come, and she knew even at a distance that the sentence of the doctor in Williamsburg had been life, not death. It was in the briskness of step, the set of powerful shoulders, the jaunty upthrust of head, and, as he came closer, the absence of pain and worry from lips and eyes. To her embarrassment he took both her small earthstained hands in his big ones and bent low in a courtly bow.

"Mistress Custis! It's such a pleasure to see you again!"

Martha hoped the edges of her sunbonnet hid the flaming of her cheeks, which felt as if they had turned the bright hue of her crimson poppies. "How good of you to come, Colonel!" she returned politely. "Jacky has been reminding me of your promise. That's why I put my servant on watch for you."

He could stay only a few hours, it developed. Bishop would be waiting for him across the river with the horses. His business in Williamsburg had taken him longer than expected. In fact, it was not finished now. He must ride back to Williamsburg, have another conference with the acting Governor, for Dinwiddie had left for England the preceding November, then rush on to his regiment at Winchester, stopping briefly perhaps in Fredericksburg to see his mother and sister and at Mount Vernon.

So, thought Martha gratefully, watching as Jacky proudly rode his pony around the paddock for the benefit of the guest, he made a special trip of about sixty extra miles to keep his promise to a small boy . . . or . . . As she bustled about giving hurried orders to the servants for a festive meal, washed the soil from her hands, removed the sunbonnet and, after brushing her hair smooth, substituted a frilly cap of lace and ribbons, she dared only briefly to speculate on what other reasons might have brought him.

Yes, he told her when they had retired to the parlor after the sumptuous dinner, he had consulted the eminent Dr. John Amson, and the news had been surprisingly good. The doctor's long experience with ailments of this kind had convinced him that fears were groundless and that the new symptoms meant little. He would soon be back in robust health. This was no news to Martha, though she responded with the proper pleasure and congratulations. She had known from the moment she first saw his face.

He seemed in no more hurry to leave than during their encounter at the Chamberlaynes'. But finally, when the afternoon was so far advanced that he must go soon if he was to cross the river and reach an "ordinary" (the common word for "inn") before dark, he reached the real purpose of his visit. He spoke haltingly, for he was not gifted with glib speech, but his words were clear, simple, and straightforward. He was twenty-six years old, and unmarried. Mistress Custis was a widow, beautiful, with charms that many men would certainly be unable to resist. She must have known that he had been attracted to her at their first meeting. In fact, he wanted to make her his wife. Of course she need not decide at once, that was too much to expect. But he did not want to leave for the uncertainties of a dangerous western campaign without making his proposal. He would be returning as soon as possible, and he would hope then to receive her answer. That is—he gave her a disarmingly boyish smile—unless she gave him a refusal now.

Martha did not refuse. Neither did she give her consent. In spite of the pounding of her pulses she managed to keep her voice calm and steady. She appreciated the great honor he had paid her, and, yes, she would give the proposal her earnest consideration. She had been much impressed by his attitude toward her children, and she knew they would benefit from such an arrangement. She would look forward to his return, hopefully in the near future, when she would tell him her decision.

Mercifully the children arrived then and appropriated the guest for the short remaining time of his stay. When he left he again took both her hands, not only bowing but laying his lips briefly on each one. She watched him go, striding down the path toward the river, Jacky clinging to his hand, Cully in their wake. At the dock he turned, sensing perhaps that she was watching, and raised his arm in a parting salute. Slowly she went back into the house.

So this was what people, what Papa, had meant, when they talked about being "in love." The touch of one person was like fire coursing through your veins. His absence, even for a short while, meant unutterable loss. But colors were suddenly brighter, the fragrance of flowers sweeter, you could not breathe deeply enough to absorb all the intoxicating essence of the world around you, and you felt yourself one with all the mystery of creation.

She did not tell anybody. It was like the first knowledge that you were succoring another life within yourself, something to be savored alone for a while before sharing it. Besides, she wanted to wait until she had given her answer. But she did yield to one temptation. She wrote a letter to her agent in London, Carey and Company, ordering "one genteel suite of cloathes for myself to be grave but not to be extravagant and not to be mourning."

Before sealing the letter she added another order of a more intimate nature, blushing as she wrote, "I have sent a night gown to be dide of a fashionable couler fitt for me to ware and beg you wont [she meant will] have it dide better than that I sent you last year but was very badly done. This gown is of a good length for me."

Another letter was dispatched soon after the Colonel's arrival in Winchester, ordering from Richard Washington, his kinsman in London "by the first ship bound for Virginia . . . as much of the best superfine blue cotton velvet as will make a coat, waistcoat and breeches for a tall man, with a fine silk button to suit it . . . six pairs of the very neatest shoes . . . and six pair gloves . . ."

He came to the White House again the first week in June, having been sent to Williamsburg to procure such equipment as he could from John Blair, the acting Governor of Virginia, in preparation for his western campaign. At first, while the delighted children were present, conversation was about ordinary matters, the progress of crops on both their plantations, affairs in Williamsburg, Jacky's increasing prowess on his pony, Patsy's amusing attempts to repeat new words she had learned. His attention to the children, thought Martha, already reflected something of the pride and affection of a father. As her eyes met his over their heads, she was conscious of their mute question and wondered if her own were as mutely revealing. Then, when dinner was over and Molly came to take the children away for their rest, Jacky beguilingly resistant, she knew the moment had come.

They sat for a while in silence, and she sensed once more his innate shyness and—could it be in one so glamorized?—self-depreciation.

"Have you—considered—decided"—he was as embarrassed and tongue-tied as a schoolboy—"what I spoke to you about on my previous visit . . ."

"Yes, Colonel?" she prompted helpfully but without lifting her eyes from her knitting.

He cleared his throat. "You may recall, Mistress Custis, that I made you a—a proposal. I asked you to—to become my wife."

"I do recall that, Colonel," she replied composedly. For some perverse reason she was determined not to make it easy for him. If he really wanted her . . .

"And have you—have you come to a decision?"

"I have, Colonel." Still she did not lift her eyes, just kept on knitting.

"And—your answer is—?"

She did lift her eyes now and looked straight into his. It was not like her to be coy or hesitant. "My answer," she said simply, "is yes."

Suddenly he was on his knees beside her chair. The knitting fell out of her hands, for he had taken both of them in his and was covering them with kisses. Then just as suddenly he was on his feet, giving her a dignified and courtly bow.

"My dear Mistress Custis," he began with stilted gallantry.

"The name," she interrupted, smiling, "is Martha, but everybody calls me Patsy."

He started over, returning her smile and relaxing, his voice boyishly, tenderly grateful. "My dear—Patsy, you have made me a very happy man."

There was little time for making plans. He must hasten back to the frontier to take part in the offensive he had long been urging. He had obtained most of the supplies he sought from the burgesses. This time, he hoped, the attack on Fort Duquesne would result in victory, not disaster, like the fiasco with Braddock. At the end of this campaign, he told her, he planned to retire from military service. On the way back to Winchester he would stop briefly at Mount Vernon and start plans for remodeling the house for his new family. His neighbor and close friend, George William Fairfax, who had recently returned from England, would take charge of the improvements that must be made. Yes, and he was declaring himself a candidate for burgess from Frederick County. Though he had failed to win the election three years before, he had friends working for him now who thought he might succeed.

"So," he told her, smiling, "you will not be the wife of a soldier but of a farmer, landholder, and family man, also, hopefully, a member of the Assembly."

Martha breathed a sigh of relief. To have him always with her, not away somewhere, in danger! It would be heaven. But, oh, the days and weeks and months of fear and worry before heaven could be reached!

At least she could share the prospect of future happiness with her family. She mounted her horse—Foxglove it was now, for Graylegs had been long gone, and the beautiful roan that had caused her encounter with Daniel was getting old—and rode to Chestnut Grove. Mama received the news of the engagement with her usual calm but slightly caustic acceptance.

"So—Colonel Washington, the military hero. Well, one hears good things about him and some not quite so good. They say he has an eye for pretty women, rich ones most of them, and has been turned down by some of them. How can you be sure, Patsy, that he's not marrying you for your money and lands? After all, you are one of the richest women in Virginia."

Martha's amusement was tinged with irritation. "And how can he be sure," she retorted, "that I'm not marrying him to get a manager for my estate? After all, I certainly need one."

But Mama was really highly pleased with the news. The Washingtons were an old and distinguished family in Virginia, though not among the wealthiest. The first Washington to reach Virginia, John, had arrived about a hundred years before. He had been an important member of the House of Burgesses. His father, Lawrence, Mama understood, like her own grandfather, had been a preacher in England, but because he was a royalist he had been deprived of his parish when Charles II was in exile. Yes, it would be a respectable marriage, though not with one of the *very first* families like the Custises. Martha listened, humoring her mother and glad she was pleased. For herself she could not have cared less whether her future husband's ancestor arrived in Virginia with a coat of arms or just a simple frock coat.

It was with relief that she left Chestnut Grove and rode toward Eltham, her sister Nancy Bassett's home. Of course Frances Dandridge, always wisely practical, must temper her warm approval with a dash of cold water. But—was Mama right? Was the Colonel more interested in her fortune than in herself? Had she imagined the warmth which had seemed to flow between them from their first meeting, like interlocking rays of sunlight, charging every touch and glance with magic? No! She would not believe it. Impulsively she spurred Foxglove to a canter, increasing the pace to a brisk gallop, finding relief from her unease in swift motion.

Nancy, bless her, was comfortingly exuberant. What exciting and fascinating news! Her favorite sister to be married to the most popular hero in all Virginia! When was the wedding going to be? Could she help plan it? Had Martha sent to England yet for materials for her wedding dress? It should be silk brocade, shouldn't it, trimmed with— what? Lace or lutestring? And would it be at St. Peter's or at the White House?

Martha laughed. The wedding was a long time away, she reminded.

The Colonel had gone campaigning, and no one knew when he would return. But her sister's enthusiasm helped to quiet her doubts. Burwell Bassett was even more reassuring. Spending much time in Williamsburg, he was fully apprised of colony gossip.

"Congratulations, sister. So the Colonel has at last succumbed, and about time. He's twenty-six years old, to my knowledge. And, though he has a reputation for sensitivity to female charms, never before has he been known to commit himself. On his trip to Boston two years ago, I understand, his name was linked for a time with the beautiful Mary Phillipse, heiress to some fifty thousand acres of New York land. Charms and fortune notwithstanding, the Colonel evidently made no proposal. Perhaps her reputation as a dominating personality discouraged him. Anyway, he has shown good taste in his final choice."

Martha breathed a sigh of relief. No need to worry that he would be marrying her for her wealth, if he had avoided alliance with a Mary Phillipse! But it was Burwell Bassett who inadvertently aroused another nagging worry, one that was to haunt her life for years to come.

"Funny! I heard a bit of gossip once. Probably nothing to it, but somebody said, *sub rosa,* that the Colonel had sort of a yen for the wife of his friend and neighbor, George William Fairfax of Belvoir, she who used to be Sally Cary of Ceelys." Aware suddenly that he might have been guilty of an indiscretion, Burwell hastily tried to negate the idea. "Silly rumor, nothing to it, I'm sure. You know how foolish gossip gets started. And even if it were true, some schoolboy infatuation . . . Of course it was all over long ago." He gave a nervous laugh.

Martha echoed his laughter. "Of course," she returned lightly. But as she rode home, slowly now, hands slack, Foxglove choosing his own leisurely pace, she kept remembering. A hedge of dogwood in full bloom conjured a vision of a tall, slim figure all in white. A swirl of golden dust shot through with sunlight suggested that same figure whirling and dipping through the figures of a dance. The voice of a woman greeting her from a passing carriage might have been that of Dorothea Spotswood. "She *is* beautiful, isn't she? That is Sally Cary . . . clever . . . fascinating . . . surrounded by admirers . . . half of them would-be suitors . . ."

A rumor. But suppose it was true. How, she wondered, could any man once even boyishly enamored of the tall, fair, scintillating Sally

Cary Fairfax fall in love with the short, moderately pretty, slightly plump Martha Dandridge Custis?

She was nearly home when her innate common sense reasserted itself. What matter? Of course Colonel Washington had had other romantic attachments. Had not she herself been happily married? But it was she, Martha Custis, whom he had chosen to become his wife. Responding to her change of mood, Foxglove sprang to swiftness, and they raced along the side road and down the lane to the White House, her scarlet riding coat a bright streak of color against the greens of poplars and catalpas.

There followed months of waiting, of expectation, of agony, of disappointment, of preparation for a fulfillment which kept moving further into the future. Surely, she thought, he would keep her informed about his plans and actions. All through the rest of June and almost to the end of July she awaited a letter, but none came. When one finally arrived she tore it open, eagerness mingled with apprehension. Had he perhaps changed his mind? It was dated July 20 and was very short. Strangely enough, it did not contain even a salutation.

"We have begun our march for the Ohio. A courier is starting for Williamsburg, and I embrace the opportunity to send a few words to one whose life is now inseparable from mine. Since that happy hour when we made our pledges to each other, my thoughts have been continually going to you as to another Self. That an all-powerful Providence may keep us both in safety is the prayer of your ever faithful and affectionate friend."

Relief? Disappointment? What had she been expecting? Impassioned words of love such as Daniel Custis would have written? Again common sense banished any doubt and uncertainty the words might have aroused. This man was not another Daniel Custis, devoted solely to home and family. He was a public servant, with tasks demanding complete dedication. She should be grateful that he had spared time for even this brief message. And there were words in it to reread and cherish: ". . . life now inseparable from mine . . . happy hour when we made our pledges . . . another Self . . . ever faithful and affectionate . . ."

It was well she could not know of much longer missives that the Colonel was sending to a woman other than his affianced wife, at least two of which were to be preserved by their recipient and discovered in

England in her effects some hundred years later, letters which contained some poignantly revealing passages:

"To Mrs. George Fairfax, Camp at Fort Cumberland, September 12, 1758.

"Dear Madam: Yesterday I was honored with your short but very agreeable favor of the first inst. How joyfully I catch at that happy occasion of renewing a correspondence which I feared was disrelished on your part. I leave to time, that never failing expositor of all things, and to a monitor equally faithful in my own breast, to testify. In silence I express my joy; silence, which in some cases, I wish the present, speaks more intelligently than the sweetest eloquence.

"If you allow that any honor can be derived from my opposition to our present system of management, you destroy the merit of it entirely in me by attributing my anxiety to the animating prospect of possessing Mrs. Custis, when—I need not tell you, guess yourself. Should not my own Honor and country's welfare be the excitement? 'Tis true, I profess myself a votary of love. I acknowledge that a lady is in the case, and further I confess that this lady is known to you. Yes, Madame, as well as she is to one who is too sensible of her charms to deny the Power whose influence he feels and must ever submit to. I feel the force of her amiable beauties in the recollection of a thousand tender passages that I could wish to obliterate till I am bid to revive them . . . You have drawn me, dear Madame, or rather I have drawn myself, into an honest confession of a simple fact. Misconstrue not my meaning; doubt it not, nor expose it. The world has no business to know the object of my Love, declared in this manner to you when I want to conceal it . . ."

Fortunately Martha would never know of this missive or of others written during the months of anxious waiting. She was grateful for his brief letters telling of his whereabouts and the details of the western campaign. She sympathized with his frustration over the slowness of the military movement and the insistence of the new British General, John Forbes, on cutting a new route to Fort Duquesne through Pennsylvania instead of following Braddock's old road, as he had forcefully—stubbornly, it seemed—recommended. She rejoiced over his election as burgess from Frederick County, which loyal friends had promoted after he had left Winchester for Fort Cumberland, winning by a large majority in spite of his enforced absence. And the news that pleased her most was that the work on his house, Mount Vernon, was proceeding well under the direction of his friend George William Fairfax, including not only repairs but also the installation of new carpets and furnishings in preparation for the coming of his bride.

Though all his letters were as brief and devoid of emotional content as the first, that did not worry Martha. Her concern was wholly for his safety. As the regiments probed deeper and deeper into the wilderness and his letters ceased, she awoke to each new day with both hope and apprehension. She rode frequently to Eltham, less to confer with the excited Nancy about plans for her marriage than to hear from Burwell Bassett news gleaned on his latest trip to Williamsburg.

Though the fabrics had arrived for her wedding gown and were being fashioned into creations after the latest London style, Martha regarded them with only casual interest. Why think of silks and brocades when *he* was struggling over mountains, through swamps, perhaps being ambushed, killed? She sought comfort in the fabled prophecy of the Indian chief, that he could not die in battle, but she did not really believe it.

Days, weeks, months crawled by. October. Forbes was pushing forward, reported Burwell, but Washington had written Governor Fauquier that the road was indescribably bad, the weather more and more inclement. There was little hope of reaching Fort Duquesne before winter.

November. Again Washington had written Fauquier: ". . . we expect to move on in a few days, encountering every hardship that an advanced season, want of clothing, and no great stock of provisions will expose us to." Washington had been given a brigade and had been ordered to clear a road toward Fort Duquesne . . . He was chopping down trees and building bridges and causeways over streams and marshy ground . . . The nearer he and his troops came to the fort, the greater was the danger of an ambush . . .

"Unless they reach their goal by the first of December, when most of the troops' terms of service are due to expire," said Burwell, "there's not much hope of victory during this campaign."

"And suppose they do reach it," thought Martha, "there's no assurance that it will mean victory instead of defeat—and death." Thank heaven she was not looking forward to being a soldier's wife! Once this terrible uncertainty was over, if he remained safe, there would be no more such campaigns. He had promised to resign.

Then . . . the news spread through Virginia, penetrated even to remote plantations, like the White House. Fort Duquesne had fallen without a battle! It had been found burned, deserted. By the light of its flames the French troops had departed, some by water, some on foot, never to return to the Ohio country. The war was over. Washington and his Virginia troops had been in the vanguard of the strange assault. All over the colony he was once more being acclaimed as a hero.

Relief, yes, but not release from all worry. When would he come? Or —would he? It had been six months since she had seen him, and never more than a few hours at a time. She had a hard time remembering even how he looked. Would the bond she had felt from their first meeting still be between them? Had she promised to spend the rest of her life with a comparative stranger? Anticipation changed to panic.

It was late in December when he came, and she had no warning. Apprised of his approach by an excited servant, when he rode into the yard she was standing in the open door, shivering from the December cold and even more from trepidation. He flung himself from his horse and came toward her. Standing there small and lovely in her bright-flowered calico, she could not know that to the weary soldier who had come to her through mud and wilderness she was the picture of homely well-being and contentment, a comforting contrast to any dreams he might be conjuring of tall, slender, alluring but unattainable beauty. He took both her small hands in his big ones, and in spite of their coldness she felt enveloped in warmth.

She looked up into his face. How could she have thought she had forgotten its features? Its rugged lines seemed as familiar as if she had known them all her life. He's tired, she thought, as she had done that day in Williamsburg at her first sight of him. Yes, and he's been sick again. He needs someone to take care of him. All her doubts vanished. She drew him with her into the comfort of the warm firelit house.

He could not stay long, no, not even for the approaching festivities of Christmas, though he looked regretfully at the greens and festoons and gift-laden tree which awaited the holiday. He must go on to Williamsburg the next day to try to persuade the Governor to provide warmer clothing and better equipment for the ragged men of his regiment who had been assigned to spend the bleak winter months at the site of Fort Duquesne—now renamed Fort Pitt—on the icebound Ohio. But that evening, a child on either knee, he sat with her by the fire while they discussed plans. He told her, to her great relief, that he had already resigned from the army. She would be the wife, not of a soldier but of a planter, also a burgess. His eyes glowed in the firelight, the weariness gone momentarily from his face. His could hardly wait to get settled on his beloved estate at Mount Vernon, finish the improvements on the house, put all his plans for the farm into operation. And he wanted the wedding to take place as soon as possible. Would the first week in January be too soon? Could she manage it?

Martha gasped. No more than two weeks to get ready! Her mind raced. Invitations to dispatch, food to prepare for—how many guests? Thirty? Forty? Surely that many, with her relatives and his and all their friends, plus dignitaries wishing to honor the most popular man in all Virginia! The ceremony could not be at St. Peter's, which was unheated in the winter. She was glad. There would have been ghosts of her first marriage in St. Peter's. It must be here at the White House. At least, thanks to the importunate Nancy, she had her wedding dress ready.

"Yes," she replied composedly after only a moment's hesitation. "I can manage it."

When he had gone the household—all three households, in fact—sprang into frenzied activity. Fires in the cookhouses were kept blazing. The White House was dusted, swept, scoured from top to bottom, for every room would be needed for guests, as well as extra accommodations at Chestnut Grove and Eltham. Messengers were dispatched with invitations, since mails were infrequent and undependable. The Reverend David Mossum was notified. Nancy came up from Eltham and stayed, relieving Martha of many routine details. Mama, of course, was generous with advice and efficient management. Christmas had to be observed for the children's sake with due festivities, but it had become of secondary importance.

Martha labored over the names George—she still found it hard to speak, even to think the name—had given her. One invitation she found especially difficult to write: "Mr. and Mrs. George William Fairfax." The Fairfaxes, she knew, were George's closest neighbors and friends. Of course they must be invited. But—subject her own imperfect, probably misspelled script to the eyes of the impeccable and elegant Sally? Finally she dashed it off carelessly, in an impulse of defiance. I hope they don't come, she thought guiltily.

The day came, Wednesday, the sixth of January 1759. It started with light snow flurries but soon cleared. She stood in front of the mirror while Nancy and Sally, her maid, with Mama looking critically on, applied one festive garment after another. "Tighter," she directed as they laced the stiffly boned stays. She was used to the feeling of imprisonment now, and today she wanted to look her best. Impossible to be slim and tall like the fabulous Sally Fairfax, but at least she could disguise indications of growing plumpness. With "Oh's" and Ah's" they slipped over her head the gown of yellow brocaded grosgrain silk, arranging the rich point-lace ruffles about its neck, running admiring fingers along its trimmings of pink lutestring. It was indeed a beautiful gown, its open-front skirt revealing the lustrous folds of a white and silver petticoat of quilted satin. Her high-heeled white satin slippers, a diminutive size five, were embroidered in gold and silver. As a final touch Nancy looped about her freshly powdered hair the Custis pearls which Daniel had given her as a wedding present. She wore other pearls about her neck and on her round white arms.

"Beautiful!" approved Mama, while lamenting that Papa was not there to see.

"Whee!" Jacky's round-eyed admiration was less formal but more expressive. Patsy, who had also been brought in by Molly to view the bride, was speechless with delight.

Both children had been overjoyed at news of the wedding, Jacky's exuberance exploding with high-pitched glee. "Jolly good! Hear that, Patsy? That tall man, the Colonel, is going to be our new father!" Patsy, while less vociferous, was equally delighted.

They were outfitted almost as lavishly as the bride, looking very much as in their portrait painted by John Wollaston two years before, Jacky like a little old man in his silk waistcoat ruffled at neck and wrists, long satin coat, velvet knee breeches, silk stockings and velvet slippers; Patsy a tiny model of adulthood in low-necked gown, narrow bodice and full skirt, eyes unnaturally slanted, to Martha's displeasure, as in all of Wollaston's paintings.

Martha descended the stairs to a scene of such color and splendor as had seldom been seen even in tidewater Virginia. Governor Fauquier, who had arrived in Williamsburg the preceding June, had come in full dress of scarlet cloth embroidered with gold, impressive in his bagwig and gleaming dress-sword. Other military officers were equally resplendent. Silks and satins shimmered, velvets and brocades glowed richly, diamonds glittered. By no means least among the brilliant assemblage was Washington's man Bishop, standing outside the door, tall and dignified, dressed in his scarlet uniform of a soldier in the royal army of George II, booted and spurred, his hand on the bridle rein of his master's charger, both of them legacies of the ill-fated Braddock.

To Martha it was all a blur of color, movement, confusion. Even the figures of her three bridesmaids in their rainbow silks, all of them close friends from the neighborhood, seemed to merge into one. But the tall figure who stood waiting for her in the drawing room before the Reverend Mr. Mossum she saw clearly. He was wearing his uniform of the Virginia regiment, a suit of blue cloth, coat lined with red silk, over an embroidered white satin waistcoat, with white gloves, oversize to fit his huge hands, gold shoe buckles, a straight dress-sword.

Standing beside him under the crystal chandelier with its four lighted candles, Martha felt very small compared with his more than six feet of height, but she drew herself up to her full five feet slightly plus, glad of her high heels and of the fashion of coiffure which was beginning to dictate a high pompadour. For the second time she repeated the solemn vow pledging herself to one man "until death do us part," this time with far more soberness and understanding. For before she had been little more than a child. Now she was a woman, and the man beside her awakened emotions and loyalties which she had not known existed.

"For better for worse, for richer for poorer, in sickness and in health . . ."

Though such a prospect seemed far removed from the comfortable milieu, there might well have been added, "In peace and in war, in victory and in defeat."

After the ceremony she moved among the guests, the thoughtful and proficient hostess. There was George's family to meet—his brother Augustine from Westmoreland, his brother Charles from Jefferson County, and from Fredericksburg his sister Betty, Mrs. Fielding Lewis, who looked so much like him that Martha was startled.

"I know." Her new sister-in-law flashed a merry smile. "Give me a wig and a cocked hat and a uniform, and I'll play Colonel Washington for you. I've often done it."

George's mother had not come from her home in Fredericksburg.

"She thinks she's too old for such a journey," explained Betty with a wry smile, "but if you ask me, she just wants to make her son bring his bride to *her*. She's a rather independent soul, as you will discover."

Martha was not sorry. Mary Ball Washington, she judged from reports, was formidable as well as independent. Better to make her acquaintance in less confusing surroundings. Neither was she distressed at the absence of two other invitees, the George William Fairfaxes. She could not imagine Sally in any role except that of star, and this was *her* day, Martha's. Besides, there was that foolish rumor . . .

All the people she cared about most were there, relatives and friends, her brothers William and Bartholomew to stand in her father's place; Mama with ten-year-old Elizabeth, and little Mary, a child of three; Nathanael and his wife Dorothea; neighbors like the Chamberlaynes.

As the afternoon progressed more candles were lighted in all the sconces, and fires glowed in every fireplace until, when supper was served, the house was ablaze with lights. Everything gleamed and glittered—white arms and shoulders, jewels, crystals and silver on the long supper table, the scabbards of dress-swords. The Negro servants marched in, bearing polished pewter dishes. The faces of the kitchen helpers shone. It was a bountiful feast, terrapin and venison, Chesapeake Bay oysters, crab, wild turkey, followed by a mountainous array of ices and other sweets. After supper there was dancing, and Martha noted with surprise that her husband excelled in the art, every form from minuet to quadrille, and that before the evening was over he had danced with every lady in the party.

Perhaps it was her servant Cully who long afterward would give a questioner the most eloquent description of the day's festivities.

"And so, Cully, you remember when Colonel Washington came a'courting of your mistress?"

" 'Deed I do, master. He was dar on'y fo' times afo' de wedding, for you see he was in de war all de time. We couldn't keep our eyes off him, he seemed so grand. An' Bishop 'peared 'mos' as grand as he."

"And the wedding, Cully?"

"Great times, sah, great times! Shall never see de like agin. Mo' hosses an' car'ges, an' fine ladies an' gen'lemen dan when Missus was married afo'."

"And Colonel Washington, how did he look, Cully?"

"Neber seed de like, sah! Neber de likes of him, tho' I've seed many in my day. He was so tall, so straight, so han'some! An' he set a hoss and rid wid such an air! Oh, he was so grand! Ah, sah, he was like no one else. Many of de grandest gen'lmen in gold lace was at de weddin', but none looked like de man hisself!"

"And your mistress?"

Cully raised both hands and his eyes turned toward the sky. "Oh, she was so bootiful an' so good!"

For three days the festivities continued. The morning after their first night together in the bridal chamber, beautifully decorated with evergreens and holly—not the room she had shared for nine years with Daniel—Martha donned her "second-day dress," a flowered silk over a ruffled white petticoat. Many of the guests lingered on. In fact, it was almost a week later that the wedding party prepared to leave. They were not going to Mount Vernon at once. It was decided that until after the coming Assembly, George's first as burgess, they would live in the Six-Chimney House in Williamsburg. A welcome interlude, Martha felt, before breaking the intimate ties with family and moving far away into a life of newness and strangeness.

Sitting in the Custis coach with her children, the six horses prancing in eagerness to be off, her liveried black postilions mounted and ready to take the lead, Martha looked back on the twenty-seven years of her life. There was the White House, where she had spent her happiest and saddest years. There, gathered in the portico, was her family, Mama, her brothers and sisters, Nancy, fun-loving William and sober, studious Bartholomew, ten-year-old Elizabeth, and little Mary, not yet three. They would be the last guests to leave. Beside her on his big charger, with Bishop attending, was her husband, ready—impatient— to escort the coach on its journey.

Martha gazed at him, enthralled. What a superb figure he was on a horse! Yes, the two *were* like a magnificent statue, carved out of the same stuff. Marble, perhaps? No, marble was too cold, lifeless. Bronze. Warm and golden in sunlight.

She felt a moment of panic. This man she had married was a hero, his name honored throughout Virginia. How could she, a simple back-country woman, become the sort of wife he needed? He should have someone like—yes, like the beautiful, competent, scintillating Sally. But the moment passed as she remembered with sudden relief that he was resigning his commission. He was going to be a farmer, a plantation owner, a country squire like Daniel, like her father. She need not worry. She was going into the same kind of life she was leaving.

The driver flicked his whip. She waved to the group at the portico. The statue of the horseman sprang into motion. With a great flurry the coach and its escort rolled and pounded up the driveway and into the road.

"We're off!" shouted Jacky gleefully.

"Yes," said Martha Dandridge Custis Washington. Perhaps it was fortunate that she could not see where that road was leading.

7

Were there ghosts of the past at the Six-Chimney House which seemed to resent her newfound happiness? Not memories of Daniel. She sensed somehow, having known him so well, that his love and approval still surrounded her. It was the sight of the garden, frozen in winter bareness and neglected by indifferent gardeners, which summoned a vision of a grotesque figure with flapping garments and wig awry, uttering accusing comments.

"So—what's going to happen to my precious garden now you're no longer a Custis? Left to run wild or die, most likely! And those grandchildren of mine? You're so pleased that your new husband is fond of them! I'll wager he'll want to adopt them and make them little Washingtons. Then the name of Custis will be as dead as my garden!"

Martha was walking with George among the imported trees, the leafless shrubs, the plots of exotic perennials strewn with dead leaves and weeds.

"So this is old John Custis's famous collection!" he exclaimed. "For years I've been hearing about it." His eyes lighted with eagerness. "It's superb. Listen, Patsy, we mustn't let it go to ruin. We'll find a better gardener, restore it to what the old codger tried to make it and keep it that way. Don't you agree?"

"Oh, yes!" Martha felt swift relief. A gust of January wind seemed to erupt into a throaty chuckle. But the ghost still lingered. Mingled with her delight in watching her husband's increasing affection for her children was that sense of another nagging problem. *Then the name of Custis will be as dead* . . . She could almost hear old John speak the words. Finally she decided to broach the subject.

"Would you like to adopt the children?" she asked George after Molly had borne them away to bed after a lively romp during which he had played roles of prancing steed, jouncing chariot, and, stretched full-length on the carpet, a mountain to be climbed. "Already they think of you as their father. Perhaps it's only fair that they should bear your—our name."

He considered for what seemed a long time. "No," he said at last. "It wouldn't be fair. They are Daniel's children. Custis is a noble name, and it's theirs by right. I can love and care for them just as much. Besides," he smiled down at her, "there's plenty of time for children to bear my name."

So, if there were ghosts, they were exorcised. The restless figure no longer roamed the garden. They spent three months at the House of the Six Chimneys, the happiest of Martha's life.

No more worry about debts, accounts that would not balance, servants who would not respect a woman, irresponsible factors, orders to London that might result in shoddy and overpriced merchandise. George, the overly methodical, the competent, the scrupulously honest, assumed full responsibility for the Custis business affairs, both hers and the children's. Though the General Court would not sit in chancery until April, when he could assume formal administration of the estate, already he had acquainted himself with the details. Martha's personal estate of one third would belong to him, and he would become the guardian of the two thirds allotted to the children.

Since the active social season in Williamsburg did not start until the meeting of the Assembly in late February, George and Martha had time for leisurely planning, also for getting acquainted. It was a joyous honeymoon. They spent long hours discussing new furnishings for Mount Vernon, for with the departure and remarriage of Anné Fairfax Washington, widow of George's brother Lawrence, the house had been left nearly bare. What should Martha take from the White House and what should be ordered from England? George had already chosen the paint and wallpaper for many of the rooms, including their bedroom, but the latter must be furnished and decorated according to Martha's taste. Though she could not make decisions until she reached there, they could indulge in excited speculation. It was well that she had sent orders for dress materials, fans, jewelry to London, so that she would do George credit as his bride as soon as the *Cornwall,* captained by Thomas Hooker, should arrive loaded with chests of merchandise.

One consignment came while they were in Williamsburg, and to Martha's delight it contained toys for the children. There was a wee coach-and-six, with a little stable for the horses. For Patsy there was a tiny corner cupboard and a walnut bureau for her dolls. Martha took more pleasure from George's enjoyment over the children's excitement than from their enchantment with the new treasures.

Together she and George compiled a list of new merchandise to be ordered from London, and while he wrote she stood by his side, her hand resting lightly on the ribboned queue of his hair as she looked over his shoulder.

> 1 Salmon-colored Tabby [watered silk] of the enclosed pat-
>   tern, with Satin flowers; to be made in a sack and coat.
> 1 Cap, handkerchief, and Rucker with Ruffles, to be made of
>   Brussells lace or Point, proper to be worn with the above
>   negligee; to cost 1 lb. 20.
> 1 piece Bag Holland, at 6 s a yard.
> 2 fine flowered Lawn Aprons.
> 2 prs. women's white silk hose . . .

He laughed. "I'd like to see my Cousin Richard's face. One of the last lists I sent him was for shoe brushes, a saddle and bridle, cotton velvet for a coat, waistcoat, and breeches for a tall man, double-channeled pumps, gloves larger than the middle size, and so forth."

The present list continued through "white sattin Shoes of the smallest size, fashionable hat or bonnet, Women's best kid gloves, 1 dozen round Silk stay laces, sewing silk, a silver Tabby velvet petticoat, 2 handsome breast flowers, hair pins, pickles, cheese, green tea, raisins, almonds, sugar, mustard," and other items. The bachelor had indeed turned into a provident but indulgent husband.

After the Assembly met on February 22, life quickened its tempo. In addition to the usual round of teas, receptions, balls, and other festivities Martha, as the wife of a new burgess who was also a popular hero, felt an obligation to do much entertaining. George discovered to his pride and satisfaction that he could bring members of the Assembly to

Six-Chimney House with or without forewarning and find Martha and her servants prepared to extend hospitality. She became acquainted with prominent burgesses. Many were interested in George as the most conspicuous of the young legislators and wanted to become acquainted with him more intimately.

Among them were Edmund Pendleton, in his late thirties, tall and thin, a skillful lawyer who could outwit almost any opponent; Richard Henry Lee, about George's age and also a new member; his brother Francis Lightfoot Lee, even younger than George, shy, scholarly, keen. The Lees had grown up near George's brother Austin's house in Wakefield, and George had known them in boyhood. There was Peyton Randolph, who seemed cold and unapproachable when you first met him but kind and affable on closer acquaintance. But the burgess who interested Martha most was George Mason, who was six years older than George and one of his near neighbors at Mount Vernon. His wife Anne was only a little younger than Martha, and she looked forward to their becoming good friends.

It was George Mason who told her about the honor paid her husband by the Assembly on Monday, February 26, when the work of the body had just been getting underway.

"Too bad you couldn't have been there, Mistress Washington. During a lull in the arguments, somebody got up, cried, 'Mr. Speaker,' and offered a resolution. I wish I could remember the exact words, but it went something like this: 'Resolved that the thanks of the House be given to George Washington, Esquire, late Colonel of the First Virginia Regiment, for his faithful service to His Majesty and this Colony, and for his brave and steadfast behavior, from the first Encroachments and hostilities of the French and their Indians, to his Resignation.' There was a roar of 'Ayes'! Then while the Speaker leaned forward in his chair to add his thanks, your husband got up and—what do you suppose happened?"

Martha waited, pink-cheeked and eager, hoping Mr. Mason could remember just what George had said. How she wished she could have been there to share this moment of his triumph!

Mason slowly rose to his feet, obviously trying to emulate the stance of his much taller and slenderer friend, cleared his throat a few times, then slowly sat down again, clapping his hand on his knee and bursting into laughter. Martha stared at him in bewilderment. What—?

"That was what happened, dear lady. He stood up, uttered a few unintelligible sounds, was absolutely tongue-tied."

"Oh!" Martha looked at her husband, distressed. Though he made a perfunctory attempt to join in the laughter, she could see that he was embarrassed.

Mason sobered. "It was a case where silence was more eloquent than speech. The Speaker rose gallantly to the occasion. 'Sit down, Mr. Washington,' he said, smiling, 'your modesty is equal to your valor, and that surpasses the power of any language that I possess.' "

Martha gave her husband a reassuring smile. "Good!" she said comfortably. "It's much better to be modest than boastful, and actions mean more than glib talk."

It was not the first time she had found him embarrassed over honors paid him. Soon after their marriage she had found a paper thrust carelessly into the pocket of a coat she was sending to be mended. It was an imposing-looking document, with a long list of names appended.

"What's this?" she had asked him. "It looks very important."

"Oh—that." He had dismissed it with a gesture. "It's a testimony my company officers gave me on my retirement. Nothing much."

"May I read it?"

"If you wish. But—don't believe all it says. My men were prejudiced."

Martha had read with mounting excitement. "In our earliest infancy you took us under your tuition, trained us up in the practice of that discipline which alone can constitute good troops, from the punctual observance of which you never suffered the least deviation. Your steady adherence to impartial justice, your quick discernment and invariable regard to merit, wisely intended to inculcate those genuine sentiments of true honor and passion for glory, from which the great military achievements have been derived, first heightened our natural emulation and our desire to excel . . ."

When she had read to the end her eyes were wet. "Oh, this is wonderful! Why didn't you tell us—" But George had disappeared. Carefully she had laid the paper away where it would not be lost.

George was restless during the long argumentative days of the Assembly. He was anxious to be gone to Mount Vernon and busy himself with spring planting. Only one legislative matter really concerned him, the continuation of his old regiment for western service and provisions for it. Once the bill for this was passed on the second of April, he applied for leave of absence for the remainder of the session.

Came days of frenzied activity—leaving Six Chimneys with proper gardeners and other servants; journey to the house on the Pamunkey; assembling of furniture, clothing, toys, personal possessions of a lifetime; packing of trunks, chests, boxes; arranging for the management of the plantation; deciding which servants to take and which to leave at the White House. Only now did Martha fully comprehend the competence of the man she had married. What seemed to her impossible confusion resolved itself into order. To the man who five years earlier had almost singlehandedly conducted a regiment over mountains, through swamps, unbroken forests, hostile ambushes, the matter of transporting his new family, their servants and baggage across the Pamunkey, the Rappahannock, and the Occoquan, along some hundred and twenty miles of well-traveled roads, was simple routine. To Martha, who had never traveled farther than Williamsburg and was leaving her whole life behind, it was exodus to a new world.

But in Fredericksburg, where they stopped to visit Betty and George's mother, the seasoned soldier discovered to his chagrin a sad omission in his planning. He had made no more preparation at Mount Vernon for their coming than if he had been arriving alone! Hastily he dispatched an attendant with a letter to his overseer, John Alton.

"Jno: I have sent Miles on today, to let you know that I expect to be up tomorrow and to get the key from Colonel Fairfax . . . You must have the house very well cleaned, and were you to make fires in the rooms below it would air them. You must get two of the best bedsteads put up, one in the hall room, and the other in the little dining room that used to be, and have beds made on them against we come. You must also get out the chairs and tables, and have them very well rubbed and cleaned; the staircase ought also to be polished in order to make it look well. Enquire about in the neighborhood and get some eggs and chickens, and prepare in the best manner you can for our coming . . ." A tall order for a man to execute in just twenty-four hours, no matter how great his zeal or how efficient the staff at his disposal!

From the moment she entered it Martha felt almost as much at home at Millbank, Betty Washington's house, as at Eltham, her own sister's. Fielding Lewis, Betty's husband, was building Millbank on an eight-hundred-acre tract in Fredericksburg so his wife could be near her mother. If Martha had been unused to luxury at the White House and Six Chimneys, she might have been overawed by the mansion's magnificence. Even the spacious entrance hall with its wide-sweeping mahogany staircase and its carved lotus leaf ornamentations, designed by Italian artists, was impressive.

"We ran out of ideas for ornamental designs"—Betty laughed—"so we asked George here to help us out. See what he came up with." She pointed to a stucco fresco illustrating Aesop's fable of the crow and the fox, adorning the drawing room mantel.

And had Betty been less gay and friendly, Martha might have found her a bit awesome, she was so tall and majestic in appearance.

"You look so much like George!" she marveled again.

"Wait! You haven't seen my act!" Betty disappeared, to reappear presently with a long blue cape about her shoulders, a tricornered military cap perched on her head, powdered curls tied in a queue, and in her hand a stout cane in lieu of a sword. "There!" she boasted triumphantly. "All I need is a horse, and I'll wager his troops would present arms!"

The resemblance was certainly striking. All burst into laughter and clapped.

Betty was the second wife of Fielding Lewis, his first having been an aunt of George's, Catherine Washington. Fielding was a distinguished and wealthy merchant, a vestryman and magistrate in his county, and a burgess as well. Martha found him agreeable and friendly, attractive in spite of his slightly crossed eyes, and she fell in love with the children. Betty had been fruitful during the eight years of her marriage, having already borne four sons, with another child obviously on the way. Martha became enamored with little George Washington Lewis, aged two. Her own children were joyously absorbed into the nursery family. Seeing George's delight in his young nephews, Martha hoped that the next time they came there would at least be the prospect of a Washington addition to the brood.

She wished they could stay at Betty's or go directly to Mount Vernon. She dreaded her first meeting with George's mother. Her information about her was meager. To all Martha's questioning George had uttered only a laconic "You'll see." "Formidable," "independent," were the words of description she had heard. But, Martha consoled herself, the mother of two people like George and Betty, who had borne and raised them, presumably endowed them with many of her characteristics, could not be too unapproachable. And, as they crossed the Rappahannock to the farm on the other side, her spirits rose. She became excited. She was about to enter the scenes of George's boyhood, not the place where he was born—that was Wakefield, thirty-five miles away on Pope's Creek—but the farm called "Pine Grove," where his father had moved the family when George was very young.

"Takes me back," George reminisced. "I used to cross by this ferry to go to a little school in Fredericksburg, the Reverend James Marye's. I never had much schooling, you know. First I went to a funny old fellow named Hobby, a church sexton, whose real business was to bury people, not teach them. And he certainly didn't—much. You should have seen me, carrying my little hornbook, wearing my little plum-colored coat. I've never felt so big since. Then later I lived with my half brother Augustine for a while and went to a Mr. Williams's school. He taught me the mathematics I needed to do surveying. But you might as well know, Patsy"—he laughed disparagingly—"you didn't marry an educated man. I'm not like my father or my brother Lawrence, who went to school at Appleby in England." He smiled wryly. "If I'd had proper schooling, perhaps it would have smoothed off a country boy's rough edges, made him a gentleman like Fielding Lewis or Daniel Custis."

"Oh, but you *are* a gentleman!" Martha protested stoutly. And suddenly she wondered who or what had made him so, a country boy to be sure, bereft of his father at age eleven, shunted about from mother to brother to brother, wanderer in the wilderness, tough soldier, yet with all the dignity and courtly manners of a first family scion. Who had taught him the graces of gentility? His brother Lawrence? Hardly. He had not lived long enough. His mother? She would soon find out.

Ferry Farm seemed small beside the estates of White House and Eltham, but its fields were models of perfection. Every scrap of land, even close to the house, was thriftily cultivated. Though it was only April, neat rows were bursting into green leaf. Slaves, diligently hoeing and weeding, barely looked up as the newcomers approached. "She has no trouble," thought Martha, "keeping her servants obedient." The nearer they came to the inevitable meeting the more hesitant and unconfident she felt. The house, too, was small and starkly bare, its dormer windows suggesting eyebrows raised in what might be either surprise or disapproval.

Mary Ball Washington. A woman whom future generations would have difficulty in evaluating. Forbidding? Dictatorial? Stern? Frugal to the point of parsimony? Demanding? Devoid of emotion? Intensely righteous? Yet by one of her descendants she could be called "the rose of Epping Forest" and "the reigning belle of the Northern Neck." At age sixteen she would be described in a letter by one peer as "Sweet Molly." "Mamma thinks Molly the comliest Maiden she knows. She is about 16, is taller than me, is verry sensable. Modest and loving. Her Hair is like unto Flax, Her eyes are the color of Yours, and her chekes are like May blossoms." Could this be the same person of whom one of her son George's playmates would write later: "I was more afraid of her than of my own parents; she awed me in the midst of her kindness; and even now, when time has whitened my locks, and I am the grandfather of a second generation, I could not behold that *Majestic* woman without feelings it is impossible to describe."

"Welcome, son. Welcome, Mistress George Washington. I was expecting you. Come in."

Martha's first emotion was awe. Looking up at this tall, imposing woman so like George and Betty in face and figure yet so different, she felt indescribably small and insignificant. Her next was embarrassment. Though she had dressed so carefully, choosing a simple silk gown and petticoat figured with green velvet leaves and pink flowers, a mobcap of plain gauze topping her unpowdered hair, beside this woman in homespun wool and slat sunbonnet she felt like a peacock flaunting her fine feathers in a barnyard. But more poignant than either emotion was surprise. For George did not kiss his mother as her brothers would have done after a long absence from Frances Dandridge. He stood stiffly at attention, as if in the presence of a superior officer, lips compressed as when she had first seen him, but this time not from weariness or illness.

"Thank you, dear madam," he said with the courtesy he might have accorded a stranger.

The house was as neat inside as out and as devoid of ornament. Martha absorbed every detail with eagerness, knowing that here George had spent many years of his boyhood. The large hall, used also as a dining room, had painted walls hung only with a mirror, no pictures. She counted eleven leather-bottomed chairs ranged with mathematical order against the walls. A door at the rear opening into Mary Washington's bedroom revealed portions of a narrow bed, a chest of drawers, and a rush-bottomed chair.

Mary Washington conducted them into the parlor at one side, a room also starkly neat and unadorned except for a large book in the exact center of a small table and, yes, an incongruous item amid its simple environs, on one wall an escutcheon bearing an elaborate and colorful coat of arms.

While George and his mother discussed details of the farm's management Martha sat on one of the hard mahogany chairs, her straightness of posture dictated less by her iron-stiff stays than by the unbending mien of the calmly impressive figure seated on the other side of the clean-swept fireplace, her only motions the swift interplay of her vigorous knitting needles.

"But she has a beautiful voice," thought Martha, "sweet, like music. And with that auburn hair and those blue-gray eyes, so like George's, she must once have been very attractive."

Presently George left at his mother's request to inspect some of the fields. She was especially anxious this year to grow good crops, since there were many destitute families in the area, and she wanted more than her usual funds and produce for her neighborhood charities. After a brief, perfunctory exchange of amenities with Martha, she herself left to superintend preparation of dinner. Curious, Martha approached the table and examined the book. It was Sir Matthew Hale's *Contemplations, Moral and Divine*. On the flyleaf was written "Jane Washington" and, just beneath, the words, in bold but cramped writing, "and Mary Washington." Jane, Martha knew, had been Augustine Washington's first wife, mother of Lawrence, Augustine (usually called Austin), and her namesake Jane. The book was well worn. Riffling through the pages, Martha shuddered. Sin . . . punishment . . . hell. The words seemed to leap at her. Hastily she replaced the book.

She moved away and stood looking at the escutcheon, which bore a rampant lion and a shield with two lions and a fleur-de-lis, above one of the lions a broad bar, half red and half gold. Flamboyant in its bold coloring, it seemed to emphasize the frugal simplicity of the rest of the room.

"The Ball coat of arms."

Martha turned, startled. Mary Washington had reentered with an almost eerie quietness. "It's very—impressive."

"Yes. George's children need not be ashamed of their heritage. I hope they will learn about their ancestor John Ball, who four hundred years ago rebelled against the British nobility for their oppression of the common people. They called him the 'mad preacher of Kent.' Everywhere he went rousing the poor yeomen, taking for his text, 'When Adam delved and Eve span, Who was then the gentleman?' He was put in prison and finally beheaded."

"How very brave!" said Martha. "I am sure George has inherited his courage."

"George has always been a good boy," conceded his mother.

They returned to the seats by the fireplace, Mary Washington stopping on the way to replace the book in the exact center of the table.

"Tell me more about him," urged Martha eagerly. "What was he like as a—child?" She had been about to say "boy" but suspected that to this woman he was still a boy and always would be.

Mary Washington regarded her new daughter-in-law with tentative approval. Her tongue, usually frugal with words, loosened, for this was obviously her favorite subject.

"Yes, he was a good boy, honest, truthful, and"—she hesitated—"for the most part obedient."

She told of the time when as a mere lad he had attempted to tame one of her prize horses, a blooded steed which her husband had bred, a beautiful but fierce sorrel colt. George boasted that if some of his friends would help him confine the animal and put a bit in his mouth, he would mount him. They drove the colt into a narrow enclosure. Startled and angry, the horse rushed madly about, but George curbed him, riding without a saddle. They had a frightful struggle. Finally in one last desperate attempt to be free the colt burst a blood vessel and fell, dying.

"They came in to breakfast," recounted his mother. "I asked them if they had seen the colt, my favorite. And what did my son do? Deny his foolish act? No. 'Your favorite, madam,' he said, 'is dead.' He told me the whole story. I admit I was angry at first, but not for long. 'It is well,' I told him, 'for while I regret the loss of my favorite animal, I rejoice in my son who always speaks the truth, as I taught him to do.' "

Martha nodded. "I don't wonder you are proud of him." But, she asked herself sagely, proud of his being truthful or of having taught him?

Mary Washington continued, her pleasant, melodious voice keeping pace with her clicking needles. Somehow she had the faculty of making another woman feel useless sitting with idle hands.

Yes, he had always been a good boy, industrious, obedient. Imagine, surveying his brother Lawrence's land at Mount Vernon when he was little more than a child, but becoming so skilled that he was appointed a public surveyor when only sixteen! There had been one crisis, though. When he was not yet fourteen his brother Lawrence had wanted him to go to sea, perhaps join the British navy.

"I was appalled, but what could I do? Lawrence was not my son. He had always had his own way. And he was my boy's hero. George was overjoyed. I wrote to my brother Joseph in London asking his advice. Lawrence got George a midshipman's warrant. The boy was all ready to depart in a British ship of war, his luggage all on board, when the letter from my brother arrived. He advised strongly against the idea. I forbade my son to go, and"—she nodded with satisfaction—"of course he obeyed. I had taught him to be obedient."

Martha was surprised at the sudden change in the woman's grim hawklike features. There was warmth in the gray-blue eyes. The thin lips curved upward. The knitting fell idle in her lap. "But you, my dear, have accomplished something that even I was unable to do. You made him leave the army."

"Oh, but I didn't," protested Martha. "It was his own decision. I wouldn't—"

She might not have spoken. "That awful wilderness! Those perils by storm, flood, Indians, the killing! When he was invited to go with that Braddock I rushed to Mount Vernon to dissuade him, argued, pleaded, told him how much I needed him. For almost two days he hesitated. But this time he did not obey me. It was he who began arguing with me, reminding me how I had commended him to God, who had defended him from harm, begging me to yield. I did and returned home heavyhearted. But"—the thin lips tightened—"I am sure if I had continued to insist, he would have obeyed me."

Again the needles began their swift motion. "Thank God, now such worries are over. My son has a wife"—she smiled approvingly, if a bit condescendingly—"a very acceptable and, I am sure, capable young woman. There will be no more warfare in his life."

A bell sounded, loud, insistent. At the first stroke Mary Washington put aside her knitting and rose. "Dinner is served," she said. "We always eat precisely on the hour."

Martha looked at her watch, suspended on a gold chain from her neck. The hands pointed exactly to three in the afternoon.

"Oh! George . . . Should we send someone—?"

"He'll be here," said his mother confidently. "I taught him to be always punctual."

He was. When they went into the hall he was standing by the table. He smiled at Martha's look of surprise. "You feared I'd be late, my dear? Not in this house." His eyebrows lifted in a humorous quirk. "It's said around here that the neighbors set their timepieces by the ringing of her bells. And never, never is she a fraction of a minute late for church. Oh, she taught us all to be on time!"

The meal was ample in quantity but simple. There was a plain soup, just one kind of meat. A fish course, sweet potatoes, and corn cakes completed the menu. Though a slave hovered in the background, Mary Washington served. Obviously she made no difference in her life-style for guests, even one she might logically wish to impress. In a society of damask cloths, silver services, tables loaded with multiple delicacies, she served her simple food on homespun in a few pewter dishes and made no apologies. In an age of dissipation, of cosseted females pampered by multitudes of slaves, she served no liquors, not even wine, and industriously shared in the tasks set her servants.

Martha gazed at her in wonder, her first aversion turning to growing appreciation. She knew she could never love this woman—in fact, she doubted if her own children really did—but already she could admire her, respect her. Left a widow with four sons and a daughter, the oldest only eleven, she had become teacher, mentor, as well as successful breadwinner, agriculturist, manager, dispenser of charity, paragon of self-sufficiency and independence. Her George, Martha sensed, was very much his mother's creation. She had taught him well, endowed him with many virtues—honesty, truthfulness, orderliness, punctuality, filial obedience. But she had not taught him the most endearing of his qualities, the refinement and courtliness of a gentleman. Then who—?

"It's time we should go," said George when the meal was finished.

Instantly Mary Washington rose. She made no attempt to detain them. Another of her unusual habits, Martha discovered, always receiving visitors with a cordial welcome but never asking them to stay once they seemed ready to leave, in fact speeding them by every facility in her power. Honesty again! She believed them sincere when they said it was time to go.

Back to Betty's across the river, organizing the caravan of carriages, horses, children, servants, baggage. The heavy stores of furniture and other household effects were coming by river barge. As they traveled north, stopping overnight at Williams's Ordinary in Dumfries, passing by the town of Colchester on the Occoquan, Martha felt more and more excited, yet fearful and uncertain. She was entering a new world. Would this Mount Vernon ever become home, like Chestnut Grove and the White House and Six Chimneys? Could she acceptably fill the role of plantation mistress, hostess, society matron, wife of a popular hero, among the women of this exclusive Northern Neck, one of whom, she knew, was the incomparable Sally Cary Fairfax?

"There it is! There's Mount Vernon!" George's huge hand made a wide, sweeping gesture. But it was not the sight of broad green fields, a white house in the distance surrounded by small outbuildings which after a brief glimpse riveted Martha's attention. It was the look on George's face, the sound of his voice. Just so an angel opening the gates of Paradise to a newcomer might have announced with joyful pride, "Here's Heaven!"

They drove up to the west entrance of the house, the coachman sensing the importance of the occasion and urging the horses to a final flourish. Descending, Martha found herself surrounded by smiling black faces. Little Patsy was handed down into eager waiting hands. Jacky was already out of the carriage and exploring. The door was wide open, but Martha stood still, waiting. She wanted George beside her when she went in for the first time. Only when she felt his hand cupping her elbow in a firm grip did she move forward, mount the steps, and enter the house which was to be her home for the next forty-three years, then become a living memorial of those years in the following centuries.

It was not a large house, rather small compared with either the White House or Six Chimneys, unpretentious beside Eltham or the Fielding Lewises' Millbank. Entering a long hall with a sweeping stairway at the right, Martha was aware of two rooms at each side, but George did not let her more than glimpse them. He led her straight through the hall to the open door at the other end.

"Oh!" she exclaimed, gazing in delight at wide sloping lawns descending in a series of green terraces to a broad, shining river.

"You like it?" demanded George with the eagerness of a small boy displaying his most precious treasures.

"Oh—yes!" Martha could find no words to express her delight. It was early April, with spring at its loveliest. There were trees in bloom—dogwood, redbud, magnolias. The grass was an emerald carpet, smooth as velvet. But it was the river which captured her eyes. Beside its sparkling, sweeping grandeur the Pamunkey was a sluggish, meandering stream, the Rappahannock a mere creek.

George pointed toward the right. "See that point of land down there, with the building of rose-red brick? That's Belvoir, the Fairfax house. I've told you about them."

Yes, George had spoken often of the Fairfaxes. Already she knew many of them by name. There was William Fairfax, who had built Belvoir. He had come to Virginia to oversee lands of his cousin Lord Fairfax, and at his death two years before George had grieved for him like a father. There was Lord Fairfax himself, who had been granted vast land holdings by Charles II which had once included all the Northern Neck and thousands of acres east and west of the Blue Ridge. He had become a veritable patron of George when the latter was only a boy of sixteen, choosing him to accompany him into the wilderness of the Shenandoah and giving him the responsible job of surveying his lands. There was William's son George William, who was George's closest friend, his companion in western exploration, his comrade in the French and Indian War, keeper of the keys of his estate, manager in charge of repairs during the last busy months. There was George William's sister Anné (Nancy), who had been married to Lawrence Washington and who after his death had become Mrs. George Lee. With Nancy's marriage and the death of Lawrence's only surviving child, Sarah, Mount Vernon had come to George. And, of course, there was Sally Fairfax.

"Funny! I heard a bit of gossip once . . . that the Colonel had a sort of yen for the wife of his friend and neighbor, George William Fairfax,

*she who used to be Sally Cary . . . Silly rumor! Nothing to it, I'm sure
. . ."*

Martha remembered the comment, almost word for word. In fact, it
had been lingering like a sleeping serpent in the Eden of her happiness.
Was it a silly rumor? With all his talk about the Fairfaxes George had
scarcely mentioned Sally, yet from his telling he had spent almost as
much time at Belvoir as at Mount Vernon. Was there a reason for his
silence?

"You'll be seeing the Fairfaxes soon," said George. "Once they know
we're here they'll be coming."

"And I'll know," thought Martha. "I can tell when I see them
together."

But no time now to worry about rumors! There was her new house to
examine; boxes and chests to be unpacked, orders given to the servants
(it would take consummate tact to create harmony between George's
servants and those she had brought with her); planning where her
furniture could be combined with that left in the house by Lawrence's
widow.

The house was small, to be sure, only four rooms on each floor, and
the upstairs was still in the process of construction. George had arranged for the house to be raised from its original story and a half to
two and a half. His orders to John Alton had been complied with. Beds
had been set up in two of the downstairs rooms. Table and chairs,
dutifully polished, were in a third room used for dining. But surely John
Alton was not responsible for other features of welcome which indicated beyond a doubt a woman's hand: the linen sheets on the beds,
beautifully hemstitched and embroidered; flowers in all the rooms chosen with taste to blend in color with the walls; the dining table embellished with lace doilies, silver, glassware. And when she went to the
cookhouse to consult with one of George's servants about the evening
meal . . .

"Nem mine, ma'am. Dinnah, she all planned. Miz Fairfax she come
tol' us what we's to have. An' her peoples come totin' all sort o' stuffs
befo' time to start cookin'. She sez you-all be so tired out from trabble
you-all mus' rest. We's doin' fine, ma'am."

Martha smiled. "How kind of Mrs. Fairfax! But tomorrow I will be
here to discuss plans for the day—*early.*"

She was upstairs examining the room, newly papered, which would eventually be their bedroom, when the expected guests arrived. Fortunately she had found time to change from her calico traveling gown into a decent silk. As she descended into the hall she heard voices in the parlor to the left of the stairs. Her soft slippers made no sound on the uncarpeted stairs. She stood in the parlor door for some time before her presence was detected, regarding the three occupants of the room. Sally. Martha had forgotten how tall and slender she was. Surely a pair of big hands could almost join fingers together about that narrow waist! But of course she had borne no children. She was talking, gesturing eagerly, her expressive features alight with animation. George William. A man in his mid thirties, impressive in height and mien, patrician features set in sober lines, dark, heavy brows arching over keen, penetrating eyes. He was standing a little away from the other two, listening but taking no part in their conversation. George. Martha could see his face plainly, but, though he was turned in her direction, he did not see her, for his attention was focused on the other woman. To her, familiar now with every nuance of his expressions, his face was nakedly revealing.

"Ah! Your wife, my friend! The beautiful bride. You must introduce us."

Instantly George became the courtly, attentive and—yes, proud husband. Taking her arm and leading her into the room, he presented her formally to their guests. Martha, lifting her head high and drawing herself to her full diminutive height, became the poised and smiling hostess.

"Mr. Fairfax—and Mistress Fairfax! How kind of you to come!" She was surprised that her voice betrayed nothing of the coldness within her. It sounded warm with friendliness. "Welcome to our home!"

"Not Mistress Fairfax! Sally. We're close neighbors, you know, and we're going to be friends. I'm sure we have met before, too, in Williamsburg."

"Thank you—Sally. And I certainly appreciate all you have done to make our homecoming pleasant. We must have you come to dinner once we get settled."

They sat and talked, about the house, the fields, the crops, weather. Then . . .

"Before you came," George said to Martha, "we were speaking of a play Sally acted in last year, Addison's *Cato.* She played the part of Marcia."

"And a perfect Marcia she was," interposed George William gallantly. "But I'm sure, George, you could have played a better Juba. I remember you once read the part."

George smiled and quoted:

> "The virtuous Marcia towers above her sex,
> True, she is fair, oh, how divinely fair!
> But still the lovely maid improves her charms
> With inward greatness, unaffected wisdom
> And sanctity of manners."

"You actually remember the words!" marveled Sally.

"Yes, and others of the score which I might well have uttered while you were playing the part." Again he quoted:

> "Oh, Marcia, let me hope thy kind concerns
> And gentle wishes follow me to battle!
> The thought will give new vigour to my arm."

"Bravo!" George William clapped his hands. "A pity you weren't there to play it! I declare, when we first went into the wilderness together, I never would have guessed you'd ever be quoting poetry. You were such a raw, ignorant little fellow! Sally's a good teacher. You haven't read all those books and studied all those plays together for nothing."

Martha sat listening, smiling woodenly, feeling the conversation wash over her like water over a motionless stone, a small insignificant stone, scarcely bigger than a pebble. They were talking in a foreign language. She had never heard of Addison or of a play called *Cato.* She felt bereft, excluded. They belonged to a different world from hers, these Fairfaxes, and George was a part of it.

So . . . it was true, that rumor which she had tried so hard to make light of. Her husband had been—*was now*—in love with another woman. She had seen it in his face. And it was that same woman who had taught him the graces of cultured thought and living which made him so attractive.

Politely the guests drew her into the conversation, and she responded with apparent ease and composure. Yes, they had had a pleasant journey. No, she was not tired. They must not think of leaving so soon. Of course she was delighted with the house and could hardly wait to get it settled for real entertaining. But all the time her mind was struggling, questioning. Did Sally share George's—should one call it infatuation? No. It might have been that when he was a youth, but now he was a man. Her face and manner were unrevealing, features beautiful and animated, voice sparkling with wit. But Martha doubted if she ever showed any really deep emotion. And George William, what of him? Did he realize the feeling his young friend had for his wife? If he knew, there was no sign of resentment. His manner toward George might have been that of a proud and indulgent older brother.

Suddenly Jacky came bounding into the room. "Papa!" He went straight to George. "There's a new little colt in the stables, and the groom says I can have him for my own if you say so. Can I, Papa?"

"Jacky!" rebuked Martha. "See, we have visitors, our neighbors, Mr. and Mrs. Fairfax. This is our son, John Parke Custis."

Obediently Jacky acknowledged the introduction by courteously extending a grubby hand. Patsy, always his shadow if possible, bobbed a curtsy, then went to George and climbed on his knee. Back at George's side in the circle of his arm, Jacky was assured smilingly that the colt could indeed be his.

"Oh, thank you, Papa!"

Martha glanced from George's smiling face to that of Sally. She had been wrong. As Sally gazed at the two children, her face revealed deep emotion, hunger, even envy. It was plain that she desperately longed for the children that in her ten years of marriage she had been unable to bear.

Martha drew a long, releasing breath. She could live with this new knowledge, distressing though it had seemed. Suppose her love for George was greater than his for her. She was his wife. This was their home. She had given him these children whom he certainly loved like a father. She would give him more, she hoped.

When the visitors rose to go she smiled warmly at Sally. "Thank you so much for coming. I know we are going to be good friends as well as neighbors."

8

Martha plunged immediately into the exciting work of settling her new home. She highly approved recent acquisitions of furniture which George had secured from England, for the pieces he had felt able to afford were of the best workmanship. After visiting Belvoir she could see that his taste had been educated by his friends, for the furniture he had chosen was in the same style (thanks again to Sally?).

There were two large, square mahogany tables which could be moved together for a company meal, with a dozen mahogany chairs, fitted with pincushion seats covered with horsehair. Just a year before their marriage there had arrived from England a bedstead with carved and fluted mahogany pillars, pieces of yellow silk and damask furniture, and six more mahogany chairs with arched backs. Especially did Martha admire a little mahogany gaming table with two sets of counters for the game Quadrille. But even after her furnishings from the White House arrived by barge, with some of the dishes and glassware broken, she found other things were needed. Many of the pieces she had brought because of sentiment rather than usefulness, including the little black country-made walnut stretchered table on which she and George had been served their wedding breakfast.

One of the delightful tasks was the choosing of furnishings for their new upstairs bedroom. Though they discussed the problem together, had begun to do so back in Williamsburg, George insisted that she make the decisions. The decor should be blue, or blue and white, she determined, after seeing the wallpaper which George had ordered in August 1757. They sat down together to make out the order.

But all such plans had to be interrupted by a trip he made in April to appear before the General Court for qualification as administrator of the Custis estate. All was arranged without difficulty. Returning home in May, George showed Martha a copy of the letter he had dispatched to the London merchants, Robert Carey and Company, together with the order for new merchandise which they had decided on together:

"Gentlemen: The enclosed is the minister's certificate of my marriage with Mrs. Martha Custis, properly, as I am told, authenticated. You will therefore for the future please to address all your letters which relate to the affairs of the late Daniel Parke Custis, Esq. to me, as by marriage I am entitled to a third part of that estate, and invested likewise with the care of the other two-thirds by a decree of the General Court, which I obtained in order to strengthen the power I before had in consequence of my wife's administration."

Martha smiled up at him with satisfaction. She was only beginning to realize how fortunate she and the children were to have this honest, meticulous guardian of their interests.

Skipping over the parts of the letter dealing with tobacco prices and prospects, her eyes lingered over the list of goods to be shipped. George's handwriting was bold and easy to read, and this part seemed to have been written with a fresh quill:

> 1 tester Bedstead 7½ feet pitch, with fashionable bleu or bleu and White Curtains to suite a Room lined with the Ireland paper.
>
> Window Curtains of the same for two windows; with either Papier Maché Cornish to them, or Cornish covered with the Cloth.
>
> 1 fine Bed coverlid to match the Curtains; 4 Chair bottoms of the same; that is, as much covering suited to the above furniture as will go over the seats of 4 chairs (which I have by me) in order to make the whole furniture of this Room uniformly handsome and genteel.
>
> 1 Fashionable Sett of Desert Glasses, and stands for Sweet Meats, Jellys, etc., together with Wash Glasses and a proper stand for these also.

2 setts of Chamber, or Bed Carpets—Wilton.
4 Fashionable China Branches, and Stands, for Candles.
2 Neat Firescreens.
50 lbs. Spirma Candles.

Again she skipped, for she was not interested in "a pretty large assortment of grass seed—amongst which let there be a good deal of Lucerne and St. Foin, especially the former, also a good deal of English, or Blue Grass . . ." But she smiled delightedly at the next items, which included men's handkerchiefs, stock tape, silk, thread, and worsted hose, "all the above stockings to be long and tolerably large."

1 Suit of Cloathes of the finest Cloth, and fashionable color, made by the enclosed Measure.
Half a dozen pairs of Men's neatest Shoes, and Pumps, to be made on Colonel Baylor's last; but a little larger than this, and to have high heels.
6 pr. Men's Riding Gloves, rather large than the middle size.

Added to these personal male items were orders for a book on gardening and one on horses, plus—a title which made her laugh aloud—*A New System of Agriculture*, or *A Speedy Way to Grow Rich.*

George, she was discovering, was not only faithful guardian, generous provider, but also efficient household organizer. Without his tactful management she would have found it difficult to combine their two sets of servants into one harmonious and efficient whole. The domestic staff finally numbered fourteen. There was Breechy, the waiter, with Mulatto Jack his assistant as well as "jobber." Doll, the cook, had Beck for her scullion. Jenny would superintend the washing, and Mima the ironing. Sally, of course, was Martha's personal maid. Her seamstress would be Betty. It was decided now that Jacky was old enough to have his own boy, named Julius, his senior by six years. Even Patsy would have her own little maid, Rose. Molly would preside over all these denizens of the nursery. Billy and Bishop, George's personal servants, and John Alton, the white steward, brought the number to fourteen.

Of course there were other numerous servants ministering to household needs: the weavers, spinners, five carpenters, four tanners, and some of the farmhands whose work related to both field and house.

Days soon settled into a routine which was to persist with few changes through all the years of their living at Mount Vernon. George and Martha both rose early, by sunrise in summer, two hours earlier in winter. Before breakfast Martha would give her household orders, then after breakfast spend her hour at devotions, a time with her door closed, never to be interrupted. Then followed gardening, needlework, overseeing the spinning, weaving, sewing, visiting the servants' cabins to check on sickness, clothing, and other needs. Meanwhile George was spending the hours before breakfast writing letters or visiting the stables and kennels. Then, after a frugal meal of corn cakes, honey, tea or coffee, he would mount his horse and ride over his farms, directing his overseers. Dinner, as in his mother's house, was at three. George would always return home at a quarter of, punctual as a clock, in time to change his riding clothes for more formal dress, powder his hair, and appear at the table, like Martha, faultlessly attired.

Once they were settled there were very often guests, sometimes just for dinner, but often remaining overnight or longer. Martha found the new faces bewildering. Besides the Fairfaxes and the George Masons, whom she already knew, there were Dr. James Craik and his wife, also the Carlyles from Alexandria. Sarah Carlyle was a sister of George William Fairfax and almost as charming and intellectual as the incomparable Sally, yet Martha found her less awe-inspiring. Never, she knew, would she feel completely at ease with this nearest neighbor whose dazzling, tantalizing manner aroused such doubts and unanswerable questions. Yet they were together, sometimes, it seemed, constantly, the two families visiting back and forth at least two or three times each week.

Martha expected to find Lord Fairfax, cousin of George William, proprietor of the huge six-million-acre grant from the King, graduate of Oxford, long a patron of her husband, a formidable guest. But when he arrived one day from Greenway Court, his home in the Shenandoah, she was pleasantly surprised. He was short, stout, almost roly-poly, and in spite of his brusque manner and lowering brows there was a twinkle in his eyes. He reminded her a little of old John Custis, whose soft heart had been encased in such a forbidding crust.

"So this is the little lady who took a good surveyor and soldier out of the wilderness and made him a gentleman farmer!" Gruffness of voice was belied by a nod of obvious approval. "Well, if the wild horse must be stabled, I can't conceive of a fairer hand to do the taming."

"Thank you, sir," replied Martha demurely. "I assure you that any bit and bridle this horse wears will be of his own choosing."

"Bravo!" The twinkle brightened into an appreciative gleam. "A clever brain as well as a fair hand! Congratulations, George, on your good taste!"

For Martha it was a rare moment of triumph, less for the compliment than for the pride she saw in her husband's eyes. And, to crown her satisfaction, Sally was there to see it.

Besides neighbors of the Northern Neck who came, there were relatives from farther away, George's brother John Augustine and his wife Hannah from Westmoreland County, his brother Austin and his wife from Wakefield, George's birthplace.

They lived in a small, enclosed world of neighbors, relatives, friends, with little encroachment of outside events. Even the continuation of the French and Indian War which had once been George's chief concern seemed to arouse in him only passing interest.

"I am now, I believe," he wrote his cousin Richard Washington, "fixed at this seat with an agreeable consort for life and hope to find more happiness in retirement than I ever experienced amidst a wide and bustling world."

All his energies were expended in improving the plantation, restoring buildings, adding to the livestock, especially thoroughbred horses for hunting, accumulating more workers—shoemakers, tailors, smiths, wheelwrights, masons, charcoal burners, millers, hostlers—experimenting with new methods of planting, draining, ditching, fertilizing. But he still found time to plan further decorations of the house with Martha and to send off more orders to the agents in London. While he had left to Martha the furnishing of the upstairs bedrooms, he concerned himself personally with adornments for the parlor.

With this order were included personal items. For George "a light Summer Suit made of Duroy, 2 beaver hats at 21 shillings each; a piece of black satin ribbon for his queue; a red morocco sword belt; Irish linen for shirts; and a ream of writing paper." Martha especially wanted a salmon-colored tabby silk with satin flowers for a negligee and coat, with cap, handkerchief, tucker and ruffles of Brussels lace, to cost no more than twenty pounds. Her further needs were two flowered aprons, silk and cotton hose, black and white satin shoes ("of the smallest fives"), a fashionable hat or bonnet, six pairs each of kid gloves and mittens, a pound of shaded sewing silks, a black mask.

As with all orders to London, this one went on to include numerous items, both luxuries and necessities, which British colonies were required to import: pickles, anchovies, capers, olives, salad oil, cheese, tea, wine, mustard, salt, white sugar candy, broadcloth, buttons, buckles, halters, bridles, nails, medicines.

Like all the Virginia planters, George grumbled each time he sent an order because of the absurd selfish laws of Great Britain forbidding the manufacture of many goods in her colonies, in order to secure a monopoly for her own merchants. Colonists must depend on London tailors and dressmakers not only for fine fabrics but for their manufacture into many garments for men, women, and children.

"We could manufacture many of these things ourselves," he fumed, "if they didn't have such silly laws. They make virtual slaves of us. Sometime we may surprise them and rebel."

And it required all his sharp persistence to make sure that the goods imported were of decent quality.

"Tis a custom, I have reason to believe," he wrote once to the Messrs. Carey, "when they know goods are bespoken for exportation, to palm sometimes old, and sometimes very slight and indifferent goods upon us, taking care at the same time to advance the price." He made it plain that he would not be duped by such practices.

Remembering her own experiences as a defenseless widow, Martha noted with relief the far better quality and lower prices of their present importations.

By the end of summer she was completely the mistress of Mount Vernon. Every inch of the eight rooms with halls had been scoured and polished to her satisfaction. The tester bed with "bleu" accessories had arrived and been arranged with an eye for taste and comfort. The long-neglected gardens were replete with new growths, colorful blooms to keep every room bedecked, herbs for the kitchen, many planted and nurtured with her own hands. And to her husband's delight and surprise her interest extended beyond the house, the outbuildings, the servants' cabins. Sometimes she rode with him on his daily visits to the fields, her scarlet riding habit a bright foil for his plain blue coat and black knee breeches. Already her visits to the slave cabins had made her a familiar figure to the field hands, and black faces lighted, white teeth gleamed at her appearance.

She took interest in the growth of the estate. George, she soon learned, had a passion for acquiring land, and eventually the estate would consist of about four thousand acres separated into several farms. Each farm had its overseer, and more than two hundred servants were employed in the different fields. Noting her interest, George would share with her his problems.

"This year isn't a fair test," he said after that first season. "There wasn't time to prepare the land, and much of it was leased to tenants. Next year it will be different. We'll find out if tobacco is really a profitable crop."

Autumn came. Before the trees burst into red and gold splendor and the first frosts came the tobacco was cut, hung in barns, and, at just the right time between dampness and dryness, put in hogsheads, which were inspected and stamped and made ready for shipment to England, subject to all the vagaries of heavy freight charges, possible piracy, duties, imposts, subsidies, handling charges, commissions of merchants, and other costs. But the colonists were not allowed to ship their produce to countries other than England and Scotland. In spite of the risks and uncertainties, George was infinitely relieved. Now he could turn surveyor again and try to determine the true bounds of his Mount Vernon tracts of land.

Martha decided not to go with him when he went to Williamsburg for the fall session of the Assembly. Even the prospect of spending time with her family on the Pamunkey could not tempt her away from her pleasurable duties as mistress of the new household.

But after he had gone she discovered suddenly that she was distressingly lonely and—yes, homesick. It was not wholly George's absence. She wanted to see her own family, especially her mother and her sister Nancy. The following weeks seemed like as many months. But when George rode into the yard soon after the Assembly adjourned on November 21, even the bleak browns of the fading autumn acquired a golden glow. He had waited long enough to see that the tobacco on the Custis plantations—allotted to Jacky—was inspected and delivered to the ship for export, then had hurried home. And he brought news. Martha's sister Nancy Bassett was coming for the holidays.

It was the happiest Christmas Martha had ever spent, the first in her new home. George's delight in the children's excitement and Nancy's presence were its crowning joys. Patterns of holiday celebration were established which would prevail, whenever possible, for the next half century. Christmas greens were brought in to deck the house, pine, spruce, cedar, holly and boxwood cuttings. Servants climbed on long ladders to twine them about doors and windows, over chandeliers. Fires in the kitchens glowed red-hot for the preparation of mince and pumpkin pies, roasting chickens with oyster dressings, ducks and geese crackling over turning spits. To Martha's amazement George proved himself a master chef when he began to mix his holiday eggnog several days before Christmas, a noble concoction containing a quart of milk, one of cream, a dozen eggs, a dozen tablespoons of sugar, a pint of brandy, a half pint of rye whiskey, a fourth-pint of Jamaica or New England rum, and a fourth-pint of sherry. He kept tasting it from time to time as it sat in a cool place, to make sure it was progressing properly. The coach and six took the family to Pohick Church on Christmas morning (shivering in spite of their heavy clothing). The servants came in their best clothes for gifts and money and sweets. Neighbors arrived. There was a huge dinner. Presents were dispensed from a glittering tree.

For Martha only one flaw marred the texture of the holidays for a moment: a touch of envy. Nancy, after just two years of marriage, was expecting her second child. Surely, Martha thought, by this time . . .

It was well that the Christmas holidays were full of bliss, for the New Year had troubles in store. They began at once.

"Tuesday 1," George wrote in his diary on January 1. "Visited my Plantations . . .

"Called at Mr. Posey's in my way home and desired him to engage me 100 Bar'l of Corn upon the best terms he could in Maryland.

"And found Mrs. Washington upon my arrival broke out with the Meazles."

Measles! But it was a children's disease! Martha could not believe it when a few days after illness developed the red blotches began to appear. Nancy remembered when she and the boys had had a bout with it in childhood. How had Martha escaped? There had been an epidemic among the children in the slave cabins during December, and Martha had made special visits to take them broths and herb teas and other delicacies, not dreaming that she was in danger of contagion.

"It must be you never had it," observed Nancy, "and how lucky it is that I've had it and I'm still here to nurse you! It can't be very serious, unless—she gave her a shrewd, half-questioning glance—"that is, as long as you're not pregnant."

But with Martha it *was* serious. On January 4, George sent word to the Reverend Charles Green, who was physician as well as rector of Pohick Church which the family attended, to come the next morning. He gave her the usual treatments, bled and physicked her, and on the fifth George recorded that she "appeared to be something better," but she was still very ill. Green had hardly left before Sally Fairfax and George William's sister Hannah arrived bringing broths, jellies, nourishing soups, and other delicacies. The day was so cold, with high winds, that George insisted on sending them home in the chariot.

Martha should have been grateful for Sally's continued attentions during the following days, but the sight of her lovely concerned face, smooth fair skin, and faultless apparel aroused only a wretched consciousness of her own blotched features, untidy hair, and general déshabillé. The frequent and prolonged visits with Sally both at Mount Vernon and at Belvoir were hard enough when she looked and felt her best, but now . . . She managed, however, as usual, to present a smiling, appreciative, and outwardly friendly aspect, despising herself for the hypocrisy and knowing she should be genuinely grateful.

Worry over the children was no aid to recovery. When they came down with a mild form of the disease, in spite of Nancy's protests she persisted in leaving her bed frequently to check on their condition. When Nancy had to leave for home finally on the twelfth, George going with her in the chariot as far as Port Royal below Fredericksburg, where Burwell Bassett was to meet her, she could not let them see how sick she still was or how desolate she felt.

There were other troubles that winter besides Martha's continued illness with several relapses. Four of the Negroes died. Some of George's tobacco in the sheds at Alexandria was exposed to wet. Heavy rains broke the dam at his mill on Dogue Run, and it had to be rebuilt prematurely. The new plow George had designed so hopefully proved too heavy for the horses to pull. But spring finally came. To Martha's disappointment she was still too unwell to accompany him to Williamsburg for the Assembly, but he brought back news of the family. Most exciting was the fact that he had rented Six Chimneys to her brother

Bartholomew Dandridge. It was good to know that old John Custis's exotic shrubs and trees would once more have good care.

It was a spring of much planting at Mount Vernon, too. George grafted row upon row of cherries—black Mays, Carnation, Bullock Hearts—plums, nuts. The cherries and plums, he noted in his diary, came from George Mason's. Gunston Hall, the Masons' estate below Belvoir, was famous for its blackheart cherries. Never would Martha forget her first sight of them. They were planted in four rows, two on each side of the drive at the north end of the house. She had arrived by the river, so had entered at the other side. Presently Mason had taken her to see the north front of his grounds.

"Now," he directed, "stand in the center of the doorway. How many trees do you see?"

"Why—four," she replied.

"Now—stand close to the side of the doorway and tell me how many you see."

She gasped with surprise. "Why—so many I can't count them!"

It was like magic. So carefully had the trees been aligned in rows twelve hundred feet long that if one stood two feet to the right or left of the doorway's center there were vast rows of trees, a whole forest stretching away into the distance.

It was a trick of planting that had caused George Mason hundreds of amused chuckles.

Trees, flowers, crops, grass, puppies, colts, pickaninnies . . . everywhere on the plantation Martha saw signs of new-springing life—except, where she longed for it most, in her own body. But at least she was feeling like her old self, and spring was a season of hope.

"I must do myself the pleasure of congratulating you," she wrote Nancy in June, "on your happy deliverance of, I wish I could say boy, as I know how much one of that sex was desired by you all. I am very sorry to hear of my Mama's complaints of ill health, and I feel the same uneasiness on the account that you are not well but hope that Mr. Small's prescription will have the desired effect. The children are now very well, and I think myself in a better state of health than I have been for a long time, and don't doubt but I shall present you a fine healthy girl when I come down in the fall, which is as soon as Mr. Washington's business will suffer him to leave home. I am very much pleased to hear Betsy continues to grow a fine hearty child."

Martha expressed dutiful regrets when that summer of 1760 George William and Sally decided to take a trip to England. With the death of an uncle George William had become heir to the Fairfax estate of Towelston in Yorkshire. Previously he had made a journey to convince this uncle that, though his father had married a woman from the West Indies where he had been stationed in the British Navy, the offspring of that union was not black! The uncle, convinced of the purity of his nephew's blood, had made a will in his favor. Now it was necessary that George William attend to business connected with his inheritance.

"Why don't you go with us?" he suggested to George when he and Sally came to Mount Vernon to discuss their plans. "I know you've always wanted to see England, and you have relatives there."

Martha's fingers, busy with her knitting, stilled. They felt paralyzed. Time seemed to stop while she waited for what seemed an eternity for George's answer. She did not even glance at him, afraid that he would be regarding Sally and that the revealing look would be on his face.

"No," he said at last. "Much as I would like to, it would be impossible. The plantation needs all my attention. Besides," he added, "Mrs. Washington would not be able to go now. An ocean trip would be too much for the children, at least for Patsy, who isn't at all strong."

Martha began knitting again, furiously. New life seemed to permeate her whole body. He had not even considered going without her! Still, she was almost ashamed to feel such relief when she stood on the landing beside George and waved good-bye to the couple on the deck of the British ship. Somehow the grass seemed greener, the August sky bluer, the flowers and fruits of a brighter hue. Her only worry was that George might miss the intoxicating gaiety of the social life at Belvoir.

In October, to Martha's delight, they all went to Williamsburg for the fall Assembly, traveling for the first time in style with the chariot and six, attendants resplendent in the Washington white and scarlet livery. It was Martha's first visit home since her marriage, and she reveled in the reunion with family far more than in the whirl of social gaiety in the capital. Her greatest joy was in holding and petting Nancy's new baby girl. Her own children were getting too big now for cuddling, and she hadn't realized how empty her arms had felt. Returning to Mount Vernon, she knew that only one thing remained to make her life near perfection.

Why, she kept wondering as months passed, did she not bear George the child he must long for? Was there some ill fortune in childbearing here at Mount Vernon? Laurence in his lifetime had lost three children, and a fourth, also born here, had died later. But of course that idea was foolish. Laurence's wife Anné had at least conceived. Could it be the fault of one of George's severe sicknesses, perhaps the smallpox in those evil swamps of Barbados or the bloody flux spawned in the wilderness morasses? Or, as Nancy suggested, had her own bout with measles affected her ability to bear children?

Not that George ever expressed regret for lack of a child of his own. He could hardly have been a more considerate and loving father to a little Washington than to the two small Custises. The only complaint he ever made was due to what he called her overindulgence and lack of discipline. Reared by Mary Washington's rigid code of conduct, he could not condone a laxity which permitted tantrums and other unpleasantries of behavior. Nor, having himself escaped with sheer willpower from the tentacles of a possessive mother, could he approve her eternal vigilance and anxiety.

"Let them alone sometimes," he urged her. "Don't keep them tied to your apron strings. Suppose they do fall down and cry. They'll pick themselves up. And they'll get over a little stomach ache without your worrying yourself sicker than they are."

Almost Martha reminded him, in a sudden burst of temper, that they were *her* children and he could not possibly know the natural concern of a parent, but she stopped herself in time. George, she remembered humbly, always said "the children" or "our children," never "Mrs. Washington's children" or "my stepchildren." She did protest mildly that Patsy had always been delicate and needed special supervision and loving care. Secretly, however, she agreed with him. She *was* too lenient and overprotective. She proved that to herself when in the summer of 1762 she let George persuade her to go with him to visit his brother John Augustine and his wife Hannah in Westmoreland County, leaving Jacky at home with his new tutor from England, young Walter MacGowan, and the nurse Molly. John Augustine had a new son, who would be christened Bushrod after his mother's family.

The other Washingtons seemed prolific enough, thought Martha ruefully. Austin, who after many illnesses had died in the spring, had left four children. Bushrod was John Augustine's third. Betty, Samuel, and Charles all had children. Only George . . .

The trip was not a success, even though Martha had her delicate little Patsy with her.

"My dear Nancy," she wrote on August 28, "I had the pleasure to receive your kind letter of the 25 of July just as I was setting out on a visit to Mr. Washington in Westmoreland, where I spent a weak very agreabley I carred my little patt with me and left Jackey at home for a trial to see how well I coud stay without him Though we were gon but won fortnight I was quite impatient to get home. If I at aney time heard the doggs barke or a noise out, I thought their was a person sent for me.

"I often fancied he was sick or some accident had happened to him so that I think it is impossible for me to leave him as long as Mr. Washington must stay when he comes down—if nothing happens I promise myself the pleasure of comeing down in the spring as it will be a healthy time of the year. I am much obliged to you for your kind invitation and assure yourself nothing but my childrens interest should prevent me the sattisfaction of seeing you and my good Friends I am always thinking of and wish it was possable for me to spend more of my time amongst. It gave me great satisfaction to hear of your dear billy's recovery which I hope will be a lasting one . . ."

Yes, Nancy at last had got her boy.

George might have reason to criticize her for her overprotectiveness, but in some ways he was fully as indulgent of the children. It was he rather than Martha who insisted on ordering for them so many luxuries from London, like the list he sent Robert Carey a few years after their marriage, which included the following:

"For Master Custis, eight years old, a handsome suit of Winter Cloathes; a suit of Summer ditto, very light; 2 pieces Nankeens with trimmings; 1 silver laced hat; 6 pair fine Cotton Stockings; 1 pr fine worsted ditto; 4 pr. Strong Shoes; 1 pr. neat Pumps; 1 p. gloves; 2 hair bags; 1 piece ribbon for ditto; 1 p. silver Shoe and Knee buckles; 1 p. Sleeve buttons; a Small Bible neatly bound in Turkey, and John Parke Custis wrote in gilt letters on the inside of the cover; a neat Small Prayer Book bound as above, with John Parke Custis as above; . . ."

The list that year for little Patsy reflected a doting father's special indulgence of a small daughter:

"For Miss Custis, 6 years old, a coat made of fashionable Silk; a fashionable Cap or Fillet with big apron; ruffles and Tucker—to be laced, 4 fashionable dresses to be made of Long Lawn; 2 fine Cambric frocks; a sattin Capuchin hat and neckatees; a Persian quilted coat; 1 pr. pack thread stays; . . . Fashionable dressed Doll to cost a guinea, 1 Do. at 5 s; a box Gingerbread, Toys and Sugar Images and Comfits; a neat Small Bible, bound in Turkey, and Martha Parke Custis wrote in the inside in gilt letters; a Small Prayer Book, neat and in the same manner; . . . 1 very good Spinet, to be made by Mr. Plinius, Harpsichord Maker, in South Audley Street, Grosvenor Square. It is begged as a favor that Mr. Carey would bespeak this instrument as for himself or a friend, and not let it be known that it is intended for exportation. Send a good assortment of spare strings to it."

Surely a man who loved children so much, thought Martha, should have some of his own. Yes, it was the one thing necessary to make her happiness complete. Well—perhaps not the *one* thing. If she could only see George look at her just once, even, as she had seen him look at Sally!

9

Days . . . months . . . years. Time flowed by like the river, turbulent with spring floods, subsiding into sluggish summer calmness, whipped into unrest or icebound by winter storms and cold. And, like the river, life at Mount Vernon changed in tempo with the seasons.

Spring was a time of furious activity. Fields sprang from dead brown to luxuriant green. Fruit trees blossomed. The seines at the fisheries were heavy with shad and shoals of herring, which, with corn pone, turnips, onions, and lentils, were a main source of nourishment for the hundreds of servants, "my people," as George always called them. The house must be scrubbed clean of winter grime and soot. Spinning wheels hummed, doling flax now instead of wool. Looms creaked, turning out hundreds of sturdy summer garments, also for "my people." Shrubs and trees unfurled their leaves, changing from tender red to filmy green like gossamer, then to bold emerald. Martha's gardens soon became a riot of blossoms, white, yellow, lavender, pink. Bluebells rimmed the riverbank. Dandelions flecked the lawns with bits of gold.

It was the time of year Martha loved best. She abounded in energy, seemed to imbibe strength from the land's fever of creativity. She almost begrudged the hour of devotions spent indoors, sure she could have worshiped far more joyfully outside, but the closed door was all that ensured against interruptions. At least she could open the windows wide to the fragrances and breezes and bird carolings. Once a gorgeous butterfly came and lighted on the page of her Book of Common Prayer.

The only flaw in this burgeoning of creativity was its lack in her own body.

Summer was more languorous, certainly not conducive to activity. One sweltered within the prison of stifling stays and layers of petticoats, even the thinnest calicoes and gauzes becoming steaming compresses long before the onset of the day's full heat. Rising at four as usual, she performed as many duties as possible before breakfast, then agonized for George, making all his rounds of the farms in the blaze of the mounting sun.

But summers were not devoid of social life. The river abounded in pleasure boats as neighbors journeyed back and forth for dinners or to Alexandria for balls, races, theater parties. There were water sports. George kept a handsome barge for these, manning it on special occasions with black oarsmen in livery. And sometimes there was great excitement, as when on July 20, 1762, the ship *Unity* arrived at the Mount Vernon wharf, discharging trunks, boxes, crates, with all the variety of articles ordered by George the year before, ranging from salt, saddles, augers, almonds, to shoes, hair bags, silks, egrets for Martha's headdresses.

The children, Patsy now six, Jacky eight, were duly excited. Jacky donning his new silver-laced hat, shoes with silver buckles, and one of his "handsome suits," and marching about the house attended by his fourteen-year-old servant Julius resplendent in a new suit of livery with the Custis arms. Patsy was more interested in her "fashionable dressed Doll to cost a guinea" than in the "Persian quilted coat" and "pack thread stays" which would signal her promotion into miniature womanhood. ("Not stays this soon!" deplored Martha, who had reluctantly yielded to the prevailing custom. That frail little body was far too thin already.)

There was less youthful interest in the "neat Small Bibles" and prayer books, even with names inscribed in gilt letters, but the harpsichord, released from its crate and voluminous wrappings, was set up in the parlor and duly admired by all. Jacky, instead of its owner, Miss Custis, was first to test its quality of tone, his violent strumming eliciting only mild reproval from the indulgent Martha and silent wincing from George.

"A good thing I ordered extra strings!" he muttered, wishing no doubt he could remove the young musical aspirant from the stool and administer the bodily chastisement he had so often resented as a child.

In spite of the fact that rain withheld its blessings that summer and he was still deeply in debt, George sent off another order to London, including not only necessities but also luxuries, such as four dozen knives and forks "properly disposed of in neat mahogany cases for decorating a sideboard." No dolls this time or gingerbread toys, but, at the suggestion of the new tutor, Walter MacGowan, Latin grammars, dictionaries, and other titles in the classics. Jacky was to be immersed, much against his will, in the fountainheads of culture. Patsy, of course, being a girl, would fare more leniently, learning reading, writing, spelling, sewing, dancing, music, Bible texts, plus refined deportment and elegance of carriage. But even at these gentler pursuits Martha guarded her jealously. For this indulgence George did not chide her, since he was as concerned as she about the child's delicate health.

Autumn. A time of waning growth but of rich, satisfying fulfillment. Next to spring it was the season Martha loved best. Life was colored with crimsons of maples, golds of oak and sassafras, coppers and bronzes of beeches. There was almost as much activity as in the spring. Fruits must be gathered and preserved or dried—cherries, plums, pears, apples, quinces, grapes. Apples were turned into cider. George, who prided himself on his fruit trees, was embarrassed to find that he must order three barrels of apples from New York in the fall of 1762. The tobacco was harvested and hung in the tall barns. As usual, in those early years, the crop fell far short of George's expectations.

"I have not succeeded in any one sort which I proposed to plant," he wrote his merchants in that same year. He was beginning to doubt that his land was best suited to growing tobacco. The crop on Jacky's estate to the south was always far better.

Fall was the hunting season. It was the one feature of autumn and early winter that Martha did not enjoy, though she suffered the onslaught of guests with good-natured hospitality. They kept open house for weeks, and Mount Vernon, with its superior dogs and stables, attracted sportsmen from miles around. At first Martha sometimes rode to the hounds with some of the bolder women guests, but she found most of them would prefer sitting in the parlor or on the terraces exchanging gossip and recipes. Besides, once Jacky was permitted—reluctantly on her part—to ride with George, it terrified her to watch him. A miniature of George in his short blue hunting jacket, scarlet waistcoat, buckskin breeches, velvet cap, flourishing his little whip, the boy would attempt recklessly to follow him, an impossible goal, for George was an unrivaled horseman.

"He loved to feel a horse under him," commented George Mercer, one of his oldest friends from wilderness days, "to ride at breakneck speed, leaping fences, turning obstacles with the hounds yelping—that must have been the charm."

George prided himself on his horses. As years passed the names of many of them—Chinkling, Ajax, Valiant, Magnolia, Blue Skin—became famous throughout the Northern Neck. Blue Skin was a full-blooded Arabian. His hounds also would be immortalized by future historians—Vulcan, Ringwood, Singer, Truelove, Music, Sweetlips, Forrester, Rockwood. And he did not stint himself when it came to a horseman's accessories. One order to London included "a man's riding saddle, hogskin seat, large plated stirrups and everything complete; a very neat and fashionable Newmarket saddlecloth; a riding frock of handsome drab colored broadcloth, with plain double-gilt buttons, a riding waistcoat of superfine scarlet cloth and gold lace with buttons like those on the coat."

Glorious as autumn was, Martha was not sorry when the bright colors vanished even when winter storms kept the family housebound, when fires were kept glowing on the huge hearths and the family became a tight little entity secure from outside intrusion. Not that all color had disappeared. There was still the holly, great bunches of scarlet berries flaunting their lavish hues against the deep blue of the winter sky. Of course winter had its duties too. Ice must be cut and stored in the icehouse under heavy layers of straw. It was hog-killing time, with fires blazing under great caldrons of boiling water, then sausage, soap, lard to be made and stored, bacon and hams to be cured. It was a huge task. After sales and deductions for overseers, in 1762 George reckoned the total pork for use by "my people" at 6,632 pounds.

Then by March the river would once more be in spate, fish would start to run, sap to flow. Plowing would begin. And the cycle of the years would start all over again.

Social life—entertaining, travel—changed little with the seasons. Except for those brief housebound intervals it persisted without interruption, varying only in methods of transportation, by river when feasible, by chariot during winter and spring floods. Often Mount Vernon was filled with children when Mr. Christian, the dancing master, came. After an afternoon of dancing candles would be lighted and the young people would play at "Button to get Pawns for Redemption" or "Break the Pope's Neck." Always when dinners were served at Mount Vernon the tables were loaded.

Not so all the festivities they attended. George disgustedly recorded in his diary one occasion which seemed to him sadly deficient:

"Went to a ball at Alexandria, where Musick and dancing was the chief Entertainment however in a convenient room detached for the purpose abounded gt plenty of bread and butter, some biscuits, with tea and coffee, which the drinkers of could not distinguish from hot water sweet'ned.

"Be it remembered that pocket hdkchiefs served the purposes of Table cloths and Napkins and that no apologies were made for either. I shall therefor distinguish this ball by the stile and title of the Bread and Butter Ball."

Needless to say, when some years later George built his own house in Alexandria on a lot at the corner of Pitt and Cameron streets, for use during court sessions, elections, and social occasions, there was no such paucity of refreshment when Martha entertained. Though it was too small a house to hold balls or large parties, her teas and little dinners were as lavish and faultless as the more elaborate functions at Mount Vernon. She loved the little house and found it far more comfortable and homelike than Gadsby's Tavern and certainly more enjoyable than visiting in the mansions of friends like the Carlyles, the Fitzhughs, the Ramsays, the Fitzgeralds.

So rarely was the family alone at Mount Vernon that George's diary reported the unusual fact with surprise. Day after day, year after year it detailed what sounded like a continuous parade of visitors, usually just dining but sometimes staying several days. It often taxed Martha's ingenuity to find room for family and guests in the small dining room. An estimate covering seven years of the period following her marriage noted two thousand guests who had visited Mount Vernon.

Once more there was visiting back and forth between Mount Vernon and Belvoir, for the Fairfaxes returned from England in 1763. Almost to her own surprise Martha was more relieved than disturbed by their arrival. George had read her a letter from George William written from his estate in Yorkshire. They were finding it unpleasantly cold in England. He and Sally had been sick, but they hoped to regain their health at a place called Buxton Wells. "In the meantime," he went on, "should be glad to know your and Dr. Green's determination about leaving that part of the world, for I assure you 'tis our greatest inducement, and will turn the scale very much whether we come back or not."

Martha had been shocked. Had George actually been considering going to live in England, been talking about it to other people? Did he miss Sally so much that he would give up everything he had here, his beloved Mount Vernon, just to be near her? But nothing more had been said about the possibility, and now the Fairfaxes were back again. Relief was mingled with resignation. If George must have Sally nearby to complete his happiness, better in this country than in some cold, foreign land! George directed the opening of Belvoir for their coming, went to the dock to meet their ship, so she was spared the sight of their meeting. Would that look be in his eyes? Better not to know.

Her first visit to Belvoir proved less disturbing than she had expected. The Fairfaxes might have been gone two days instead of two years. If Sally had changed, it was only to have accentuated features already inherent in her personality—vivacity, wit, pride, a certain brittle sophistication. She was extremely conscious of having traveled far, hobnobbed with the rich and intellectual, patronized the best shops, all but rubbed shoulders with royalty.

"Martha, my dear, you must see all these things I brought back! You have no idea of what really inferior dress materials our agents send us!" She exhibited yards and yards of lustrous silk, ribbons and rich laces, at least a half dozen negligees, one of gray lutestring, another of black silk, and a white silk nightgown.

Martha duly admired and listened with appropriate responses of interest to accounts of life as experienced by the nobility of England, or, at least, aspirants to it, for it was obvious that Sally's hopes were set on a title for George William in the event of Lord Fairfax's death.

"You have no idea what is considered big over there! We think we have mansions here. You should see Towelston, it's really palatial. And York's Grand Assembly Room. Why, it's three times as long as the Apollo Room in Raleigh Tavern! Even Bruton Church, which we think is so imposing, is nothing beside York Minster."

Martha's attention strayed. She was really more interested in what George and George William were discussing, and while keeping her eyes dutifully fixed on Sally's animated features, her ears were cocked toward the men still seated at the dining table. George William was telling of the jubilation in London over the signing of the Treaty of Paris the preceding February, bringing to an end the war between France and England. England was at last supreme in North America.

"What a joyful climax it must have been for you!" he observed. "After all, it was you who really began the war by your regiment's attack on Jumonville back in 1754. And you gave five years of your life to the struggle. You must count it a real personal victory."

"Yes," agreed George, "peace will be of great benefit to our colony. Our trade should flow in a more easy and regular channel than it has done in the past."

George William stared at him, nonplussed. "Is that all you're thinking of—trade? I'll be bound! You—the heroic soldier who challenged every freeborn Englishman to rise up and attest the rights and privileges of our King—now turned into a planter, trader?"

"I hope so," returned George seriously. "I intend to spend the rest of my life living at peace, rendering the service of a good citizen to my neighborhood and colony, developing my land—"

"Land, yes!" George William's eyebrows rose quizzically. "I hear you keep adding to it constantly, even investing in that western gamble known as the Dismal Swamp and getting yourself more in debt with every venture. What are you trying to be, another Lord Fairfax?"

George shifted uneasily. His friend had evidently probed a sensitive spot. "It's good land," he objected firmly. "I've visited it several times. And now that the French are finally ousted, our future lies in the west. I hope the British government has the sense to see where its best interests lie."

The talk shifted back to England. The death of George II had brought his grandson to the throne, a young man of twenty-three, the first King of England with a German background, and no one yet knew what the accession of George III might mean to the colonies.

"Georges!" thought Martha. How many of them there were! Her own George, George William, and now another King named George! Well, at least this one was across the ocean and could have little influence on their lives.

"There's a rumor going around England," said George William with a twinkle in his eye, "that the new King is slightly mad."

Sally also had been at least half-listening, for she broke in hastily, eyes flashing. "Colonel Fairfax—please! Don't ever apply such a rude word to our sovereign. It—it's disloyal, unpatriotic. Sick, perhaps, but certainly not mentally unsound."

George smiled at her—tenderly, or was it teasingly? "Spoken like a loyal Britisher, madam. I take it the King can do no wrong. But you can't say the same for some of his subjects. Our factors in London cheat us, underpay us, send us poor-quality merchandise, postpone our payments for months, even years. And now British merchants are refusing to accept payments in paper currency issued by our colony. The British Board of Trade is demanding currency reform. At the Assembly in May, Governor Fauquier told us all efforts to evade the Board's decision would be fruitless and incur His Majesty's displeasure. It's really alarming and is likely to set the whole country in flames."

Talk shifted again, to crops this time. George was beginning to think it was not profitable to grow tobacco on his land and was thinking of turning to wheat and other crops. He was trying all sorts of experiments, with fertilizers, cow dung, marl, mud from the marshes . . . Martha turned her attention back to Sally, who had embarked on an eloquent and clever description of a reception they had attended at the mansion of the Duke of York.

On the way home Martha heard George chuckle several times. Finally he said, "Well! Our Sally seemed to have come down with quite a severe case of British-itis. I think she has a yen for becoming Lady Fairfax."

Martha felt a sudden warmth of relief. He had said "*our* Sally." And he had spoken of her jibingly, almost with criticism. He might still be in love with her, probably was, but at least she had been taken down from her pedestal. Martha could accept a renewal of the old intimate relationship with more equanimity.

But it was not quite the old intimate relationship. True, there was just as much interchange between Belvoir and Mount Vernon, borrowing back and forth, dinners two or three times a week, overnight visits, and the two families often meeting at other plantations. But as dinner talk and conversation on porch or terrace changed increasingly from crops and land to politics, George and George William were sometimes in frank if polite disagreement.

At first there were only rumors. Report of a change in British policy reached Virginia in May 1764. George Grenville, Chancellor of the Exchequer, had made a long speech to Parliament urging that the colonies contribute to the cost of defending them. He suggested that it might be proper to charge some stamp duties to the said colonies. At Mount Vernon and neighboring plantations there was instant shock and challenge. All the taxes imposed in any colony had been by laws of its own Assembly, chosen by the people who had to pay the taxes. Were the colonists not British subjects, protected by the same rights as other Englishmen? Did that not include the right of taxation by representatives of their own choice? Shades of Runnymede! Heaven knew what a struggle Parliament had had to ensure that the taxpayer had the right of his own taxation! Richard Henry Lee, Washington's friend from childhood and fellow burgess, expressed most of the colonists' first reaction.

"Can it be supposed," he wrote a friend in England, "that those brave adventurous Britons, who originally conquered and settled these countries meant thereby to deprive themselves of that free government of which they were members, and to which they had an unquestionable right?"

"It's a reasonable move on the part of Parliament," insisted George William stiffly. "During the war with France, England has increased her national debt to 130 million pounds—and a good part of it in our defense."

Martha felt the atmosphere grow tense. The Washingtons were entertaining at a neighborhood dinner, with guests from both Belvoir and Gunston Hall. She looked apprehensively at George, who, as usual, was sitting across from her at the middle of the table. She saw his lips tighten.

"As for their defending us," he said, the quietness of his voice belied by the steeliness of his eyes, "we defended ourselves and are still doing it from western marauders—yes, and paying for it. All through the war we bore an equal part in the fighting, and though they mocked at our crude equipment and disciplines, we proved ourselves the equal of any man in the King's pay."

"*Touchez.* Well said. I should know that, Colonel, having fought beside you." George William smiled even while he continued stubbornly. "But you still must admit that we've been a great expense to the Mother Country, much of it," he repeated the words pointedly, *"in our defense."*

"In defense of her own interests, you mean," retorted George Mason dryly. "Making sure we colonists can't even trade with each other without sending our produce first to England. English merchants must be our middlemen. English ships must carry our goods. Even the smoking tobacco sold in Boston and New York has been first to England!"

Another George, thought Martha idly. All three of these men named George. Couldn't their mothers and fathers have thought of any other names? But of course all of them must have been christened in honor of whichever George was on the throne when they were born, the First or Second. And now there was another . . .

As if echoing her thoughts George William Fairfax lifted his wineglass in challenge. "Come, gentlemen, I offer a toast. God save our King, George the Third."

"Hear, hear!" applauded Sally. Glass held high, she looked from one to the other as if daring them to show reluctance.

Martha felt a moment's panic as George proceeded to finish his handful of nuts before complying. But then he obediently lifted his glass, and the other guests followed suit. "To the King, George the Third!" he agreed, smiling.

Relieved, Martha led Sally and Anne Mason to the terrace for more feminine talk, leaving the three men to what might or might not be a continuation of argument. She took a perverse pleasure in knowing that Sally would have preferred to remain with the men, perhaps even participating in their political discussion, certainly making sure that no further disparagement of British policy remained unchallenged. Sally was never at her best in conversation with other women, managing somehow to convey the impression that she was above their trivial interests. Now she sat tapping one velvet-slippered foot while Martha and the lovely auburn-haired Anne Mason talked of remedies for children's croup and proper discipline for refractory servants and a new recipe Anne had discovered for making perfume out of flowers.

"You dry your violets in a sunny window," she directed, her pretty face alight with housewifely fervor. "Add to them some bay salt. Then dry rose petals and add them to the violets, with a layer of bay salt between each layer of the dried flowers. Lavender and verbena can be used too. Stir it all together in a jar every day for a month. Then close it tightly and put it away. When you open it, it will make your rooms as fragrant as a garden."

"Lovely!" enthused Martha. Then, feeling herself remiss as a hostess, she skillfully led Sally to describe the management of the Fairfax mansion in England.

George was only mildly concerned with problems created by rumblings overseas, for most of the new measures were galling chiefly to the northern colonies. The so-called "Molasses Act," passed by Parliament in 1763, aroused ferment mainly in New England, which now had to pay a duty of three cents a gallon for molasses imported for their distilleries from sources other than the British West Indies. Agents in Boston were given leave by "writs of assistance" to enter any premises they wished in search of smuggled goods. There followed instant horror, protest, defiance. But that was New England. Virginia had no need of molasses.

However, Grenville was not finished. In 1765 he proposed that colonists be required to use revenue stamps on all their commercial paper, legal documents, pamphlets, and newspapers and that soldiers stationed in the plantations to enforce the act should be billeted on the people. The act was passed in March but news of it did not reach Virginia until the Assembly was meeting in May. George went to the Assembly alone but left Williamsburg early to attend to the grafting of his cherry trees. Most of the other members had left also, so that out of the total of one hundred and sixteen burgesses only thirty-nine were present when, as George Johnston of Fairfax County told George later, "all hell broke loose."

"You should have been there, Colonel!" he chided, stopping on his way home to Belvale, his plantation just south of Alexandria. Johnston was a respected friend and one of George's legal advisers. "Of course we were disturbed last year by the threat of taxation and made our protests, and when news came of the actual passing of the bill we were stunned. It stirred up a tempest! But, by heavens, we were ready for it! Remember that young burgess from Hanover that I introduced to you last year, the one who made such a powerful speech to the Committee on Courts of Justice?"

George nodded. "Yes. Patrick Henry. Rather a young firebrand, he seemed."

Martha, who was presiding over the tea table, also remembered this Patrick Henry. He had been pointed out to her on the street in Williamsburg. He had seemed to her uncouth and untidy, certainly not a gentleman. Why, there in the capital he had been clad in buckskin leggings as if he were back home on the frontier!

"Firebrand?" Johnston winced as he imbibed too hasty a gulp of his hot tea. "Perhaps. But sometimes it takes a firebrand to kindle a good blaze. Henry somehow anticipated the passing of this stamp act, while the rest of us were fooling ourselves that it was only a rumor, and he was ready for it. He had prepared a set of resolutions. I myself made the motion that he present them. And did they rouse a turmoil!"

"What were they?" demanded George. "Surely last year we made strong protest against the passing of such laws and sent it to the Crown."

"Not so strong as this!" Johnston took a sheet of foolscap from his pocket. "Well, briefly the Resolutions stated," he began reading, " 'that from the first His Majesty's colony of Virginia had possessed and enjoyed all the privileges, franchises, and immunities at any time enjoyed by the people of Great Britain; and that this, their freedom, had been explicitly secured to them by their charters; that the taxation of the people by themselves or by persons chosen by themselves to represent them was a distinguishing characteristic of British freedom, without which the ancient constitution of the realm itself could not subsist.' "

"Hear, hear!" George set down his cup to clap his hands. "Well stated!"

"But that's not all. Listen to what followed: 'Resolved, therefore that His Majesty's liege people of this most ancient Colony have uninterruptedly enjoyed the right of being governed by their own Assembly in the article of their Taxes and internal police, and that the same hath never been forfeited or in any other way given up, but hath been constantly recognized by the Kings and People of Great Britain.' "

George had not picked up his cup. He was listening with mounting excitement.

"But just listen to the last resolution, Number Five!: 'Resolved, therefore, that the General Assembly of this Colony have the *only* and *exclusive* Right and Power to lay Taxes and Impositions upon the Inhabitants of this Colony, and that every Attempt to vest such Power in any Person or Persons whatsoever, other than the General Assembly foresaid has a manifest Tendency to Destroy British as well as American Freedom.' "

George gasped. "But that—that might be called treason!"

"So it was," said Johnston. "You should have heard the furor. But Henry was equal to it. He talked like—like a Cicero, or a Demosthenes, thundering, eloquent. Finally, gesturing defiance, he called the act tyranny and shouted, 'Caesar had his Brutus, Charles the First his Cromwell, and George the Third—' But before he could finish, the Speaker shouted, 'Treason!' And others echoed, 'Treason, treason!' Then Henry did finish, triumphantly. 'And George the Third,' he shouted, 'may profit by their example. If *this* be treason, make the most of it!' "

Even as George's lips tightened, his eyes gleamed. "Daring young cub! Surely most of the Assembly would not stand for that! What happened then?"

"He went on speaking," said Johnston, "but with more moderation. He had made his point, and he didn't want the Assembly prejudiced against his Resolutions because Speaker Robinson had accused him of treason. He apologized and vowed his loyalty to the King. A vote was taken and—would you believe it?—his Resolutions were approved by twenty to nineteen, just by one vote!"

Martha looked from one to the other of the two men, her eyes fixing anxiously on George. Though she did not understand just what had happened, she realized that it was something of tremendous importance, also that there was inner conflict behind those tight lips and gleaming eyes.

"You're right," said George at last. "It's hard to believe. They must have been carried away—"

"They were, even the old guard that voted against the Resolutions, like Peyton Randolph. After the meeting he stomped out, and somebody heard him say, 'By God, I would have given five hundred guineas for a single vote!' That would have meant a tie, of course, and you know how Speaker Robinson would have voted to break it. I wonder," Johnston suddenly looked hard at George, "if you had been there, Colonel, how would you have voted?"

Martha's hand, reached out to take one of their cups for refilling, drew back. Vaguely she realized that at the moment nothing could have been more unimportant to the two men, perhaps to herself, than tea, even the rare India tea which had come from London with the last shipment.

George was silent for a long moment. "I—I really don't know," he said at last.

"Well—you don't have to decide—not yet, that is." Their guest visibly relaxed. "There's more you haven't heard. All *that* took place in the Committee of the Whole. The next morning the Assembly met to receive the report, and, while they passed the Resolutions, they toned them down considerably and completely cut out Number Five, which had threatened non-obedience. Patrick Henry had gone home then, so his eloquence was a matter of memory. At least we have sent our protests to the Crown. Now we'll just have to wait and see what happens."

Martha drew a sigh of relief. George smiled, the restless gleam gone from his eyes. He was once more the genial and punctilious host. "Have another cup of this good tea, Johnston. It's a new brand, the latest delicacy out of India via London. And try another piece of Mrs. Washington's spiced gingerbread. It's famous."

Martha's hand closed over the curved handle of the silver teapot, embossed with the Washington coat of arms. Life had returned to normal. After all, what did a bill passed by some men across the ocean have to do with the pleasant, remote, well-ordered life of Mount Vernon?

10

These were the happiest years Martha had ever known. She lived a carefree life, but certainly not an idle one. The children were growing and learning, handsome and intelligent both of them, even though spoiled, and, except for Patsy's delicate health, they gave her no worries. Though she dressed simply when at home, as fitted her activities, when she went visiting to neighboring plantations or drove with George to Annapolis or Alexandria or to Pohick Church on Sundays in their chariot and four, with black postilions in the white and scarlet livery of the Washingtons, she dressed richly and in a style becoming the wife of a respected and successful planter, an influential burgess, and, since 1762, an honored vestryman of Truro Parish whose calm, competent judgment was relied upon for a fair settlement of all church problems.

True, the summer after the disruptive Assembly had its setbacks on the plantation. After good early rains, which freshened the corn and started the hemp, which was one of George's trial grains, winds blew steadily from the west and southwest, and drought followed. There was rust on the wheat crop. It was ironic, because farms farther inland were blessed with rain. At least, if he had to buy corn next winter, he could procure it from nearby farms! In spite of having a large plantation, he was always having to buy, it seemed. One year he was chagrined because, although he had over a hundred cows, he had to buy butter!

But the summer also had its satisfactions. George had a new assistant, Lund Washington, a distant relative who had been a playmate on the Rappahannock. He could leave on business or spend more time with guests and know that the plantation was in good hands. Also, with a new election occasioned by Governor Fauquier's dissolving of the Assembly due to his displeasure over the Resolutions, George ran again for burgess, this time from his own county of Fairfax, and won by a large margin.

Though agitation over the Stamp Act was spreading through the colony like wildfire, involving many of the soberer leading planters as well as young hotheads like Patrick Henry, George seemed to take no sides. He listened with equal concern to resisters like Johnston and staunch British supporters like George William Fairfax. His neutral position was evidenced in a letter he wrote a friend in September 1765.

"The Stamp Act imposed on the Colonies by the Parliament of Great Britain engrosses the conversation of the speculative part of the Colonists, who look upon this unconstitutional method of taxation as a direful attack upon their liberties . . ." Though admitting that the tax was "unconstitutional," he spoke of the attack on *their*, not *our*, liberties. He manifested no excitement, no emotion except distress when his old friend and former military aide George Mercer, a popular man in the colony, was made distributor of the new stamps for Virginia and immediately encountered not only opposition but also hatred. He was burned in effigy. Arriving in Williamsburg from England with the hated stamps, he was almost mobbed until he agreed not to proceed further with their distribution without the assent of the Assembly. Then he became hero instead of villain.

Another George! thought Martha, glad that her own bearer of the name was content to remain uninvolved in the disagreeable fracas. She doubted if many of the present generation of babies would be christened after this encumbent of the British throne.

Whether the result of colonial furor or of a more reasonable leadership in Parliament typified by William Pitt, in May of 1766 the ship *Lady Baltimore* brought the long-hoped-for news. The Stamp Act had been repealed! The House of Commons had voted overwhelmingly, the Lords less enthusiastically, and royal assent had been given.

"There!" Sally Fairfax's brilliant eyes were triumphantly challenging. "I guess now you can see that our good King is both wise and just—yes, and magnanimous!"

George agreed that the King had acted with wisdom but reminded her that there had been no admission that the law was unconstitutional or tyrannical, also that Parliament had served notice that, if need be, it would declare colonial laws of no effect. At least, thought Martha with pardonable satisfaction, George was no longer a prisoner of Sally's ideas and loyalties, however much his emotions might still be held captive.

With the new year, 1767, life continued to flow smoothly and serenely at Mount Vernon. George was growing no tobacco now on his farms, only wheat, corn, hemp, flax. He decided to develop weaving as a major industry, since the lack of specie to purchase English cloth was increasing the demand for homespun. But Martha was no longer responsible for the plantation weavers. There was a professional weaver, Thomas Davis, to direct the work. In fact, she was carefully protected from most of the worries that beset George. *Her* worries were all for the children: Jacky's laziness and increasing appetite for fine clothes and other luxuries (though even George was inordinately proud of the boy's handsome appearance, skilled horsemanship, and unfailing good nature); Patsy's mysterious malady that caused so many weakening attacks.

It was chiefly for Patsy's sake that in August George took the family to Berkeley Springs, where he had gone in a vain attempt to restore his beloved brother Lawrence's health and he himself had gone during an illness in 1761. The place was far less crude than in earlier days. They lived in a cottage instead of a tent, food was plentiful, with veal, mutton, pork, and venison. Since they had brought along the Mount Vernon cook, it was well prepared. But the celebrated waters, whether drunk or bathed in, seemed to do little for Patsy except bring on fits of shivering, and Jacky was so bored with the place that Martha was glad when they returned home the second week in September. Life once more resumed its comfortable, satisfying tenor.

Even the passing by Parliament of what were called the Townshend Acts, which fixed taxes on paints, glass, paper, and tea and spread another furor of alarm through the colony had little effect on Martha's sense of well-being. Once more conversation about the dinner table grew hot with debate, though George Johnston was no longer there to participate, having died in the summer of 1766. But others, including George Mason of Gunston Hall, were ready and willing to challenge the Fairfaxes' defense of British policy.

"Violation of the fundamental rights of Englishmen!" . . . "Tyrannical to levy taxes without the consent of the people!" . . . "Ruinous if we get Governors and other officers who are no longer dependent on our votes for their salaries!" . . . "Have you heard what they did in New York? When the Assembly refused to vote salt, vinegar, and beer for the troops billeted there, saying they were not allowed the King's troops in Europe, what did General Gage do? Suspend the Assembly until it complied with all the requirements for the billeting of troops!"

"Well," objected George William hotly, "and why shouldn't we pay for the troops that are sent here for our defense?"

"Defense from what?" shot back Mason. "From the oppressors that they are here representing? If our rights are lost, I ask you, what remains?"

George listened, asking himself the same question, but unwilling as yet to commit himself. Time, he felt, would give the answer. Protest, of course. Look what it had done for them before. Parliament had proved reasonable. Wait and see. Besides, he was completely engrossed in his new plans for the plantation. Already he could see advantages in the shift-over from tobacco to wheat. So hopeful did he feel about the coming season that he was more lavish than usual in his invoices from London. He even decided to order a new chariot, for the old one was becoming shabby and prone to breakdowns. George was very specific in his list of requirements.

It must be "in the newest taste, handsome, genteel . . . of the best seasoned wood and by a celebrated workman. The last importation which I have seen, besides the customary steel springs have others that play in a brass barrel, and contribute at one and the same time to the ease and ornament of the chariot . . . green being a color little apt, as I apprehend, to fade, and grateful to the eye, I would give it the preference . . . A light gilding on the mouldings, that is round the panels, and any other ornaments that may not have a heady or tawdry look (together with my arms agreeable to the impression here sent) might be added, by way of decoration."

A pity, George felt, that the chariot was not there for their spring trip south! But they made the journey to Eltham and Williamsburg without mishap. Though he took no active part in the discussion, he agreed heartily with the action of the Assembly that spring of 1768 begging King and Parliament for repeal of the Townshend Acts and for the "security and full enjoyment of all our natural and constitutional rights and privileges."

Martha stayed with the children at Eltham, a visit of pure joy unmarred by the tumult of debate rocking the Assembly. Nancy had given birth to another daughter, Frances, the year before, her sixth child, and Martha developed an almost fierce affection for this new and most lovable baby. Now thirty-seven, she had long since given up hope of bearing George a child, and this little "Fanny" seemed to fill the long-felt emptiness. She felt replete with pleasure when in late May they returned home.

It was well that she had this season—yes, these years—of serene, untroubled enjoyment, for her state of pure contentment would soon be ended.

In fact, it did end almost immediately on their arrival. "My dear," said George the first evening when, for a wonder, there were no guests, "I think we have an important matter to discuss."

"Yes?" She settled herself comfortably with her knitting. Something about new plans for the house, no doubt. Then, suddenly aware of his unwonted soberness, she felt a slight unease. "Yes?" she repeated.

"The time has come, my dear, when we must plan for our Jacky's further education."

"Oh—yes, of course." She felt swift relief. The children's tutor, Walter MacGowan, had left for England in March. "I do hope," she said, "that you will be able to find another tutor as able and worthy as Walter."

George cleared his throat. He well knew what grief he was about to cause her. "I think, my dear," he said gently, "that the boy is too old for tutors. He is almost fourteen, and the environment here at home is not conducive to study. In spite of MacGowan's attempts, he remains deplorably ignorant."

While in Williamsburg, George continued, he had heard of a school for boys conducted by Jonathan Boucher, a clergyman and rector of excellent repute. It was right here in Virginia, in Caroline County. Better than his going to England as so many of the colonists' sons—in fact, George's own two half brothers—had done. Of course Martha would appreciate having him near. Mr. Boucher had a little plantation and grew food for his twenty or thirty students. There would be plenty of fresh milk for him, eggs, and butter, so Martha need not worry about his welfare. George had written Mr. Boucher a letter on the thirtieth, the day they had arrived home, and perhaps Martha would like to read it.

At first she could not see the words, so blurred were they. Then slowly she began to read, her thoughts insisting on interjecting themselves among the boldly inscribed sentences:

"He is a boy of good genius, about 14 years of age, untainted in his morals, and of innocent manners. *(Oh, yes, he was all that, and also so good-natured and handsome!)* If he comes to your school he will have a boy, well acquainted with house business, which may be made as useful as possible in your family to keep him out of idleness, and two horses, to furnish him with the means of getting to church and elsewhere as you may permit; for he will be put entirely and absolutely under your tuition and direction, to manage as you think proper in all respects. *(Oh, dear, how could a man, a strange man, possibly give him all the care he needed, especially if he was sick!)* . . . I do not think it necessary to inquire into and will cheerfully pay 10 or 12 pounds a year extraordinary to engage your peculiar care and a watchful eye to him, as he is a promising boy, the last of his family and will possess a very large fortune; add to this my anxiety to make him fit for more useful purposes than a horse racer. *(Yes, George was right, of course. The boy had shown more interest in horse racing and other amusements than in his studies!)*"

Martha endured both agony and hope until the answer came. Perhaps this Mr. Boucher would be unable to take Jacky. When the letter arrived, hope at first won—Mr. Boucher expressed doubt because he might soon move his school to Maryland. Then it plummeted into agony—for at present he would be delighted to have Jacky for a pupil.

"You, sir, seem so justly sensible of the vast importance of a good education that I cannot doubt of your heartily concurring in every plan that might be proposed for the advantage of your ward; and what I am more particularly pleased with is the ardent desire you express for the cultivation of his moral as well as his intellectual powers. I mean that he may be a good as well as learned and a sensible man."

Martha should have been heartened by this promise, but all she could think of were the months of his absence when who knew what sickness or accident might befall him. Since that unhappy visit to the Austin Washingtons, when she had suffered agonies of worry, she had never been separated from either of the children for more than a few nights. Then in June, a month before he was due to leave, something happened that made the coming separation seem even more tragic.

On the thirteenth they rode to Belvoir where the Fairfaxes were entertaining a number of guests. Since they would not be away overnight the children were left behind. Returning the same day, Martha immediately began preparing to entertain the Fairfaxes and their guests on the fifteenth. Suddenly Patsy was taken very ill. She gave a strange cry, then fell to the floor, where, after lying rigid for some seconds, she began to jerk about, eyes rolling, face twitching, little flecks of foam gathering at the corners of her mouth. Fortunately George was in the house, and Martha's agonized cry brought him running. When he arrived the violent motions had stopped, and the child was lying limp and motionless, the only sign of life little convulsive gasps which soon settled into heavy, stertorous breathing. Giving a curt command to one of the servants to summon a doctor, he picked her up, carried her upstairs, and laid her gently on her bed.

"Oh, God help us!" Martha was almost inarticulate in misery and terror. "What is it? What—what shall we do?"

"Wait for the doctor," he told her with all the assurance he could muster. "She seems to have had a fit of some kind, probably nothing serious. It might well be the hot weather. Perhaps"—he saw her helpless need for action—"some cool cloths on her forehead?"

"Oh—yes!" Relieved, she sent Molly for a basin of water and some soft cloths, then sat by the bed sponging the child's damp forehead, while the nurse hovered over them, her dusky features as expressive of anguish as Martha's pallor.

Dr. Rumney, the local physician, arrived. "Ah, yes," he said, looking grave, "the falling sickness. Has she had attacks of this kind before?" No, they assured him, nothing like that, though she had always been delicate and subject to frequent illnesses. He was able to relieve her symptoms, and she recovered sufficiently so he felt justified in leaving the next morning. On the fifteenth they entertained the guests as planned, and Patsy was her usual sunny self, charming in a new gown of pink lutestring bedecked with lace and ruffles, showing a petticoat embroidered with chenille in a pattern of bright flowers, a really grown-up outfit for the twelve-year-old just emerging into womanhood.

As usual Martha was the competent and gracious hostess, making sure that the dinner served was perfection, the linen tablecloth spotless, the silver polished, the crystal goblets sparkling, the wines ice-chilled, the meats turned on the spit to just the right degree of succulence. But if one stern eye noted the progress of the small dusky servants bearing platters and salvers and porringers from cookhouse to serving tables, the other anxiously followed the slender, rose-clad figure as it flitted gaily among the guests. Though Patsy seemed to have recovered completely from the strange attack (indeed, she herself had no memory of it), the doctor had warned that similar spells might follow. Never again would Martha feel safe letting the child out of her sight.

In July she watched George and a half-eager, half-reluctant Jacky set off for Mr. Boucher's domain in Caroline County, accompanied by his body servant, his two horses, much luggage, but minus, doubtless due to his own carelessness (or intention?), the Latin and Greek textbooks he would soon be needing. Martha managed to stifle her tears until they were out of sight, then shut herself in her room so her grief would not further excite Patsy. July . . . and she might not see him again until Christmas! This time her keen pleasure in George's return from a journey was tinged with vague disappointment. She had been nursing a secret hope that Jacky might be so homesick that George would have brought him back.

She waited anxiously now for the first letter. It came, not from Jacky but from Boucher, who reported that the young gentleman had enjoyed perfect health except for a few days of stomachache. "I at first took it for the colic," he wrote, "but since think it more likely that it might be owing to worms." Worms—Jacky! It had obviously been a mistake for Boucher to mention such a possibility. What was for him a normal child's complaint was to Martha a misfortune of the first magnitude. She endured tortures until other letters reported a long period of robust health.

George was as concerned as she about Patsy. He could not have loved her more had she been his own flesh and blood. His eyes glowed with pride as they followed her riding the little mare he had given her, her red riding habit and little feathered hat flashing across the fields in a bright streak of color; or dipping and whirling and pirouetting through the steps of a country dance or minuet; or making daily visits to the servants' cabins with fruits and broths and jellies for the old and ailing. All on the plantation loved her. They called her "the dark lady" because of her brunet complexion, brown eyes, and dark curling hair. Already she was giving promise of rare beauty. He watched her as carefully as Martha, making sure that there was always someone with her in case she had another seizure. And he was even more extravagant than Martha in the luxuries he ordered for her from London. In the invoices sent that year were included "a very handsome and fashionable saddle with bridle and everything complete," also a smelling bottle, gloves, satin pumps, a "neat pocket looking glass, a book with a version of Psalms and Hymns set for the spinet, a young lady's black furred riding hat with a white feather."

Because of Patsy, Martha was even more reluctant to see George leave on his various missions—to his lands in the Dismal Swamp in October, to the Assembly in Williamsburg in November—but she dared not risk for the child the excitement of travel, and of course she could not leave her. With the death of Governor Fauquier, for whom she had always had a unique affection because of his attendance at her wedding, a new Governor, the Baron of Botetourt, had arrived and immediately dissolved the Assembly. Another election campaign for George! But he won easily. In addition to the office of burgess he was also warden of Truro Parish, justice of the Fairfax County Court, all duties which made him one of the busiest and most distinguished citizens of the Northern Neck.

But Christmas in that year of 1768 was all Martha could have wished. Jacky returned, boisterous and healthy, unscathed by evidences of debility, whether colic or worms or maternal supervision, raring for the holiday hunts. It was a gala season. But to Martha's dismay it was at home, not at school, that Jacky fell sick and was not able to return to his classes until the end of January. This time his departure aroused resignation rather than intense grief. And by then Martha had other more pressing worries. Patsy had another severe attack, more prolonged than the first, and, while she recovered again into what seemed normal health, the threat of recurrent attacks was ever present. Doctor Rumney made frequent visits but, though charging generous fees (one of his bills was for nineteen pounds!), he was unable to effect a cure.

"Why not try an iron ring?" one of the neighbors suggested. "It's supposed to draw out spasms from the body when everything else fails."

George found the idea repugnant. It seemed to savor of witchcraft, but, seeing the desperation in Martha's eyes, he consented. At least it could do no harm. So in February he noted in his diary: "Joshua Evans, who came here last night, put an Iron Ring upon Patcy (for Fits) and went away after breakfast." But, as he had expected, Martha's hopes were again dashed. In April, when the family was driving to Captain McCarty's for a visit, Patsy had a seizure in the carriage, and of course the trip had to be abandoned. But, as each time before, she recovered, and Martha, hopes rising, felt that this one might be the last. Perhaps it took the iron ring a long time to work. Or perhaps they would discover a new doctor or treatment that would be more effective.

Meanwhile her greatest comfort was in her hour of devotions each morning and in the worshipful, though lengthy and monotonous services in Pohick Church on Sundays. Even the accompanying noise and confusion of the churchyard—clatter of carriage wheels, cracking of whips, shouts of masters to their accompanying slaves, excited neighing of horses vying with each other for priority, as one visitor expressed it, "steed threatening steed with high and boastful neigh"—could not penetrate her mood of spiritual exaltation. Kneeling on the hard bench, repeating the old familiar prayers, she was able to absorb worries as well as self into a fervency of hope and faith.

George's participation in the church was of necessity more practical. As one of the twelve vestrymen, "twelve lords of the parish" some satirically called them, he helped fix the amount of tithes, choose and pay the rector, provide for the poor, fix the boundary of lands on the public roads, present to the county court persons guilty of profanity, drunkenness, gambling, Sabbath-breaking, failure to attend church. And in this year of 1769 he and his fellow vestrymen had another important duty, planning for a new church, for the old frame building —erected in the 1600s on the south side of Pohick Run about two miles from Gunston Hall—was beyond repair. At the first parish meeting there was hot disagreement over the site of the new building. Martha heard the argument continued around the dinner table.

"Close to the same spot," insisted George Mason. "It's there that our fathers worshiped, there many of them are buried. It's a sacred place."

"No," objected George, "it's no longer the center of population. Things have changed."

It was the first time in Martha's memory that the two had disagreed.

She sympathized with Mason. She would have felt the same about St. Peter's, where she had worshiped as a child. But it was George who had his way. At the next meeting he presented a paper showing a map with the exact location of all houses in the district, their distances from the suggested sites indicated, and his argument won the day. The new site would be on a main road closer to the homes of the majority of worshipers. Practical considerations triumphed over sentiment. It would always be so in matters where George was concerned. But his meticulous work was not finished. He drew a ground plan of the building for the architect, sketched with China ink on fine drawing paper, an artistic creation which would long outlive him.

Martha awoke from her absorption with Patty's illness to discover that events far beyond the bounds of the plantation or of Pohick Parish were impinging on her life. In the conversation around the dinner table she heard more and more frequently names like Boston, New York, Philadelphia. Always before they had seemed as strange and faraway as London.

"My dear," said George one evening in early April when they were sitting in the parlor bathed in spring fragrances from an open window, "I think you should know something of the content of these papers I have received from Dr. David Rose in Maryland. It may concern you almost as much as it does me and others of our friends."

Martha was surprised. The papers had come some days ago, and she knew George had been sober and preoccupied since their arrival. It was something about politics, she supposed, this business of taxation which the men seemed always to be talking about. But how could it possibly concern her? She had spent long hours in the garden, and she was tired. Moreover, she had just come downstairs after seeing Patsy settled for the night, and she still feared the child had a slight fever. But dutifully she put aside her knitting and tried to focus her attention on what George was saying. Yes, it *was* something about politics and taxation. This Dr. Rose, it seemed, was suggesting that people get together and agree not to buy things from England that they could get along without until England stopped taxing them against their will. It sounded like a good idea until, suddenly, she became fully aware of its implications.

"You mean—not buy things anymore from England?" she repeated, eyes widening in unbelief. "What things?"

"Whatever we can get along without," he replied calmly, "especially those things that are taxed in these Townshend Acts, paint, paper, glass, tea. And it might well extend to other items, cloth, sugar, wines, laces—in fact, most of the luxuries we import from London."

"But—" Martha's head whirled. How could they possibly get along without such things? No more silks, laces, sugar, perfumes, powders for one's hair . . . *tea!* Why, life wouldn't be the same at all!

George smiled ruefully at her dismay. "Don't worry. Nothing has been decided yet. It will be discussed at Assembly next month. But I thought you ought to know. I'm sending these papers along to George Mason. He's very wise, and I depend on his opinion"—he grimaced—"on most matters if not on where to put our church. Perhaps you'd like to hear these comments I am sending along with the papers."

Martha listened attentively while he read. She wished she had Sally's brilliant mind so she could understand exactly what his words meant.

"At a time when our lordly Masters in Great Britain will be satisfied with nothing less than the deprivation of American freedom, it seems highly necessary that something should be done to avert the stroke and maintain the liberty which we had derived from our ancestors; but the manner of doing it to answer our purpose effectually is the point in question."

Martha nodded. That seemed simple enough. Even she, a woman and not a very intellectual one, could understand what he meant. But he hadn't finished.

"That no man should scruple, or hesitate a moment to use a-ms in defence of so valuable a blessing, on which all the good and evil of life depends, is clearly my opinion; yet a-ms, I would beg leave to add, should be the last resource."

Arms! But that meant guns, killing! Surely she couldn't have heard right. The April breezes no longer felt soft and balmy, and the spring fragrances had given way to febrile odors from the distant marshes. Seeing her shiver, George got up and closed the window.

"Anyway," he told her cheerfully, "there's nothing to change our way of living yet. Look what our protests did before. Parliament will probably be reasonable. Meanwhile we won't worry."

George Mason responded promptly after receipt of the papers and George's letter, and, though he did not attend the May Assembly because of poor health, George took his suggestions with him. Mason agreed in urging the policy of non-importation which was already being practiced by some of the northern colonies. "We may retrench all manner of superfluities," he wrote, "and confine ourselves to linens, woolens, etc, not exceeding a certain price." He sent a long list of these "superfluities," including all luxuries of goods and dress, alcoholic beverages, beef, pork, butter, cheese, candles, confectionery, pewter, watches, clocks, mirrors, carriages, upholstery, trinkets, jewelry, gold and silver, silks except sewing silk, cambrics, lawn, muslin, gauze, stockings, shoes, saddles.

On receipt of the carefully worded protest and appeal to the Crown to repeal the hated Townshend Acts, Governor Botetourt promptly dissolved the Assembly, whereupon the burgesses adjourned to the Apollo Room of the Raleigh Tavern and drafted the non-importation agreement binding the colony to exclude from purchase all the luxury items listed by Mason, adding paint and tea. But when George returned home late in May he still hoped, trusted, that Parliament would be reasonable.

Martha was too busy entertaining guests to listen with more than half an ear to the news from Williamsburg. Jacky had arrived with the Reverend Jonathan Boucher, his teacher. Walter MacGowan, returned from England, had come to report his acceptance for holy orders. Doctor Rumney was visiting, fortunately not because of Patsy, but socially. Mrs. John Bushrod, mother of Austin's wife, was there, and Mrs. Warner Washington. It was a full house. And the following days were too full of planned festivities to allow for worry about what King and Parliament might be doing in far-off England. There was a race at Cameron to attend, followed by a barbecue in Alexandria. Then there was a trip to Towelston, the home of Bryan Fairfax, George William's half brother, where George was to stand as godfather to Bryan's third son by his wife Elizabeth, the younger sister of Sally. But for George none of these events, not even the outcome of the momentous Assembly, was as worthy of mention in his diary as the item first recorded on his return from Williamsburg:

"Found my wheat much better in general than ever it was at this season before."

For Martha the most important event of that summer was another trip to Berkeley Springs in the hope that Patsy's health might be improved. To her delight Jacky was permitted another visit home before the family left. Somehow he managed on any pretext possible to get away from school. Mr. Boucher made frequent dubious reports of his scholastic progress—or lack of it. Boucher assured them hopefully that Jacky was "far from being a brilliant genius" but that he gave promise of becoming "a good and useful man."

George prepared for the trip with his usual meticulous thoroughness, even making a list headed *Packing Memorandum,* which included items ranging from "Blew coat, Buff Vest and Breeches" to "Dressing Gown, Razors, etc." They left in the chariot on July 31, finishing the trip of some ninety miles as the crow flies but much longer by the road, on August 6. Once more they occupied the cottage loaned by George Mercer, soon getting it into condition for entertaining, for Lord Fairfax, George William and Sally were already there, also other friends and relatives. They had brought along their own cook, but a butcher and baker were resident at the springs.

Martha hopefully urged upon Patsy the spring water which attendants served in dripping goblets to one invalid after another, scarcely bothering to rinse them in the spring's basin between servings. George also was seeking the benefit of the waters, since he was suffering a recurrence of malaria. On the ninth of September, beset by chills and other discomforts, they started home. Though the old chariot broke down before they had gone a mile, it was soon repaired, and on the twelfth they were back in comfort at Mount Vernon, Patsy no worse but to Martha's dismay apparently no better. Neither was George, for he noted in his diary a return of the ague on September 23, a disappointing piece of ill luck "just at the beginning of the hunting season."

Since the Governor had dissolved the Assembly George had to stand for another election, but again he won easily. Governor Botetourt called the Assembly for November 7.

"You're going with me this time," George told Martha. "We can take Patsy to see that new doctor in Williamsburg. And," he added with self-conscious pride, "it will be the first time we have taken the new chariot to Eltham and the capital."

Martha smiled to herself. She knew what satisfaction George would take in driving down the Duke of Gloucester Street in his new conveyance, perhaps even encountering on his way the splendid coach of the Governor, who, as he had told her, sported a regal carriage with arms of Virginia on its panels, drawn by six magnificent cream-white horses, servants in green and red and gold livery. Well, George also had a beautiful chariot now, and no wonder, for it had cost 315 pounds. She had seen the invoice. Fortunately it had been ordered long before these troublesome non-importation vows were likely to go into effect. Its intricate carvings, gilded panels, diamond-cut glass, green leather finishings were all that he had specified, "in the newest taste, handsome, genteel." It had arrived early in the year, but this was the first time the family had taken it on such a journey.

They left on the last day of October, taking seven horses. No risk this time of the new equipage's becoming mired in the mud and remaining immobile for humiliating hours or days! They spent two days at Fredericksburg, visiting Betty and George's mother, stopped at the school in Caroline County to see Jacky, who begged to go with them.

"Please! I haven't been to Eltham for ages, and it would be fine education for me to be in the capital for Assembly," this latter a shrewd appeal to "Papa's" desire for his political enlightenment. Martha could not resist his pleas, and George could not resist Martha. Jacky went with them to Eltham, where George left him and the others, promising to return on the weekend and take them to Williamsburg.

His report of the first session was surprisingly optimistic. Except for one small item it would have been exuberant. Governor Botetourt had been amazingly conciliatory. He brought assurance that His Majesty's present administration did not propose to lay further taxes on America to raise revenues, and that they intended to propose in the next session of Parliament to take off the duties on glass, paper, and colors, such duties not in the interest of commerce.

"But," George added with significant emphasis, "the tax on tea would remain. And the Governor made it plain that this must not be regarded as an admission that Parliament had no right to levy taxes on America. I guess all we can say is that we have a reprieve."

But it was enough to make the Assembly season gayer than it had been for years. Martha and the children went back with him to Williamsburg, where the Lewises had opened their town house. George's diary recorded a succession of dinners, teas, balls, receptions, theater parties, and he took pride in presenting his handsome foster son at many of them.

"I and J. P. Custis suppd at Mrs. Campbell's . . ."

"Dind with Mrs. Washington etc at the Speaker's by Candlelight . . ."

"J. P. Custis and I dind with others at the Govr's . . ."

At one reception at the Governor's Palace, Martha, looking across the room from her seat with women friends, saw George talking with a man she had never seen before. He was tall, almost exactly the height of George, so that the two towered over all surrounding persons. He was slim, very straight, as muscular as George and younger by at least ten years. His face, like George's, showed the ruddiness of outdoor life. But he was not nearly so handsome, she thought with satisfaction. The two were engaged in serious conversation, and the stranger was doing most of the talking, which was natural, for George was never a glib speaker.

"Who was that young man you were speaking with?" she asked her husband at the first opportunity.

"The new burgess from Albemarle County," he replied. "His mother was a Randolph, one of the first families. And he's a real scholar, graduate of William and Mary." As always, George's tone betrayed a wistful admiration for those with superior education. "I believe he was sort of a protégé of old Governor Fauquier. He has some new and rather interesting ideas, about people's rights, not only those with money and property and good parentage, but all people"—his voice grew thoughtful—"just—just because they *are* people. What's that? His name? Oh—didn't I tell you? He is Thomas Jefferson."

The Assembly dragged on. George was especially interested in securing rights that the veterans of his western campaign had to 200,000 acres of bounty land, and he took an active part in petitioning for the legislation. He was finally given the responsibility for surveying and certifying the lands' distribution. It was December 21 before Assembly was able to adjourn. Eager to get home, George wanted to start the day before adjournment, foregoing the most elaborate function of the season, the ball given by the Speaker and burgesses in honor of the Governor.

"I hope you don't mind missing it," he apologized to Martha.

No, she did not mind. For her the pleasure of the trip had ended on finding that the new doctor could give no help to Patsy. Besides, the ball would have been a disappointing anticlimax. The wives of the burgesses had entered into an agreement in an excess of patriotism to wear to the ball nothing but homespun, even though the colony was hopeful that the hated taxes would be repealed, and there was still that one on tea! The principle of British right to tax remained. The stout-hearted ladies were determined to fulfill their vow. Martha would have turned with regret from the beautiful rose-colored gown of figured damask she had brought for the occasion to a dull, coarse blend of flax and wool. Still, it would have been interesting to see the Governor's face when confronted with nearly a hundred women so attired, though, from reports, he rose gallantly to the occasion with the comment that the feminine beauty of Virginia adorned anything it wore. Even London in its *Chronicle* celebrated the event in a couplet expressing more amusement than chagrin:

> Not all the gems that sparkle in the mine,
> Can make the Fair with so much lustre shine.

11

Tea! Who would have supposed such an ordinary staple of life could suddenly have become so important—or its lack such a deprivation! Once the last supply from England was gone, nothing could take its place. Martha tried raspberry leaves, loosestrife, goldenrod, yeopan, sage, but none proved a decent substitute. Tea was one of the chief topics of conversation, too, for, though Parliament had voted to take the hated tax off paper, painters' colors, and glass, they had left it on tea.

George was adamant in his support of the non-importation agreement reached in the spring of 1770, and of course tea was one of the prohibited "luxuries." Cheap cloth, shoes, stockings, and horse furnishings were to be allowed. Cheerfully, if reluctantly, Martha resigned herself to the prospect—at least temporarily—of no more silks and furbelows from London, even putting aside some of those already acquired, for, as George insisted, one should not give even the appearance of noncooperation with the boycott.

"I could wish the covenant to be ten times more strict," he averred.

There was shock at the spring Assembly over news from Boston. On the fifth of March, British troops had fired on a crowd of some sixty rioters who had mobbed a squad of soldiers. Three of the rioters had been killed, two others fatally wounded. The outrage of New England over this "Boston Massacre" had spread even to remote Virginia. Colonies heretofore widely separated by distance and interests were beginning to feel a growing cohesion of alarm. Still, for the Mount Vernon family, Boston was far away that year of 1770. George's chief interest was administering the western claims of lands for his former regiment, a task which took him to Fredericksburg during the summer. Martha's was a continued attempt to find help for Patsy. For two years now the girl had been having these intermittent seizures, and she had one on the way to Fredericksburg in July. Hopefully they took her to Dr. Hugh Mercer, a Scotch physician who had established a practice on Princess Street. Martha's pleasure in the visit with Betty was marred by disappointment when this doctor also proved unable to give effective treatment.

She returned home in August only to face another maternal worry. Mr. Boucher in his correspondence with George was advocating a tour of Europe as a proper feature of Jacky's troubled educational career. At seventeen, the minister complained, the boy was "constitutionally too warm, indolent and voluptuous." Jacky was definitely spoiled, and George was almost as much at fault as Martha. The boy had been showered with luxuries. Martha was almost sick with worry. It had been hard enough learning that Boucher was moving his school to a new curacy in Annapolis, across the broad expanse of Chesapeake Bay. But now—across an ocean! She knew suddenly how Mary Washington must have felt when her beloved George was likely to become a seaman. No wonder she had written to her brother in England for confirmation that it would be disastrous!

But to her immense relief George did not encourage the project. Though his objections were practical, not sentimental, they were firmly stated. Fifteen or sixteen hundred pounds a year, Boucher had said their trip would require? Why, that would exceed the boy's annual income! He could not permit recklessness with Jacky's property.

But the problem of Jacky persisted. Later in the year there was more correspondence with Boucher. Over in Annapolis there would be great temptations for a youth interested chiefly in dogs, horses, and guns—and, possibly, other diversions. George wrote Boucher asking that the boy not be permitted to sleep anywhere but under the teacher's own roof, "unless it be at such places as you are sure he can have no bad example set him; nor allow him to be rambling about of nights in company with those who do not care how debauched and vicious his conduct may be."

Fortunately Martha was not present when the reply arrived, and George was able to protect her from its worst implications by reading parts of it aloud. Boucher enlarged on Jacky's love of ease and pleasure. The letter was long and disturbing. There was certainly no assurance in Boucher's statement that "I must confess to you I never did in my life know a youth so exceedingly indolent or so surprisingly voluptuous. One would suppose Nature had intended him for some Asiatic Prince."

Martha was having worries enough without these further suggestions of venal temptations engulfing her handsome and problematic son. The time had come when, like most young adults subjected to dangers of travel, he should be inoculated for smallpox. Martha was terrified at the idea, and Jacky, always good-natured and amenable, acceded to her wish that it be postponed as long as possible.

Though she wanted Jacky to have the protection of inoculation, she could not bring herself to consent. If only, she expressed it, he might be inoculated and out of danger before she knew about it! George took her at her word and connived with Boucher to have it done without her knowledge. They were getting ready to leave for Eltham and Williamsburg in April when the news came. Boucher had taken Jacky to Baltimore and had the task performed. The boy had made a steady recovery with only eight "pocks"—pustules—developing. In fact, he had "such strong Symptoms of Health as we almost find inconvenient at this scarce Season of the Year, and dear Markets." George would have postponed the trip south until assured of Jacky's full recovery. Always Jacky's welfare and Martha's serenity of mind were his first priorities.

There was no Assembly that spring of 1771 because Governor Botetourt had died the preceding autumn, but George had business connected with Jacky's estates, and they wanted to consult Dr. Carter, a new Williamsburg physician, about Patsy's malady. The doctor did prescribe "fitt drops," four boxes of which were secured at a cost of one pound and five shillings. Perhaps George realized that this remedy also would be ineffective, for he accompanied the purchase with other thoughtful little items designed to appeal to a young girl, a "blewstrand Necklace, a song book, the Bullfinch, and a parrot." He also indulged himself by acquiring four of Lord Botetourt's notable cream-white carriage horses which came up for sale, an expensive transaction which involved the selling of four of his own horses and trading two more.

Still hopeful that the "fitt drops" might prove the long-sought elixir,

Martha yielded without reserve to the pleasures of Eltham and the capital. There were evenings at the theater in Williamsburg, one of them featuring the musical drama *The Beggar's Opera*. But for Martha the crowning joy of the trip was to reach home and find Jacky waiting, completely recovered from his inoculation and showing not even a single pockmark. And her fears about the possible European trip were set finally at rest. George cannily decided that the boy was far more in need of tutelage in basics like arithmetic and spelling than of exposure to the cultural benefits of Europe. Jacky, he told Boucher, did not know enough of mathematics to make even a good surveyor, as was necessary for a landed proprietor, and his spelling, as evidenced by one of his letters which he returned with corrections, was appalling.

"I was in a hurry when I wrote," Jacky excused himself cheerfully, protesting that he could write as good English and spell as well as most people, but acknowledging that he always put off everything to the last. And all he could do was to "pomise" that he would do better in the future.

George was becoming disillusioned with Boucher's school, also with Boucher, whose letters were filled more with verbiage than with content and who exhibited a tendency to tipsiness on occasion. Jacky, he thought, should be sent to college. Boucher recommended King's College in New York, where he believed the boy would stand "a better chance for receiving that liberality of manners which is one of the best uses of travel, mixing occasionally with truly well-bred people." For himself Jacky was less interested in acquiring such "liberality of manners" than in equipping himself in proper attire to meet such "well-bred people." He was impatient for the non-importation agreement to end so he could order "a crimson dress suit with velvet lining, a pearl colored half dress suit and jewelry and fittings of like quality."

For the present, however, Jacky was to remain with Boucher and acquire such knowledge as the clergyman's questionable talents and the youth's happy-go-lucky temperament permitted, while George busied himself with other important concerns. His mother was becoming unable to manage Ferry Farm profitably. He and his brother Charles and Fielding Lewis decided that she should move to Fredericksburg as soon as a suitable house could be found and that George should take over the management of the farm through an overseer. It had always been his property, left him by his father. The new terms were generous on his part to a fault.

A new Governor arrived in Williamsburg, the Earl of Dunmore, who promptly dissolved the Assembly. Another election. And when George returned home in November from his trip to Williamsburg he found Martha struggling with a household containing ten guests.

"I wonder," he asked her good-naturedly, after dutifully welcoming them and listing their names in his diary, "am I a planter or an inn-keeper?"

At least there was a respite from guests at the beginning of 1772. On January 26 snow began to fall. Three days later it was "up to the breast of a tall horse everywhere." There was no sign of roads. It became a struggle to feed, not company, but the stock and the fires that kept the house decently habitable. "At home all day alone," he wrote in his diary over and over, then "ditto," "ditto." It was February 21 before the Potomac was open to boats. Starting for Williamsburg on February 25 for the Assembly which had begun on the tenth, George had to turn back and wait a day, he found the waters of Accotink Creek so high. Little of importance to him happened at the Assembly, and he lost more than he gained by the trip, paying a surgeon-dentist-baker four pounds to extract several of his teeth, a further detriment to this weakest feature of his otherwise superlatively strong body, for he had begun losing his teeth at age twenty-two.

But the year was producing assets as well as liabilities. Martha was as relieved as he when the non-importation agreement was sufficiently relaxed to permit the old-time generous orders to London, and George took full advantage of the change. New invoices included as fine and expensive luxuries as he had ever ordered: a "White Sattin quilted Coat, 2 handsome Caps of Minionet Lace, one to wear in dress, the other with a Nightgown, 4 handkerchfs of Jackanot Muslin, 15 yards of fash'ble ribbon, a Blew Sattin Bonnet . . ." Nor had George stinted himself, ordering "a gentleman's hunting cap covered with black velvet to fit a pretty large head, cushioned round or stuffed to make it sit easy thereon, a silk band and handsome silver buckle to it," also "a riding frock of a handsome, drab colored broad cloth with plain, double gilt buttons and a riding waistcoat of superfine scarlet cloth and gold lace." Inclusion of "1 Doz'n Breakfast Tea Cups, with a Tea Pot, Milk Pot,

Sugar Dish, and Slop Bowl to each Set . . ." indicated expectation of an early repeal of the hated tax on tea.

It was Jacky, however, who added to the family possessions treasures far more valuable than scarlet coats and teacups. Arriving on vacation in May, he brought with him an Annapolis painter named Charles Willson Peale, a former saddle craftsman who had studied painting under Copley in Boston and Benjamin West in London. Boucher had sent the young man with a letter of recommendation. Surely the Washingtons would want portraits of their whole family at the hand of this artist whose work was becoming quite the fashion in Maryland and Virginia and as far north as Philadelphia.

George was by no means delighted. He felt it an unnecessary expense, and he was far too busy and too impatient to spend time in an idle sitting. But the rest of the family insisted. He must wear his colonel's uniform, Peale decided, with his sword and gorget and a rifle over his shoulder. That was how his host of admirers remembered him and knew him best.

"In other words," George commented wryly to Martha, "I ceased being of interest and importance when I stopped being a soldier and turned planter. I thought that was just when I began to live."

Dutifully he donned his old militia uniform, dark-blue coat faced with red, its bright metal buttons bearing the number of his regiment (22nd) cast on them, dark-red waistcoat and breeches. Cocked hat covering unpowdered hair, sash over left shoulder, crescent-shaped gorget hanging from his neck, rifle projecting beneath his left arm, he seemed suddenly to have sloughed off fourteen years. Martha gasped. It was exactly as she had first seen him, striding down the street in Williamsburg, ramrod-straight, towering over all the bedecked and bedizened dignitaries in his entourage while she . . . She sighed. She wouldn't even attempt to get into her wedding dress.

But young Peale did not share her self-derogation. With enthusiasm and admiration for "one of the most beautiful women in Virginia" he painted her in a lovely miniature, insisting on simple dress, unpowdered rich brown hair, nothing to mar the sweet serenity of her regular features, dark eyes softly aglint, lips slightly curved in a little, secretive Mona Lisa smile. It was the way George saw her each morning across the breakfast table, before she donned the high caps and lacy furbelows which were the custom of the day. That George liked her best this way might be inferred from the fact that he was to wear such a miniature around his neck during all the trying years yet to come.

He hated the sittings, first of a long succession of such apparent necessities. He was embarrassed, self-conscious, and at times sleepy.

"I am in so grave, so sullen a mood," he wrote Boucher, "and now and then under the influence of Morpheus, when some critical strokes are making, that I fancy the skill of this gentleman's pencil will be put to it in describing to the world what manner of man I am."

Peale certainly discovered one of his subject's qualities, that of physical strength, when one afternoon he and some other young men were engaged in the outdoor sport of "pitching the bar." George suddenly appeared among them, asked to see the pegs marking where the others had thrown, and, without taking off his coat, held out his hand for the missile.

"No sooner did the heavy iron bar feel the grasp of his mighty hand," Peale wrote later, "than it lost the power of gravitation, and whizzed through the air, striking the ground far, very far, beyond our utmost limits. We were indeed amazed, as we stood around all stripped to the buff, with shirt sleeves rolled up, and having thought ourselves very clever fellows, while the Colonel, on retiring, pleasantly observed, 'When you beat my pitch, young gentlemen, I'll try again.'"

Martha was amused but also surprised on hearing of the incident. It was one of the few times that she had known of George's willingness to "show off." For her the most memorable feature of Peale's visit was his painting of miniatures of the children, Jacky's almost girlishly beautiful with its handsome but immature features and shoulder-length curling hair; Patsy's revealing all the gentle sweetness and sparkling liveliness which so endeared the "dark lady" to all who knew her. Little did Martha realize what treasures they would soon become . . . or that the present year was a deceptive time of calm before a rising tempest.

It was a happy autumn. Patsy seemed better. The "fitt drops"? The iron ring? In September they journeyed to Annapolis with both Jacky and Patsy. At the home of Mr. Boucher and his new wife, who had been Eleanor Addison, they were entertained lavishly along with other guests who included Benedict Calvert, his wife, and two of his ten daughters, Eleanor and Betsy. The Calverts were respected Maryland colonists whose home was called Mount Airy, a plantation in St. Mary's County. It was a far more momentous meeting than either George or

Martha suspected, for in the rush of festivities neither of them noticed the amorous glances a suddenly awakened Jacky was casting at lovely young Eleanor Calvert.

On the way home from Eltham that fall they stopped in Fredericksburg where George's mother was already installed in a house, near enough to Betty's, only four streets away, so her daughter could reach her quickly in case of need, yet far enough to preserve her independence. Mary Washington did not like the house. It was too small, she remarked, making pointed comparisons with both Millbank and Mount Vernon, and she missed all the extra furniture which her sons had necessarily disposed of. Martha thought it was an excellent house, well-built and with beautiful woodwork, certainly large enough for one woman and her few servants. As usual, George left her a generous gift, this time fifteen pounds.

"She probably thinks we should have insisted on her living with one of us," he remarked cryptically to Betty, "but we both know it's the last thing she would want."

As if loath to reveal the misfortune it had in store, the new year, 1773, continued the final gay beneficence of the old. Even the weather was propitious, as mild as the former winter had been severe. Nothing to portend that the months ahead would produce major problems, almost unbearable sorrow, increasing political upheaval!

It was March when the first problem reared its head. George was determined that Jack must leave Boucher's school and go to college. (Even Martha conceded that, now the boy was a strapping eighteen, he should no longer be called "Jacky.") But what college? Not William and Mary, to Martha's disappointment. George had confirmed reports of its mismanagement. The choice was between Philadelphia College and King's College in New York. Boucher recommended the latter because it was in "the most fashionable and polite place on the continent." To Martha it sounded as far away as London. But she resigned herself to the inevitable. At least it was *not* London! Then at the end of March when plans were complete for George's taking him to New York, Jack exploded a bombshell. He announced that he was engaged to be married. The girl was Eleanor Calvert, usually called Nelly.

George was incensed. Silly young cub! And just when there seemed to be a chance of getting some solid knowledge into his flighty head! Martha was more hurt than surprised or angered. He had not confided in them about a matter which would affect his whole future! It was small consolation when he explained cheerfully that he had been unable to devote himself properly to his studies for the last year because he had been so terribly in love.

George wrote Benedict Calvert a tactful letter. He had no objection to the match, but feared, as he had discovered the boy's fickleness, that he might change and injure the young lady; or that he might be precipitated into a marriage before he had bestowed a serious thought on the consequences. He hoped that for a time at least Jack might continue his education. Calvert was in hearty agreement. Wisely George and Martha accepted the fact of Jack's engagement. They visited the Calverts and entertained them at Mount Vernon. Martha was so charmed by the lovely Nelly that secretly she wished they could be married at once. Then there would be no need of Jack's leaving for college. Perhaps he and Nelly could live right there at Mount Vernon, and—happy thought—she could become a doting grandmother. But not yet. In May, tears held stubbornly in check, she sent him off to spend two days at Mount Airy before George should pick him up and take him up the coast to that strange foreign bastion of learning, New York.

Could she have followed their progress, she would have been as surprised as Jack, for it was a triumphal journey. George's reputation as a military hero was not confined to Virginia. And at King's College they were warmly received. Jack was duly enrolled, given a large parlor and two bedrooms, one for him and the other for his servant, who would cook his breakfast, clean his rooms, and care for his two horses, the gray and the bay. George even secured him permission to dine with the faculty, "a privilege," Jack boasted, "that is not allowed any but myself." Certainly the careful planter had adequately prepared the soil for the reception and germination of choice seeds of knowledge. At least, George thought with satisfaction, the boy was too far away to yield to the temptation of marriage on sudden impulse.

Slowly the household returned to near normal. Martha could almost forget that Jack was over two hundred miles away instead of less than fifty. It was June, the month in the year she loved best, when her gardens were at their peak of brilliance, when the enervating heat of summer had not fully arrived, when everything in the world displayed growth and fruition, nothing of decay or death. Patsy seemed better than usual. There was a rose-bloom in her cheeks. Martha refused to wonder if it might be the flush of fever. Nelly Calvert had come to visit with one of her friends, and Martha tenderly contemplated the growing affection between these two lovely and lively girls who might sometime become sisters.

On the eighteenth John Augustine Washington, George's favorite brother, arrived with his wife and two children, and an air of festivity prevailed. On the nineteenth George remained with the family all the morning, and they enjoyed a long and bountiful dinner. Patsy especially seemed in unusual health and high spirits. When dinner ended at four, all departed to various activities, George to his postponed round of the farms.

"You promised to show me Jack's last letter," Nelly reminded Martha.

Martha willingly agreed. She loved talking with this beautiful girl about the subject dearest to both of them. While the other guests wandered about the gardens she took Nelly up to her bedroom and opened the lacquered box which held all the letters Jack had written her from school. Meanwhile Patsy, bored by this eulogizing of a teasing brother who seemed less than hero, went to her own room to change her dinner dress for something less formal. Suddenly Nelly looked startled. "What was that noise, like something falling! I'm sure I heard something. I'll go and see." Presently she returned, running, face white with fright. "It's—Patsy! She—"

Martha did not wait to hear. Oh, dear, another attack! And she had seemed so much better. Yes, there she was, lying on the floor. Molly also came running, and together the three of them lifted the recumbent figure to the bed. Swiftly Martha gave Molly orders for the other servants. One must ride to find the Colonel. Another must take a fast horse and go for the doctor.

For Nelly's sake she tried to conceal her own anguished fear. "We'll just try to keep her as comfortable as possible. She has had attacks like this before, and they don't last—"

But this attack seemed different. There was no thrashing of limbs, jerking, stertorous breathing. She was just lying still, terribly still. With mounting apprehension Martha leaned over the bed, smoothing back the curling hair, speaking urgently, trying to rouse her. "She must have fainted," she thought, not knowing whether to feel more relieved or alarmed.

George rushed in. Fortunately he had been no farther than the stables. He took one look, raised one of the limp wrists to feel its pulse, placed his cheek close to the gently parted lips. He had been on battlefields and knew death when he saw it. He fell to his knees. Tears ran down his cheeks. It was the first time Martha had ever seen him weep. Standing on the other side of the bed, she felt a swift surge of relief. His lips were moving. He was speaking. Surely he would be able to rouse her, bring her out of the fainting fit. She loved her "Papa" so much that she had always come running when he called. Martha leaned closer to hear what he was saying. Then suddenly life seemed to drain from her body. He was repeating the prayers for the dead.

It was soon over. George made all the arrangements, notified Jack and the relatives around Williamsburg, had the body made ready for burial. A coffin was procured from James Connelly in Alexandria. Clothes for the first mourning were ordered from Williamsburg. Those for the second mourning were put on an invoice to London. Martha would have "a Black Silk Sacque and Coat; a suit of fash'e Linnen to wear with it; a White Silk Bonnet; 8 pr. Women's White kid Mitts, to fit a small hand and a pretty large arm; 1 Handsome Fan, Prop'r for Second Mourning; 1/2 Ream best large Folio Paper Mourning." For George there would be "A genteel Suit of Second Mourning, such as is worn by Gentlemen of taste, not those who are for running into the extreme of every Fashion, a genteel Mourning Sword, with Belt, Swivels, etc." A pall that belonged to George but loaned in Alexandria was recalled. The Reverend Lee Massey, who had become rector of Pohick Church after Dr. Green, was asked to read the service.

George wrote to Burwell Bassett telling of the death and begging him to persuade Martha's mother to come to Mount Vernon. "It is an easier matter to conceive than to describe the distress of this Family; especially that of the unhappy Parent of our dear Patsy Custis, when I inform you that the Sweet Innocent Girl Entered into a more happy and peaceful abode than any she has met with in the afflicted Path she hitherto has trod . . . This sudden and unexpected blow I scarce need add has almost reduced my poor Wife to the lowest ebb of misery; which is increased by the absence of her son."

Jack was as helpful as possible from a distance. He wrote describing life in New York, careful not to emphasize any carefree social aspects. "All was going on well in this agreeable manner till last Thursday, the day I received Papa's melancholy letter giving an accnt of my dear, and only sister's death . . . I have put myself and Joe into deep mourning."

But no condolences could assuage Martha's grief. Unlike George, she had been unable to weep. Her world had changed. Skies were less blue. The gardens seemed to have lost their bright colors. Yet to some stimuli her senses had become more painfully acute. The scents of white jessamine blossoms were overpoweringly sweet. She could hardly bear the fragrance of the white musk-cluster roses. The Madonna lilies, tall and stately, reminded her of the lovely bride that Patsy could never become. However, to George's surprise she revealed unexpected reserves of strength. She would not yield to her grief. She would continue with life as before, performing her usual household duties, inviting guests, riding with George about the farm. One day his diary recorded, "Rid with Mrs. W. to Muddy Hole, Doeg Run, and mill plantations." Nine days after the burial she went with him to dine at Belvoir.

The Fairfaxes, George William and Sally, were soon leaving for England, this time with no plans to return. George William had become more and more unhappy in the atmosphere of growing hostility toward England. Also his affairs relating to his inheritance there were still tangled. Health was a problem, and both he and Sally felt that English doctors might be more qualified to treat their ailments.

Martha felt no relief at Sally's leaving. She was happily secure in her own position, whatever emotions George might still harbor toward this early and probably abiding love of his life. She would genuinely miss Sally as nearest neighbor and friend, especially since the death of the lovely red-haired Anne Mason. Sally had been especially kind since Patsy's death. Unbending from her tall, superior aloofness, she had taken Martha in her arms and, eyes brimming, had said, "At least you have had a beautiful daughter to enjoy. How fortunate you are, my dear!"

On the eighth of July, George and Martha dined for the last time at Belvoir and the following day they went there again to see the Fairfaxes set sail for England. Martha did not even bother to look to see if that old revealing look of hopeless adoration was for a last time in her husband's eyes.

Belvoir seemed empty and deserted after they had gone. It had been left in George's care for rental. To make up for what must be his loneliness, Martha insisted on entertaining as usual. Perhaps the fact that Nelly Calvert had been there at the time of Patsy's death made it natural for her to assume the role of daughter in Martha's affection, helping to fill the emptiness, and she returned with her sister Betsy for another visit the day after the Fairfaxes left. George's brother Sam, now married to his fourth wife, and his brother Charles, with their children, came for brief visits. But no guests, young or old, could bring even slight healing for Martha's aching grief. Always her ears were attuned to the familiar sound of light, running feet, her eyes searching vainly for a slender figure flitting gaily through the house, garbed in the rose color they both loved.

Only during the hours spent in church did she feel some measure of release from grief. The new church building was completed now, a lovely square brick edifice on the border of a forest that extended almost to the edge of the Mount Vernon lands. One could look out of its windows into the lofty greens of ancient oaks, chestnuts, and pines. George's pews, numbers 28 and 29, were near the high pulpit and, looking up into the serene, kindly face of the beloved Lee Massey, Martha could feel herself merged into a state of being where there was no life, no death, no beginning, no end. Even in the quiet of her chamber words did not hold such assurance.

"I am the resurrection and the life . . ."

"Come unto me, all ye that labour and are heavy laden . . ."

But when George returned in October from a trip to Annapolis for the races, bringing Jack with him, the frozen core of her grief, covered all these months with a brittle crust of cheerfulness, melted. For the first time she was able to weep. Relieved, George felt himself forced to consent to Jack's extending his leave from college. Yes, he should go with them on the fall trip to Williamsburg. To Martha's delight, it was arranged also for Nelly Calvert to go with them. They went first to Eltham and remained there while George went on alone to Williamsburg. For Martha the visit was a blending of joy and sorrow. Nancy also was in mourning, having lost her oldest daughter that same year. But it was a joy to see her favorite niece, Fanny, now six; to visit Bartholomew

Dandridge with his family of five; to introduce the lovely Nelly Calvert to her future relatives.

Martha even enjoyed the days in Williamsburg, where she and Nelly lodged at Charlton's Tavern and Jack was given twenty pounds to exhibit the glories of the capital to his fiancée, among them the new statue of Lord Botetourt, mourned as "best of governors and best of men," standing impressively in the piazza of the capital. "Fortunate, perhaps," commented George wryly, "that his tenure as Governor was so brief. With the tensions fast developing in the colonies his popularity might have evaporated like a morning mist."

Returning home on December 9, George recognized defeat. He could not dispel that new contentment in Martha's eyes. He wrote President Cooper at King's College:

"At length I have yielded, contrary to my judgment, and much against my wishes, to his quitting College; in order that he may enter soon into a new scene of Life, which I think he would be much fitter for some years hence, than now; but having his own inclination, the desires of his mother, and the acquiescence of almost all his relatives, to encounter, I did not care, as he is the last of the family, to push my opposition too far; and therefore have submitted to a Kind of necessity . . ."

Christmas without Patsy? For Martha it would have been unbearable but for the presence of Jack and Nelly. The gifts they had ordered from London for Patsy were given to her. And the excitement of the young couple over their coming wedding could not fail to lend an atmosphere of gaiety to the holiday.

But Martha refused to attend the wedding in February at Mount Airy. She would not intrude on a scene of joy in her mourning black nor run the risk of marring the joyful occasion with tears. George and Lund Washington would go, and they would take with them a letter expressing her joy in the event:

"My dear Nelly: God took from Me a Daughter when June roses were blooming—He has now given me another daughter, about her age when Winter winds are blowing, to warm my heart again. I am as Happy as One so Afflicted and so Blest can be. Pray receive my Benediction and a wish that you may long live the Loving Wife of my happy Son, and a Loving Daughter of Your Affectionate Mother, M. Washington."

The year of misfortune, of sorrow, was ended, and a new one had begun. It showed all the promise of happiness and prosperity, nothing to mar its prospects. George had every reason for satisfaction. The patenting of western lands for his regiment was nearing completion. The hateful British taxes had all been removed except the one on tea. His debts to London creditors would have been discharged except for charities to needy friends. His plans for additions to the Mount Vernon house had already resulted in large orders of bricks, shingles, window glass, paint, oil, hardware. There seemed to be no cloud on the horizon.

His diary did not even note a strange incident that took place in Boston Harbor on the night of December 16, 1773. The fact that some rowdies dressed as Indians had dumped a boatload of tea into the ocean seemed curious but unimportant. Surely it could have little effect on the lives of George and Martha Washington!

12

Tea! Here it was again, become suddenly the most important topic of conversation. There seemed to be no way of getting rid of it, thought Martha with less amusement than exasperation. You refused to buy it, banished it from your table, then suddenly it was back, not in your English china cups, but on every lip, dominating everyone's interest. Those queer people up in Boston had found a way to get rid of it. When three ships arrived from England, they had allowed all the cargo to be landed except the tea. Then, when the Governor had refused to let the ships leave until the duty on tea was paid, some of them had dressed up like Indians one night and thrown the tea into the water, 342 chests of it, they said. What a huge cup of tea that must have been! When morning came there was tea at high tide on all the beaches for miles around. But it had done them more harm than good. England was outraged. Boston must be punished.

At first George was not especially excited about this "Boston tea party" and its possible results. He was too much involved in other problems—sale of his mother's farm on the Rappahannock; additions to the house; an accident that plunged the cherished chariot into the river; a calamitous frost which destroyed half his wheat. In fact, he wanted to stay at home from the Assembly that spring but found that county affairs required his attendance. He and Martha set off in the rescued and refurbished chariot on May 12, arriving in Williamsburg on the sixteenth.

Martha had been terribly lonely since Jack's wedding. She had hoped the bridal couple would make their home at Mount Vernon until a house could be provided for them, and George had offered every inducement, but they had chosen to remain most of the time at Mount Airy. The house seemed indescribably empty, the shouts and poundings of the workmen echoing eerily through the silence. She looked forward eagerly to reunion with family, yes, even to the gaiety and excitement of the capital, even though she was sure she could never feel really gay again.

There was excitement in Williamsburg, yes, but gaiety was muted by shock and consternation when news came from the north. Parliament had voted to close the port of Boston to all vessels after June 1, 1774, until the town paid for the destroyed tea and convinced the King that it would be loyal and obedient. Report of the passing of this Boston Port Bill reached Williamsburg on May 19.

"The Parliament of England," declared Landon Carter, the respected burger from Richmond County, "have declared war against the town of Boston. This is but a prelude to destroy the liberties of America."

Though George was not included in the small group of young leaders like Thomas Jefferson and Patrick Henry who met in white-hot heat to formulate counteraction, he was just as thoroughly alarmed.

"But why?" Martha was puzzled. "What has Boston to do with us? Why should it matter to us if their port is closed?"

"Because," he told her, "if England can close her port at the King's inclination, she can do the same to Alexandria or Yorktown or Norfolk at the slightest pretext. In fact, she might have done the same thing to Charleston, which is much nearer home, but they were permitted to send the tea back to England without paying the duty. We're all in this together, and we can't put up with it."

"But—how can we help it?" wondered Martha. "What can we do about it?"

The first sign of action came on May 24. The Assembly had voted, he told her, to set apart the first day of June as a day of fasting, humiliation, and prayer, to implore divine interposition for averting the calamity which threatened destruction of their civil rights and the evils of civil war.

War! The word coursed through her body in a wave of coldness. But of course it would not come to that. Impossible! The colonists were themselves Englishmen. Fighting—killing—your own people! Parliament would again be reasonable. In fact, many of its leaders like Edmund Burke had argued against the Boston Port Bill.

Prayer? Fasting? The day following the vote Governor Dunmore dissolved the Assembly. It was getting to be a habit of governors, not only in Virginia but also in other colonies. And, as usual, the members immediately flocked to the Apollo Room. Ironical, humorous, they opined that praying that His Majesty and Parliament might be inspired with wisdom and justice should be considered an act of disloyalty! They adopted a resolution calling for the appointment of representatives from the various colonies to meet in a congress to decide on future action.

Oddly enough, opposition to the Governor did not extend to social ostracism. The next day George took breakfast with him at the Palace. That evening a grand ball had been scheduled to honor the Governor's wife, the Countess of Dunmore, who had just arrived from England with her daughters, the Ladies Catherine and Augusta. Virginia hospitality triumphed over politics. The Apollo was hastily made ready for the most festive event of the capital's most festive season. George and Martha with most of the other burgesses and their wives attended, elegantly powdered, perfumed, dressed to the hilt, if not in the latest London styles, at least in silks and brocades and laces acquired before the non-importation agreement. Now that all but the tax on most luxuries had been revoked, homespun was no longer rigidly espoused. Burgesses who in the morning had been most bitter in their condemnation of the Port Bill now made courteous obeisance to the wife of the man who had just dissolved their House!

"The arrival of the Countess gave inexpressible pleasure," declared the Virginia *Gazette* the next day.

"Went to church and fasted all day," George wrote in his diary on June 1.

The fires of opposition blazed down the coast, igniting emotions, whipping up protests and resolutions, welding disparate colonies heretofore strongly independent and competitive into a unity of grievance. Stiff-necked Yankees, pious, frugal Quakers, opulent Church of England plantation squires, all suddenly spoke the same language. Started in New England, Committees of Correspondence were becoming powerful agencies for promoting unity among the colonies.

Though as slow and wary in making up his mind as in expressing himself in speech, once committed, George was unwavering. When Bryan Fairfax, staunchly loyalist like all his family, wrote that appeal to King and Parliament should be "unaccompanied with any threats or claims" and that any new inclusive non-importation agreement should be postponed "till the effect of a petition be tried," George responded with hot impatience.

"Have we not tried this already?" he wrote. "Have we not addressed the Lords and remonstrated to the Commons? And to what end? Did they deign to look at our petitions? Does it not appear, as clear as the sun in its meridian brightness, that there is a regular, systematic plan formed to fix the right and practice of taxation upon us?"

He was even more specific in a letter to George William Fairfax.

"What is it we are contending against? Is it against paying the duty of three pence a pound on tea because it is burdensome? No, it is the right *only* we have all along disputed. And to this end we have already petitioned in as humble and dutiful a manner as subjects could do. What hope then from petitioning? Shall we whine and cry for relief when we have already tried it in vain? If I was in any doubt as to the right to tax without our consent, I should most heartily concur with you that to petition, and to petition only, is the proper method to apply for relief, but we should then be asking a favor and not claiming a right."

Martha, to whom he showed this letter, knew how much it had cost him to differ so radically with his old friend.

Always before he had assumed that difference with Britain could be adjusted. Never had he thought of America as separated in any way from England. Now his views were changing. A denial of their fundamental rights, he believed, would justify complete separation.

Back at home in July, Martha viewed these developments with alarm. Already they were disrupting the even tenor of Mount Vernon life. Discussion, planning, sometimes hot argument were as regular fare at the dinner table as soup, fish, fowl, corn, pumpkins. Guests were always present, perhaps Mason, Bryan Fairfax, Edmund Pendleton, one of the Randolphs. The usual familiar toast at the end was no longer given: "To the King and Queen, the Governor of Virginia and his

Lady, and success to American trade and commerce." Instead George
would rise, extend his glass, bow gravely to each person present while
saying, "Your health, sir; Your health, madam."

Once Lord Fairfax was there from Greenway Court, just when
George had received word from a friend in London that more tea ships
were about to sail.

"Well, my lord," he could not resist challenging, "and so the ships,
with the gunpowder tea, it seems, are on their way to America!"

Lord Fairfax looked puzzled. "But, Colonel, why do you call it gunpowder tea?"

"Why, I am afraid, my lord, it will prove inflammable, and produce
an explosion that shall shake both countries."

"Impossible!" The doughty loyalist choked, and his gaunt, rawboned
face turned so red that Martha, seated beside him, was so alarmed she
had the temerity to reach up and pound him on the back.

Her only pleasure that summer of 1774 was in the presence of Jack
and Nelly, who had come for a visit, a long one, she hoped, and when
George took Jack to Williamsburg for the convention of July 28, she
was overjoyed when he left Nelly behind. They were back within two
weeks, Jack, who had hoped for excitement, disappointed, for the chief
business had been to select delegates from Virginia to the Congress,
which was to meet in Philadelphia on September 5. Seven men had
been selected, Richard Henry Lee, Patrick Henry, Richard Bland, Benjamin Harrison, Edmund Pendleton, Peyton Randolph, and—Martha's
heart sank when she heard the name—George Washington.

Perhaps she sensed, though unconsciously, that it marked the end of
an era, like the auction held at Belvoir on August 15, confirming the
suspicion that George William and Sally would never return to America. George and Jack, with Dr. Craik, rode over, and George bid in a
number of items: a mahogany shaving-desk, an oval looking glass with
a gilt frame, twelve mahogany chairs, three crimson window curtains, a
large Wilton Persian carpet, two candlesticks, a bust of Shakespeare, a
folding fire screen lined with yellow, a mahogany spider-leg tea table, a
Japanese bread tray, pillows (would George recall that Sally's head had
once rested on them?), a fire iron, shovel, tongs, and other small articles. The Fairfaxes had already given them their Blue Room furniture
suite. They would need extra furniture when the contemplated additions were finished.

George's plans for the new construction were now complete. There was to be an addition at each end of the house, extending its length by forty-four feet, on the south side a library with a small stair leading off it to his and Martha's new bedchamber; on the north a two-story reception or banquet room for entertaining their constant guests. A master joiner named Lanphier was already at work on the library. George begrudged the time he must spend away from these projects on tiresome conventions, having to leave much of the fascinating oversight to Lund Washington.

To Martha's dismay George had invited that strange uncouth backwoodsman Patrick Henry to come to Mount Vernon on August 30, stay overnight, and go with him to Philadelphia. Edmund Pendleton was to do the same. George Mason came also, but illness was preventing his being a convention delegate. While repelled by his carelessness of dress and manner—though his simple gray suit did make him look like a parson, if not a gentleman!—Martha was impressed by Henry's charm and eloquence. At dinner she found herself hanging on his words. Beside the sedate, conservative Pendleton he was like a hunter's horn compared with a willow whistle. She felt a thrill go through her body when he said suddenly—words that were to inflame the coming Congress and meld their disparate factions—"I tell you I am not a Virginian, I am an American!" But she was not so thrilled with the conversation that followed.

"I recall something you said in the House of Burgesses, Colonel Washington," said Patrick Henry, "when news came of the passing of the Boston Port Bill. I wonder—do I remember it correctly? Something about a thousand men—"

"Yes," said George calmly. "What I said was, 'If need be I will raise one thousand men, subsist them at my own expense, and march myself at their head to the relief of Boston.'"

Martha felt his eyes on her, anxious, apologetic. Of course he had not told her about making such a statement. Mason and other friends would have carefully refrained from telling her. Only this crudely outspoken stranger had been so thoughtless. Mason was hastening now to relieve any shock she might have felt.

"An impulsive reaction on the Colonel's part, I'm sure. Words uttered in haste without real forethought or intention."

Martha smiled. Her lips felt stiff, and she knew the color had drained from her cheeks. But to her relief her voice sounded clear and natural. "Colonel Mason," she said firmly, "Colonel Washington never acts impulsively or without forethought. If he made a statement to the burgesses, I am sure he meant exactly what he said, and rightly so."

Glancing from Mason back to George, she felt the color rush back to her cheeks. Had she imagined it, or had there been in his eyes something of that revealing look she had once seen him give Sally? Or perhaps it was just gratitude for her understanding.

And she did fully understand. She demonstrated that in a letter she wrote to a relative in England who had deplored George's "folly" in siding with those he termed "the rebels."

"Yes, I foresee consequences," she told him, "dark days and darker nights; domestic happiness suspended; social enjoyments abandoned; property of every kind put in jeopardy by war, perhaps; neighbors and friends at variance, and eternal separations on earth possible. But what are all these evils when compared with the fate of which the Port Bill may be only a threat? My mind is made up; my heart is in the cause. George is right; he is always right. God has promised to protect the righteous, and I will trust Him."

After dinner on August 31 Mason left for home, and the other men loaded their baggage, mounted their horses, and, accompanied by their servants and led mounts, started for the ferry. Martha stood in the door and watched them, eyes fixed on the tallest and straightest of the figures until they moved from sight. She was used to seeing him ride away, to other farms, to Alexandria, to Williamsburg, to mysterious lands in the west, even to this same "foreign" Philadelphia which he had passed through when taking Jacky to New York. But this journey was different. He was going, she sensed, not just to another place but into a strange new realm of activity, fraught with possible danger and leading along paths where she might not be able to follow. She hoped she had been able to hide the uncertainty and fear she was feeling. She would have been relieved could she have known of a letter Edmund Pendleton wrote to a friend:

"I was much pleased with Mrs. Washington and her spirit. She seemed ready to make any sacrifice, and was very cheerful, though I know she felt very anxious. She talked like a Spartan mother to her son going to battle. 'I hope you will all stand firm, I know George will,' she said. The dear little woman was busy from morn until night with domestic duties, but she gave us much time in conversation and affording us entertainment. When we set off in the morning she stood in the door and cheered us with the good words, 'God be with you, gentlemen.' "

She need not pretend any longer. She was indescribably lonely. The hammers of workmen echoed like resounding heartbeats through the otherwise empty house. Husband and children gone. No near neighbors she wanted to visit, now that Anne Mason was dead. She would even have welcomed Sally with her bright, brittle perfection. No one with whom she could share her tumult of emotion. No one? She went upstairs to the blue and white room, closed the door, though there was little chance of interruption, and for the second time that day sat down with her Bible and her Book of Common Prayer. Long habit told her where to turn.

"Let not your heart be troubled . . ."

"God is our hope and strength . . ."

"O God, merciful and compassionate, who art ever ready to hear the prayers of those who put their trust in thee; Graciously hearken to us who call upon thee, and grant us thy help in this our need . . ."

There! She was ready now to assume her regular duties again. She must make the rounds of the cabins and see if there were any of the servants who needed help. She made these visits more often than usual now, for she knew how they missed the bright, loving presence of their "dark lady."

She waited anxiously for word from George. Though Governor Spotswood had long ago arranged a post that was carried southward to Virginia, it was slow, irregular, uncertain. News spread more rapidly through postriders and travelers, stopping at "ordinaries." But a letter finally came by messenger. "My dear Patsy . . ." Since his stepdaughter's death George had reverted to Martha's old nickname. He had arrived in Philadelphia on September 4. The Congress was meeting in a place called Carpenters' Hall. Peyton Randolph had been chosen Speaker. George was meeting many delegates from other colonies and finding those from Massachusetts surprisingly congenial. There was a young lawyer named John Adams, a man somewhat short and stout with a wide, scholarly brow and keen, whimsical eyes. And there was another Adams, Samuel, boldest of all the New England leaders, steely-eyed and hawk-nosed, younger than George, yet with a palsied hand and prematurely gray hair.

The Congress dragged on. George wrote little of his own part in the proceedings, and she knew he probably said little. But she could see him moving among these important people, tall and ramrod-straight, as impressive in velvet waistcoat and ruffled stock as in blue soldier's uniform, unconsciously drawing attention to himself and exciting admiration from both friends and strangers. Astutely she knew that he would be respected more rather than less for his unwillingness to flaunt his opinions in bursts of public eloquence. Quietly and patiently he would let people know what he thought and what course he was willing to pursue.

It was October 20 when he came riding home. The two months of his absence had seemed like two years. Though Martha was duly grateful for the handsome pocketbook which he brought her, his presence was all she would ever ask or want. Of course she was interested in learning what this Continental Congress had decided. Its greatest achievement seemed to lie in this very word, "Continental," for through their delegates the colonies had for the first time "united" in a common agreement. They had reaffirmed a program of non-importation of luxuries from England. They had declared united support for Massachusetts, which was so heavily oppressed. They would resist all threats of transporting any citizen to London for trial. They would go to the defense of Boston if need be. And they were to meet again at another congress in Philadelphia in the spring if there was still need.

It sounded harmless enough. Mostly words, more petitions, even stricter limits on orders to London. Martha was used now to going without tea. In fact, she was finding "Hyperion tea," made with raspberry leaves, a beverage very delicate and tolerably satisfying. She was keeping at least sixteen spinning wheels in constant operation and cheerfully confining her own garments to homespun. In fact, two of her dresses she was very proud of, the silk stripes in their fabric being made from ravelings of silk stockings and old damask chair covers. All the servants were wearing domestic cloth, except for the coachman's scarlet cuffs, which, she took care to explain, had been imported long before the non-importation agreement.

To her relief life again became almost normal. Jack and Nelly came for visits, with Nelly's sister Betsy, and once more the house was alive with young people. George was immersed in the farms, in his mother's affairs, those of George William and other friends needing help, in his building project. He examined every inch of the new library wing, conferring with the architect Lanphier, admiring, criticizing, discussing with Lund Washington plans which to Martha's sensitive ears presaged future absences.

And indeed the period of normalcy was short-lived. Though Martha knew that Virginia counties were organizing militia groups, drilling with new uniforms and makeshift weapons, it seemed to have nothing to do with George and Mount Vernon. Until one Sunday in January 1775 . . .

After the service at Pohick Church, George Mason and some others came back with George, and they talked together all that afternoon and evening. Martha heard words which struck fear to her heart. Ammunition . . . weapons . . . armed defense of colonial rights . . . arming without risk of arrest . . . money for explosives. Soon after this George was asked to train some of these upstart militia groups. He came back one day wearing the new uniform affected by the Fairfax County Independent Company of Volunteers, a blue coat, "turned up with buff, with plain yellow buttons, buff waistcoat and breeches, white stockings," together with flintlock and bayonet, cartridge box and tomahawk. At her gasp of dismay he smiled reassuringly.

"Don't worry, Patsy. All this militia training is just a precaution. We have no British soldiers here and are not likely to. In fact, we have reason to believe the regiments in Boston will soon be recalled."

Martha nodded, her fears somewhat allayed. After all, Virginia was not Boston, and, except for that hot-tongued Patrick Henry, men were reasonable, upholding their rights in calm protest, not hotheads dressing up like Indians and dumping tea in the ocean.

But it was George's London merchants, always hopeful of renewed commerce, who gave such cheerful assurances. Other news from England was not so good. The King had made a belligerent speech in Parliament in November, saying: "You may depend on my firm and steadfast resolution to withstand every attempt to weaken or impair the supreme authority of this Legislature over all the Dominions of my Crown."

People came pouring into Mount Vernon, grimly sober men as well as the bevy of young people. Often they remained closeted with

George until midnight and had to be entertained overnight. One visitor whom Martha disliked at sight was Charles Lee, who claimed to be a general of the British army but declared his sympathy with the colonies. Martha could not decide which she disliked worse, his boorish manners or his troupe of equally ill-mannered dogs that he insisted on feeding in the dining room. Before leaving he borrowed fifteen pounds from George.

In March, George was off to another convention in Richmond to select delegates to a second Continental Congress. This time he returned after only about two weeks' absence. Yes, he announced wryly, he was to be a delegate again. There had been hopeful developments. Public opinion in England seemed to be turning toward the colonials. It was predicted that Lord North was becoming more reasonable, that the greater part of the military was to be removed from Boston, and only the fleet left to enforce the blockade.

He did not tell her of the fiery speech made by Patrick Henry, who had boldly argued that Americans must fight to retain their liberty, who had swept on in a burst of eloquence which had resulted in a vote putting the colony into a posture of defense. But the final majestic words were etched into his own memory as indelibly as they were to be inscribed in the annals of history.

"Is life so dear, or peace so sweet," the magnificent voice had thundered, "as to be purchased at the price of chains and slavery? Forbid it, Almighty God! I know not what course others may take; but as for me, give me liberty or give me death!" Nor did George mention to Martha that he had written John Augustine his own "full intention to devote my life and fortune to the cause we are engaged in."

Martha sighed. Another long absence. Before it had been two months. But at least there was some respite. He need not go until June. And now it was April, loveliest of all seasons on the Potomac, when the spring plowing was over, the wheat was green, corn planting was under way, the herring were running, and every plot in her garden was riotous with color. Still, the throng of visitors, the influx of disturbing news, the excited conversations, precluded real enjoyment. The obnoxious Charles Lee came again, and Martha's insistent courtesy to every guest was tested to the limit. Another British officer, Horatio Gates, professed himself eager to defend the colonies if need arose. But Martha noticed that George was only mildly polite to them both. She welcomed other guests with more enthusiasm—Walter MacGowan, Dr. Craik, Jack and Nelly, George Mason, George Augustine Washington and his son Billy, even Bryan Fairfax, who argued heatedly for more patience and moderation in both speech and action.

Bryan, together with Major Gates, was there on the day in April when news came from Williamsburg. At the behest of Governor Dunmore the Captain of a British armed schooner had landed with fifteen marines, had gone to the magazine in the town and taken all the colony's powder. Bryan was distressed but hot in defense of the British action. Major Gates, ambitious for personal prowess, was delighted. George said little but counseled patience and wise conduct. The raw recruits he had been training were certainly ill equipped to challenge such an indignity, powder or no powder.

While they were arguing, even more shocking news came from Alexandria. Blood had been shed in Massachusetts. On April 19 a British infantry force had met a volunteer company in a town called Lexington and, when they refused to disperse, had fired, leaving eight dead and ten more wounded. They had then marched on to another town, Concord, and there had been more fighting. Boston was virtually at war! George rode posthaste to Fredericksburg to calm the six hundred men of his militia trainees who had rushed to arms.

May. And it was almost time for George to leave for Philadelphia. Martha knew how he hated to go. The new addition on the south side was enclosed and glazed, but not finished on the inside, and a new chimneypiece for the dining room had just arrived. Though his plans were specific to the last inch of plaster and Lund Washington was a careful supervisor, half his pleasure had been in seeing them take shape.

The brief respite in balmy April was past. May had come rushing in on a blistering wind from the south, with a burst of unusual heat. Like the hot passions, thought Martha, that seemed to be withering all the pleasant normality of living, turning friends into foes, neighbors into strangers. She begrudged the time spent with the constant flow of guests, leaving George and herself no time for talk or privacy. On May 3, with Major Gates still there, Richard Henry Lee arrived with his brother Thomas, also Charles Carter of Cleve. They spent hours in parley, on the lawn during the day, at dinner, in the parlor late into the evening. There was time only for the briefest of parting words after the guests had gone to their rooms, for George must leave early in the morning.

She was up at sunrise, making sure a sumptuous breakfast—roast fowl, ham, venison, fish, corn cakes, jellies, maple syrup, her best substitute for tea—would be properly prepared. When George came down, she smiled up at him, hoping to hide her surprise and dismay. He was wearing his uniform, blue and buff coat, gorget, triangular hat with black cockade, small gilt-handled sword, rich gold epaulettes.

"But—" she began, then stopped. "You're going to a Congress," she had been about to say, "not a training ground." Instead she commented lightly, "How well it becomes you! You'll be the handsomest man there."

This time he was taking the chariot, for he was picking up other delegates in Alexandria. Again Martha watched him go. This time she refused to yield to fear or sadness. It was just one more of the trips he was constantly making. Surely this Congress would be no longer than the first, which had lasted two months. When he returned it would probably be July, in the lushness of summer, the time on the plantation he loved best, with all nature rushing toward harvest. Perhaps she could surprise him by having the new bedroom all ready, carpet laid, the furniture from their old room in place, and the library downstairs ready for him to have the bookshelves put in.

Again long days—weeks—of waiting. George's letters told little. Outside Philadelphia the Virginia delegates had been met by about five hundred welcoming citizens and military officers and conducted into the city in an admiring parade. This time they were meeting in the State House. Many of the delegates seemed friends now instead of strangers, especially Sam and John Adams from Massachusetts. Sam was a radical, who dared even to mention the fear-fraught word "independence." John was a brilliant but more cautious lawyer, strong for the cause of liberty but less pugnacious. A new member was Dr. Benjamin Franklin, returned from England just in time to be elected to Congress from Pennsylvania. George was still voting with the majority for all measures seeking reconciliation, but he had little faith in their success.

In fact, his letters became more and more discouraging. New York was soon to receive a British garrison like Boston. He had been named to a committee to consider what measures Congress should take to counteract this danger. Then . . . Congress had authorized the raising of ten companies of riflemen to march to Boston under the command of the chief officer of that army, only as yet there was no chief officer. One had yet to be chosen. Martha felt a sudden thrust of uneasiness at this point, until she read what followed. The logical choice would be Artemas Ward, Commander in Chief of the Massachusetts troops in front of Boston. Or John Hancock, who was called the wealthiest man in New England. George was sure he expected to be named to the post and wanted it, though George could not see why any sane man would covet the *honor* of such a duty. Better for any man to renounce that sort of "honor" when he considered the weakness of the colonies!

"Of course," thought Martha with infinite relief, "somebody from New England would naturally be chosen to take charge at Boston. Certainly no one from Virginia!"

But what followed was not so reassuring. He was evidently being mentioned as the most experienced of the young soldiers, the member who had displayed the greatest familiarity with military matters. He was doing his utmost to restrain his friends from recommending his election. Some of the delegates, including John Adams, seemed to feel that the only way to unite the colonies in a common effort was to place the army under the direction of a man who represented not just New England but the Congress and the continent.

Martha closed her eyes. She could almost hear the words with which John Adams placed in nomination a name for Commander in Chief of the combined armies of the thirteen colonies. ". . . a gentleman from Virginia . . . whose skill and experience as an officer, whose independent fortune . . ."

Lund Washington brought her the letter. It had been delivered by special messenger. Lund's kind face was eager. "It's a thick one this time. It must hold news. Perhaps it tells when he expects to come home."

"Perhaps," said Martha. She smiled but made no motion to break the seal. "If there's any news in it, Lund, you'll be the first to know."

She took the letter upstairs, entered her bedroom, and closed the door. She opened it with steady fingers and read:

"Philadelphia, June 18, 1775. My Dearest: I am now set down to write you on a subject which fills me with inexpressible concern and this concern is greatly aggravated and increased, when I reflect upon the uneasiness I know it will cause you. It has been determined in Congress, that the whole army raised for the defence of the American cause shall be put under my care, and that it is necessary for me to proceed immediately to Boston to take upon me the command of it.

"You may believe me, my dear Patsy, when I assure you, in the most solemn manner that, so far from seeking this appointment, I have used every endeavor in my power to avoid it, not only from my unwillingness to part with you and the family, but from a consciousness of its being a trust too great for my capacity, and that I should enjoy more real happiness in one month with you at home, than I have the most distant prospect of finding abroad, if my stay were to be seven times seven years. But as it has been a kind of destiny, that has thrown me upon this service, I shall hope that my undertaking it is designed to answer some good purpose. You might, and I suppose did perceive, from the tenor of my letters, that I was apprehensive I could not avoid this appointment, without exposing my character to such censure as would have reflected dishonor on myself, and have given pain to my friends. This, I am sure, could not, and ought not, to be pleasing to you, and must have lessened me considerable in my own esteem. I shall rely, therefore, confidently on that Providence, which has heretofore preserved and been bountiful to me, not doubting but that I shall return safe to you in the fall. I shall feel no pain from the toil of the danger of the campaign; my unhappiness will flow from the uneasiness I know you will fear from being left alone. I therefore beg, that you will summon your whole fortitude . . ."

There was more. She might want to move into the little house they had built in Alexandria, or go to her friends and relatives on the Pamunkey. As life was always uncertain, he had made a will . . .

She reread the letter, certain words leaping out at her, searing her consciousness, as if written in fire. ". . . whole army . . . under my care . . . proceed immediately to Boston . . ." *Immediately.* He was not coming home before leaving. *Boston.* As far and as strange as London, or Rome, or—or Timbuktu. Where there was fighting already, bloodshed, Englishmen from over there coming to kill other Englishmen here.

But there were words which she read over and over, capable of healing the searing pain, like—how did the good Book put it?—balm.

"Balm in Gilead." *My Dearest.* It was the first time he had ever called her that, and it banished forever the ghost of a bright, slender, scintillating figure whose presence even an intervening ocean had not quite exorcised. Two words that made whatever the future might bring—separation, danger, perhaps death—at least bearable.

". . . not doubting that I shall return safe to you in the fall." It was June now. October? November? Only four or five months of waiting. ". . . summon your whole fortitude and pass your time as agreeably as possible." Not agreeably, but, yes, with fortitude.

It was well she could not know that it would be over six years before he would see Mount Vernon again.

13

"Philadelphia, June 23, 1775. My dearest: As I am within a few minutes of leaving this City, I could not think of departing from it without dropping you a line; especially as I do not know whether it may be in my power to write again till I get to the camp in Boston—I go fully trusting in that Providence, which has been more bountiful to me than I deserve and in full confidence of a happy meeting with you sometime in the fall—I have not time to add more as I am surrounded with Company to take leave of me—I retain an unalterable affection for you, which neither time nor distance can change my best love to Jack and Nelly, and regard for the rest of the Family concludes me with the utmost truth and sincerity. Yr. entire G. Washington."

Comfort in the letter's salutation, none in its content. He was gone, each moment taking him farther away and into greater danger. She almost wished she were superstitious, so she could believe the old Indian's prophecy, though there was a bit of comfort in remembering it: *The Great Spirit protects that man and guides him. He will become the chief of nations. He cannot die in battle.* But even if it should prove true, there was an even greater danger—in case of defeat, the prospect of a traitor's death, the hangman's noose.

Presently the green chariot with its four horses was returned. He wanted her to have its use, to travel, to "pass your time as agreeably as possible." He had bought riding horses and a phaeton in Philadelphia. She wept when there also arrived a purchase she had suggested in one of her letters—"two suits of what I was told was the prettiest muslin. I wish it may please you. It cost 50/ a suit, that is 20/ a yard."

She busied herself furiously, for fortunately the plantation demanded constant labor and supervision from both Lund Washington and herself. There were the spinning, weaving, flour mills, the feeding and care of hundreds of servants, the building, the harvesting, and, as always, the guests. George had written Burwell Bassett, Jack and Nelly, his brothers Sam and John Augustine, urging all to visit her, to keep her from being lonely. As if any human presence, even Jack, could fill even a minim of the void!

Letters finally came. He was living with his officers in a place outside Boston called Cambridge, in the very comfortable house of a loyalist who had deserted it and fled to Boston. Billy, his favorite servant, whom he had secured in 1768, was with him, also his military "family." Two young men he had liked best in Philadelphia, Joseph Reed and Thomas Mifflin, were his secretary and aide. Charles Lee, whom she would remember, was a new Major General in the army and was already beginning to be difficult, demanding pay for his services. Martha smiled grimly, knowing that George had refused to accept any remuneration as General except bare expenses. Did Lee take his dogs with him, she wondered. Before their arrival there had been a terrible battle with the British at a place called Bunker Hill, where, in spite of the colonists' stupendous bravery, the British had won a victory, though with terrible loss of life. George was struggling with baffling problems —undisciplined and untrained troops, indifferent officers, lack of food, clothes, ammunition, and other equipment. The British army was holed up in Boston and, surprisingly, making no move to engage in hostilities. They had tasted the temper of the resisters at Bunker Hill.

Then suddenly the war—for at last it could be called that—came close to home. Governor Dunmore, who had taken refuge with his family on a British ship in York River, was threatening to devastate all the great river houses whose owners had dared to attend the Philadelphia Congress or take up arms.

"There are rumors," Lund told Martha anxiously, "that British ships will come up the Potomac, burn Mount Vernon, and carry off the General's wife as prisoner."

"Nonsense!" She laughed at the idea. "What on earth would the

Governor want of me, a harmless woman? Why, I know the man, have eaten at his table, danced with him."

When neighbors, alarmed for both her and themselves, suggested that she should move out of danger, at first she indignantly refused, but when George Mason sent her a message one morning advising her to retire away from the coast, she reluctantly yielded.

"I sent my family many miles back in the country," Mason wrote George, "and advised Mrs. Washington to do likewise, as a prudential movement. At first she said, 'No; I will not desert my post;' but she finally did so with reluctance, rode only a few miles and plucky little woman that she is, stayed away only one night."

And that was one night too long, she scoffed. In ensuing correspondence George upheld her decision. On August 20 he wrote Lund: "I can hardly think that Lord Dunmore can act so low and unmanly a part as to think of seizing Mrs. Washington by way of revenge on me."

" 'Tis true," Lund wrote back reassuringly on September 29, "that many people have made a stir about Mrs. Washington's continuing at Mount Vernon, but I cannot think her in any sort of danger. . . . She does not believe herself in danger, nor do I. Without they attempt to take her in the dead of night, they would fail, for ten minutes notice would be sufficient for her to get out of the way . . . She sets off next week with her son and daughter down the country . . ."

Martha hated to leave even for a brief visit at Eltham. There was the new mantel to install, the new bedroom to be finished, for surely he would be home by Christmas. But her mother and Nancy were anxious, and she wanted to allay their fears. Before leaving she packed George's account books and diaries and other papers, together with the best silver and some of the more valuable possessions, so they could be moved quickly in case of emergency. With Jack and Nelly she set off in the middle of October in the chariot. There was comfort in being with family again. Nancy's three surviving children out of the seven she had borne—Burwell, John, Fanny—seemed almost like her own. It was reprieve from loneliness if not from fear.

She was still at Eltham when the letter came. A horseman had ridden with it from Cambridge to Mount Vernon, together with one for Lund, who had sent him on posthaste to Eltham. Martha broke the seal with trembling fingers, knowing it must be important. As she read, excitement mounted, her eyes brightened, color flamed into her cheeks.

"What is it?" demanded Nancy. "It must be good news to make you look like that."

Martha thrust the letter into her hand. "He wants me to come. I'm to go to Cambridge, to be with him." Words tumbled from her lips. "Isn't it wonderful, Nancy? He wants me! Oh, there's so much to do! We must go back to Mount Vernon at once!"

"But—" Her sister was reading. "Wait, love, not so fast! He doesn't really expect you. He writes of the terrible difficulties—the winter coming—the long journey. Why, it's hundreds of miles—maybe a thousand!"

Martha was not even listening. She would have started immediately for Cambridge had she had her way, but reason asserted itself as Burwell Bassett, Jack, and others convinced her of the necessary procedures. Of course she must notify George that she was coming, so he could arrange for her journey. She must wait until she heard further of his plans. And the courier must rest before starting back with her reply, both he and his horse, for they had traveled six hundred miles with only brief interruptions. She agreed, wrote the letter, saw the horseman away on his mission, and insisted on returning immediately to Mount Vernon, which itself took five days of travel.

Then—days, weeks, of waiting, but not of idleness. There was the household to leave for winter, clothes to prepare for the cold northern climate, food to pack and take, great hampers of hams, bacon, jellies, flour, nuts, dried fruits, salted fish, for surely George and his officers would welcome such delicacies. And finally, about the middle of November, the message came. It was arranged. George had planned all the stages of the journey, escorts, stopping places. Jack and Nelly could come with her. No more waiting. Trunks, boxes, hampers—all had been packed for days. Within hours they were ready to go, Martha, Jack, Nelly, Martha's maid Sally, coachman, postilion in white and scarlet livery, Jack's servant on his mount, the baggage wagon, the chariot with its four beautiful white horses, the mounted escort sent by George. As they swept out of the gate Martha did not look back. She had eyes only for the road ahead. No matter if it was long, six hundred miles through cold, snow, winter winds, strange places, probably dangers. She who had never been farther north than Alexandria, ten miles from home, faced the road ahead without the slightest hesitation. She would have done the same knowing that it led into an uncharted wilderness or across an ocean or into the thick of battle, if George wanted her and was at the end of it.

After Alexandria all was strange. The road passed through forests, beside fields, through villages and little towns, where people came out to stare at the unusual cavalcade. When it was learned who was traveling in the coach, groups gathered along the roadside or peered out of windows to watch it pass. The wife of the Commander in Chief, "Lady Washington," was traveling to be with her husband in the battlefields to the far north. Though Martha would have been horrified at the idea, it had been whispered through the colonies that she was a Tory, a loyalist. She would have rejoiced that this journey quelled such rumors once for all. Days passed in rattling, bone-grinding, dust-ridden discomfort, nights in strange "ordinaries" battling lumpy beds, soil ground into the pores, poor food, noisy rowdies. But at least there was satisfaction in knowing that each grueling mile brought them nearer the goal.

Philadelphia at last! On November 22 the Pennsylvania *Gazette* reported: "Yesterday the Lady of his Excellency General Washington arrived here, upon her way to New England. She was met at the Lower Ferry by the officers of the different battalions, the troop of light horse, and the light infantry of the 2nd battalion, who escorted her into the city."

Martha was amazed, embarrassed. Surely this impressive welcome by soldiers, this triumphal band salute, was not for her! The chariot ran the gamut of waving crowds, smiling faces, shouts of "Lady Washington!" But she was also conscious of hoots and scowls, and once a sharp missile flew against the chariot, barely missing its opened window, for Philadelphia was at least half loyalist. It was her first frightening exposure to the intense conflict of emotions sweeping the colonies, not words, as in arguments around the dinner table; not letters, like the one from Jonathan Boucher: "You are no longer worthy of my friendship. A man of honor can no longer without dishonor be connected with you. With your cause I renounce you; and now, for the last time, subscribe myself, Sir, your humble servant, J. B." No. Here was deadly violence.

For both Nelly and herself the hugeness of the city, dwarfing Alexandria and Williamsburg into mere villages, was bewildering, but Jack, superior in experience, was in his element, pointing out landmarks,

Carpenters' Hall, the State House where Congress was in session, mansions where he and his stepfather had been entertained.

Joseph Reed, George's handsome, young military secretary, who had returned from Boston, met them at the ferry and conducted them to his home, where Martha, welcomed by his lovely, delicate English wife, was made to feel instantly at home. Deathly weary after a week of travel, she reveled in a hot bath, fresh clothes, a clean, comfortable bed. But there was little time to rest. Philadelphia ladies, anxious to show hospitality, came to call, also members of the Continental Congress who had not brought their wives to the city. The caller who impressed Martha most vividly was the wife of the Congress President, Mrs. John Hancock, who had been the fascinating Dorothy Quincy of Boston. It was her husband, Martha remembered, who had expected to be named Commander in Chief.

The patriots of the city proposed giving a ball in her honor at the City Tavern. Oh, dear, thought Martha, could she possibly do credit to this husband who had suddenly become so important that his wife was honored like an English noblewoman—"Lady Washington"! Dutifully she and Nelly extracted their best gowns from the baggage and summoned a hairdresser. But a committee arrived to request in great embarrassment that she not attend such a ball. The Puritan Samuel Adams had advised Hancock that such a celebration at this juncture would be unwise since Congress had requested the people to abstain from "vain amusement." The committee begged Martha to "accept of our grateful acknowledgment and respect due to you on account of your connection with our worthy and brave General, now exposed on the field of battle, in defense of our rights and liberties."

"Of course," said Martha, smiling at the embarrassed petitioners and putting them courteously at ease. "I understand perfectly, and I appreciate your esteem and concern. Your desires are agreeable to my own sentiments." She was really relieved to have a quiet evening with the Reeds.

November 27 and on the road again. More roadside crowds, pealing bells, cheers, shouts of "Lady Washington!" How wonderful that George was so popular! She did not realize that some of the acclamation was for the plucky little rosy-cheeked woman smiling at them from the chariot, daring to travel these hundreds of miles to spend the winter with an army in eye-to-eye confrontation with a powerful enemy.

At Trenton there was another escort, this time from Elizabethtown, to conduct the party to Newark. George had warned them not to enter New York, a rabid royalist city. A mounted escort took them across the Hudson at King's Ferry above New York. More towns with strange names—New Rochelle, New Haven, Hartford. They were in New England now, and it was well into December. Occasional snow. Bumpy, icy roads, cold that penetrated even woolen blankets and garments. Drafty inns, with skimpy fires and damp sheets. Tired, straining horses. Teeth chattering both from cold and jolting wheels. Even Jack, novelty and adventure behind, turned grim and taciturn. Nelly, always delicate, looked wan and sickly. Only Martha remained intrepidly cheerful. Every mile was bringing them nearer . . . nearer . . .

Springfield. Ironic name for a town locked in winter's cold, its fields bare and brown! But at least it was Massachusetts, the foreign land that had suddenly become home because George was there. At one of the long succession of inns they were met by Colonel George Baylor, son of an old Virginia friend, sent by George to conduct them through the lines and into Cambridge.

It was late afternoon of Monday, December 11, when the chariot drew up in front of a big yellow house. Colonel Baylor dismounted, threw open the door with a cheerful "Here we are!" Martha saw a tall figure emerge from the house, break into a run. Then his arms were about her. Weariness, strangeness, the discomforts and perils of nearly a month's harrowing journey were forgotten. No mistaking the look in his eyes now! He had not expected she would dare to come. After fifteen years he was only beginning to discover the depths of character in this woman he had married. For Sally Fairfax his look had shown mere boyish adulation. Here was the mature, humble devotion which could come only with long trial and experience.

Her reception by officers and aides was almost as overwhelming as in Philadelphia. The General's wife—come six hundred miles to be with them for the winter! And such food she had brought, promise of a holiday season of festivity instead of military gloom and monotonous army fare! Almost from the moment of her entering it the house was transformed from a barracks into a home. Once rested—and that took no more than one night—she was absorbed into activities entirely new but which for all her life, it seemed, she had been preparing. She became housekeeper, dietician, hostess, seamstress, mother-adviser not only to the young aides and officers but to soldiers in the surrounding camp, patient, comforting helpmate to the harassed man struggling from dawn to midnight with almost insuperable problems.

"Pooh!" Stoutly she disclaimed any expressed admiration of these unexpected activities. "It's nothing more than I've always done. I'm just an old-fashioned Virginia housekeeper."

She was surprised and delighted by the house. It was a fine mansion with a wide hall and spacious rooms. A hundred—two hundred—years later it would be known as Longfellow House, long the home of the New England poet Henry Wadsworth Longfellow. To the right of the front door was George's office, with a connecting staff room. Here, where letters, dispatches, conferences were evincing the birth-pangs of a new nation, the poet would one day immortalize the exploit of a Boston man who in that year of 1775 had just made himself a hero:

> Listen, my children, and you shall hear
> Of the midnight ride of Paul Revere . . .

Martha was given one of the large rooms to the left of the hall for receiving guests and entertaining. And she and Nelly did receive them, immediately, constantly. There was the charming young wife of Thomas Mifflin, George's handsome aide-de-camp, and Mrs. Morgan, wife of the Philadelphia doctor who was Director General to army hospitals. There was Kitty, wife of Nathanael Greene, whom Congress had made a Brigadier General. Martha was immediately attracted to Kitty, niece of the Governor of Rhode Island, a sprightly young woman whose beauty and friendliness made her a special favorite with the young officers and soldiers. Her attraction for Martha was by no means lessened by the discovery that Kitty's infant son had been christened George Washington Greene.

Days passed before she found time to write letters to friends and relatives back home. One went finally to her young friend Betty Ramsay at Alexandria:

"I have waited some days to collect something to tell, but alas, there is nothing but what you will find in the papers. Every person seems to be cheerful and happy here. Some days we have a number of cannon and shells from Boston and Bunkers Hill, but it does not seem to surprise anyone but me; I confess I shudder every time I hear the sound of a gun. I have been to dinner with two of the generals, Lee and

Putnam, and I just took a look at poor Boston and Charlestown from Prospect Hill, Charlestown has only a few chimneys standing in it; there seems to be a number of very fine buildings in Boston, but God knows how long they will stand; they are pulling up all the wharfs for firewood. To me that never see anything of war, the preparations are very terrible indeed, but I endeavor to keep my fears to myself as well as I can . . ."

The room at the left of the hall soon became a favorite resort for young officers and soldiers and a center of sociability. Her coming seemed even to have helped relieve one of George's most grievous problems, the fact that many of his soldiers, enlisted for three-month periods, anxious to be home for Christmas and discouraged by the stalemate of activity, had failed to reenlist. Perhaps it was the cheerful atmosphere at headquarters and the presence of its friendly presiding hostess who took a motherly interest in all of them that helped turn the tide. But by Christmas fully ten thousand men, in response to George's stirring appeal, were held in reserve.

If only she could bring as much cheer and comfort to George as she seemed to do for the young aides and soldiers! He looked ten years older since leaving Mount Vernon. Hearing him discuss his problems with his officers, she agonized over his futilities and her helplessness. Still, pressured though he was, he had taken time to arrange every step of her journey with such meticulous care, write Lund each week at such length about details of the house and farms, even provide thoughtfully for indigent neighbors and strangers in need.

"Let the hospitality of the house," he had written Lund, "with respect to the poor be kept up. Let no one go away hungry. If any of this kind of people should be in want of corn, supply their necessities, provided it does not encourage them in idleness."

The short enlistment terms of his men, Martha knew, were only one of George's worries. Lack of discipline, jealousy among his subordinates (often *in*subordinates), futile attempts to get action from Congress, rivalry among the colonies, dearth of clothing, of food, of arms and ammunition, colonial poverty, absence of soldiers on the slightest pretext taking their weapons with them, constant criticism—his predicament was overwhelming. He was barely surviving in a hand-to-mouth existence. Though Congress had authorized the issue of two million dollars in paper money with "the faith of the colonies behind it," it had depreciated instantly, and merchants were unwilling to take it. Though he was without artillery or ammunition, only ten cartridges to a man, Congress wrote that he should be bombarding Boston! Night after night Martha lay wakeful until the small morning hours, knowing he was down in his office still struggling with letters, orders, dispatches, methods of organization, plans for the seemingly impossible.

"The reflections on my situation and that of this army produces many uneasy hours when all around me are wrapped in sleep," he wrote Joseph Reed. "Few people know the predicament we are in on a thousand counts; fewer still will believe if any disaster happens to these lines from what cause it flows. I have often thought how much happier I should have been if, instead of accepting a command under such circumstances, I had taken my musket on my shoulder and entered the ranks; or if I could have justified the measure to posterity and my own conscience, had retired to the back country and lived in a wigwam."

Fortunately the British troops in Boston, first under General Gage, then under General William Howe, were ignorant of the helpless state of the encamped adversary. Otherwise they could have delivered a crushing blow at almost any time in the past months. Remembering the mettle of the foe at Bunker Hill, they had postponed attacking and settled for the winter into their comfortable Tory stronghold, assaulting the rebels with no more serious artillery than a satire called *The Blockade of Boston*, whereupon Mercy Warren, the brilliant wife of the President of the Massachusetts Provincial Congress, countered with a play called *The Blockheads, or The Affrighted Officers*, with women as characters, giving them names like Captain Bashaw, Lord Dapper, Shallow, Dupe, and Simple.

Martha made Christmas as gay a celebration as possible with her food and gifts. Distressed to learn that Christ Church, deserted by its Tory members, had been used for a barracks and boarded up, she had it cleaned and put to rights for a service on New Year's Day, about which one lady who attended wrote, "Mrs. Washington, Mrs. Gates, and Mrs. Custis entered together and were shown to a seat in front of us, the Royal pew. Do you think the name prophetic? Our Queen looked very well in peach-colored satin which is worn on all State occasions, and she glanced most kindly upon us, wishing us 'the compliments of the season' in quite an audible tone." Martha would not have liked the designation "Queen." It smacked too much of British royalty.

She planned an even more festive celebration for Twelfth Night, which was also their wedding anniversary. At first George frowned on such merrymaking, then, realizing that amusement might raise the spirits of his men, he let the day be observed in due style with cakes, candles, dancing, and general rejoicing.

Martha's days settled into a steady routine. Each morning except Sunday she attended sewing sessions where some of the camp women knitted or worked on clothing for the troops. Afternoons, when there were no visitors to entertain, she helped in the office, transcribing George's orders or correspondence, for he always required a copy to be kept of everything he wrote or dictated. He was surprised and touched the first time he found her there.

"Colonel Harrison had so much to copy," she explained apologetically, wondering if he would disapprove. "I know my spelling is terrible, but I promise to be careful."

He gave her a tender, appreciative smile. "Of course, my dear. You make a very fine assistant secretary, though I'm afraid Congress may not come across with the appropriate pay. You write a much better hand than young Baylor—and I'd challenge Harrison here to do better."

Only six hundred miles to home and Virginia? It seemed at least a thousand. Massachusetts, with its cold winds, its ice and snow, its people with strange, clipped speech, was another world. Sometimes she felt exiled, forgotten, by all friends and relatives.

"My dear Sister," she wrote Nancy on the last day of January, "I have wrote to you several times in hopes that would put you in mind of me, but I find it had not had its intended affect and I am really uneasy at not hearing from you and have made all the excuses for you that I can think of, but it will not doe much longer, if I doe not get a letter by this night's post, I shall think myself quite forgot by all my Friends. The distance is long yet the post comes regularly every week.

"The General, myself, and Jack are very well. Nelly Custis is I hope getting well again . . . hope noe accident will happen to her in going back,—I have not thought much about it yet god knows where we shall be I suppose there will be a change soon, but how, I cannot pretend to say . . .

"winter here been remarkably mild. The Rivers has never been frozen hard enough to walk upon the Ice since I came heer, My dear

sister, be so good as to remember me to all enquireing friends—give my
Duty to my mama, and love to my brothers and sisters Mr. Bassett,
your Dear Children and self—in which the General, Jack and Nelly,
join me. I am, my dear Nancy, Your ever affectionate sister, Martha
Washington."

A mild winter? She spoke too soon. In mid February, when willows
could be dripping gold in Virginia, this northern world was plunged
suddenly into bitter cold and locked in ice. When George returned one
day from riding to Lechmere, one of the heights overlooking Boston,
the determination in his face chilled her even more than the cold. She
knew that the more or less comfortable impasse in the struggle was
over. The Charles River, he reported, was frozen all the way to Boston,
a new bridge to the city. The next day he called his generals together.
Was not this the time, he suggested, to make a general assault across
the ice, rather than wait until the British got reinforcements? The
officers did not agree, and he could not persist. Presently it was too late,
for by February 20 the snow had disappeared and the hard freeze
ended. But Martha knew it was only a postponement.

There had been triumphs as well as frustrations. An officer named
Henry Knox, a former Boston bookseller, had ridden in the dead of
winter to Lake Champlain, collected about twenty pieces of heavy
artillery left by the British, and achieved a miracle—transported them
on sledges drawn by eighty yoke of oxen three hundred miles, over
snow, thin ice, through mud, slush, swollen creeks, and delivered them
at strategic points outside of Boston. Meeting Knox, Martha wondered
less at his achievement. He was a big, powerful man, as tall as George
and half again as heavy, perhaps fifteen years younger, and when his
wife Lucy came to join him, she knew she had found another friend.
Lucy was cheerful, energetic, garrulous, and so plump she made
Martha feel delightfully slim and trim.

The days moved swiftly, frighteningly, toward the inevitable climax.
She saw almost nothing of George. He was rushing about conferring
with officers, attending to voluminous correspondence, but she knew by
the excitement in his eyes, the grim tightness of his lips, how serious
was the coming confrontation. If it failed, the American cause would
probably be in ruins, himself a hunted traitor. Even without his letter
to Burwell Bassett, she could guess its implications:

"I thank you heartily for the attention you have kindly paid to my landed affairs on the Ohio, my interest in which I shall be more careful of, as in the worst event they will serve for an asylum." If only that *were* the worst event! was Martha's reaction. A cabin in the wilderness seemed like heaven compared with a traitor's noose.

At least there might be no mansion at Mount Vernon to return to. Lund wrote that Dunmore had moved ships, five large ones, up the Potomac. People were moving out of Alexandria with every wagon, cart, packhorse obtainable. He was packing up china, glass, and other valuables in barrels, ready to move them out of harm's way. But it was Mount Vernon now that seemed strange and far away. Here was the crisis that would determine the future.

Leap Year gave an extra day of grace before the cold dawn of a March 1 that portended long-delayed operations. Report came that General Howe was determined to attack at last, regardless of loss, if the rebels so much as broke ground. And they would break ground. By March 2 George had fortified Lechmere Point to the north of Boston and Lamb's Dam in Roxbury. But it was whispered through the camp, even reached the women sewing in the parlor, that these movements were only a blind. The real action would take place later when, under cover of darkness, Dorchester Heights to the south of Boston would be occupied. Though the ground there was frozen too hard for retrenchments, men had been working for weeks behind the lines making frames to be filled with fascines and bundles of hay and used as cover for men under fire.

Before leaving on the night of March 2 George came upstairs to bid her good night. His step was light, buoyant, eyes clear and calm, lips no longer grim. He was a man of action, and now the long months of grueling preparation were to be translated into deeds. This was the George who had broken roads through uncharted wilderness, had had two horses shot from under him yet kept fighting on foot, had ridden to bring reinforcements through darkness so thick he sometimes had to lead his horse, drop to his knees, and feel his way along the road.

"Don't wait up for me," he said as he kissed her. "I may be late. And don't worry."

Not wait up? Not worry? Well she could not know how many years of just such nights lay ahead! She hoped Nelly in the next room was asleep, and she would not wake her. The girl was four months pregnant and should be protected from worries. Martha hoped Jack was with her and not out somewhere enjoying the excitement. She did not want them with her. At a time like this she wanted to be alone.

Soon there came the sound of cannon fire, not spasmodic as usual, she had become used to that. This was fighting in earnest, from the new emplacements in Roxbury to the right, from those to the east, left of Cambridge, at Prospect and Cobble hills, General Greene's command. Poor Kitty, trying no doubt to quiet the fears of George's little namesake! Surely even a baby could not sleep through those cannon booms. The British were responding, as expected, with heavy bursts of gunfire.

Other women were awake that night. One of them was Abigail, John Adams's wife, whom Martha had not yet met but felt she already knew because of her reputation for patriotic loyalty. Abigail, down at the Adams farm in Braintree to the south of Boston, had been writing to her husband at the Congress in Philadelphia:

"I have been kept in a continual state of anxiety and expectation ever since you left. It has been said 'tomorrow' and 'tomorrow' for this month, but when the dreadful tomorrow will be, I know not." Then had come the sound of cannon. She had gone to the door and listened. Not the usual idle booms. The house shook, This was *it!* She returned to her candlelit desk and kept on writing. "No sleep for me tonight . . ."

There was comfort for Martha in knowing that she was only one of many such women, listening, agonizing. Dawn came at last, Sunday, and the guns were silent. Perhaps a reprieve. George returned at dawn and slept. The day passed quietly. Sunday night was like the preceding, with the American guns challenging the British to respond.

It was night on the fourth of March when George's plan was consummated, a clear night with a full moon. The bombardment was heavier by ten times than on the two nights preceding, drawing attention away from the three hundred tons of heavy equipment, the lines of infantry and riflemen, all moving silently toward Dorchester Heights. Again George returned at dawn, this time well satisfied. He would like to see General Howe's face, he admitted, when he looked up and saw those mortars and howitzers staring down at him, commanding the whole town! Fortunately he wouldn't know how little powder they possessed!

He would have been even more satisfied could he have heard the words spoken by the astonished General: "My God! those fellows have done more work in one night than I could make my army do in three months!"

"It was like the work of the genii of Aladdin's wonderful lamp!" exclaimed one of the British officers, adding with chagrin, "Why didn't we occupy those heights ourselves?" It was a question to be asked with stern censure by their superiors in England. How could Howe and his men have been so stupid, letting themselves be fooled all night by cannon fire from other directions when two thousand men, hundreds of wagons and oxcarts with timber, bales of hay, crowbars, hatchets, and other tools, to say nothing of huge quantities of heavy ordnance, had been gotten unobserved to the top of nearby hills!

It was a brilliant tour de force. The British and their Tory supporters in the town were surrounded. What would they do? Attack? An alert was ordered all the way around the American lines. But no attack came. There seemed to be confusion in the town. Troops were embarking. Making ready to attack by sea? Impossible that night, for a furious storm roared in from the south. Days passed, and still the intentions of the British forces were in doubt. Finally a great stir was visible. People were rushing about the streets, Redcoats marching to the wharves, equipment loaded into tumbrils, rowed out to the moored ships, crammed into holds. Were the British evacuating Boston? George was not sure. It might be a ruse calculated to make him relax his forces.

More days passed. Then on Sunday, March 17, a day of favorable winds, action started. The wharves were thronged with Redcoats. They were seen to enter boats and start for the moored vessels, to climb aboard. Why? To make the long-expected assault on the Dorchester fortifications? Or to leave Boston? Then, as the vessels moved majestically toward the open sea, sails bellying in the wind, a great shout arose. The British were going! Still George was not sure. They would keep a sharp lookout until the ships were actually out of sight. Monday, though they were still dangerously close, he entered Boston for the first time since, twenty years before, he had come as a Virginia Colonel seeking rank in the British army. Now he was attempting to defeat that army. After noting the damage done, the equipment left behind, the desperate condition of the remaining populace, ravaged by hunger, exploitation, disease, including smallpox, he returned to Cambridge. It was not until March 27, after dinner, that a messenger brought the long-awaited news. The fleet had set sail from Nantasket. Except for three or four vessels, all were standing out to sea.

"It is with the greatest pleasure," George wrote John Hancock, "that I inform you that on Sunday last the 17th inst., at about 9 o'clock in the forenoon the Ministerial Army [He had always refused to call it the army of His Majesty the King!] evacuated the town of Boston, and that the forces of the United Colonies are now in actual possession thereof. I beg leave to congratulate you, Sir, and the Honorable Congress on this happy event, and particularly as it was effected without endangering the lives or Property of the remaining unhappy inhabitants."

It was George who should be congratulated, thought Martha, not Congress, which had been of precious little help! She would be somewhat mollified on learning that Congress had decreed a gold medal to the victor, the die to be cut by Duvivier of Paris and to bear the words "The American Congress to George Washington, Commander in Chief of its Armies, the Assertors of Freedom: The Enemy for the first Time Put to Flight—Boston Recovered, 17th March, 1776." The gold, she felt, might have been put to better use in providing some warm clothes for the poor soldiers that winter!

Her joyful relief over George's triumph was tinged with unease and further worry. The struggle was only beginning. General Howe was not defeated. He had gone—where? To Halifax, to refresh his worn-out troops who, as one person put it, had been "harassed with severe duty and bad living"? Or to New York, a city of strategic importance to the British? Even before ascertaining his destination George dispatched to New York all his army not needed to garrison Boston, and now he was making preparations to move his headquarters there. No easy task, moving nine or ten thousand troops with all their equipment some two hundred miles! Then, too, he must spend time submitting to celebrations and an address by the Massachusetts Assembly praising his achievements and voicing hope:

"May the United Colonies be defended from slavery by your victorious arms. May they still see their enemies flying before you."

Harvard College also had bestirred itself to confer on him the second degree of Doctor of Laws granted by that institution.

Martha saw little of him. He spent much time in Boston, but he did not allow Martha to go with him, having found smallpox in at least fourteen homes. His secretaries went back and forth and kept her well informed. One incident they reported all found amusing. One day George had picked up his landlady's little daughter and put her on his knee. "Which do you like better," he had asked her, smiling, "the Redcoats, or my provincials?" "Oh, the Redcoats," she had replied promptly. George had laughed. "Ah, my dear, they look better, yes, but they don't fight. The ragged fellows are the boys for fighting."

Martha's days were filled with preparations for leaving. Jack and Nelly would be returning to Mount Airy to be at her home during the time before the baby arrived. And she herself? Much as she longed for Mount Vernon the thought of more months of separation from George was almost more than she could bear. Then came happy reprieve.

"I'm arranging for a house for us in New York," he announced amid these days of grueling detail.

Martha's spirits soared. He wanted her with him! Spring, which here in the north had seemed so slow in coming, the trees only now beginning to bud, became all at once balmy and redolent with promise. Days passed in a flurry of activity, packing, visiting her new friends, entertaining.

One of Martha's visitors during these last days in Cambridge was Mercy Warren, whose three-volume work on the American Revolution would in future years become a standard source of authority. Though Mercy had met George and perceived that "in his character was blended a certain dignity with the appearance of good humor," she had not visited Cambridge since Martha's arrival, probably too busy caring for her five sons, the youngest only ten, to take many trips. However, in January she had written headquarters inviting Martha to take refuge in her home in Plymouth in case of emergency.

Far from being intimidated by this visitor of superior intellect, Martha was her usual gracious and friendly self, perhaps surprising this New Englander who had had little contact with southern culture.

"I was received," Mercy wrote her friend Mrs. John Adams after her visit early in April, "with that politeness and respect shown in a first interview among the well bred and with the ease and cordiality of a much earlier date.

"If you wish to hear more of this lady's character," she went on, "I will tell you I think the complacency of her manners speaks at once of the benevolence of her heart, and her affability, Candor and gentleness, qualify her to soften the cares of the Hero, and smooth the rugged paths of War . . . I did not dine with her, though much urged. She desired me to name an early hour in the morning, when she would send her chariot and accompany me to see the deserted lines of the enemy, and the ruins of Charlestown. A melancholy sight, the last, which evinces the barbarity of the foe, and leaves a deep impression of the suffering of that unhappy town."

Though Martha and Mercy Warren would not meet again for many years, a friendship was formed that day which was to grow more and more intimate through long correspondence.

So short would be their separation that Martha felt neither lonely nor bereft when George rode away on April 4. He was to go by way of Providence and the towns along Long Island Sound to observe the progress of his troops. Martha, Jack, and Nelly, with the servants and baggage, would go later by chariot through Hartford and New Haven, an easier but not a shorter route. George, of course, had arranged all the details, postilions, mounted guards, overnight stops.

Morning came. The baggage was packed, the chariot waiting. She roamed through the rooms for a last look. Four months had turned them into a genuine home. Last of all she paused on the threshold of the downstairs office, strangely bare now of papers, secretaries, waiting messengers, subordinate officers. But the room still seemed dominated by the familiar uniformed figure sitting at his desk, the man who through nine months of travail had planned, suffered, labored, struggled against incalculable odds to bring the dream of a new nation into being. Would there remain an abiding memory of that presence when seven decades later another would sit, perhaps in the same spot, and celebrate in poetic language the fulfillment of that dream?:

> Thou, too, sail on, O Ship of State!
> Sail on, O UNION, strong and great!
> Humanity with all its fears,
> With all the hopes of future years,
> Is hanging breathless on thy fate!

"Come, Mama, what are you waiting for? The chariot's ready."
"Yes, yes, Jack, I'm coming."

14

New England in April was a sleeping beauty come to life. Inured to the
dead browns of winter, Martha's gaze reveled in vistas of trees springing into tender green, pinks and creams of cherry and apple blossoms,
golds of willows and forsythia. But it was not a pleasant journey. Even
George's careful foresight could not prevent the discomforts of soggy
rains, muddy roads, drafty inns, jolting wheels, or protect poor Nelly
from the increasing distress of a difficult pregnancy. Since Nelly had
lost her first baby, Martha worried. And certainly no one could have
predicted that midway in the journey Jack would be taken sick, necessi-
tating a delay of some days in discouragingly makeshift quarters.

It was April 17 when they arrived in New York. George had been
there four days. The family was soon installed in a house known as
Mortier's, a small but pleasant enough place some two miles uptown
from the fort at the Battery, with a garden and a view of the Hudson
River. After they had purchased a feather bed, bolster, pillows, bed
curtains, crockery, and glassware it was tolerably comfortable. But there
was no congenial society, no amusement, as in Cambridge. Life in New
York was too tense. Jack fretted, Nelly languished, and Martha lived
only for the few minutes, seldom hours, when the harried Commander
in Chief returned from his headquarters down on lower Broadway.

Conditions, she knew, were critical. Howe with his fleet might be
descending on New York at any moment. It was rumored that the King
was hiring soldiers from German princes to augment his forces. Incred-

ible outrage that, employing mercenaries to quell freeborn Englishmen possessed of all the rights their ancestors had fought for! Thirty thousand soldiers the British claimed they would have in America by the end of June, while George had in New York only 6,717 fit for duty! In addition he was contending with his usual problems, acute shortage of arms, slow recruiting, short enlistments, depreciated currency, lack of discipline, and, one of the worst headaches of all, smallpox! News of ravages of the disease was spreading panic through the city. Both soldiers and civilians were inoculating themselves by ignorant and dangerous methods. George issued strict orders for a swift isolation of suspects and prohibition of all unauthorized inoculation.

"You must go home," he said to Martha, returning one midnight, face tight-lipped and drawn with weariness. "I can't have you running the risk of contracting the disease. And it's going to get worse. We may have a real epidemic."

Martha stared at him in consternation. Her hands trembled as she set before him the late supper of tea and milk toast which was often his simple night repast. Go home! Later, of course, if fighting really started. But not now! Not when he needed her so much. Who would be waiting for him at the end of a grueling day, make sure he had a nourishing meal, do all the little things for his comfort that no aide, no matter how loyal and efficient, could possibly do? But she knew she would worry him even more by staying, unless . . . The very thought sent cold fright coursing through her body. She couldn't! But—yes, if it meant staying with George, being able to accompany him next winter into another camp . . .

"No," she said. "I'm staying. And"—she drew a long breath—"I'll be inoculated."

It was George now who stared, remembering her terror over Jack's experience. Brows raised quizzically, he patted the now steady hand dropping a big lump of sugar in his tea. "Very well, my dear. We'll wait —at least until Dr. Morgan gets here. You're probably not in much danger now, so far from the center of camp."

She could see he did not trust her courage to act on this impulsive decision, and she was right. On April 29 in a letter to his brother John Augustine detailing his plans for fortifying the city of New York and the Hudson River, he added, "Mrs. Washington is still here and talks of taking the smallpox, but I doubt her resolution."

After Jack and Nelly left for Mount Airy in May, Martha was both relieved and lonely. Six months pregnant and extremely delicate, Nelly should be with her parents. Jack, now come of age, must attend to the business of settling his estate. Though George and his "family," secretaries and aides, were in and out and she faithfully saw that they were well fed and assisted in every way possible, time dragged. Her days were tense with waiting . . . waiting for news which, when it came, portended only disaster, the loss of Quebec, reinforcement of British troops in Canada, a confirmation that indeed England was employing German mercenaries, seventeen thousand of them . . . waiting for the day she dreaded, when Dr. Morgan would come to fill her body with those live but deadly agents of disease. George was still skeptical of her courage. Very well. She would show him. She did. She was inoculated for smallpox on May 18. On the twentieth they left for Philadelphia, George feeling that affairs were in such a crisis that he must consult with Congress. They arrived on the twenty-third well before the disease, whether light or severe, could work its havoc.

John Hancock, President of Congress, had written on May 21 inviting George and Martha to be his guests while in Philadelphia. But when they arrived, he sent a regretful note. He was suffering from a severe attack of gout. George was just as well pleased. He had not forgotten the chagrin on the face of this New Englander when he had been passed over for the choice of Commander in Chief. He would prefer not to accept favors from him. They took other lodgings, and Martha settled herself grimly for her ordeal. It proved far less severe than she had feared.

On May 31 George again wrote his brother: "This is the 13th day, and she has few pustules. She would have written to our sister Betty but thought it prudent not to do so, notwithstanding there could be little danger of conveying the infection in this manner." How silly, Martha chided herself, to have been so worried about her own well-being when *he* was constantly having to make decisions meaning life or death for thousands!

Each night, after long days consulting with Congress or conferring over dinner with his Virginia friends who were in the city—Richard Henry Lee, Francis Lightfoot Lee, Thomas Jefferson, Benjamin Harrison—he would return to the room always weary and harassed. But on one night he came with a light step and an almost youthful zest in his manner. Triumphantly he held aloft a paper, the resolution passed by the Virginia legislature on May 15, drafted by George Mason, Edmund Pendleton, Patrick Henry, with the assistance of Thomas Jefferson. Dicky Lee was soon to present it to the Continental Congress.

"Listen to this!" he read to her. "Resolved unanimously that the delegates appointed to represent this colony in General Congress be instructed to propose to that respectable body to declare the United Colonies free and independent states . . ." Of course, he continued, it would arouse a furor. But the fire would have been kindled. Surely all knew by this time that they could expect no justice from Great Britain. They must conquer or submit to impossible terms and their concomitants, such as confiscation, more taxation, military occupation, hangings.

Fortunately he was striding up and down the room, back toward her, so he did not hear her faint, terrified gasp or see the stricken look on her face. She saw him suddenly through a blinding haze, proud powdered head suspended somewhere in midair, a noose about his neck.

When he turned again the mist had cleared, and she managed a thin smile. "Independence!" Her voice broke on the word, then steadied. "I know. As you say, it's the only way."

George completed his business with Congress and returned on horseback to New York on June 4, leaving her to finish her convalescence under proper care in Philadelphia before going on to Mount Vernon in the chariot. She was almost relieved when he sent word of rumors that Mount Vernon might be less safe for her than New York. Lord Dunmore had gathered a band of some five hundred loyalists and established a fortified camp on an island in Chesapeake Bay, intending to use it as a base for forays all along the bay and its tributaries. She had no fear of Dunmore, but the threat meant that she could join George again in New York. She was back in the Mortier house once more by the sixteenth of June.

The situation there was even more tense than when she had left. Though the British fleet had not yet arrived, it was expected momentarily. Bad news continued to come from Canada. Worse yet, though George tried to keep it from her, she overheard his aides worrying about a plot against his life. A man named Thomas Hickey had been arousing loyalists in New York, also corrupting members of Washington's own guard. There was a plan to poison him, seize his staff and send them to England for trial. Desperately worried, Martha breathed a sigh of relief each night when George returned safely.

Life during these anxious days had its mitigating features. Kitty Greene was in New York, having left her baby with her family in Rhode Island. Lucy Knox was there also, settled with her husband on lower Broadway, and the three women enjoyed a semblance of their sociability at Cambridge. There were fresh faces among the aides and officers. One newcomer, young and energetic, appealed especially to Martha's motherly interest. He was almost the same age as Jack, and both had recently been students at King's College. His name was Alexander Hamilton.

Jack himself provided another happy relief from tension with a letter written to George while she was in Philadelphia. "Honored Sir," it began and expressed the sincerest pleasure to hear that "my dear Mother has gone through the smallpox so favorably. I do with the most filial affection congratulate you both on this happy event, as she can now attend you to any part of the Continent with pleasure, unsullied by the apprehensions of that Disorder."

But it was the rest of the letter which atoned for all the worry and frustration his waywardness had caused them.

"I am extremely desirous (but I am at loss for words sufficiently expressive) to return you Thanks for your parental Care which on all Occasions you have shown me. It pleased the Almighty to deprive me at a very early period of my Life of my Father, but I can not sufficiently adore his Goodness in sending me so good a Guardian as you Sir; Few have experienced such Care and Attention from real parents as I have done. He best deserves the Name of Father who acts the part of one. I first was taught to call you by that Name, my tender years unsusceptible of the Loss I had sustained knew not the contrary. Your Goodness (if others had not told me) would always have prevented me from knowing I had lost a parent. I shall always look upon you in this Light, and must intreat you to continue your wholesome advice and reprimands whenever you see occasion. I promise you they shall not be thrown away upon me, but on the contrary be thankfully received and strictly attended to . . ."

Martha read and reread the letter which, she knew, had given George great satisfaction. At last Jack was growing up. And about time, a father already!

But there were few such rifts in the menacing clouds, and suddenly events moved with terrifying swiftness. On June 28 Thomas Hickey was hanged. About nine o'clock on the morning of June 29 flags of warning were raised, for the long-expected British ships were sighted. Within minutes the harbor was a veritable forest of masts, as one observer said, "like a wood of pine trees trimmed." By the time George sat down to write a dispatch to Congress, forty-five ships had come in. By two in the afternoon almost a hundred rigged vessels had arrived.

"Make all possible preparation," was the grim order of the Commander in Chief. Another quickly followed: "The women must go."

Unlike Kitty and Lucy, Martha made no protest. George had enough to harass him without having to worry about her safety. She would make it as easy for him as possible, getting ready to leave the following day, June 30, even though it was Sunday, a day she did not care to travel, stopping with friends in Philadelphia as he wished, because Lord Dunmore was still menacing the Potomac plantations. When George made a rush trip from headquarters and took her in his arms to say good-bye, she even resisted the almost irresistible impulse to cling to him and weep, managing to hold her tears until she was in the chariot and out of sight. Even then weeping was a luxury she could not afford, for people might notice. Seeing the General's wife in tears, they would fear the cause was lost. But restraint would have been less possible had she known that it would be nine long months before she would see him again.

Once more there were crowds along the road, excited faces at windows, shouts of "Lady Washington!" Dutifully Martha smiled and waved, but it was a stiff smile, and there was more anxiety than gaiety in the eyes that watched her passing. News of the threat to New York had swept down the coast ahead of her. The glamor of patriotic resistance had turned suddenly into nervous awareness of the proximity of war.

In Philadelphia, Martha settled in the lodgings arranged for her on Chestnut Street. There was no dearth of company. Dorothy, wife of John Hancock, and other wives of congressmen came to call and invited her to their homes. A new friend was Eliza, Mrs. Samuel Powel, whose husband was one of the most wealthy and respected men in Philadelphia. Perhaps ten years younger than Martha, Eliza was gay, charming, keenly intelligent, fluent of speech, fashionable in dress. At first awed by this paragon of superior attainments, as she had once been by Sally, Martha soon found herself thoroughly at home in the imposing family estate in the center of the city, with its four mansions, its gardens adorned with statuary, its profusion of lemon, orange, and citrus trees. It was a friendship which would grow richer and more intimate through the years.

Philadelphia was agog with excitement. The very day of Martha's arrival Congress was taking a final vote on the momentous resolution proposed on June 7 by Richard Henry Lee and seconded by John Adams, but, after furious debate, laid on the table for three weeks while delegates from thirteen woefully disparate colonies argued hotly, consulted, condemned, criticized, agreed, and a young man from Virginia, Thomas Jefferson, shut himself away at a desk getting the proposed document into final shape.

On Monday, July 1, the voting started. George was there, in spirit if not in person, for he had sent three letters urging the resolution's adoption. That day the voting was inconclusive, nine to four for independence. New York had refused to vote. Pennsylvania and South Carolina had voted nay. Delaware had been undecided. Congress was adjourned until the following day.

Tuesday, July 2, it was done. Twelve states had voted "Ay," with New York's vote guaranteed. Congress agreed unanimously that "these United Colonies are, and of right ought to be, Free and Independent States; that they are absolved from all allegiance to the British Crown . . ." Still there were minor points in the Declaration to be worried and chewed over, some spat out, some digested, while Jefferson squirmed in agony, fearing for the life of his Preamble, especially its dangerous "all men are created equal" (anathema to patrician landowners) and its "life, liberty, and the pursuit of happiness" ("life, liberty, and *property*" was the common slogan). But miraculously it passed.

"When, in the course of human events, it becomes necessary for one people to dissolve the political bands which have connected them with another, and to assume, among the powers of the earth, the separate and equal station to which the laws of nature and of nature's God entitle them, a decent respect to the opinions of mankind requires that they should declare the causes which impel them to the separation.

"We hold these truths to be self-evident, . . ."

On July 4, Martha heard the bell in the State House steeple begin to peal and the crowd thronging the streets break into cheers. The church bells started ringing. She had gone to visit Dorothy Hancock. The two women looked at each other with relief and satisfaction.

"It's done," said Mrs. Hancock, drawing a long breath. "John will have just signed the document."

"The very first name." Martha nodded, smiling. "John Hancock."

But there was trouble as well as satisfaction in the look they exchanged, for both knew it was a declaration not only of independence but also of war. There was no chance of reconciliation now. And the result would brand both of their husbands either victors or traitors.

With other women Martha was in the crowd thronging the State House yard on July 8 when, at the hour of noon, Colonel Nixon of the Philadelphia Associators read the Declaration. Troops saluted. There was a tremendous medley of huzzas. She wished she could have been in New York the following day when, news of the act having been rushed to the Commander in Chief by express rider, at six o'clock in the evening, uniforms spruced up, bayonets fixed, all George's men not on pressing duty marched into formation and listened to a loud voice proclaiming the strange and startling words, "When, in the course of human events . . ." and ending with the challenge, "And for the support of this Declaration, with a firm reliance on the protection of Divine Providence, we mutually pledge to each other our lives, our fortunes, and our sacred honor." Someone told her afterward that George had listened to the reading sitting astride his horse with the troops around him in a hollow square. She heard also that he had officially condemned the action that night of the Sons of Liberty who swarmed over the fence on the Bowling Green, climbed up on the majestic statue of George III, garbed like a Roman emperor a third larger than life, and with ropes and bars and axes hewed it to the ground, triumphantly cutting off its head. But since the gold-plated statue contained some four thousand pounds of lead which could be molded into precious bullets, his censure had been not unmixed with satisfaction.

It was well that she had some good news from New York that summer, for most of it was bad. Martha was torn between alternatives—to return home or to stay in Philadelphia. Her first grandchild was due. Lund Washington was urgently demanding her presence to cope with problems at Mount Vernon, and Virginia was free from threat of attack at least temporarily. However, she lingered. In Philadelphia she was at least many miles nearer George, and President Hancock brought her news from New York as soon as Congress was apprised.

"I am still in this town," she wrote Nancy on August 20, "and no prospect of leaving it. The General is at New York. He is well and wrote me yesterday, and informed me that Lord Dunmore with part of his fleet was come to General Howe at Staten Island, that another division of Hessians is expected before they think the regulars will begin thare attack on us. Some hear begen to think, thare will be noe battle after all . . . I thank God we shan't want men, the army at New York is very large and numbers of men are still going there is at this time in the city . . . I do, my dear Sister, most religiously wish there was an end to the war."

There was one piece of good news that summer. Jack wrote from Mount Airy: "Nelly was safely delivered of a fine daughter . . . a strapping Huzze . . . I wish you were present." Elizabeth Parke Custis had been born on August 21.

Suddenly it was time to go home. She would have known even without George's advising her to do so. She could not help him here, and she was needed there. The new wings must be finished so that all would be ready if—no, *when* he returned. And now there was the new grandchild to welcome. It was with hope, if not anticipation, that she began to pack.

Fortunately John Hancock did not tell her the latest news, or the hope would have turned to despair. On August 22 General Howe, having occupied Long Island, had made an overwhelming attack on the five thousand Americans set to oppose him and had utterly routed them, with the loss of four hundred killed and wounded and a thousand taken prisoners. Martha had left Philadelphia before rumors of the engagement reached the city—that the Commander in Chief had been furious because his men had fled in panic, had raged forward among them striking out at the fugitives with the flat of his sword, would have charged straight into the British lines, actually seeking death, if an aide had not checked him by seizing his bridle. But, remembering Boston, she would have grimly relished the account of what followed—how, to prevent Howe from cutting off his lines of retreat, George had taken ten thousand men across East River in a black night of drizzling rain with all their stores and arms, leaving a small guard to keep up a deceptive bombardment from the breastworks, the enemy completely unaware of their retreat. The British commander had been as astonished the next morning to see Brooklyn Heights empty as, previous, to see Dorchester Heights occupied. It had been a masterly retrieval from complete defeat.

The Calverts met Martha's chariot in Baltimore and accompanied her to Mount Airy. Even her delight over baby Eliza could not hold her there long. She was like a hungry mare sniffing the scents of home pasture. Jack rode with her the rest of the way.

Never had Mount Vernon seemed such a haven of beauty, of peace, of security. The gardens were a riot of bloom. After the dusty streets of Philadelphia the lawns sloping down to the river were a lush expanse of green. A dogwood on the east lawn was turning a brilliant orange-red. The magnolias were covered with bright scarlet seed. Soon the locusts would be flaming yellow. Grapes were ripening. A hundred tasks were waiting, butter to be churned and put into pots, jams and jellies preserved, flowers and herbs hung up to dry, apples turned into cider and apple butter, carrots and onions and eggplant stored, nuts gathered in readiness for George's after-dinner snacks. The spinners and weavers had grown lax. Lund had done well directing the servants, but nine months without the mistress's oversight had resulted in grave deficiencies. She tackled all this multiplicity of duties with zest and vigor, and both staff and servants, overjoyed by her presence, rallied in support.

Work on the additions had been progressing and, though George had been apprised of all details in Lund's weekly reports, she enlarged on them enthusiastically in her letters. George's library on the south side was completed except for the bookshelves and his own finishing touches. Their bedroom above, with its little stair coming up from the library to give them privacy, was ready for occupancy. Already the big bed with its freshly laundered hangings of white dimity was in place. She had brought up the desk she had given him for a wedding present which had belonged to old John Custis, its drop leaf inlaid with white holly, bearing the Custis coat of arms with its motto, "Victory be Thine." His shaving and dressing table was already in place in his little dressing room beyond the bedroom.

But, oh, he should see the "new room," the great dining hall which was still in process of construction! The ceiling had been finished at last, its decorations of carved stucco the finest she had ever seen, hand-

somer than any of Colonel Lewis's at Kenmore House. And the Palla-
dian window was exactly as he had designed it, just as noble and beautiful. You could stand outside and look through it to the new
chimneypiece. She could hardly wait for him to see it all . . . if! Always the word hung in the air like a vulture sensing the proximity of
death.

For distance did nothing to allay worry. News from the north continued to be bad. George's letters reported little but continued retreats.
September had seen him constantly withdrawing from positions on the
island of Manhattan, fighting all the way, sometimes angry at his men's
cowardice, sometimes encouraged by their staunch resistance. In November the British captured Fort Washington, causing the Continental
army to flee across the Hudson to New Jersey. The enemy was now in
full possession of New York.

Fortunately Martha was not told the extent of George's discouragement and near despair, how his generals were becoming insubordinate,
his men were deserting by the hundreds, whole companies leaving
when their terms expired; how he had barely three thousand men remaining when he reached Princeton; how Charles Lee had disobeyed
orders and remained with fully half the army in a safe post, leaving the
British to pursue George through New Jersey. Martha would have nodded grimly at this bit of news. She had never trusted Lee. She was
almost pleased to hear in December that he had been taken captive by
the British and that most of his troops had managed to reach George
beyond the Delaware.

On December 10 George wrote Lund from his encampment near
the Falls of Delaware: "I wish to heaven it was in my power to give you
a more favorable account of our situation than it is . . . I tremble for
Philadelphia . . . no time to send the horses I promis'd. Mrs. Washington must therefore make the old grays serve her a little while
longer."

Martha felt like weeping. Thinking about horses for her, when all his
objectives, including his life, were in jeopardy!

To his brother he was even less hopeful: "In a word, if every nerve is
not strained to recruit the new army with all possible expedition, the
game is nearly up."

The British believed it was. Fearing for Philadelphia, Congress had
moved to Baltimore but before going had "conferred on Washington

full power to order and direct all things relative to the operations of war." On Howe's offer of pardon hundreds of patriots rushed to take the oath of allegiance. The rebellion seemed to be over. But Martha, though terrified, could have told them they did not know George. Difficulties only stiffened his determination. Faced by what seemed certain defeat, he was exploiting all the delegated authority conferred on him by Congress, justifying any excesses with the claim, "A character to lose, an estate to forfeit, the inestimable blessing of liberty at stake, and a life devoted must be my excuse." During December he collected six thousand men and was ready to make his move against the Hessians whom Howe, secure and exuberant in his luxurious quarters in New York, had strung along the eastern shores of the Delaware.

Christmas. Martha flinched at the mere thought of holiday festivity. Deck the house with greens and berries when George was flirting with death, perhaps shivering in a tent on another riverbank? Cook turkeys and hams and pies and prepare the usual rich, steaming eggnog when he and his men might be feeding on crusts and water? She even resented the gay flamboyancy of the holly branches pruned to provide fresh cuttings. Last holiday season they had at least been together. It was not loneliness she felt now as much as fear and foreboding. Where would he be next Christmas? Languishing in some British prison awaiting execution, or, if he was lucky enough to escape to those western lands he talked of, hiding away in some wilderness hut? If so, she would find some way to join him, leave everything behind, yes, even that new precious baby of Jack's!

But of course she must reveal none of these fears. Friends, neighbors, would be coming. Servants and staff would expect the usual gifts and festivities. Christmas must be observed at Mount Vernon. The house was decorated with boughs of pine and cedar and spruce and holly. Over glowing fires in the cookhouse spits and roasting pans and kettles steamed and boiled and sizzled. The eggnog with its quart of milk, quart of cream, dozen eggs, sugar, variety of spirits, was prepared, cooled, aged, even though George was not there to taste it frequently, making sure it reached the proper stage of maturity.

She got through the day, honoring staff and servants with gifts and feasting, greeting guests, smiling assurance that all was well, finally mounting the new little staircase which George had never seen to the new bedroom where he had never slept beside her, dropping wearily into the big four-poster made especially long and wide to accommodate his muscular six-foot-two body. She felt lost in its expanse. Sleep when it came was fitful, disturbed by troubled dreams. They would have been far more troubled could she have known what George was doing all that long night.

Soon John Augustine, his wife Hannah, daughter Jane, and son Bushrod came for a visit. Bushrod, age fifteen, was a law student at William and Mary College in Williamsburg, and George's favorite nephew. Martha tried not to feel slightly jealous of George's pride in Bushrod, who was acquiring the education he had so much wanted for his stepson. Not that he had the same affection for him as for Jack. George loved Jack like his own son. But Bushrod had one advantage: his name was Washington.

They were still there when the news came which turned the bleak holiday season into one of joyous festivity. George's letter disclosed only the bare facts with little emphasis on his own incredible feat. He had crossed the Delaware on Christmas night with a portion of his troops and surprised the Hessian garrison at Trenton. It was as decisive a victory as his conquest of Boston. George Mason, who had gleaned more details of the coup from accounts sent the Virginia legislature, shared them with the family at Mount Vernon.

"Can you believe it—ten hours of perilous passage of that stormy river swept by wind and snow, in pitch dark, surrounded by floating ice, getting twenty-five hundred men of his own division safely across, not a man or gun lost! It was an incredible feat! Then marching nine miles through driving snow and sleet to Trenton, two men frozen to death during the march, his only loss! When General Sullivan sent word to him that the guns were wet, all he said was, 'Then tell them they must use their bayonets, for the town must be taken!' And it was. The Hessians were completely surprised. Their commander was mortally wounded, and nine hundred of them surrendered."

News continued to be good. When the British General Cornwallis had come with eight thousand men to rout him from Trenton, George had let him come all the way to the Delaware doing nothing except put a small stream between his men and the advancing army. Then when Cornwallis had put his army to bed on the other side of the stream, confidently believing that he had "run down the old fox and could bag him in the morning," George had worked his old trick, keeping campfires burning and a small detachment audibly working on the ramparts, moving his main force on the road north. On January 3 he had met the British at Princeton and routed them. It was even rumored that he had shouted at them, "An old-fashioned Virginia fox hunt, gentlemen!" Then he had withdrawn to the heights of Morristown, New Jersey. The defeated Cornwallis had returned sheepishly to New York.

Hopefully Martha waited for an invitation to join George in his new winter quarters, but it did not come. He was living in small space, he wrote, in the Morristown tavern, with only two upstairs rooms over the bar. Besides smallpox, there were epidemics of septic sore throat and dysentery against which there was no inoculation. Also he was fearing that Howe might move to take Philadelphia before waiting for spring. She assured him that she was ready to come anytime and kept on waiting patiently. Finally the summons came, in March, and she set forth immediately, Jack going with her as far as Baltimore. At Philadelphia she was met by George Lewis, son of George's sister Betty, who had attached himself to his uncle's staff.

"The General has been sick," he told her, "terrible sore throat, high fever. At one time we all gathered around his bed, despairing of his life."

Oh, if she had only known! She would not have stayed that extra day at Mount Airy enjoying that new grandchild. She refused to stop now in Philadelphia, though her friends urged her. The horses did not move fast enough. She was tempted to climb to the driver's seat and urge them on herself. Then what relief when, a few miles out of Morristown at a place called Pluckemin, she saw him waiting, looking thin and pale and tired but at least able to be up and about! She did not wait for George Lewis to hand her from the coach but jumped down and ran toward him, almost stumbling over her long full skirts, but the familiar arms were there to steady her, enfold her.

"Are you all right?" he demanded. "Did you have a good journey?" Then, after they had assured each other of their mutual well-being, "How is everything at home? How are Blueskin and Magnolia and Sampson?"

Martha laughed merrily, so great was her relief. He *would* think first, not of his new grandchild or his other human dependents, but of his favorite horses! She would have been even more amused had she known the surprise her arrival caused. The woman at whose house George had been waiting looked out the window, saw her descend from the carriage and, because she was so plainly dressed, thought she must be an attendant of the great lady . . . until she saw the General's arms go around her!

This woman was not the only one who evidenced surprise at a first meeting with Martha. One Morristown matron recorded: "I was never so ashamed in my life. We thought we would visit Lady Washington, and as she was said to be so grand a lady, we thought we must put on our best bibs and bands. So we dressed ourselves in our most elegant ruffles and silks and were introduced to her ladyship. And don't you think we found her *knitting and with a specked* [checkered] *apron on!* She received us very graciously, and easily, but after the compliments were over, she resumed her knitting. There we were without a stitch of work, and sitting in State, but General Washington's lady with her own hands was knitting stockings for herself and husband!

"And that was not all. In the afternoon her ladyship took occasion to say, in a way that we could not be offended at, that at this time it was very important that American ladies should be patterns of industry, because the separation from the mother country will dry up the sources whence many of our comforts have been derived. We must become independent by our determination to do without what we cannot make ourselves. Whilst our husbands and brothers are examples of patriotism, we must be patterns of industry!"

"She seems very wise in experience," commented another of these visitors, "kindhearted and winning in all her ways. She talked much of the sufferings of the poor soldiers, especially of the sick ones. Her heart seems to be full of compassion for them."

Martha soon involved them and others in her knitting and sewing circles and was as much at home in the cramped quarters in Morristown as in the spacious mansion in Cambridge. The officers and aides were once more her "family," and she mended for them, cooked her hams and puddings and hot breads for them, mothered them, tended them when sick, new ones among them now, including the young captain whom she had seen briefly in New York, Alexander Hamilton. Brilliant and popular he was, boyishly handsome, and a favorite with the ladies, but Martha suspected that he thought a little too well of himself.

Surprised not to find George's favorite Joseph Reed among them, she was horrified when George reluctantly told her of a letter he had inadvertently opened from Charles Lee to Reed obviously in reply to one Reed had written Lee. In it Lee had agreed with Reed's appraisal of George as to his "fatal indecision of mind" resulting in "eternal defeat and miscarriage" and had been flattered by the suggestion that he, Lee, would be a far more able Commander in Chief.

"And what did you do?" demanded Martha indignantly.

The only thing possible, he told her bitterly. Enclosed the letter in one to Reed, apologizing for having opened it in the mistaken belief that it was official business. Seeing how hurt he had been by this defection of a trusted and beloved colleague, Martha ached for him. But she was also furiously angry with these two disloyal and selfishly ambitious subordinates who so compounded his difficulties. She had never liked or trusted Charles Lee, but Reed, whom George had loved like a son . . . !

It was a time of tense waiting. When would the British attack, and where? Howe seemed to be content extending his winter in New York into spring. Reports came of his gay life there, housed in loyalist mansions, days filled with dancing, card playing, and, it was rumored, dalliance with a bold and obliging mistress, while George struggled endlessly with his problems of administration—desertions of his troops, delay in pay for his soldiers so that he had had to pledge funds from his own estate, inability of Congress to supply his men with decent clothing so that a sixth of them were practically naked, a third without blankets.

Martha eased his life as much as possible, presiding graciously over the dinner table where the senior officers and brigade majors of the day were often his guests. There was quite a bit of gaiety, for many New York and New Jersey families had taken refuge in these western hills, and Martha made all welcome. Mrs. Cox, wife of Colonel John Cox, would describe long afterward to her grandchildren her visits with this sociable wife of the General who, as soon as breakfast was over, "would bring out her fathomless mending basket, from which she was content to mend and darn from morn to noon, from noon to dewy eve." And Mrs. Theodorick Bland, who had come from Virginia to join her husband, wrote home that "the General's worthy lady seems in perfect felicity by the side of her 'old man,' as she calls him."

Indulgently Martha encouraged George in joining gay riding parties after dinner when the day had brought no unusual report of dire calamity, even though most of his companions would be admiring women not incapable of a bit of flirting. She would have smiled amusedly at Mrs. Bland's description in that same letter of those rides, when "Washington throws off the hero and takes on the cheery, agreeable companion—he can be downright impudent sometimes—such impudence, Fanny, as you and I like."

Martha had long since ceased to be jealous of George's attractiveness to women or of his undeniable interest in feminine beauty and intelligence. Sally Fairfax had cured her of that. She could sit contentedly knitting and watch him dance an evening out with lovely Kitty Greene without a qualm of resentment. And she knew that a riding party, whether with men or women, an hour of throwing ball with his junior officers, released memories and foretastes of the life he so desperately longed for, a yearning she so intimately shared. They shared it one night in April, sitting in their small Morristown bedroom after a long and grueling day, the windows open to the scents of spring. George, writing a letter to Edmund Pendleton, laid down his quill.

"The lilacs will be purple in the north grove," he said musingly, "and the tulips and daffodils are in full bloom. I hope Lund has turned the water from Doeg Run into the Mill Race."

"And I hope"—Martha applied even more energy to her knitting—"that the servants are getting along with the housecleaning. This would have been a good day to open all the windows wide and let the musty smells of winter out."

They looked at each other and smiled. Then George took up his quill pen and wrote briskly:

"That the God of Armies may enable me to bring the present contest to a speedy and happy conclusion, thereby gratifying me in a retirement to the calm and sweet enjoyment of domestic happiness, is the fervent prayer and most ardent wish of my soul."

15

Strange! It did not seem like coming home, returning to Mount Vernon in early June that year of 1777. Home was where George was, whether a borrowed mansion, a hired lodging, or two rooms in a village tavern. But of course she plunged into the waiting duties with her usual diligence and efficiency and with only a few variations in routine. It was noticed that some days, especially after letters had come to Lund or herself from the north, she spent longer than the customary hour at her morning devotions and her face revealed less of its usual serenity when she emerged. The gardener also was surprised at finding her down on her knees in the flower garden, her skirts of brown homespun in dull contrast with the brilliant reds and yellows and pinks of roses, spider-flowers, snapdragons.

"It's good to feel close to something living and growing," she said once, looking up with a smile, "there's so much dying in the world."

She herself came to life when Jack brought Nelly and the baby for a visit, though she almost envied Nurse Molly her happy privilege of constant attendance on the cooing, cuddly Eliza, now nearly a year old. It was a disappointment that Jack seemed unwilling to make Mount Vernon his permanent home but was looking for a place he could call his own. Near Mount Vernon, she hoped, instead of Mount Airy! She should be glad, she supposed, that he was showing independence in his new maturity, but, oh, the house was so silent and empty without them!

In fact, she felt so bereft when they left that in August she journeyed by chariot to Eltham. Even reunion with family brought no surcease from worry. Discouragement continued to follow her from the north, where George was desperately trying to save Philadelphia from occupation by the British. Her brother Bartholomew roused alarm over a formidable enemy fleet which appeared in Chesapeake Bay, with only meager defenses to prevent its encroachment on the whole inland river area. But even more worrying to her was the fact that Nancy was unwell and the doctors in Williamsburg seemed helpless either to diagnose her ailment or to effect a cure. It was hard to recognize in this wan, prematurely aging woman the gay, sprightly, fun-loving sister who had been closer to her than any other member of her family. She returned to Mount Vernon even more troubled than she had left it, taking with her Nancy's two boys, aged twelve and thirteen, promising their mother that they would receive the smallpox inoculation under her supervision. It was one service she could render her concerned sister, who had lost so many of her children. She was glad of the boys' presence, even though their sickness and convalescence brought anxious moments, and sent them home with a mingling of regret and relief.

"I have the very great pleasure of Returning you your Boys as well as they were when I brought them from Eltham," she wrote Nancy on November 18. "They have had the small pox exceeding light and have been perfectly well for this fortnight past . . . They have been exceeding good Boys indeed, and I shall hope you will lett them come to see me when ever they can spare so much time from school . . . The last letter I had from the General was dated the 7th of this month—he says nothing hath happend since the unsuccessful attack upon our forts on the Dalawar—Nelly Custis has ben over the river this three week—Jack is just come over, he tells me that little Bet is grown fat as a pigg . . ."

Martha lived for the letters from George, even though they contained more bad news than good. In September his troops had suffered a crushing defeat at Brandywine. Later that month the British had occupied Philadelphia. In October he had seemed close to victory at Germantown, only to experience a disheartening reversal. But the news was not all discouraging. A few days later General Horatio Gates and his troops had thoroughly routed the forces of General Burgoyne in

their march from Canada, taking his whole army as prisoners. George
was hearty in his praise of Gates and ordered a *feu-de-joie* to celebrate
the event. He evinced no jealousy of this subordinate who was winning
victories while he himself was suffering only defeat. For him the cause
was all-important.

When would he call her to join him? She waited in an agony of
expectation. If only she could be there to brighten Christmas for all of
them! But December brought only the report that he was moving with
his army to a new headquarters more secure from attack, a wooded
region about eighteen miles northwest of the occupied city of Philadelphia, a place called Valley Forge. The month brought other news which
portended not only a lonely but a grief-stricken Christmas. Her beloved
sister Nancy had died. Stoically she went through the motions of holiday preparations, the cooking of foods which could have only a bitter
taste, the hanging of greens and holly and bright crimson decorations
which should have been swathed in black. Only in her room during her
morning retreat and in the sleepless night hours did she allow herself
the luxury of tears.

But life has a way of emerging persistently out of death. On the last
day of that troubled month and year Nelly gave birth to her second
child, another girl, and as soon as it seemed safe for Jack and his family
to travel across the river from Mount Airy, the lonely house was once
more blessed with young life.

"Another Patsy," thought Martha gratefully as her empty arms enclosed the warm bundle, for the baby had been named Martha after
her.

But even this inducement could not hold her at Mount Vernon a
moment after George gave her leave to join him. The chariot had been
packed for days, waiting only for the last-minute supplies of hams,
cheeses, dried fruits, preserves, salted fish, nuts, to be brought from the
storehouses. She waited impatiently. George's letters were full of explanations for the delay. There were few houses in the bleak Pennsylvania
valley. His men were camping in tattered tents until they could fell
trees and build their own log huts. Unwilling to be better housed than
his troops, he also was living in a tent. There were constant rains.
Provisions were scanty. Horses were dying for lack of feed. The soldiers
had spent Christmas Day looking for food to prevent starvation. The
following week they had built a thousand log huts.

"To see men," he reported, "without shoes (for the want of which their marches might be traced by the blood from their feet) . . . marching through frost and snow and at Christmas taking up their winter quarters within a day's march of the enemy, without a house or a hut to cover them . . . is proof of patience and obedience which in my opinion can scarce be parallelled."

The only house available to him, he wrote, would be small and uncomfortable, worse even than the tavern at Morristown. As if she cared about that! She would have been glad to share a tent with him.

The summons came at last, and he sent an aide, Colonel Meade, to meet her below Wilmington.

"I had nothing but kindness on my journey," she wrote back. "The travelling was pretty rough. I found snow in crossing Delaware, and at an inn on Brandywine Creek, at a ford where I lodged, the snow was so deep in the roads in some places that I had to leave the chariot with the innkeeper and hire a farm sleigh to bring me here. The General is well but much worn with fatigue and anxiety. I never knew him to be so anxious as now, for the poor soldiers are without sufficient clothing and food, and many of them are barefooted. Oh, how my heart pains for them!"

Now she learned of a development which had etched new small lines of bitterness about George's lips. It was not he who told her but his indignant aides. It was the story of disloyal, ambitious Charles Lee all over again. It was Gates now who was doing the maneuvering instead of Lee. What had Washington been doing, according to the gossip he and his henchmen promoted, while Gates had been conquering forts and taking a whole British army prisoner up in the north? Losing at Brandywine and Germantown, Philadelphia, retreating, shilly-shallying, refusing to attack! An Irish adventurer named Conway was one of Gates's henchmen and at the center of the intrigue intended to unseat George from his post and force the appointment of Gates in his place. The movement was already known as the "Conway Cabal." Its technique was underhanded, its chief tools slander and innuendo. A letter from Conway to Gates, intercepted and sent to Washington by one of his loyal officers, had contained the words: "Heaven has determined to save your country, or a weak General and bad Councellors would have ruined it."

Like the aides, Martha was furious. What had George done to combat these underhanded attacks? Apparently nothing. He could erupt in violent temper often enough, as when one of his servants was discovered in perfidy, but now, when personally belittled, humiliated, he had endured the calumny in cold and contemptuous silence. However, both she and the indignant aides were underrating him. The very day of her arrival, February 9, he and the loyal Alexander Hamilton were preparing a crushing statement which was not only a vigorous defense of his own actions but a blistering, yet scrupulously courteous indictment of Gates and the "incendiary" Conway.

"Their own artless zeal to advance their views has betrayed them," was his only spoken comment.

Martha settled into the routine of the wretchedly inadequate camp with her usual cheerful acceptance of the inevitable. Housed with George in two little rooms in a small but snug stone house owned and occupied by the Isaac Potts family at the head of the bleak valley, her colored maid Oney in attendance, she was almost ashamed to live in such tolerable warmth and comfort when outside, all up and down the clusters of cheerless huts men were shivering over little smoking greenwood fires, their shoeless feet leaving bloody tracks in the snow, sometimes nothing but a thin blanket to cover their naked bodies, or even no blanket at all, a bit of meat a luxury, many days passing without bread.

"For some days past there has been little less than a famine in the camp," George was writing. "A part of the army has been a week without any kind of flesh, and the rest three or four days. Naked and starving they are, we cannot enough admire the incomparable patience and fidelity that they have not been, ere this, excited by their sufferings to a general mutiny and desertion."

Martha did what she could. A young girl who lived near the Potts house which was Washington's headquarters was to write of her years later: "I never in my life knew a woman so busy from early morn until late at night as was Lady Washington, providing comforts for the sick soldiers. Every day, except Sundays, the wives of officers in camp, and sometimes other women, were invited to Mr. Potts' to assist her in knitting socks, patching garments, and making shirts for the poor soldiers when materials could be procured. Every fair day she might be seen, with basket in hand, and with a single attendant, going among the huts seeking the keenest and most needy sufferers and giving all the comfort to them in her power. I sometimes went with her, for I was a stout girl sixteen. On one occasion she went to the hut of a dying sergeant, whose young wife was with him. After she had given him some wholesome food she had prepared she knelt down by his straw pallet and prayed earnestly for him and his wife with her sweet solemn voice. I shall never forget the scene."

Life was not all misery. For George's birthday she helped some of the "family" plan a surprise party. There was a "feast" of fowl and boiled parsnips, mugs of rum and water to toast his health, and, rare luxury, a whole package of tea, secured from somewhere for five pounds cost a pound. During the dinner General Knox's artillery band came and serenaded him outside the house, then were invited in to join the festivities. It was the first time his birthday had been observed on February 22. Virginia still used the old-style calendar, which dated his birth on February 11. Pennsylvania was one of the first states to change to the new calendar. As they enjoyed the meager fare, serenaded him, danced, toasted, they little realized that they were setting a precedent for such observances over the next two hundred years.

"The General is in camp," Martha wrote Mercy Warren on March 2, "in what is called the great valley on the Banks of the Scuylkill. Officers and men are chiefly in hutts, which they say is tolerable comfortable; the army are as healthy as can well be expected in general. The General's apartment is very small; he has had a log cabin built to dine in, which has made our quarters much more tolerable than they were at first."

Tolerable! A mild word indeed to describe the situation!

She managed tasty if frugal dinners for officers and aides and wives. There were not only new faces about the table but unfamiliar languages. Not all the foreigners in the ranks, she discovered, were adventurous opportunists like Conway. There was Du Portail, an engineer from the French army, whose genius had helped create this city of a thousand log huts without benefit of nails or proper tools. There was Baron von Steuben, a German soldier who had arrived in February knowing not a word of English but who had become overnight an invaluable instructor in military techniques. With him was his secretary Pierre du Ponceau, who translated the Baron's German into French, whence one of George's aides turned it into English. Von Steuben was soon able to swear at the troops in all three languages, yet in spite of his severity of discipline and Prussian rigidity the troops came to love him. And there was the most intriguing personality of all, Marie Joseph Paul Yves Roch Gilbert du Mortier, the Marquis de Lafayette.

Handsome, slender, red-haired, blue-eyed, no more than twenty, obsessed with a passion for human freedom, he had been stirred by the Declaration of Independence and the colonies' bold resistance to tyranny and had determined to volunteer in their struggle. Threatened by his noble family of Noailles with incarceration in the Bastille for his "mad" decision, he had got away in a ship purchased with his own money, leaving behind a sympathetic young wife and their child. He had arrived in Philadelphia the preceding July. In three days he had charmed a Congress soured on foreign opportunists into making him a Major General. In three months he had got himself wounded in battle and by Christmas had endeared himself to the whole army. He arrived at Valley Forge in April. George, Martha could see, loved him like a son, and she gladly took him to her own heart.

In fact, she preferred many of these late arrivals to some of the original officers, especially one. For Charles Lee also appeared, on a prisoners' exchange effected by George, and was greeted almost as a hero. George rode out to meet him, and Martha reluctantly presided at a dinner in his honor, replete with delicacies that could be ill spared, plus his ubiquitous dogs.

Spring came finally. The mud following the terribly wet season dried, and the hills enclosing the valley burst into green. Gradually supplies increased. General Greene, sacrificing his superior military status for the good of the cause and love of his chief, became quartermaster in place of the ineffective General Mifflin, and food which surrounding farmers had been stubbornly routing to the British luxuriating in Philadelphia was intercepted and diverted. There was promise of clothing for the troops from New England. There was even increasing hope that the recognition of the new country by the French government might soon bring military help. John Adams, sent as an envoy to Paris, had been promoting the American cause there for months.

So pervasive was the spirit of rejuvenation that some of the soldiers decided to give a play, choosing the popular Addison's *Cato*. In spite of lack of proper costumes, scenery, and sufficient rehearsals, it was a gala occasion. George and Martha, with other officers and wives, attended. As Jubo poured out his fervent avowals to Marcia, Martha stole a glance at George. Was he remembering his emotions at seeing Sally Fairfax receive the passionate vows of love in the same play? The faint twinge of jealousy, supposedly conquered long ago, subsided. Suppose he was. What did it matter? Memories were poor things to encourage and comfort a man or keep him warm at night.

To their surprise and chagrin Congress, still haunted by the puritanism of Sam Adams and his ilk, was horrified at this display of gaiety and passed a resolution beginning, "Whereas religion and good morals are the only solid foundation of public liberty and happiness," and forbidding any soldier to attend a theatrical performance under pain of dismissal from service.

This bit of gaiety was mild indeed beside the elaborate fete taking place at about the same time in Philadelphia, planned by a dashing young British officer, John André, to honor Sir William Howe on his resignation and return to England. There were regattas, balls, fireworks, boats, barges, galleys, gay with the flags of all nations—yes, including the new Stars and Stripes! All this while at the same time at Valley Forge nearly three thousand men were barefoot and almost naked.

For both George and Martha spring roused conflicting emotions, for George a keen homesickness for Mount Vernon, for Martha the disquieting knowledge that she must soon return there, leaving him behind.

"Remember," he said to her on the last day of April as they sat together in the little upstairs room before the candles were lighted, "where we were four years ago on this day?"

"Yes," said Martha promptly, for it had been a most unusual day. "There was not a single guest, just the two of us sitting down at the table together."

He moved restively. "The fish would be running now. I hope the servants are making good hauls off Sheridan Point."

But this April 30 was to prove an even more memorable one in their lives, for at that very moment a message was arriving by express from a man named Simeon Deane, who had left Brest on March 8, arrived in Falmouth on Casco Bay on April 13, hastened to Boston, then rushed to York, where Congress had fled from Philadelphia. Deane, so George's message read, had delivered to Congress five packets. One of them contained the text of a treaty, signed on February 6 at Versailles, declaring the recognition by France of a new nation called the United States of America.

Spring had come indeed. In George's face Martha saw the miracle of renewal. Gone were the fine lines of harassment and tension, the grim tightness of lips. He seemed almost as young and vigorous as on the day she had first seen him.

"I believe no event was ever received with more heartfelt joy," he wrote Congress.

There must be a celebration. The next morning the brigades were called together to listen to the reading of the news. There was a triumphant salute of thirteen guns, shouts of "Long live the King of France!", a grand review of the troops. Services of thanksgiving were held at the chaplain's quarters, and Martha was surprised and touched when she left with George to hear, amid the cheers and huzzas, shouts of "Long live Lady Washington!"

Incredible that out of this winter of despair should spring such hope and vigor, that those half-starved, ragged, hopeless derelicts could turn into such clean, almost decently garbed (thanks to Congress's belated appropriation of some meager funds), smartly marching figures, the pride of Von Steuben's meticulous, if galling, Prussian training! But there was anxiety in the women's mood of reveling. For spring meant renewed military action, danger, separation. Wonderful, of course, that the French had become their allies in the struggle for freedom! But summer loomed ahead, and France was thousands of miles away. It was time to leave their men once more, endure months of torment, wondering, waiting.

Mount Vernon again. It was June when Martha arrived. In spite of the mounting heat she embarked on a frenzy of housecleaning, for if hopes were realized, this year might see the end of the terrible war, and George would be coming home. All must be made ready for him. News was encouraging. The British had left Philadelphia for New York. The Continental army had pursued them and a battle had occurred at a place called Monmouth Court House. The battle had almost been lost. General Lee, ordered to move forward with six thousand men to attack General Clinton's troops, while Washington held his main body ready to strike, had again disregarded the command. To his amazed horror George had met his own soldiers of the advance corps retreating with the enemy in pursuit. His wrath had been terrible to see.

"I never saw the General to such advantage," Hamilton reported. "He instantly took measures for checking the enemy's advance. He directed the whole with the skill of a master workman, but his own presence brought order out of confusion, animated his troops, and led them to success." And LaFayette would remember: "Amid the roar and confusion of the conflict I took time to admire our beloved chief mounted on a splendid charger as he rode along the ranks amid the shouts of the soldiers, cheering them by his voice and example, and restoring to our standard the fortunes of the fight. I thought then as now that I had never beheld so superb a man."

But for Lee's treachery it might have been a full victory instead of a partial one. Martha could not help being pleased when Lee was court-martialed for his disobedience. The summer dragged on, the war a stalemate. By autumn Martha feared there was no hope of decisive action before winter. Of course she would join him in another camp if he permitted. But for the first time she dreaded the prospect. Memories of Valley Forge were still with her, and this year she was torn by conflicting loyalties. Her mother had been seriously ill. Jack, to her delight, was purchasing an estate on the river not far above Alexandria. Nelly, pregnant with her third child, might be needing a mother's care.

"I am very uneasy at this time," she wrote brother Bartholomew in November. "I have some reason to expect that I shall make another trip to the northward—the pore General is not likely to come to see us from what I can see here . . . If I am so happy as to stay at home, I shall hope to see you and my sisters here as soon as you are at leisure. Please to give little Patty a kiss for me. I have sent her a pair of shoes . . . in a bundle for my Mamma . . . I cannot tell you more news than this. I have had no letter since he came from the camp . . ."

Her fears were realized. George was not coming home, so she would be joining him at a new place called Middlebrook. Early in December she started for Philadelphia, where George had been invited to meet with Congress. Arriving on December 17, five days before he did, though entertained at the sumptuous home of Henry Laurens, former President of Congress, and feted by her many friends, she was unhappy both for the delay and for the spirit of gay, almost wanton profligacy pervading the city. Surely there could not have been more luxury and dissipation under General Howe than now, when General Benedict Arnold was in command of the Continental forces here. When George arrived he also was scandalized by the lack of sober dedication to the cause. Congress, by now a different group from the original body, was engaged in petty quarreling, hemming and hawing, deferring, straining his patience almost beyond endurance.

"It appears to me," he wrote Jack Custis in January, "that idleness and dissipation seems to have taken such fast hold of everybody that I shall not be at all surprised if there should be a general wreck of everything."

But to win the support he must have, it was necessary to conform. For more than a month they attended dinners, teas, soirees, receptions, while he struggled to stir the reluctant Congress to action, also gave hours of his time, fuming, to sitting for his portrait by Charles Willson Peale, commissioned by the Executive Council of Pennsylvania. *Portraits, parties,* when his soldiers were not getting decent pay, when Continental currency was depreciated almost to nil, when the British were invading the south as far as Georgia, when up in the encampment his men were facing almost as much discomfort and deprivation as at Valley Forge!

It was over at last, and early in January they were at Middlebrook. Martha as usual accepted conditions as she found them. There were only two frame houses in the settlement, neither with a completed upper story. George had commissioned some of the army carpenters to finish off a room for her upstairs. Since the workmen were still there, she smilingly suggested a few improvements.

"She came into the place," one of them remembered, "a portly-looking, agreeable woman of forty-five, and said to us, 'Now, young men, I care for nothing but comfort here. Would you fit me up a buffet on one side of the room and some shelves and places for hanging clothes and storing things on the other.' We went to work with all our might. Every morning about eleven she would come up the stairs with some refreshment, and after she and the General had dined, we were called down to eat at their table. We worked very hard, nailing smooth boards over the rough and worm-eaten planks and stopping the crevices in the walls. We then consulted together how we could smooth the uneven floor and take out or cover over some of the huge black knots. On the fourth day, when she came up to see how we were getting along, we had finished the work, made the shelves, put up the pegs in the wall, built the buffet. 'Madam,' I said, 'we have endeavored to do the best we could. I hope we have suited you.' She smiled and said, 'I am astonished! Your work would do honor to an old master, and you mere lads. I am not only satisfied but highly gratified by what you have done for my comfort.' "

As with all other encampments, even terrible Valley Forge, this became home, the aides, officers and wives her "family." Kitty Greene was there with her three babies, the last one named Cornelia, also Lucy Knox, stouter and jollier than ever. Martha missed young Lafayette, who had gone to France to hasten the promised aid. In spite of worries and discouragements there were times of jollity and amusement in which even the harried Commander in Chief participated. On the first anniversary of the French alliance the Knoxes celebrated with a ball at Pluckemin which the whole countryside attended. George opened the cotillion with Lucy Knox, light-footed and graceful in spite of her rotundity. Later the Greenes entertained in their house on the Raritan, large enough for several couples to join in minuets and quadrilles. Kitty, lithe, volatile, more than a bit of a flirt, was in her element.

"Ooh! I could keep on dancing without stopping for ever so long!" she lilted.

"How long?" someone teased.

"Forever, if I had the right partner." Mischievously she turned to George, who excelled both in dancing and in endurance. He accepted the challenge, nodded to the fiddlers, motioned to another couple, and swung her into a brisk quadrille. When the second couple dropped out, exhausted, another took its place. On and on they danced, and hilarity mounted. Wagers were made as to which would drop out first. An hour passed . . . two . . .

Martha, whose dancing had barely outlasted the first hour, watched indulgently, glad that George was enjoying a surcease from worry. Fortunate, she thought, that it was he who was being paired with the glamorous Kitty instead of one of the young officers whose competition for her attention must sometimes irk her husband. Poor sober, stodgy, Quaker Nat Greene, so terribly in love with his wife, so proud of her beauty, her cleverness, yet never quite approving her bold flaunting of charm. Of course George was in his element, too, never immune to the lures of a pretty woman. But Nat would never be jealous of his idol. Three hours. It was Kitty who finally yielded, dropping with prettily appealing exhaustion into a chair, younger admirers than her partner hastening to revive her with fans and cooling drinks. Relaxed features tightening again into lines of tension, George soon took Martha home with the excuse that he still had letters to write.

She had personal worries of her own. Weeks had gone by with no word from Jack and Nelly. Where were they? At the White House, Mount Airy, or their new home near Alexandria? And the new baby due in March, this very month! She became frantic with anxiety.

"Dear children," she wrote on March 19, "I hear so very seldom from you, that I don't know where you are, or whether you intend to come to Alexandria to live this spring or not. The last letter from Nelly she says both children have been very ill; they were, she hoped, getting better. If you do not write to me I will not write again . . . Give the dear little girls a kiss from me, and tell Bett I have got a pretty new doll for her, but I don't know how to send it to her . . ."

News came soon. The new baby, Eleanor (another Nelly), had arrived on March 21. The Custises were settled in their new home, to be called Abingdon. And spring, which had come early after an almost snowless winter, infected the whole camp with new life and activity. Fruit trees were in bloom on the tenth of April. Lund wrote that on Valentine's Day the peach trees had been in bloom.

By the last of May she was at Mount Vernon, again marking time, but the summer, though filled with anxiety, was not lonely. Nelly had been ill following the birth of her little namesake, unable to nurse her. Mrs. Anderson, wife of George's English steward, had just had a baby, and Elizabeth Washington, Lund's wife, had arranged for the baby to come to Mount Vernon to be nursed. Holding the little dark-haired mite, Martha could almost believe it was Patsy returned to her, and when Nelly recovered enough to pay a long visit with Jack she found a measure of contentment. Holding little Nelly or rocking her in the cradle which had held her own four, she could almost forget the discouraging news coming from the north.

George was experiencing only disappointments and delays. Would Lafayette be successful in persuading the French to send more reinforcements, and would they arrive in time? Finances were in perilous condition, and the British had sent from New York cartloads of counterfeit Continental bills to worsen the depreciation. Hope for the reconquest of Savannah by American troops and a French fleet under the Count d'Estaing were dashed when in October the joint attack failed. He faced another winter of hardship. But the war was not lost.

He was unbeaten. He had no reason to be ashamed of his summer's campaign when on December 1 he opened winter quarters once more in Morristown.

Martha started early, for George wanted her to travel partway before the roads became bad. She arrived in Philadelphia in a snowstorm and, while waiting for orders from George, was snowbound by another blizzard which made traveling impossible until after Christmas. In spite of friends, it was a frustrating holiday, apart from her families both at home and at headquarters. It was the last of December before she arrived in Morristown.

If, for her, Christmas had been frustrating, for George it had been devastating. Waiting for huts to be built, soldiers had lain down crowded together, feet to an outdoor fire, to keep from freezing. One man set down in his journal: "Severe snow storm . . . No bread and but half allowance of rice." No mild winter this time! By early January snowdrifts were four to six feet deep, with temperatures sixteen degrees below zero. Bread had been scarce before the big storm. Now, as George put it, the soldiers "ate every kind of horse food but hay."

"Poor fellows!" Nathanael Greene wrote in a letter. "They exhibit a picture truly distressing—more than half naked and two thirds starved. A country overflowing with plenty are now suffering an Army, employed for the defence of everything that is dear and valuable, to perish for want of food."

Martha felt guilty to be housed in better quarters than they had known since Cambridge, a large white house belonging to the widow of Jacob Ford, with a parlor and office and four big bedrooms. But the site was not without danger. Far from the main encampment, it was hazardously near the British outposts, and when alarms sounded, as they sometimes did at night, George's Lifeguard posted in log huts nearby entered the house, even the bedrooms where Martha and Mrs. Ford lay buried under the covers, to take posts with their muskets at the open windows until troops from headquarters should arrive. But modesty was the least of her concerns. Not even at Valley Forge had she seen George so harassed and discouraged. General Clinton had sailed from New York with a large fleet, presumably to join the British forces at Savannah and move upward toward Charleston. There was a disheartening dearth of officers. General Benedict Arnold was being court-martialed for unwise administration of Philadelphia. Raids by British troops into New Jersey resulted in severe losses and might well have reached Morristown except for the depth of the snow. The adverse weather was of some advantage!

But the snows finally melted, giving place to sloughs of mud. Then in May came sudden hope in a letter from young Lafayette, who had arrived in Boston.

"Here I am, my dear General," he wrote with his usual ebullience, "and in the midst of the joy I feel in finding myself again one of your loving soldiers, I take but the time of telling you that I came from France on board of a fregatt which the king gave me for my passage. I have affairs of the utmost importance that I should first communicate to you alone . . ."

George wept, but they were tears of joy. Martha knew that his emotion was due almost as much to the return of this gay adventurer whom he loved like a son as to the news he might bring. He had been afraid the young Frenchman might have tired of his dedication to what seemed a hopeless cause and remain at home for good. His joy was akin to that of the prodigal's father: "This my son was dead, and is alive again. He was lost and is found." And he had returned with "affairs of the utmost importance." What were they? Just the prospect of his coming had brought a sparkle to George's eyes, lightness to his step.

They did not have long to wait. Lafayette reached Morristown on May 10. His news was indeed of the utmost importance. Six French ships and six thousand well-trained troops should arrive in America early in June. They were to participate in joint operations for the capture of New York and its defenders. His "Most Christian Majesty," King Louis XVI, had committed himself and his country to the cause of American independence.

Hope, yes. But it was still May, and the cause might well be lost before the promised help arrived. As the month progressed, with the discontent of hungry men increasing daily, the sparkle was gone from George's eyes, and the hard, stern lines in his face deepened. When on May 25 there was no meat in the camp with no prospect of any and two of his regiments were in armed, defiant mutiny, never had he been so depressed. If the other regiments joined them, it was the end of the army. Though the mutiny was suppressed temporarily, more disaster was in the offing. George was awakened late in the night of May 31 by a messenger bringing a copy of an extra edition of a newspaper.

"What is it?" asked Martha, frightened by the despair the flickering candlelight revealed. He tried to reassure her. It might not be true—perhaps it was only a rumor. But she knew he was certain that it was. Charleston had fallen, surrendered to Generals Clinton and Cornwallis with all the army's garrisons, arms, and equipment.

She saw the letter he sent to Congress along with a copy of the newspaper:

"Certain I am, unless Congress speaks in a more decisive tone; unless they are vested with powers by the several States competent to the great purposes of war, or assume them as a matter of right; and they, and the States respectively, act with more energy than they hitherto have done, that our cause is lost."

Never in all the five years had she so hated to leave him as on the day in June when she finally set out for home. He was as anxious for her safety as she was for his, for if the Carolinas fell in the wake of Charleston, Virginia would be next. But no one would have guessed when she arrived at Mount Vernon, smiling, briskly alert to every need of the eagerly welcoming household, that her calm exterior hid fears which, if revealed, might arouse distrust and further jeopardize the cause. Even to the family she was reticent about the grimmest details.

"I left the General about the middle of June," she wrote Burwell Bassett. "The last I heard from him he was going up to the North River. I got home on Friday and find myself so much fatigued with my ride that I shall not be able to come down to see you this summer and I must request you to bring Fanny up, as soon as you can. I suffered so much last winter by going late that I have determined to go early in the fall before the frost sets in. If Fanny does not come soon she will have but a short time to stay with me. We were sorry that we did not see you at camp. There was not much pleasure there, the distress of the army and other difficulties . . . The pore General was so unhappy that it distressed me exceedingly . . ."

It was well she had the comfort of young life that summer, for hope reached its nadir. Though the French arrived at Newport in July under Count de Rochambeau with a force of fifty-five hundred men, a powerful British fleet, appearing in the Sound, kept them from action.

"The flattering prospect which seemed to be opening to our view in the Month of May," George wrote bitterly, "is vanishing like the Morning Dew."

Disappointments mounted. The second division of the French fleet had been blockaded at Brest by British squadrons. General Horatio Gates, who had been sent south to protect the Carolinas, suffered total defeat in a battle with Lord Cornwallis at Camden, fleeing headlong on his horse 180 miles in three days and a half, his men retreating or scattered behind him. Now there was nothing to keep Cornwallis from invading Virginia. Martha's alarm at this news was tinctured with bitter satisfaction. Now, perhaps, people would see what kind of man George's enemies had wanted to put in his place! She felt even more bitterness, but no satisfaction, on learning that General Benedict Arnold, whom George had loved and trusted even after his court-martial, had turned traitor, arranging to give his post at West Point and his three thousand troops into British hands for the Judas price of twenty thousand pounds. She knew how George felt, suffered as if she had actually seen him shed tears when he heard the news, heard him pacing his room through the night, endlessly.

Leaving in November to join him in his winter quarters, she stopped in Philadelphia for several days, staying at the home of President Joseph Reed, whose lovely young wife had died just a few weeks before. Here she found work very much to her liking. Some of the Philadelphia women had formed an association to provide relief for the ill-clad soldiers, collecting over seventy-five hundred dollars in specie value. Lafayette had contributed five hundred in the name of his wife. Martha gladly gave a generous donation to the cause and joined wholeheartedly in the work. The Marquis de Chastellux, who had come to America with Rochambeau and was in Philadelphia at the close of November, described his visit to the home of Mrs. Bache, the daughter of Benjamin Franklin, who had succeeded Mrs. Reed as president of the association:

"She conducted me into a room filled with work lately finished by the women of Philadelphia. The work consisted neither of embroidered tambour waistcoats nor network edging, nor of gold and silver brocade. It was a quantity of shirts for the soldiers of Pennsylvania. The ladies bought the linen from their own private purses. On each shirt was the name of the lady who had made it . . . I found there Mrs. Washington, who had just arrived from Virginia and was going to stay with her husband. She is about forty, or forty-five, rather plump, but fresh and with an agreeable face."

Freshness . . . an agreeable face. Never had they seemed so welcome to the tortured Commander in Chief and his men as on the day she arrived at the camp in New Windsor on the Hudson the middle of December, cheerfully accepting an old-fashioned stone house, small and inconvenient, as her new quarters. Lucy Knox, with little Lucy and Henry, Jr., had a much bigger and better house, but George needed closer access to the river landing. Kitty had not come to camp, for Nathanael was with forces in the south. Martha was amused when she saw a note for Kitty which George added to the letters forwarded to Greene. "Mrs. Washington, who has just arrived . . . joins me in most cordial wishes for your every felicity and regrets the want of your company. Remember me to my namesake, Nat [the baby born the previous winter at Morristown]. Nat, I suppose, can handle a musket . . ."

In spite of the pervading atmosphere of gloom, Martha managed a creditable Christmas party, with beef and mutton as well as three turkeys, puddings, apples, nuts, cider, the exchange of small gifts, and an evening lightened by band music, fiddlers, dancing. The New Year was ushered in with more revelry, a thin and brittle coating for the mood of discouragement.

For Martha that year of 1781 would be a memorable one, perhaps the happiest and saddest she had ever known.

16

The new year gave no promise of being unusual. It began with the same heartaches and uncertainties which were of such win-or-lose, life-or-death import to the cause. Never had Martha seen George's spirits so low. Still, nothing, not even public apathy, could destroy his faith in the ultimate triumph of his commitment.

Martha regarded him anxiously. Six years of constant, harrowing struggle had etched deeper lines about his eyes, tightened his lips. Then came another blow, this time one that severed at one stroke the cohesion of his official "family." It happened on the afternoon of February 16, on the stairway of the small house in New Windsor, and Martha, sitting in their little parlor, overheard the whole violent exchange of words. George, deeply perplexed over the problem of getting the French commanders to send their fleet to aid Greene on the southern front, was hurrying up after taking a paper to Tench Tilghman and met his young aide Alexander Hamilton on the stairs.

"Please come to my office," he directed Hamilton in his normal tone of voice.

"Yes, sir," was the reply, "as soon as I have seen Tilghman."

George waited outside his office at the top of the stairs for what seemed an unreasonable time, and when Hamilton finally ascended, his patience was tried to the limit. His hot temper, usually under strict curb, erupted into anger. "Colonel Hamilton, you have kept me waiting at the head of the stairs these ten minutes. I must tell you, sir, you treat me with disrespect."

"I am not conscious of it, sir"—Hamilton's voice was courteous but crisp—"but since you have thought it necessary to tell me so, we part."

"Very well, sir," was the swift reply, "if it be your choice."

Martha gasped. Surely this could not be happening! But she heard Hamilton's swift steps on the stairs and the slamming of the front door. George's uncontrollable temper again! But she knew how quickly he recovered from such bouts and was relieved when he sent the distraught Tilghman to bring Hamilton back. The aide stiffly refused to come. He would continue with his duties until the chief found someone to take his place, then he would leave. Martha sighed. But she was not surprised. Hamilton was both proud and ambitious. She knew he had long chafed under an office which he considered inferior to his abilities, a mere secretary to the Commander in Chief. But—to add this personal grievance to the already intolerable burden his chief was carrying!

When Hamilton left in April to establish a law practice in Albany, Martha regretted his absence less than that of his lovely young bride Betsy, for she had come to love the cheerful, helpful girl like a daughter. She was relieved when David Humphreys returned to join the staff. Stout, jolly, a graduate of Yale who liked to write poetry, Humphreys soon filled the void left by Hamilton, without the latter's tension-rousing penchants.

April, with its burgeoning of spring outside headquarters, held only wintry bleakness within. The war had moved south with a vengeance. Arnold, the traitor, had gone with a British force to Virginia in December, where he had done much damage in the James River area and cut off supplies from Greene in the Carolinas. George had sent Lafayette with a strong detachment to the rescue. He had suffered agonies trying to persuade the French fleet at Newport to move south. A meeting with the Count de Rochambeau in March had accomplished little. Both he and Martha were desperately worried about danger to their families and friends in Virginia. News came slowly. Even Lund failed to write frequently. Concern aroused in George an almost insupportable homesickness for Mount Vernon. One evening when he and Martha were sitting together in their candlelit room, freed briefly from worrying details, he sat writing to Lund, a smile on his lips as he thought about things closest to his heart, questions he wanted answered.

"How many lambs have you had this spring? How many Colts are you like to have? Is your covered ways done? What are you going about next?" He mentioned a horse that Martha had "taken a fancy to" and urged Lund to purchase it.

Then came letters from both Lund and Lafayette which aroused not only consternation but anger almost as violent as that which had erupted against Hamilton. A British armed sloop had come up the Potomac and anchored in the river outside Mount Vernon. Some of George's slaves had fled and joined the enemy. Lund had gone aboard the vessel, taken food to the officers, and agreed to supply them with provisions, hoping that thereby he might keep them from destroying property and procure the return of the slaves.

"How could he!" George burst out furiously. "Lund—a traitor to the cause! Kowtowing to the enemy!"

Martha tried to calm him. Lund had only been trying to save Mount Vernon, she reminded. He had meant well, and—suppose it had been destroyed! Secretly she was relieved that Lund had acted just as he did.

George was still angry and wrote Lund sharply: "You ought to have considered yourself as my representative . . . To go on board their vessels; carry them refreshments; commune with a parcel of plundering scoundrels, and request a favor by asking the surrender of my Negroes, was exceedingly ill-judged, and 'tis to be feared will be unhappy in its consequences . . ."

The same day he wrote the letter, April 30, a far happier event was taking place near Mount Vernon, the birth of Jack and Nelly's fourth child, a boy, "quite hearty," wrote his mother, "and the prettiest creature in the world."

Martha could almost hear old John Custis chuckle. A male at last to carry on his precious family name! And she was delighted that the newcomer was to be christened George Washington Parke Custis. If George could not have a son of his own, surely this was the next best. Not that he was lacking namesakes! A little George Washington this or that was constantly appearing, including little George Washington Lafayette, born while his father was in France.

All family news was not so pleasant. When Benjamin Harrison, Speaker of the Virginia House, wrote George that a move was being made to provide a pension for Mary Washington, he was horrified and humiliated. Though he knew she was always pleading poverty, she had an ample income, and he had always responded to her every call for money, in fact had given Lund orders to meet her slightest need.

"Confident I am," he wrote back, "that she has not a child that would not divide the last sixpence to relieve her from *real* distress." He urged Harrison to use every means, if a bill was pending, to see that it was not passed and, if a pension had been voted, to have it withdrawn.

While lamenting his humiliation, Martha regarded this business with tongue in cheek. She keenly resented Mary Washington's lack of appreciation of his herculean task and her seeming selfishness in stressing her needs when he was under such terrific pressure.

Then suddenly it was she herself who was guilty of causing him worry, for in May she fell ill with one of her severe bilious attacks. Fortunately George was away conferring with Rochambeau when her sickness began. Everybody was helpful. Her faithful maid Oney refused to leave her side. Lucy Knox was a bulwark of strength. George Augustine, George's nephew, who had become an aide on the departure of Hamilton, was solicitously attentive. The Lifeguard scoured the countryside to bring fresh meats and vegetables . . . as if she could bear even the sight of them! Her one concern was to get well before George returned, and she did manage to drag herself from bed and sit at the table on the night of his return. But she could not spare him worry.

"Mrs. Washington has been sick for more than ten days, and still continues so," he wrote Lund. And to Jack, "She is still weak and low . . . very desirous of seeing you."

All was suddenly bustle in the camp. Decisions had been made. A joint attack was to be made in concert with the French against the British in New York. Martha must go—but where? Not to Mount Vernon. George would worry, with the Potomac in constant peril from marauders. To Philadelphia, of course, though in her weakened state the prospect of cloying and lavish entertainment from her kind friends roused only wearied dismay. George must not guess how ill she felt when near the end of June she prepared for departure. Smiling, mouthing cheerful encouragements, she sank gratefully against the cushions and as soon as they were out of sight let her stiff lips relax and the tears flow.

July. Still in Philadelphia, she was like a prisoner on a rack, being torn apart. In the north George waited with his army for the French reinforcements. In the south Cornwallis was in Williamsburg, having forced the Assembly to move to Richmond. Williamsburg, so close to her mother at Chestnut Grove, to brother Bartholomew, to the Bassetts at Eltham! Lafayette was there, of course, but with strength so puny he dared not attack. When he did risk a skirmish, it was to end in defeat near Jamestown.

Martha refused to wait longer. Defiantly, without waiting for George's consent, she started for Mount Vernon. Heaven to be back there again, to find the house intact (bless Lund for his complicity!), to sink at night into her own white-canopied bed, to rise in the morning with almost her old zest for the familiar tasks of the day!

August. And suddenly a message came which, like a refreshing summer rain, sent bursts of energy and excitement flowing through the whole estate. The master was coming! Plans in the north had changed. Instead of attacking New York, Washington was marching south to besiege Cornwallis, who for some reason had withdrawn to Yorktown. Martha did not understand what had made the change. It did not matter. He was coming, if only for a brief visit on his way south. For the first time, after six years and a half, he would be riding through the gate, entering his own house, sleeping beside her in his own bed.

September. He was on his way. He was marching through Philadelphia in a grand parade of French and Continental troops. He was in Chester rejoicing in the news that Count de Grasse had arrived in Virginia waters with a powerful fleet. He was at Head of Elk. Now he was like a racehorse scenting the aromas of home. He set such a pace that his companions decided not to keep up with him. News of his approach sped ahead to Baltimore, and he was escorted into an excited town by a Light Dragoon militia. Begrudging a night spent at Fountain Inn, he bowed to the necessity of numerous callers, a formal address, and the illumination of the whole town in his honor. The next morning, Sunday, September 9, he set off before dawn, taking only his servant Billy and one aide, David Humphreys, hoping to cover the sixty miles to his own plantation for an extra day before his French colleagues arrived.

Meanwhile Mount Vernon was plunged into an orgy of preparation. Jack and Nelly and the children came over from Abingdon. The house was scrubbed and polished and refurbished. Storehouses were almost denuded of hams, bacons, fowl, seafood supposed to last the winter. Fresh vegetables—sweet potatoes, pumpkins, corn, beans—were garnered in great baskets from the kitchen garden. The kitchen was a steaming, suffocating hothouse, kettles bubbling, spits turning, fires roaring, from morning to night. Ovens, usually fired only once a week, were swept, raked, reheated into glowing coals again and again for breads, cakes, tarts, biscuits, gingerbreads, roasted meats, enough to feed an army. Martha herself oversaw the whole process, not trusting the servants to use woods that would impart just the right flavors, hickory, pine, sassafras, red or white oak. With her own hands she put together her forty-egg cake, dividing whites from yolks, beating to a froth, working four pounds of butter to a cream and adding the whites a spoonful at a time, then putting in four pounds of sugar finely powdered, adding the yolks and five pounds of flour and five pounds of fruit, measuring the flavorings with meticulous precision, half an ounce of mace, one nutmeg, half a pint of wine and some French brandy.

Six years and four months. So much had happened! He had never seen the completed wings, climbed the stairs to the new bedroom, inspected his study. And the north wing, the spacious dining hall, still unfinished but built to his specifications . . . would he approve of it all? Lund was more nervous than Martha, for the construction had been his responsibility and well he knew the keen scrutiny of that eagle blue eye. Had he followed the copious directions exactly? "The chimney of the new room should be exactly in the middle of it—the doors and everything else to be exactly answerable and uniform—in short I would have the whole executed in a masterly manner." The farms, too. Lund was thorough but easygoing. He felt like a bungling pupil submitting to his stern teacher a smudged copybook.

Martha was almost glad Pohick Church had been closed for some years, most of its leaders being away and the beloved Lee Massey having resigned as rector in 1777. On this exciting day she certainly could not properly have listened to a long sermon. But dutifully she shut herself in her room as usual in the morning and read nothing but psalms of thanksgiving.

The sun was sending long shadows across the Bowling Green when the servant watching at the western gate came running. "Massa—he come!" Martha's heart raced as she stood in the door and watched him, spurring his horse ahead of his two attendants, riding along the road suddenly lined with cheering, laughing, sobbing welcomers both black and white, dismounting, then, as she ran to meet him, folding her in his long, strong arms, nearly crushing the breath from her body.

The next hours moved like the bright, shifting colors of a kaleidoscope. A sumptuous but intimate meal in the small dining room. Martha was glad he had brought only Colonel Humphreys, who was friendly and informal. Admiration of the four children he had never seen before: grave five-year-old Eliza, wide-eyed Patty, Nelly, already at two giving promise of her mother's dark-eyed beauty, chubby five-months-old "Little Wash." Hasty inspection of the new wings and, yes, to Lund's relief, at least tentative approval. Yet even tonight he was more General than excited homecomer. Before retiring he and Humphreys prepared a letter for Peter Wagener, the County Lieutenant, instructing him to muster the county militia for work on the roads. His men must not run the risk of wallowing in mud or sand. But at last there was the closing of the bedroom door at the top of the new flight of stairs, the blowing out of the candles, an ending to the long nights of loneliness.

The next morning he was all General. Even his brief ride over the farms elicited only mild criticisms and cursory comments. Already his mind was elsewhere, with the troops marching behind, the operations ahead. He made plans, wrote innumerable orders. For the entertainment of the huge company en route, including French nobility, he left the details entirely to Martha and her staff, fully trusting her competence. Though she worked tirelessly, she was buoyed by the hope and confidence that exuded from George's every word and action. For the first time in months—years—the lines of tension were erased from his face. His eyes were afire with the anticipation of victory.

Cornwallis, it was explained, had enclosed himself with nearly nine thousand British soldiers in a trap down at Yorktown. Lafayette and other Continental troops had him shut in by land. A French fleet was on its way to cut them off at sea. All that remained was for the combined forces to squeeze the pincers tight and enforce his surrender. Was it possible that the terrible war was actually near its end?

George's official family arrived at mealtime and were heartily approving of the preparations. Some must have marveled that the gracious mistress of this luxury and abundance could have just as graciously presided over the meager facilities at New Windsor and Valley Forge.

Count de Rochambeau arrived with his aides that evening and was served a sumptuous dinner. Chastellux and his staff came the next day. All were obviously impressed.

Martha's euphoria was suddenly assailed by a new worry. Jack was insisting on accompanying George on this final—it was hoped—campaign. Through all the six years she and Nelly had been relieved when George yielded to their pleas that he should not be pressed into military service, though they knew Jack had chafed under the restraint. As a member of the Virginia Assembly, they had argued, he was making his valuable contribution. But now he was both voluble and insistent: he must be in on this hoped-for triumph. He had no uniform, so, reluctantly, Martha fitted him with a wide ribbon which, worn over his dark blue coat, would mark him as one of the General's aides. She was even more worried because he had been unwell for several days. She and Nelly saw him ride away on the morning of September 12, his body servant beside him in the Custis livery, with Tilghman, Humphreys, and George's other aides. Only when they reached the west gate and Jack turned for a final wave did they yield to tears.

It was a month before they heard from him, but the letter they received was reassuring: "My Dear and Hond. Madam, I have the pleasure to inform you that I find Myself much better since I left Mt. Vernon, notwithstanding the change in my Lodging, and that the General tho in constant Fatigue looks very well; I staid a Night with my uncle in my way down, and had the pleasure to find him and Family in good Health, likewise of seeing my Grandmother . . ."

Days passed. The suspense was almost unbearable. There were rumors, some good, some bad, and letters. It was a time of interminable waiting, both at Mount Vernon and at the encampments of troops, moving slowly but inexorably toward Yorktown. There was waiting for heavy artillery, for the arrival of the French fleet under Count de Grasse, moving from the north, and another French General named Barras from the south. George was cannily refusing to attack before all was ready, preferring the slow but more certain technique of siege.

News came. At Mount Vernon they could almost see things happening, like pictures thrown in color on a wall. Alexander Hamilton, now in the blaze of military glory he had so desired, flaunting his battalion of light infantry atop a parapet in full view of the British. (Martha could just see him, cool, daring, impulsive, always inclined to a bit of swagger.) George surprising the enemy with a huge iron monster of a gun which thundered sixteen pounds of ammunition into Yorktown. De Grasse, the giant Frenchman, so huge that he called six-foot-two George "my little general," tightening the trap with his tall-masted ships. The gallant Rochambeau, whose name sounded to Yankee ears like an encouraging "Rush on, boys!", leading his French troops in perfect synchrony with the Continentals. George's men boring inexorably toward the enemy's redoubts with all-night digging of trenches. Then after days of furious fighting, on the morning of October 17, the beat of a drum and a British officer appearing on a parapet waving a white handkerchief.

"I never heard a drum equal to it," one soldier said. "The most delightful music to us all."

The joyful sound reechoed all the way to Mount Vernon. Surrender! Was it true? Until she actually heard the good news from George, Martha refused to permit celebration.

The letter came, brought by a messenger pounding through the gate and down the drive, holding aloft like a banner the sealed missive and shouting as he came. She broke the seal with trembling fingers. It contained the substance of a document which George was sending Congress and which he had been struggling over six years for the opportunity to write:

"I have the honor to inform Congress, that a Reduction of the British Army under the command of Lord Cornwallis, is most happily effected. The unremitting Army in this Occasion, has principally led to this Important Event, at an earlier period than my most sanguine Hope had induced me to expect."

Martha rushed toward the stairs to take the good news to Nelly, still in her room, then stopped, realizing she had not finished the letter. As she read on the joyous excitement turned to dismay, and she clutched the sturdy newel-post to steady herself. Jack was sick. He had caught a bad cold but had insisted on being present at the scene of triumph. Too ill to mount a horse, he had viewed the thrilling performance from a carriage. Since he had developed a slight fever, probably nothing more than a touch of camp fever, George had thought best to send him to Eltham. His close friend and camp physician, Dr. Craik, had gone with him. The illness was probably not serious. However, he would advise both Martha and Nelly to go to him as soon as possible.

Again Martha started to rush up the stairs, stumbling in her haste. "Camp fever . . . probably not serious." She knew better. In the encampments she had stood over cots smoothing dry, hot brows, patted hands that burned like fire, listened to the ravings of delirium, even helped pull a tattered blanket over one still form. Oh, yes, she knew what camp fever could be like. By the time she reached Nelly's room she had stopped trembling and was able to smile. Jack had taken a bad cold, she said, and Papa had sent him to Eltham. He thought they might like to go to him.

Nelly's first alarm subsided before Martha's calmness. "Yes—oh, yes, we must go."

Trunks were hastily packed, the chariot outfitted. Eliza, now five, would go with them; the other children would be left with Nurse Molly and Mrs. Lund. They were off within an hour.

Martha's heart sank when she saw Jack and Dr. Craik's grave face. It was all she could do to hide her fears from Nelly. The following days were an increasing nightmare.

"He—he doesn't even know me," sobbed Nelly. "He called me— Patsy."

"I know," comforted Martha. "He's not himself, thinks he's a child with his sister." At least, she thought, he had a comfortable bed to lie in, a loving wife beside him, not like those other mothers' sons, and, yes, there would be a whole clean blanket to pull up over him when the fever cooled and the delirious babblings ceased.

Dr. Craik drew her aside. He looked haggard, for he had scarcely slept an hour during the grueling siege. Martha knew he had done all he could, performed much bloodletting to reduce fever, purged, blistered, given tar-water, ginseng, ipecac.

"I think it's time the General should be told," he said wearily, "just in case . . ."

"Yes," said Martha. George was at his headquarters in Williamsburg. Knowing his tremendous task in completing negotiations, she had hesitated to burden him with family concerns, but now she sent a message by express messenger begging him to come. He did so, in record time, leaving Williamsburg late at night on November 5, bringing only his aide Humphreys and his faithful servant Billy. He was almost too late, for Jack died within a few hours of his arrival.

Martha grieved, of course. She shed many tears. *Rachel,* she thought, *weeping for her children*. For they were all gone now, the four of them, the two little ones, lovely sixteen-year-old Patsy, and now her handsome, promising Jack, sometimes wayward but always gay, genial, and, oh, so lovable. Yet she must not spend time in selfish grieving. There was Nelly, so young to sorrow, almost the age she had been when she had lost Daniel. Youth was a time for weeping. It was the young, tender plant that needed succoring, protection from storm and wind. She needed all her strength to comfort Nelly and the children. And there was George. His hour of victory must not be sullied by feelings of guilt because he had let the boy go with him against her will, or by worries about her sorrowful brooding. His growing surprise and relief over her rallying from grief was evidenced in his correspondence.

"Poor Mrs. Washington," he wrote Nathanael Greene on December 15, "has met with a most severe stroke in the loss of her amiable Son, and only Child Mr. Custis."

But on Christmas Day he wrote again, "Mrs. Washington is better than I could have expected after the Heavy loss she met with."

To her distress she discovered that the war was not over. Though Cornwallis's defeat had been a major triumph, British forces still held Charleston and New York. Somehow she had believed they could return immediately to Mount Vernon. No. Another winter at headquarters. After Jack was buried in the garden at Eltham, she and Nelly and Eliza, with George riding beside them, proceeded to Mount Vernon. They stopped in Fredericksburg to see Mary Washington, but Martha was almost relieved to find that she had gone "over the mountains" on a visit. She still felt awed in the presence of George's strong-willed mother, and she could not forgive her for embarrassing her son by her claims of neglect and poverty. It was Wednesday, November 13, when they arrived home and, during the short week he could stay, time for affairs of the estate was interrupted by accolades of congratulation from Congress, friends, neighbors, newspaper encomiums, official visitors. He must go to consult with Congress in Philadelphia, then go into camp.

"You know you need not go with me this time, Patsy. I suppose Nelly and the children need you. And I know how hard things are for you in camp."

"Do you want me to go?" She scanned his features anxiously.

"Would it be easier for you if you didn't have to bother about all those arrangements for my comfort?"

"No!" The look on his face would have been answer enough. "Of course I want you. The camp is a sorry place without you."

She nodded, satisfied, and began her hasty preparations for departure. They arrived in Philadelphia on November 26 after a journey of almost royal acclaim. While George smarted under the constant display of admiration, Martha enjoyed it, as long as it was directed at him instead of herself.

"Arrived in the city," the *Pennsylvania Journal* of November 28 recorded, "His Excellency General Washington, our victorious and illustrious Commander in Chief and his lady. All panegyrick is vain, and language too feeble to express our ideas of his greatness."

"You'd think I subdued Cornwallis all by myself," fumed George, "instead of practically looking on while others did it. And they'd better wait till the war is over before they boast of victory."

Congress as usual was being slow and uncooperative. All through December, January, February, George struggled to secure the action so sorely needed. It was late March before they were able to leave for camp at Newburgh on the Hudson. Was he more amused or annoyed by the letter he received from his mother just before leaving Philadelphia? Martha could not tell.

"My dear Georg," Mary had written on March 13, "I was truly unesy by Not being at hom when you went thru fredirceksburg it was a unlucky thing for me now I am afraid I Never Shall have that pleasure agin I am soe very unwell this trip over the Mountins has almost kill'd me I gott the 2 five ginnes you was soe kind to send me i am greatly obliged to you for it i was greatly shocht ever be driven up this way agin but will goe in some little hous of my one if it is only twelve foot squar . . ." Evidently she wanted George to build her another house "over the mountains," but why she should need to leave her comfortable home which he had provided for her or need more assurance that he would supply her needs wherever she was, Martha could not understand. Neither did George, apparently, for he put the letter away without answering it, merely labeling it, "Mrs. Mary Washington 13 Mar. 1782."

It was well Martha did not know that she would spend more time in the Newburgh headquarters than in any other camp. Surely it would all soon be over and they would be back home. Their house was small but comfortable, its seven rooms all on one floor. The living room, to her amusement, had seven doors and one window. The Knoxes were there in a house some distance away, and Martha, as well as Lucy, managed to entertain creditably in spite of grave deficiencies.

Dutifully she participated in the various social events, including a gala celebration at West Point of the birth of the Dauphin of France. Sailing with George down the river in a barge decorated with flowers and laurel wreaths, she witnessed a grand parade, attended an elaborate dinner with five hundred guests in a huge arbor, with a ball afterward. But such events were only necessary and unimportant diversions. Her deep concern was for George and his devastating uncertainty.

Was it to be war or peace? The King's speech at the opening of Parliament in February had showed determination to continue the war, but all in Britain were not agreed. Lord North, it was reported, on receipt of the stunning news of Cornwallis's surrender, had paced his room exclaiming wildly, "Oh God, it's all over! it's all over!" Even though in March Parliament had agreed to a cessation of hostilities and appointed a commission to treat for peace, George was not convinced.

"The enemy," he wrote Chastellux, "talk loudly, and very confidently of peace; but whether they are in earnest, or whether it is to amuse and while away the time till they can prepare for a more vigorous prosecution of the war, time will evince."

Instead of lightening his burdens, prospect of peace seemed to have increased them. In spite of the Articles of Confederation which had been finally ratified that very month by Maryland, the last dissentient, there was no central government powerful enough to force the states to action. His army was incensed. No provision had been made for their promised pay. There was threat of mutiny. The country seemed steeped in lethargy.

Also there were personal worries. His brother Samuel had died, leaving children by his five marriages. "How," George wrote John Augustine, "in God's name, how did my brother Samuel contrive to get himself so enormously in debt?" Mary Washington was complaining about her cheating overseer. Fielding Lewis had died, having expended his energies and much of his fortune in the cause of independence. Bartholomew Dandridge, asked to become guardian of Nelly's children, was reluctant to assume the responsibility. And Jack's financial affairs were in a hopeless muddle. Must he fight not only his country's battles but those of every individual?

There was worse shock to come. About two months after their arrival in Newburgh he received a letter from Colonel Lewis Nicola, one of his oldest and most respected officers. It was only to Martha that he vented his outrage. The letter proposed, or at least implied, that in order to end the paralysis which seemed to benumb the country's weak and incompetent republics, George should suffer his willing army to declare him *King!* Martha had never seen him so hurt or angry.

"Fool!" he blustered. "What do men think I am, an adventurer, wanting to make myself powerful, sacrificing the very principles we've been fighting for?"

He sat down and dashed off a blistering denunciation of the idea. "Be assured, sir, no occurrence in the course of the war has given me more painful sensations than your information of there being such ideas existing in the army . . . If I am not deceived in the knowledge of myself, you could not have found a person to whom your schemes are more disagreeable."

Yet he well knew the injustices festering such an appalling solution. That those who had given their all, suffered hunger, nakedness, peril of death, should be left penniless, threatened with being turned adrift with no hope of security? He would do everything possible to win justice for these men whom he loved better than himself, write hundreds of letters, urge the states and Congress to take action, harangue people right and left—everything except jeopardize the democratic principles he had fought for.

Back at Mount Vernon in July, Martha shared at a distance all his tortures of suspense. She was glad to return to Newburgh in late November, even though it meant an end to the hope of an early peace. At least she could share all the uncertainty firsthand.

George was as much tortured by the action of his men as by the inaction of the enemy, yet he could not blame them. They needed pay, and Congress was making little effort to raise money. The new commercial elements which had come into power, with business and fortunes growing, wanted to disperse the army without responsibility. No wonder the men were in a spirit of mutiny. Yet somehow he must stop them. Calling his officers together, he sternly denounced the influences inciting them to violence and assured them of his support. But it was personal loyalty to him that quelled the incipient rebellion. Attempting to read a letter from a sympathetic member of Congress, he stumbled over the words. Reaching into his pocket, he took out his new spectacles and with fumbling fingers put them on. "Gentlemen," he said, "you must pardon me. I have grown gray in your service and now find myself growing blind."

Martha wept a little when she was told of this incident. It was true. The years of struggle had taken their toll. He was looking old. Though heavier in body due to long, sedentary hours at his desk, he was haggard in the face. His light-brown hair was turning gray, and endless writing had so dimmed his blue eyes that his pen, she noticed, often slipped over the edge of the paper. But his shoulders remained square and straight, his stance that of an athlete, and always his uniform of buff and blue was immaculate.

Tension was eased when, in March, Congress passed measures providing for rewards for the troops. But peace negotiations dragged on. There was rejoicing when news came that a pact had been signed in Paris, but it was inconclusive. However, the news was confirmed by the end of March, coming by the ship *Triomphe*, sent by Count d'Estaing at the request of Lafayette. A fitting name, *Triomphe!* Surely now, thought Martha, we can go home. But no. The treaty had not yet arrived in America. The British had not left New York. A thousand duties must be discharged before George could even disband the army.

Summer brought one pleasant surprise. Friends in England were now free to write again, and a letter came from George William Fairfax. "My gratitude to heaven exceeds all description. I glory in being called an American. During the war I frequently did myself the honor of addressing a line to you, some of which I hope kissed your hand, others I know were intercepted and sent to the Minister, one of which had like to have cost me dear . . . I every moment expected a messenger to take me into custody. But times are altered, and I am now as much courted as I was before despised as an American." Sally was alive, he said, and was improving in health. Was she still as passionately loyal to the King, wondered Martha, as during the hot arguments around the table?

George hastened to reply. He hoped they would now think of returning to America and that they would make Mount Vernon their home until Belvoir, which had burned to the ground, could be rebuilt.

Martha asked herself, did she want them to return? Was it news of Sally or confirmation of George William's loyalty which seemed suddenly to rejuvenate him? Strange, stupid, to feel a stab of jealousy after all these years, and yet—she hoped they would not return.

In August they moved to an estate named Rocky Hill to be near Congress, which was in session at Princeton. To George's annoyance Congress acted as if peace were actually a reality, though terms of the treaty had not yet arrived. To his greater annoyance he discovered that they had voted an equestrian statue to be erected of him at the permanent seat of government. It was to be executed by the best artist in Europe under the direction of the minister of the country at Versailles, Benjamin Franklin.

"Imagine!" he told her wryly. "They want me represented in Roman dress, holding a truncheon in my right hand, a laurel wreath around my head. On the marble pedestal is to be represented the evacuation of Boston, capture of the Hessians at Trenton, the battle of Princeton, the surrender at Yorktown! You'd think I was another Caesar instead of a simple American who had tried to win freedom for his country."

Martha sympathized, while secretly taking pride in the honors being showered on him. Always he resented any form of adulation which smacked of royalty.

At last, on November 2, it came, news that the definitive treaty of peace had been signed on the third of September. PEACE. The final negotiations had taken so long that for some it came almost as an anticlimax. Not for Martha. When she left for Mount Vernon George riding with her in the chariot as far as Trenton, six wagonloads of papers and furnishings in their wake along with several aides and a led saddle horse for his return journey, she felt like a bride facing her honeymoon. For the first time in eight years she saw him ride away without reluctance, without fear that she would never see him again. The years of separation were over. Surely he would be home before Christmas. Already he was making plans for the new uninterrupted life together, ordering necessary household items for neighborhood entertaining, glasses for water and other beverages, silverware, a complete set of blue and white china, besides tools for the farm and books, including a French-English dictionary.

The weeks of waiting both crawled and flew. The British finally evacuated New York on November 25. The army was disbanded by order of Congress. On December 4 George parted from his officers at Fraunces Tavern in New York, a moving experience, his voice choking during his informal speech. "With a heart full of love and gratitude I now take leave of you. I most devoutly wish that your later days may be as prosperous and happy as your former ones have been glorious and honorable."

All, General Knox leading, shook his hand and received his embrace, weeping. Martha herself shed tears when David Humphreys described it to her. She pictured him leaving the tavern, raising his arm in a silent farewell, passing along the street, his officers behind him, space filled with crowds every inch of the way, features drawn taut to hide his emotion, approaching the wharf, climbing into the barge made ready for him.

Now he must go on to Annapolis, where Congress was meeting, to resign his commission. He arrived there Friday, December 19, to be feted at a grand ball. On the twenty-third he entered the old State House and in the presence of a huge crowd presented his resignation. Again he was stirred with emotion, having to grip his paper hard with both hands in order to finish reading it.

"I consider it an indispensable duty to close this last solemn act of my official life by commending the Interests of our dearest Country to the protection of Almighty God, and those who have the superintendence of them, to his holy keeping."

The days were too long . . . and too short. So much to do for this, his first Christmas at home in eight years! Nelly came from Abingdon with the four children. Cannily Martha noted the telltale yet secretive excitement which replaced the somber listlessness of Nelly's pretty face. So—Lund had been right in writing that the young widow was showing an interest in their neighbor Dr. David Stuart, a respected widower with four children. Lund seemed of the opinion that two years were too short a time for a woman to cease mourning for her husband and suggested that George might wish to interfere. He and Martha had exchanged amused smiles, not forgetting that less than a year after Daniel's death she had accepted his proposal of marriage. George had written Lund with his usual wise, good-natured tact.

"For my part I never did, nor do I believe I ever shall, give advice to a woman who is setting out on a matrimonial voyage; first because I never could advise one to marry without her own consent, and secondly because I know it is to no purpose to advise her to refrain when she has obtained it. A woman very rarely asks an opinion or requires advice on such an occasion until her resolution is fixed; and then it is with the hope and expectation of obtaining a sanction, not that she means to be governed by your disapprobation, that she applies . . ." George, Martha conceded, had a profound knowledge of the ways of women, gleaned, she thought wryly, from wide experience.

December 24. It was a beautiful day, autumn-mild. All was in readiness. The bedrooms were sheeted and blanketed for guests, fires laid on all the hearths. The house gleamed. Even the brass lantern in the hall, relic of Lawrence Washington's campaign in the Indies and one of George's prized possessions, had been freshly polished. Pantries were stocked to the ceilings with pies, cakes, puddings, jellies, candied fruits, nuts. Out in the kitchens spits were turning, ovens glowing, kettles steaming, and sweating servants, bared to the waist, black skins gleaming in the firelight, chattered and sang ditties with more than usual holiday excitement. In the new dining room a long table was laid with linen and crystal and silver which had been laid away, some of it hidden in barrels, for eight long years. Old Bishop, smartly dressed in his outmoded British scarlet uniform, had been watching at the western gate for hours, vying to be first to welcome the master.

But—would he come, as promised, in time for Christmas? Knowing how many things and people might detain him, Martha could not be sure. Yesterday he would have delivered his commission to Congress, and it was a long way from Annapolis. She could not know that he had had horses waiting at the State House door, so that after the noon ceremony, by one o'clock if possible, he could start for Mount Vernon. Once by desperate riding he had covered the distance in a single day. Impossible now with their late start, but, stopping overnight at an ordinary, they were off early on the twenty-fourth, riding hard, brooking no delays, passing homes of friends he would normally have visited.

It was late in the afternoon, dusk, when Martha heard a great commotion outside, shouts, servants running from all directions. She stood in the door and watched him come, his beautiful chestnut charger Nelson speeding ahead of his companions as if sensing the urgency of his rider and proudly conscious of the majestic picture they both made. Then he was there, and his arms were around her.

Christmas Day. It was exciting from the time they rose long before dawn. George shaved and dressed without assistance as usual, Billy having laid out his clothes the night before. He busied himself with correspondence until sunrise, when old Bishop came with his pretty daughter to bring greetings, sure of finding both master and mistress up. After visiting the stables George returned for breakfast, eating only his usual Indian cakes, honey and tea while the rest of the family, aides, and guests partook of Martha's sumptuous meal. Then came the servants, those from the house, the stables, the farms, in all perhaps one hundred and fifty of them, all dressed in their best, to bring their greetings and receive gifts of a shilling apiece. There were precious moments with the children as they slowly conquered their first awe of the tall, imposing stranger who was to be called "Grandpapa," who was soon hoisting them to his broad shoulders and eliciting squeals of delight from them over the gifts he had brought, a locket, sashes, caps and hats, children's books, a whirligig, a fiddle, quadrille boxes.

Now, at three o'clock dinner, Martha sat beside him, as was their custom, at the foot of the long table, comely but matronly in her low-cut gown of blue and white brocade over a blue gauze petticoat, powdered hair dressed high according to the prevailing fashion and crowned with a cap of fluted lace. Old finery, to be sure, saved from the era before her rigid adherence to homespun. No longer need to defy the British! Last night in the new bedroom George had removed his uniform, the blue coat with its buff-colored facings and large gilt buttons, rich epaulettes on each shoulder, the buff waistcoat and breeches, the gorget with its crescent-shaped jewel, the ivory-handled sword in its black leather scabbard with silver mountings. They would pack them away, he told her, smiling. He would have no use for them again.

She looked about her with a satisfaction she had not felt for eight years . . . David Humphreys at the head of the table carving the turkey as skillfully as he wielded a poet's or secretary's pen, the long rows of family, other aides, guests, the spaces in their midst groaning under the burden of festive foods—roast pig, boiled leg of lamb, roasted fowls, beef, fish, venison, ducks, a dozen different vegetables, pickles, jellies, pies, puddings—all fruits of the land, their own land, part of the country which George had helped make free at last. Under the damask cloth his huge hand reached for her small one and held it.

Eight years. They were over now, the terrible winters, the lonely summers, the droning drums, the guns, the killing, the dying. They were home together. This was the way life should be, *would* be, as long as they both lived. Nothing should take them away from it again. Nothing.

17

Yes, life was as it should be, the prospect of days, months, years following each other in beautiful, predictable routine, like the flowing of the river through the succession of the seasons. At least it started out that way.

Even the weather cooperated. The balm of Christmas was short-lived. Deep snow and bitter cold kept them nearly housebound for the next six weeks, ensuring a family intimacy uninterrupted by the constant influx of visitors which was soon to follow. Humphreys and Smith and Walker, George's aides, had time to help in the arrangement of his voluminous papers as well as necessary correspondence. When desk work palled even snow and cold could not keep them indoors and, while George busied himself at barns, kennels, storehouses, the aides set off on well-traveled paths for their daily exercise. Colonel Smith, who did not share Hendricks's poetic fervor for "cerulean ice" and "virgin snows," preferred to go his own way, and on one of these exploring sallies he had an unfortunate adventure.

Near the snug little cabin which had been built for the pampered old servant Bishop, the latter's pretty daughter Sarah was milking. Seeing her attempt to lift the heavy, brimming pail, the courtly young Colonel sprang to assist her. Primed by her father to be wary of strange men, especially those in military garb, she uttered a piercing scream, dropped the pail, thereby spattering him from head to foot, and ran for the cabin. Old Bishop, too deaf or obtuse to listen to the Colonel's embarrassed explanations, roared his indignation: "I'm a-goin' to tell the General! Yes, and I'm a'goin to tell the madam too, she what as good as raised my child!"

Facing the slammed door, Smith was horrified. He could not face the mirthful ridicule, good-natured though it would be, if his embarrassment was made public. And that teaser Humphreys would probably write a long poem blazoning his misadventure to high heaven! He went to his friend Billy and begged assistance.

He got it. Billy met Bishop, splendid in his red British uniform, proceeding to the mansion to seek redress for his daughter's injured innocence. He managed to persuade the irate old man that his suspicions of lechery were unfounded, and he returned home mollified. Colonel Smith gave Billy a guinea and carefully avoided the area in the future.

Of course George and Martha heard of the episode and chuckled over it, but the sensitive Smith was permitted to nurse his embarrassment in private. As soon as the roads were open at the end of February the aides left, each with a hundred-dollar bonus from George to help them find new civilian careers. Like all the rest of his men, they had received but niggardly pay for their services.

It was almost history repeating itself, thought Martha, a replay of her first coming to Mount Vernon. Now, as then, there were countless new details of housekeeping to be mastered, building improvements in process, people she had never met before having to be entertained. And, most significant reminder of all, there were two small children almost exactly the ages her own had been when she had come here as a bride. For early in the year Jack's widow had married Dr. David Stuart and had accepted George's offer to adopt the two youngest children, so Nelly, almost four, and little George Washington Custis, not quite two, were permanent members of the family. The two older girls, Betsy and Patty, spent almost as much time at Mount Vernon as at Abingdon or Hope Park, Stuart's estate. Was she really a grandmother, Martha sometimes marveled, fifty-two years old, too plump and, she feared, a bit dumpy-looking? Often these days she felt like a young mother again, just arrived here with these two babies, lovely, delicate Nelly so like Patsy, bouncing, saucy little "Wash," so like her own Jacky. George too, in spite of problems with a run-down plantation, needy relatives, lack of ready cash, seemed to have experienced a renewal of youth.

"At length, my dear Marquis," he wrote Lafayette soon after their return, "I am become a private citizen on the banks of the Potomac and under the shadow of my own Vine and my own Fig-tree; free from the bustle of a camp and the busy scenes of public life, I am solacing myself with these tranquil enjoyments of which the Soldier, who is ever in pursuit of fame, the Statesman whose watchful days and sleepless nights are spent in devising schemes to promote the welfare of his own, and the ruin of other countries, as if this globe was insufficient for us all, and the Courier who is always watching the countenance of his Prince in hopes of catching a gracious smile, can have very little conception . . . Envious of none, I am determined to be pleased with all; and this, my dear friend, being the order for my march, I will move gently down the stream of life until I sleep with my fathers . . ."

Martha begrudged the time spent in late February visiting George's mother and sister in Fredericksburg, especially since it burdened him with new worries. Fielding Lewis had mortgaged his property, Millbank, to finance the gun factory which had contributed heavily to the war, and Betty was afraid she would have to sell her home. She was deeply in debt. She hoped to save the house by selling some land and starting a school for small children. George, of course, promised to help with the payments. Martha was less sympathetic with Mary who, in spite of her comfortable house near Betty's with its well-furnished rooms, its lovely mantels, its wide, pleasant porch overlooking the box-hedged garden, her tidy income from George's farm across the river, her neat phaeton which he had given her to ride about in, was as usual complaining of poverty. George gave her ten guineas, more than he could afford.

"Yet I am viewed as a delinquent," he remarked wryly as they drove back in relief to Millbank, "and considered perhaps by the world as an unjust and undutiful son."

Never had Martha so welcomed the coming of spring. Farther north it arrived with seeming reluctance. Here it burst into a sudden glorious profligacy of new life. Or perhaps it just seemed to do so, she was so glad to be home again to stay. She rejoiced in every fresh sign of emerging color, buds swelling and tender leaves unfolding, apple and peach and cherry blossoms in a profusion of pinks and creams, tulips and daffodils in a riot of bloom, bees swarming, the red buds and lilacs great masses of lavender. Windows were flung open to let in the fresh scents and blow out the musty smells of winter. The washhouse worked overtime filling lines with curtains, sheets, blankets. And once more the house was turned upside down for spring cleaning.

"We are much in want of mops and clamps and scouring brushes," she wrote a merchant friend in Philadelphia. "Will you get me 6 of each and two cloaths baskets, 1 larger than the other."

George also was ordering merchandise from Philadelphia, for he still considered British sources out of bounds for an American citizen. His order this year contained both personal items and materials for finishing the house, including wallpaper with seventy yards of gilded papier-mâché border and eighteen Windsor chairs.

No wonder there was need of more Windsor chairs for the new piazza or that the washhouse was working overtime these days, turning out huge basket loads of sheets, blankets, towels, napery, as well as the usual daily quota of shirts, pants, petticoats, and other clothing! For spring produced a burgeoning of human as well as plant and animal life. Visitors poured in, not only the usual influx of neighbors but also friends from afar, strangers, statesmen, soldiers, inventors, merchants, sculptors, painters, preachers, people they had never heard of. George's dream of becoming once more a simple country squire was doomed. He was not only a national but also a world-renowned hero. Though dismayed, he accepted the increasing burden with his usual insistence on hospitality.

"My manner of living is plain," he wrote a friend, "and I do not mean to be put out by it. A glass of wine and a bit of mutton are always ready, and such as will be content to partake of them are always welcome. Those who expect more will be disappointed."

Overly humble words to describe the comfort and plenty of the household, yet all, family and guests, titled peer or shabby countryman, were served the same "simple" fare.

"Everything has an air of simplicity in his house," wrote the young French traveler, Brissot de Warville. "His table is good but not ostentatious; and no deviation is seen from regularity and domestic economy. Mrs. Washington superintends the whole, and joins to the qualities of an excellent housewife, that simple dignity which ought to characterize a woman whose husband has acted the greatest part on the theatre of human affairs; while she possesses that amenity, and manifests that attention to strangers, which renders hospitality so charming."

In April the Chevalier de la Luzerne described George as a "gray-coated farmer, nothing in his surroundings recalling the important part he had played in his country's history except a large number of guests, native and foreign."

In June there came a New England clergyman, William Gordon, who was writing an ambitious history of the Revolution. He stayed three weeks, working from morning till night making transcripts of George's wartime papers and developing a curious intimacy with little Wash, whose chubbiness had earned him the good-natured nickname of "Mr. Tub." In subsequent correspondence with Gordon George made humorous reference to this friendship, noting that "your friend Tub is as fat and saucy as ever," and, later, "Your young friend is in high health, and as full of spirits as an egg shell is of meat. I informed him I was going to write to you and desired to know if he had any commands; his spontaneous answer, I beg he will make haste and come here again." Already, at age three, George Washington Parke Custis was giving promise of the affability and facility of expression which would one day serve him well as lawyer and justice of the Supreme Court.

The most welcome guest of all that summer was the Marquis de Lafayette, who came in August on a tour to renew old friendships. Martha had invited his wife to come with him and, hopefully, bring her little daughter Virginie and baby George Washington Lafayette, but the Marchioness regretted that she dared not face the terrors of the ocean and invited Martha to Paris. "Thank her," Martha had instructed George, "and tell her I am too advanced in years and too much immersed in the care of the children to cross the Atlantic."

But she reveled in the visit of the gay young cavalier whom, like George, she loved almost as a son. They spent long evenings about her tea table in the coolness of the piazza talking of war experiences and old comrades. His presence charged the whole household with contagious excitement, like a brisk ocean breeze dispelling the sluggish August heat. The children wept to see him depart on his tour. When the Marquis returned in November before leaving for France, George accompanied him as far as Annapolis, where they attended a ball in his honor. George seemed unusually sad on his return. He shared with Martha the letter he wrote Lafayette soon afterward:

"I often asked myself, as our carriage distended, whether that was the last sight I should have of you? And tho' I wished to say no, my fears answered yes. I called to mind the days of my youth and found they had long since fled to return no more; that I was now descending the hill that I had been 52 years climbing, and that tho I was blessed with a good constitution, I was of a short-lived family, and might soon expect to be entombed in the dreary mansion of my fathers. These things darkened the shades and gave a gloom to the picture, consequently to my prospects of seeing you again; but I will not repine, I have had my day . . ."

"Pooh!" Martha felt like saying, but she kept her amusement to herself. Descending the hill . . . soon expect to be entombed! Never had she seen him so vitally alive, so immersed in varied interests and activities, building shelves in his study for his books and archives, finishing the new dining room, planning a better floor for the piazza with flagstones ordered from England, building a new barn and greenhouse, superintending the work on his five farms, digging a dry well to store ice, planting trees and shrubs to enclose the bowling green, experimenting with new crops, and, most ambitious of all, promoting a scheme to open the western country to trade and settlement by means of inland navigation. He made a trip west to explore possibilities.

A man who had "had his day" indeed! It was Martha, wearied with the burdens of constant entertaining in addition to her usual duties of housekeeping and attendance on the servants, who succumbed to illness during his absence. The old bilious fever again, and, as if in sympathy, both children, even the irrepressible "Mr. Tub," developed alarming symptoms. Worried, and knowing she would entrust no important responsibility to the servants, George on his return dispatched an urgent request to Sam Fraunces, that he find him a trusty steward.

"I would rather have a man than a woman, but either will do, if they can be recommended for honesty, sobriety and knowledge of their profession, which is in one word to relieve Mrs. Washington of the drudgery of ordering and seeing the table properly covered, and things economically used . . ."

For Martha a far more effective therapy for weariness than an efficient but no doubt meddlesome "steward" was the arrival on December 24 of her beloved niece Fanny Bassett, not merely for a visit, but to *stay*. On Nancy's death seven years before she had offered to take Fanny, her sister's youngest child, and bring her up as her own. Only now, with the war over and Martha settled at home, had Burwell agreed. Her coming was the best Christmas present Martha could have had. Fanny, now seventeen, helped fill two aching voids. Charmingly gay, affectionate, bubbling with enthusiasm, she was Nancy come to life again. And she was so like Patsy with her piquant, delicate features, soft brown hair, and sparkling eyes that even the older servants who remembered vowed that their "dark lady" had returned.

Once more Mount Vernon was filled with gaiety, for Fanny was popular, and young people flocked to the house. To Martha's delight George brightened perceptibly with their advent. When his august presence seemed to dampen the gaiety of a dance or play party, he would withdraw and watch the scene unobtrusively from outside the door. Slowly, as he came to be accepted, he would be welcomed into the festivities.

At least, Martha thought gratefully, her relatives were not adding to his worries, as did his own. Though hard pressed for cash, since the estate had not been run properly for eight years and he had refused to accept remuneration other than expenses for his military service, he was constantly feeling the obligation to aid his numerous relatives financially. Betty, with three sons under twenty, needed help. His mother was constantly complaining of poverty. Samuel's orphaned sons must be educated. Bushrod had needed extra money to complete his law study. And George Augustine, son of Charles, had been sent to various seaside resorts in the hope of curing a chest ailment suspiciously resembling that of George's ill-fated brother Lawrence. Of course George had borne the expense of all these travels.

But in April it was Martha who was involved emotionally in family troubles. An express came telling of the sudden death of not only her mother but also her only surviving brother, Bartholomew, both in the same week during this treacherous season for severe colds and pneumonia. It was a devastating blow, and to George's alarm it broke her resistance to the feelings of illness she had long been hiding and sent her to bed with the old dyspeptic fever. Not to stay long, however. For once more the house was full of guests, one of them a young man named Noah Webster, who wrote school books for children; another, Robert Edge Pine, an artist who had come from England with high recommendations. He wanted to paint George for his collection of

American historical portraits. To her surprise George was remarkably docile and patient during the sittings.

"In for a penny, in for a pound, is an old adage," he wrote his friend Francis Hopkinson, who had recommended the artist. "I am so hackneyed to the touches of the Painters pensil, that I am now altogether at their beck, and set like patience on a Monument whilst they are delineating the lines of my face.

"It is a proof among many others of what habit and custom can effect. At first I was impatient of the request, and as restive under the operation as a Colt is of the Saddle. The next time, I submitted very reluctantly, but with less flouncing. Now, no dray horse moves more readily to the Thill, than I do to the Painters Chair."

Martha suppressed a chuckle at sight of the two together, the six-foot-two subject and the barely five-foot artist, who with his wife and two daughters was described by Hopkinson as "a family of pigmies." But in artistry, also irritability, Pine was a giant. There three weeks, he painted all the family. While Nelly submitted with docile sweetness and looked it in her portrait, Washy and the painter endured stormy sessions. The young seraph of the finished product, holding a leafy plant stock, beatifically smiling, was a miracle of obstinate craftsmanship. Elizabeth, sometimes called Eliza, sometimes Betsy, was beautiful with her profusion of rich brown curls, a light drapery over her bosom, her father's miniature about her neck. Patty, more sober and thoughtful, was the picture of gentleness and grace.

The arrival of George Augustine in May, to give George assistance in his grueling duties as host, precipitated a sudden climax. Martha sensed the truth immediately. He and Fanny were in love! They had met often at family gatherings. Now an emotional attachment long in the bud sprang into full flower.

"Yes," Fanny confessed when Martha hesitantly broached the subject, "we've been in love for a long time. We want to get married."

Martha was half-dismayed, half-pleased. Wonderful to have her family and George's united, yet—her beloved niece joined to one in such doubtful health? The months in Bermuda and other sea resorts had effected some improvement but no cure. When Fanny could have had almost any one of the doting young swains who had been clustered about her like bees drawn to honey! "I'd never marry anybody else," insisted Fanny firmly.

"But—you're only seventeen!" Martha objected weakly. "Why not wait . . ." Remembering that she had been exactly seventeen when she married Daniel, the words trailed off into silence.

George also was disturbed, but characteristically he refused to intervene. On May 23 he wrote to Fanny's father:

"It has ever been a maxim with me thro' life, neither to promote nor to prevent a matrimonial connection . . . I have always considered marriage as the most interesting event of one's life, the foundation of happiness or misery; to be instrumental therefor in bringing two people together who are indifferent to each other . . . or to prevent a union which is prompted by mutual esteem and affection, is what I never could reconcile to my feelings . . . As their attachment to each other seems to have been early formed, warm and lasting, it bids fair to be happy; if therefore you have no objection, I think the sooner it is consummated the better." He added that he wanted them to live at Mount Vernon.

There were visits from Fanny's father and two brothers, from Charles, with much discussion. The engagement was announced. The guests went on to Abingdon, taking with them Nelly and little Washy. While they were away, on June 30, George made a singular notation in his diary:

"Rid to my Hay field at the Meadow, from thence to my Dogue Run, and Muddy Hole Plantations, and dined with only Mrs. Washington, which I believe is the first instance of it since my retirement from public life."

Indeed a memorable event, for guests continued to pour in. It was in October that one of the most important visitors arrived. Late one Sunday night, after all were in bed, they heard a great clatter, dogs barking, shouts of servants. Candles were lighted. George pulled on his clothes and hastened to meet the new arrivals, four men who had come down the river from Alexandria. Martha was soon fully in command of preparing refreshments, allotting rooms, getting the guests settled. It was a bit difficult, for two clergymen and several other guests were occupying most of the spare rooms, but as usual she managed.

They had been expecting this guest, the French sculptor Jean Antoine Houdon, whom Thomas Jefferson, then in France, had secured to carve the statue commissioned by the Virginia legislature "of the finest marble and the best workmanship." Houdon had made busts of

Voltaire and of the King of France, and his reputation was unrivaled in Europe. It was a bad time for him and his assistants and interpreter to come. George was busy preparing the lawns during this wet season and getting the house reshingled. Martha was immersed in preparations for Fanny's wedding. But Houdon went about his business with dispatch, laying out his tools, taking measurements of his subject, mixing the plaster of Paris for his masks. Since he spoke no English and sent away his interpreter after three days, Martha's duties were simple, seeing that he was well fed and comfortably bedded. It was George who endured the tedious sittings with features entombed in plaster.

It was rumored later that Houdon was unable to decide what pose to use for his subject until one day he went with George to look at a yoke of oxen someone wanted to sell him. When the man stated his price, George drew himself up angrily, whereupon Houdon exclaimed in satisfaction. Just the pose he had wanted! It was a story inspired, perhaps, by the severity of expression in the completed bust.

Houdon was still there on October 15 when, as George recorded in his diary, "After the candles were lighted, George Augustine Washington and Frances Bassett were married by Mr. Grayson." It was a simple but beautiful ceremony, with Fanny's friends Sally Ramsay and Kitty Washington acting as bridesmaids.

They saw the last of the sculptor two days later when he left with his masks on the Mount Vernon barge to take the Philadelphia stage at Alexandria. Martha was glad to see him go. She had shuddered at sight of one of the plaster of Paris creations. Life mask? It looked more like a death's-head! She would have preferred the word picture of George drawn by one of the next guests, a Mr. John Hunter, who was inspired to eloquence by his visit:

"I was struck by his noble and venerable appearance . . . He is six foot high, perfectly straight and well made, rather inclined to be lusty. His eyes are full and blue and seem to express an air of gravity. His forehead is a noble one, and he wears his hair turned back, without curls and tied in a long queue behind. Altogether he makes a most noble, respectable appearance, and I really think him the first man in the world . . .

"When I was first introduced to him, he was neatly dressed in a plain blue coat, white cassimere waistcoat, and black breeches and boots, as he came from his farm. After sitting with us some time he retired and sent in his lady, a most agreeable woman about fifty, and Major Washington, his nephew, married about three weeks ago to a Miss Bassett . . . After chatting with them for half an hour, the General came in again, with his hair neatly powdered, a clean shirt on, a new plain, drab coat, white waistcoat, and white silk stockings . . ."

Mr. Hunter thought the house very elegant and "something like Chantille, the Prince de Conde's place near Paris, only not so large."

The building program was proceeding. Perhaps the most unusual addition was an ornate mantelpiece of marble, a gift of Samuel Vaughan, a wealthy Londoner who admired Washington. Having heard of the improvements underway, he had sent the piece intended for his own house, without unpacking it, together with some beautiful porcelain vases and two bronze candelabra. It was a beautiful work of art, with three tablets under the mantel, sculptured in high relief in white marble, representing agricultural scenes—a husbandman and his wife driving a cow and a flock of sheep, a boy with plow and horses, a cottage, with a woman drawing water from a well, a child nearby eating a turnip.

"Much too elegant and costly," George demurred, "for my room and republican style of living."

It was only one of many gifts from admirers abroad. Some were much less to Martha's liking, especially the French hounds which were a present from Lafayette, who had been distressed at the deterioration of George's hunting equipment. During the war the kennels had become dilapidated, his famous hounds Vulcan and Truelove, Ringwood, Sweetlips, and others either missing or too old for service. The new arrivals were large and aggressive, hard to confine. One, another Vulcan, was a favorite with little Wash, who rode him like a pony. To Martha he was anathema, especially after one day when, entertaining a large company at dinner, she found her huge ham, pride of every Virginia housewife's table, missing from its post of honor. Puzzled, she questioned Frank, the butler. Oh, yes, madam, a ham, a very fine ham, had been prepared, but lo and behold! what should come into the kitchen while it was smoking in its dish but old Vulcan, and though they had fought him desperately with tongs and pokers, he had borne off the prize, cleanly, under their very noses. Martha's comments about the scavenger, and about all dogs, when related to George and relayed to the guests, aroused only amused laughter. She rejoiced when soon afterward George broke up his kennel, gave up the chase, and substituted a fine deer park below the house.

Another gift she found less galling: the two jacks sent by the King of Spain. They did not encroach on her domain, but they caused George more trouble than they were worth. A Spanish *arriero* had been sent to escort them. George sent a man from Alexandria to meet them in Boston. The *arriero* did not know a word of English, nor the messenger one of Spanish. George christened them "Royal Gift" and "Knight of Malta." Intended for breeding purposes, they were of dubious value at Mount Vernon.

"Royal Gift seems too full of Royalty to have anything to do with a pleibeian race," George wrote Bushrod. "Perhaps his stomach may come to him, if not, I shall wish he had never come from his Most Catholic Majesty."

Guests, guests, guests. The financial burden, to say nothing of the time and labor expended, was a severe strain on the larder and on George's meager cash supply. The farm was not yet yielding its maximum. Expenses for relatives and friends whose petitions he was never willing to refuse kept him constantly in debt. He was chagrined that with more than a hundred cows on the estate he was still forced to buy milk.

Letters, letters, letters. Once he wrote to a friend: "I can with truth assure you that at no period of the war have I been obliged to write half as much as I do now. What with letters from foreigners, enquiries about Dick, Tom, and Harry who *may have been* in some part, or at *sometime* in the Continental service . . . reference of a thousand old matters with which I ought not to be troubled more than the Gt. Mogul, but which must receive answer of some kind . . ."

The burden was lightened somewhat when in July 1786 Tobias Lear, twenty-four, a Harvard graduate, "a genteel, well-behaved young man," became secretary supreme, tutor to the children, member of the family, destined later to be trusted private secretary and adviser to the highest magistrate in the land.

With the arrival of Lear and the return of Fanny and her husband from a long visit to Eltham, George Augustine to assume the manager's position of Lund Washington, who wanted to retire to his own adjoining farm, Martha enjoyed one of the happiest summers of her life. The improvements were nearly finished. The porch floor had been replaced with British flagstones. The pine boards forming the outside walls had been cut and grooved to resemble stone, sand applied to give a rustic effect. The study had been equipped with shelves to house George's growing library and his papers. The banquet room was adorned with decorative plaster work by a master craftsman, the agricultural motif of the white stucco ornamentation on ceiling and cornice in happy harmony with the rural designs on the mantel. The gardens, kitchen and botanical, were flourishing. Humphreys, whose jovial presence added zest to much of the summer, endowed the scene with poetic glamor in his "Ode to Mount Vernon," inscribed to George.

It was well that Martha had this reprieve, for clouds of stupendous change were already gathering.

She began to notice difference in the conversation around the dinner table and in groups gathered on the porch. The men talked less of crops and land and western exploration. There were fewer stories told, less badinage and laughter. Even George's grandiose scheme for opening the Potomac and other inland waters to western settlement and trade was no longer a subject of prime interest. Talk now was of quarreling among the states over matters of trade, rebellion against authority, the issuing by some states of quantities of useless paper money, the inability of the Articles of Confederation to bring order out of chaos.

"If three years since," George once exploded, "any person had told me that at this day I should see such a formidable rebellion against the laws and Constitution of our making I should have thought him a Bedlamite, a fit subject for a mad house."

There was a change too in the personnel of groups gathering, an influx of men active in politics, Edmund Randolph, who was now Governor of Virginia, James Madison, witty and charming, member of the state legislature, James Monroe, a Fredericksburg lawyer who had been in Congress, that troublesome and uncouth (in Martha's view) Patrick Henry. And of course George Mason, always noted for his interest in public affairs. They talked of a stronger federal government able to enforce its laws, a new Constitution, a great convention. Martha was bewildered. They already had a Constitution. And why come here, as if George were a necessary ally in their plans? He had been a soldier, was now a farmer. He had nothing to do with politics. And fortunately he seemed to be doing much more listening than talking. He was writing more, however. She saw one letter he had written Madison:

"No morn ever dawned more favorable than ours did and no day was ever more clouded than the present! . . . Without some alteration in our political creed, the superstructure we have been seven years raising at the expense of so much blood and treasure must fall. We are verging on anarchy and confusion!"

Then came ominous news from the north. A farmer of western Massachusetts named Daniel Shays, reduced to acute poverty through economic conditions, had gathered several hundred of his fellow malcontents and was engaged in violent rebellion against a state government which held a tight financial grip on the producing class. Most of the rebels were veterans attempting to preserve the rights they had fought for. Their lands were mortgaged at exorbitant interest rates. Men who had risked their lives for freedom were in danger of debtors' prison. A formidable force equipped with arms, these "desperate debtors" were ousting judges from their courts, demanding justice. It was the Boston Tea Party, Lexington and Concord all over again, only this time the opponent was not a colonial power overseas but their own state government, which was imposing excessive and unequal taxes which made the British Stamp Acts and tea excises look like chicken feed.

At last George was thoroughly aroused. The whole structure which he had given years of his life to help erect was in danger. He sent off an urgent appeal to David Humphreys, now a member of the Connecticut Assembly.

"For God's sake, tell me what is the cause of all these commotions: do they proceed from licentiousness, British influence disseminated by the Tories, or real grievances which admit of redress? If the latter, why were they delayed till the popular mind had become so agitated? If the former, why are not the powers of government tried at once?"

Congress was helpless. Things were going from bad to worse. And suddenly the reason for the debacle was clear to George. The Continental Congress was impotent because it could attempt only to *influence*. And influence was not government. What was needed, as James Madison had been trying to tell him, was a strong federal government. Already there had been a meeting of a few of the states at Annapolis in September 1786. It had recommended a convention in Philadelphia for May 1787. It was plain to George that Virginia must take the lead. He hastened to write Madison, a member of the legislature, urging that "the great and most important of all objects, the federal government," be considered calmly and deliberately.

"Let prejudices, unreasonable jealousies and local interest yield to reason and liberality," he pleaded. "Let us look to our national character, and to things beyond the present period. Wisdom and good examples are necessary at this time to rescue the political machine from the impending storm."

Martha recognized the signs and sighed. Though he still pursued his daily activities, his eyes were focused beyond the five farms, even beyond the river which offered such opportunities toward the west. She had seen that look in his eyes before, and it had taken them both into eight years of the most excruciating and violent change. She was deeply disturbed and, yes, frightened. But, being the person she was, she kept silent and waited.

There was reprieve. After the beginning of December they were encased in ice, exiled from the outside world, also, happy bonus, from the encroachment of guests. She savored the weeks of peaceful incarceration to the full, and it was well she did. She would not know another time like it for the next ten years.

When news came through it was portentous. The Virginia legislature had passed the bill calling for a convention of the states. George had been elected unanimously to head the delegation. Both Governor Randolph and James Madison urged him to accept.

Martha knew he was torn between a sense of duty and a desire to avoid such unwelcome responsibility. He showed her a letter from Nelly's husband, David Stuart, containing the statement that George's "appointment appeared to be so much the wish of the House that Mr. Madison conceived it might probably frustrate the whole scheme if it was not done."

What should he do? he wondered aloud. He had told the Cincinnati, an organization of military officers whose increasingly patrician rules he was beginning to disapprove of, that private affairs and his affliction of rheumatism would prevent him from attending their triennial meeting in May, at the same time as the Convention and in the same place, Philadelphia! Accepting the other demand would be an unpardonable breach of courtesy. And yet—suppose Madison and the others were right, that his presence at the Convention might help avert possible tragedy? And, heaven knew, the freedom and unity they had fought for might be in jeopardy!

Refuse? Accept? He continued to vacillate. Though he kept asking her advice, Martha wisely kept her counsel. Secretly she smiled at his dilly-dallying, even while her heart sank at prospect of the outcome. Of course he would go. The day after Christmas he had been writing Henry Knox: "There are combustibles in every state, which a spark might set fire to." She knew him better than he did himself. He was not a man to let fires rage without doing all he could to put them out.

The new year, 1787, brought fresh anxieties as well as continued indecision. George's brother John Augustine died, his best beloved of all next to Lawrence. Samuel's sons and their education were a deep concern. Fanny's first baby died. And George himself was so afflicted with rheumatism that at the end of some days he was groaning with pain. The death of John Augustine highlighted another problem, his mother's future. She could not remain much longer in her own home. Now only two were open to her, Betty's and Mount Vernon. He discussed the matter with Martha. Horrified at the thought of having the strong-minded and outspoken Mary a part of the household, she nevertheless reserved comment. To her relief George showed her a letter to his mother which voiced her own sentiments:

"My house is at your service, and I would press you most sincerely and most devoutly to accept it, but I am sure, and candour requires me to say, it will never answer your purposes in any shape whatsoever. For in truth it may be compared to a well resorted tavern, as scarcely any strangers who are going from north to south, or from south to north, do not spend a day or two at it." She would be obliged to keep always dressing for company, or to appear in déshabillé, or be a prisoner in her own chamber, none of which alternatives would be to her liking, etc., etc.

Though seemingly undecided up to the last minute, he left for Philadelphia, as Martha had known he would, on May 9. The Robert Morrises had invited her to come too and stay at their home, but Fanny was still recuperating from the birth and loss of her child, and Martha felt she could not leave. As she watched him go, she was glad she was not superstitious. Clouds were lowering, and it looked as if a storm was coming.

The whole household eagerly awaited his letters. Six-year-old Wash was entranced by news of the reception he had received. Many mounted troops and citizens had escorted him into Philadelphia. Bells had been rung. A crowd had awaited him at his boardinghouse, but the Morrises, whose invitation he had declined, had insisted on his coming to their sumptuous home. He had gone immediately to call on the famous Benjamin Franklin, who, though old and infirm, was to be a member of the Congress. Why, Grandpapa, decided Wash exuberantly, must be a hero like Alexander and Napoleon and those other fellows his tutor Lear told him about! Martha was surprised, also disquieted. Gratifying, of course, that he was still loved and admired, but after four years all that pomp and adulation should have been finished and forgotten. Was it starting all over again?

She shed a few tears when John Augustine showed her a letter George had written soon after his arrival, it sounded so homesick. He hoped his nephew would not tax his health by working too hard in his absence, and he wished they could get some of the rain which was flooding the farms around Philadelphia. "How does the Grass Seeds which were sown with the grain, and flax, seem to come on? How does those which were sown in my little garden advance? And how does the Crops which are planted in drills between the Corn, come up, and progress?" He was sending some "Pecon nuts" to be planted, and he hoped the stray doe wouldn't get lost. Did any of them seem to be with young? He would send plans for conducting the harvest and wanted his last diary, which he had forgotten to bring, sent on to him.

His letters told little of what went on at the Convention, for the proceedings were kept secret. They knew only that he had been unanimously chosen as the presiding officer, that delegates from the different states were slow in coming, but that finally, by May 25, seven states were represented, that the Virginia Plan for union had been presented by Edmund Randolph, and that the body was struggling to agree on a new Constitution. They were told little during the months of haggling, of compromising, of near failure, of provincial self-interest in conflict with the common good, of bitter contest over the importation and representation of slaves, of almost miraculous final agreement of disparate parties to a remarkable document which would become a model of democratic government for dozens of emerging nations in centuries to come.

George returned home at sunset on September 22, having been gone four months and fourteen days. In spite of an accident near the Head of Elk, when in crossing a swollen creek on an old bridge one of his horses had broken through the weak flooring and almost dragged the other horses and chariot into the water, he was in good health and more exuberant than he had seemed for a long time. While he was not completely in accord with all the provisions of the new Constitution, he was heartily in favor of its adoption. Not that he could take any credit for it, he insisted, though he had been the first to sign it. He had made almost no speeches, expressed himself on only a few issues which he considered important, like the matters of having a strong executive, a balance of powers, and a large lower house of Congress which would be representative of more of the people.

It was from others that Martha learned about his actual contribution to the Convention, that his very presence had given the body prestige and public confidence, made it respectable in the eyes of the populace, trustworthy, that his dignity, courteous kindness and, if necessary, austerity as presiding officer, had guided the shaky deliberations through more than one near-hopeless morass.

"The constitution," he wrote Lafayette, "is now a child of fortune, to be fostered by some and buffeted by others."

Buffeted, yes. The storm of disruption was instant and intense, not only between states but between neighbors, friends. To his dismay some of his closest associates, Patrick Henry, Richard Henry Lee, Edmund Randolph, and especially George Mason, were opposed and attempting to keep Virginia from ratifying. It was a scheme to create an oligarchy, protested Henry. It said too little about human rights, said Mason.

"Feeble, shortsighted arguments," George told them. "It was the best system of government on which we could reach agreement. And," to Mason, "the human rights statements can be added later. There is always room for amendments."

But he did little talking. It was not his way. He took up his pen, using it with as much vigor and skill as he had once wielded his sword. While the battle raged life continued as usual at Mount Vernon, as routinely as the passing seasons. Guests came and went—the Philadelphia Powels, the Morrises, James Madison, Gouverneur Morris, who was soon to sail for France to become ambassador in Jefferson's place. Fanny had another baby, not at Mount Vernon this time, but at

Eltham, a girl named Maria. There was a hurricane and much rain which hurt the crops as badly as the drought of the previous summer. George sent off an order for one hundred thousand shingles. In fact, so normal were the winter, spring, and summer that Martha could almost believe normalcy would keep on forever, that she had not read that disturbing paragraph in Humphreys's letter and knew there had been similar words in many other letters:

"What will tend, perhaps more than anything, to the adoption of the new system will be an universal opinion of your being elected President of the United States, and an expectation that you will accept it for a while."

Unlike Martha, George had no illusions. When the necessary nine states had ratified the new Constitution, he knew that he must face the hardest decision of his life. When in June, after a bitter debate, Virginia, largely because of his influence, became the tenth, he sensed that the "sword of Damocles" was poised above his head, hanging by a single thread, threatening his peaceful existence. It was not long before Martha, too, was fully cognizant of his struggle. She did not need to read the letters he was writing. She had not been with him at Cambridge, Morristown, Valley Forge, without being able to tell what he was feeling and thinking.

In October 1788 he was writing: "At my time of life, and under my circumstances, nothing in this world can ever draw me from retirement unless it be a *conviction* that the partiality of my countrymen had made my services absolutely necessary, joined to a *fear* that my refusal might induce a belief that I preferred the conservation of my own reputation and private ease before the good of my country."

And in December: "May Heaven assist me in forming a judgment, for at present I see nothing but clouds and darkness before me . . . If ever I should, from any apparent necessity, be induced to go from home in a public character again, it will certainly be the greatest sacrifice of feeling and happiness that ever was or ever can be made by me."

Martha knew even better than he what his decision would be. For there were some things more important to him even than this life he loved. One was the country he had fought for, had helped create. Another was his sense of duty.

Already she was quietly making plans, deciding what must be done in the house, the gardens, the outbuildings, what must be done with the servants, what they should take with them, what they should leave behind. For they would be gone a long time.

18

"May Heaven assist me in forming a judgment!"

Whether by heaven or earth inspired, events were rapidly forcing George to painful decision. The country was polarizing into two contesting factions, those who desired a strong central government as outlined in the new Constitution, and those who hoped to restore the chief source of authority to the states. Though he assumed no leadership in the controversy, he was heart and soul with the first group, the Federalists. Some of the most violent of the opposition were in his own state of Virginia, led by the fiery Patrick Henry, who was threatening to oppose all moves to organize the new federal government unless legislation was accompanied by plans to amend the Constitution.

"He'd take us back to the old Continental Congress," complained George bitterly, "jeopardize all the freedom and unity we have struggled so hard to achieve. And," he added, "I'm sure he and his ilk want to see an advocate of destructive amendment placed at the head of government." Which would mean, as Madison, another strong Federalist, had put it, for the new government, as soon as it was born, to commit suicide.

So, Martha acknowledged silently but with cheerful resignation, it's already being decided what you—what we—must do, even though you won't admit it.

Electors had been chosen from the various states by their legislatures, and on February 4, 1789, they met to cast ballots for President and Vice President. Though it was generally known that George was the unanimous choice, the ballots would not be opened until Congress convened on March 4. Still George apparently had not made up his mind. But unhappily, like Martha, he made his preparations, applying for a necessary loan of five or six hundred pounds to pay his debts and the expenses of going to the capital of the new government in New York. He even wrote Henry Knox, who was living in that city, to buy him enough "superfine American broadcloth," which he had seen advertised, to make him a suit, also a riding habit for Martha. He paid a visit to his mother, who was still stubbornly remaining in her own house, though confined to her bed. He wrote meticulous instructions for George Augustine in case of a prolonged absence.

Congress was slow in assembling. It was April before enough delegates arrived for a quorum, and on the fourteenth Charles Thomson, Secretary of the new Congress, with David Humphreys, rode with pounding hoofs through the western gate with the announcement of George's unanimous election to the Presidency of the United States.

Martha was almost relieved when, on the morning of April 16, she saw him ride away in his carriage with Thomson and Humphreys. Though she had long known the outcome of all the hemming and hawing and dilly-dallying, now she could burst into a flurry of open preparation, pack clothes into boxes, store much of the silver in burlap and straw for leaving, sew blankets into bags to protect them from moths and dust, and a hundred other things with which she did not want to burden Fanny. The poor child would have enough to do superintending the household, tending her new baby, caring for a husband who was not well.

At least she need not take food this time. George wrote that he had secured the services of Sam Fraunces as his steward, to attend to all the purchasing and cooking. "Black Sam," as he was called because he was a West Indian and dark of complexion, was the former proprietor of the tavern where George had said farewell to his officers. Tobias Lear had written George Augustine that the amazing Fraunces "tossed off such a number of fine dishes that we are distracted in our choice when we sit down to table, and obliged to hold a long consultation on the subject before we can determine what to attack."

Martha sighed. The letters from New York sounded ominous. George's journey there had been a succession of triumphs, salutes, guns, mounted escorts, flags, arches, church bells, receptions, dinners. He had entered Philadelphia mounted on a splendid white horse, ironic contrast to his journey through the city twelve years before, when he pushed his ragged army toward a doubtful encounter at Yorktown. Thousands of spectators had greeted his barge in New York. There had been a formal induction into his new office called an "inauguration," when he swore "to preserve, protect, and defend the Constitution," and the crowd had roared, "Long live George Washington, President of the United States!" She was pleased, of course, that he was so honored, but oh, what an anticlimax to exchange this serene, happy life for such hectic ceremonies and festivities! It made her tired just to think of it.

"I little thought when the war was finished," she wrote one of her friends, "that any Circumstance could possibly happen which would call the General into public life again. I had anticipated that, from that Moment, we should be suffered to grow old together, in solitude and tranquility. That was the first and dearest wish of my heart. I will not, however, contemplate with too much regret disappointments that were inevitable . . ."

George sent his nephew, Robert Lewis, Betty's son, to be the family's mounted escort on the trip to New York. The servants gathered about the carriage, weeping, on the afternoon of May 16. Besides Robert, there were five of them making the journey, Martha and the two children, nurse Molly, and Martha's personal maid Oney. Nelly, always sensitive, shed a few tears. Not Washy, who at age eight was getting too old and streamlined to be called "Mr. Tub." He was far too excited by the prospect of life in the city to waste time in regrets. And not Martha, though she and Fanny had clung together and mingled their tears in the privacy of her bedroom. She had set off like this for too many strange destinations to consider this departure unique.

She was thankful for one small detail. George had sent back the family carriage in time for this journey. He had asked his mother to loan Martha the carriage he had given her for use during his absence. Though bedridden and doubtless unable to ever ride in it again, Mary Washington had acted with her characteristic thrifty self-interest. She would be glad to lend her carriage, but on condition that it be returned when his wife had no further use for it. Martha had taken keen pleasure in dispatching the unwelcome vehicle to Fredericksburg at the earliest possible moment.

To her amazement, as well as to young Washy's delight, it was a triumphant journey. All along the way they were met by troops, crowds, parades, conducted to sumptuous mansions, serenaded by bands and pealing bells, feasted, receptioned, saluted with guns, entertained with fireworks and musical marathons. Once she had been surprised when greeted as "Lady Washington," the General's wife. Now she was amazed to find herself even more esteemed as "Lady Washington," the President's wife.

Washy regarded her with wonder and, suddenly, respect. Grandpapa a hero, yes, though that too had been difficult to comprehend at first. But—Grandmama! Lear had provided no female counterparts of Alexander and Napoleon. "They—they're doing all this for *you?*" he demanded incredulously.

"No, dear." She smiled. "It's all for Grandpapa, because I just happen to be his lady."

She was wrong. Partly because of this self-effacing humility but more for her gracious yet simple kindliness, she was revered and honored for herself alone.

"Like her illustrious husband," reported a Baltimore dispatch, "she was clothed in the manufacture of our country, in which her native goodness and patriotism appeared to the greatest advantage."

In Philadelphia, where first of all she made purchases for the family back home—stays for Fanny, shoes for Nelly, Betsy, and Patty, a doll for Fanny's little Maria—the *Pennsylvania Packet* spoke for all the citizens when noting: "The present occasion recalled the remembrance of those interesting scenes, in which, by her presence, she contributed to relieve the cares of our beloved Chief, and to soothe the anxious moments of his military concern—gratitude marked the recollection, and every countenance bespoke the feelings of affectionate respect."

The Troops of Light Horse wanted to escort her carriage all the way to Trenton, but since it was rainy Martha insisted that they soon turn back, and she continued north accompanied only by Robert Lewis, the children and servants, and the carriage of her friend Mrs. Robert Morris, who was coming with her daughters to New York to join her husband. George met them with a beautiful new barge at Elizabethtown Point. After that Martha had eyes and ears only for him. Her dutiful

smiles for the huge crowds which met them were perfunctory. She
scarcely heard the salute of thirteen guns as they passed the Battery,
though George assured her they were in her honor, not his. He did not
look well, she worried. The lines of strain, smoothed out in the tranquility of Mount Vernon, were back in his face.

And no wonder. For, as she was to discover almost immediately, he
was coping with almost insuperable problems. His triumphal journey,
the roars of the crowds as he had taken his oath of office, the acclamation following his simple but stirring inaugural address, had been as
portentous preliminaries of struggle as the plaudits of the multitudes on
the road to Cambridge. Even during these first exercises of his Presidency people had noticed that, though only in his fifty-seventh year,
the nation's hero was looking old. The exertions of war, strain over the
fate of the Constitution, stress over the agonizing decision just made,
had all taken their toll.

"Time has made havoc upon his face," one man had written.

He now faced an uncharted wilderness of complex duties—organizing a new government, providing revenues, making appointments, setting up courts, negotiating with foreign governments and Indian tribes,
in addition to performing all the social obligations expected of a chief
executive. At least he had assistance in the organization of his personal
office with the devoted Humphreys and Lear as his secretaries. James
Madison and Alexander Hamilton became his invaluable aides in establishing proper relations with the new Congress. Though he believed in
a strong executive department, he scrupulously respected the separation of the three branches of government as outlined in the Constitution. It was the business of Congress to debate issues and make laws.
The President should not attempt to influence them in their decisions.
He would administer but he would not interfere.

One of his greatest problems was in finding *time*. Endless visitors,
calls to appear at civic entertainments, invitations to balls given in his
honor, a commencement at Columbia College where he was forced to
listen to ten student orations, levees he felt obliged to hold, public
dinners, a prevailing feeling (legacy of the presiding officers of the old
Confederacy) that the President's table was a public one and that every
important person had a *right* to be invited to it. It was a quandary. If he
extended invitations, attended endless public events, there would be no
time for important business. If he extended no invitations, kept himself

inviolate from interruptions, he might be thought to ape a king. More-over, as he expressed it, he would close "the avenues of useful informa-tion from the many." Such was the situation when on May 27 Martha arrived at the President's house at the junction of Cherry and Queen streets.

"Oh, dear," she chided herself almost at once, "I should have come earlier! No wonder he is looking so tired and discouraged, having to cope with all these domestic problems as well as with affairs of state!" But at least she was here now, and she wasted no time in assuming a housewife's responsibilities.

It was a comfortable house. In fact, the Quakers in the town called it the "Palace." It was of brick, three stories, amply lighted by many small-paned windows. The main entrance, on Cherry Street, was ap-proached by short flights of steps, one at each side of a little porch. Congress had appropriated eight thousand dollars to pay its owner, Samuel Osgood, for repairs and furnishings. Mrs. Osgood had equipped it with elegant mahogany furnishings, an ample supply of plate and china, new wallpaper, and luxurious Turkey and Wilton carpets. The east window faced Long Island, and to Martha's delight there was a well-kept garden sloping toward the river. In addition they had shipped from Mount Vernon a quantity of pictures, vases, ornaments, Sèvres china, and silver.

"I thank God the President is very well," Martha wrote Fanny soon after her arrival, "and the gentlemen with him are all very well. The house he is in is a very good one, and is handsomely furnished all new for the General [she still was not used to calling him 'the President']. I have been so much engaged since I came here that I have not opened your box or directions, but shall soon have time as most of the visits are at an end. I have not had one half hour to myself since the day of my arrival . . . My hair is set and dressed every day, and I have put on the white muslin habits for the summer. You would, I fear, think me a good deal in the fashion if you could but see me. My dear Fanny, send me by safe conveyance my black lace apron and handkerchief, it is in one of the baskets on the shelf in my closet. They were fine net hand-kerchiefs which I intended to make cap borders of . . ."

Good though she found it, the house had its deficiencies. It was too small for public purposes. Offices and reception rooms required so much space that poor Bob Lewis had to sleep in the same room with

Colonel Humphreys, who snored, also was inspired to rise and deliver one of his poetic effusions in the dead of night. And in spite of the array of competent servants, things were at sixes and sevens. Even the indomitable Fraunces was unequal to the demands of the complicated household. Martha found that out the day after her arrival.

George had invited important guests for dinner on that day, May 28, but the servants were confused and preparations had been neglected. As Senator Paine Wingate, one of the least critical of the guests, wrote: "It was the least showy dinner that I ever saw at the President's. After the dessert a single glass of wine was offered to each of the guests, when the President rose, the guests followed his example, and repaired to the drawing-room, each departing at his option, without ceremony." Once Martha assumed direction of the household, such an embarrassment would never occur again. Before summer was over, another critical senator would write of a meal there: "It was a great dinner, and the best of the kind I ever was at."

Her duties had been multitudinous at Mount Vernon. Here they were legion. The second day after her arrival, a Friday, she was scheduled for what was called a "levee," the reception of guests in the drawing room. Humphreys had sent out the invitations to officials of the new government and their wives, as well as the city's important citizens. It was a formal affair. Seated on a sofa, Humphreys by her side to make the introductions, she received the ladies with friendly welcoming smiles, while George moved about among the guests. Many she already knew, some intimately. Lucy Knox was there, also Mrs. Morris, Governor Clinton's wife, and Betsy Hamilton. Alexander, the rift between him and George now healed, was one of George's most trusted advisers. The service was faultless. Already she was in full command of arrangements. There were cakes, candy, tea, coffee, lemonade in abundance.

"It was a brilliant success," George told her gratefully.

It was with intense relief that he could relinquish into her capable hands most of the social responsibilities of the office, though he probably had no idea of their magnitude. Direction of the household was the least of her new duties. She must acknowledge visits, return calls the third day without fail. People would expect her to be faultlessly attired for all occasions. A social pattern must be set for formal dinners. Yes, and there were the children, who must not be neglected.

After two weeks she was writing Fanny: "My first care was to get the children to a good school, which they are boath very much pleased at . . ." Pleased to be back at school, or pleased with the particular dispensers of erudition which their Grandmother had chosen? She did not elucidate.

Scarcely had this letter reached its destination when Martha had far more distressing news to impart. The tragedy came suddenly. About the middle of June, George fell ill with fever and complained of soreness in his left thigh. Dr. Samuel Bard, a prominent physician, was unable to make a diagnosis. An ugly tumor developed. Rumors spread. The President had a malignant growth. No, he had anthrax, that terrible "wool sorters' " disease. Whatever his ailment, he was very ill and probably dying. To allay public concern the June 20 *Gazette* reported that he was "much better" after only a "slight fever."

He was not much better, and the fever was not slight. For days it raged higher and higher, and his pain was so acute that the slightest sound caused him torments. Straw was laid in the streets outside to mute noises, but it could not shut out the cries of water and milk hawkers or the shouts of horsemen, carriage and mule drivers. Ropes were stretched across to divert traffic and protect him from the sounds of passing vehicles and pedestrians. The ropes were stolen and had to be replaced. Never had Martha been more frightened, not even during Patsy's final attack. Then the agony had been sudden and acute. This time it was prolonged. For days on end she scarcely slept. But finally the tumor revealed itself as a deep abscess. It was opened with a large incision, and the fever slowly subsided. Only then did Martha give herself the luxury of a few hours of sleep. Recovery dragged.

But on the thirteenth anniversary of the signing of the Declaration of Independence he managed to meet some necessary obligations. The New York militia were to be paraded and reviewed, and the state Society of the Cincinnati, the group founded by American and foreign officers of the Continental army, was planning an address to him. He dressed carefully and managed to stay on his feet much of the day and to greet both groups at the door. The day was historic for another reason. That morning he signed the "impost bill" laying a duty on goods, wares, and other merchandise imported into the United States, assuring the country a measure of financial independence.

It was almost like old times, thought Martha, seeing the New York

Cincinnati marching so gallantly, with their "eagles" on their chests, many of them familiar figures. Baron von Steuben, who had taken George's place as president of the organization, delivered a brief address, and George managed to make a short, extemporaneous reply.

Even during the anxious days of his illness and long convalescence Martha was not free of social duties. People kept coming to inquire, to bring flowers, fruits, jellies, broths, messages of condolence, and she must receive them all. One of the callers she welcomed gladly for, though they had never met, she already considered her a friend. The wife of the Vice President, John Adams, had just arrived in New York and hastened to pay her respects to the "First Lady." In the beginning Martha was a bit in awe of this brilliant woman who had gone with her ambassador husband to England and consorted with royalty, but they were soon chatting like old friends in happy rapport.

"She received me with great ease and politeness," Abigail wrote her sister with frank appreciation. "She is plain in her dress, but that plainness is the best of every article. She is in mourning. Her hair is white, her teeth beautiful, her person rather short than otherwise . . . Her manners are modest and unassuming, dignified and feminine, not the tincture of hauteur about her." Later, after other meetings, Abigail was to add: "Mrs. Washington is one of those unassuming characters which create love and esteem. A most becoming pleasantness sits upon her countenance and an unaffected deportment which renders her the object of veneration and respect. With all these feelings and sensations I found myself much more deeply impressed than I ever did before their Majesties of Britain."

Martha and Abigail had much in common in addition to being the wives of the country's two chief magistrates. Both had trembled at the sound of guns at Cambridge. Both had hoped to spend the rest of their lives in quiet with their families and had been called back reluctantly to public life. And, surprisingly, back in the summer of 1776 Martha had lived in the house now occupied by the Vice President up on Richmond Hill, far more spacious and comfortable than the cramped Cherry Street abode.

"It's you who should be living up there with the fine view and garden," regretted Abigail. "This is no place for an invalid, especially in this July heat. As soon as the President is able to ride, you must come by way of Richmond Hill and make our house your resting place."

George had a bed put in the carriage and, always resistant to confinement, insisted on riding out every day. And now, moving along the tree-lined streets, past fine dwellings with broad lawns and gardens in full summer bloom, Martha was able to better appreciate the attractions of this old Dutch city which, during the preceding weeks of anguish, had seemed fraught with only crudity and raucous noise. There were fine churches, houses of many styles, Dutch, looking thrifty, white, and tidy, French with more fancy frills, English, square and sturdy like those in New England. The stores and taverns betokened an increasing postwar prosperity. An atmosphere of color, bustle, optimism pervaded the rapidly growing city. On such rides they often accepted Abigail's invitation and stopped at the Adams house on Richmond Hill, enjoying the splendid view, the broad piazza, the garden with its shade trees.

From the beginning Abigail was a staunch champion of George. "He is much a favorite of mine, I do assure you," she wrote her sister during that year of 1789, and later, after his recovery from another severe illness, she was to comment: "It appears to me that union of the States, and consequently the permanency of the Government depend upon his life. His death would, I fear, have had most disastrous consequences."

Slowly life fell into a more normal routine. The problem of excessive visitors was partially solved by the scheduled levees. George held his on Tuesdays from three to four, when he appeared in black velvet coat and breeches, hair in full dress, powdered and gathered behind in a silk bag, yellow gloves, knee and shoe buckles, at his side a dress-sword in its white polished leather scabbard. A coat covered the sword, so only the scabbard was visible. At Martha's levees on Friday evenings he appeared just as a private gentleman, mingling with the company, wearing a cloth coat and waistcoat, black small-clothes. Martha, while dressing simply, laid aside her homespun and appeared in silk, satin, velvet, and lace. It all ended at nine. Martha would rise and say, "The General always retires at nine, and I usually precede him."

"Elegance, yes," was George's description of their social role, "but always with dignity and moderation." There must be no pomp, yet the office must be properly honored and respected.

There had been too much pomp in his first levee, planned by Colonel Humphreys. The latter arranged an antechamber and a presence room. Humphreys walked through the former, the President behind him. The door of the presence room was flung open. Humphreys announced in a loud voice, "The President of the United States."

George was so disconcerted he was flustered all through the proceeding. "Well," he told his secretary angrily after the ceremony was concluded, "you have taken me in once, but you shall never do so again!"

After that he stood in a room, its chairs removed, and received the guests as they came up to him. He did not shake hands. In one hand he held his cocked hat, the other rested on the hilt of his small sword. At quarter past three the doors were closed, and he made a tour of the gentlemen, conversing with each in turn. He had a remarkable faculty for remembering names and faces. It was a simple proceeding.

There had been a great to-do about what to call him in his new official capacity. A majority of the Senate had favored "His Highness, the President of the United States of America, and Protector of their Liberties," but the Representatives had preferred the simple "President of the United States," as stated in the Constitution. Others had suggested "His Highness," "Excellency," but George eschewed all ideas which smacked of royalty. Finally a committee with his guidance had settled on the simple "The President," or "Mr. President."

Knowing that he was setting precedents, possibly for years, generations, even centuries to come, he was as cautious and punctilious in dealing with such personal details as in his deference toward the other two departments of government. If he made any suggestion for legislative action by Congress, it had to be about an issue of extreme importance, and then he made no effort to influence them. He was rigidly adamant as to observance of every detail of the Constitution.

Just as circumspect was he in making his appointments. Though many deserving and capable friends boldly applied for positions of prominence, he let it be known that he would always seek the best man for appointment, whoever he might be, as far as his judgment should guide him. Sometimes, Martha knew, he found solicitations for office acutely embarrassing, as when his nephew Bushrod, a young lawyer of twenty-seven, confidently applied for appointment as District Attorney for Virginia. In refusing, because "your standing at the bar would not justify my nomination of you in preference to some of the oldest and most esteemed lawyers in the state," he further stated his policy:

"My political conduct in nominations, even if I was uninfluenced by principle, must be exceedingly circumspect and proof against just criticism, for the eyes of Argus are upon me, and no slip will pass unnoticed that can be improved into a supposed partiality for friends or relatives."

Martha soon had the domestic arrangements well in hand. A formal dinner was served each Thursday at four in the afternoon, with ten to twenty-two persons expected beside the family. Guests might include such distinguished persons as Vice President Adams, Governor Clinton, John Jay, the French and Spanish ministers (Count de Moustier and Don Diego Gardoqui), several senators, perhaps Langdon, Wingate, Izard, and Few, and the Speaker of the House, Mr. Muhlenberg. If no clergyman was present George would return thanks. When there were other ladies in attendance, he and Martha would sit opposite each other, with one of the secretaries at each end of the table to facilitate serving and conversation. When there were no other ladies, George and Martha sat at the head and foot of the table. Or, when dinners were very informal, they would sit side by side.

Presiding over the dining room at all such gatherings was the inimitable Fraunces, delivering the delicacies produced in the kitchen by his chief cook, Hercules. Food was plain but simple. "Black Sam" was noted for his collations of roast beef, lamb, turkey, duck, and other game, his varieties of jellies, fruit, nuts, and raisins. The table was set with fine linen and china, with some central table ornament, perhaps a long mirror made in sections framed with silver and adorned with statues. The five or six waiters wore the impressive Washington livery and served with quiet, faultless precision. However, it was "Black Sam" who dominated the scene.

As Washy, grown to distinguished manhood, would later record: "When Fraunces in snow-white apron, silk shirt and stocking and hair in full powder, placed his first dish on the table, the clock being on the stroke of four, the 'labors of Hercules' ceased."

It was Washy also who would record for posterity the story of the early shad which Fraunces, knowing the President's fondness for fish, was able to secure on one of his marketing expeditions. George, served with the succulent out-of-season delicacy, regarded it suspiciously. "What was its price?" he demanded of his steward. And when Fraunces stammered, "Th-three dollars, sir," he thundered, "Take it away, take it away, sir. It shall never be said that my table sets such an example of luxury and extravagance."

Fraunces received such harsh criticism with dignified acquiescence but with tongue in cheek. "Well, he may discharge me," he was heard to say, "he may kill me, but while he is President of the United States and I have the honor to be his steward, his establishment shall be supplied with the best of everything that the whole country can afford."

The future chronicler did not comment on the fact that the viand too precious for consumption by the chief executive was doubtless devoured with gusto in the servants' kitchen.

Now, at age nine, the irrepressible Washy, storing up such episodes for future use, was sometimes an acute embarrassment to Martha. When he was present with guests she never knew what to expect. There was the time when Lucy Knox appeared wearing one of the new popular styles of headdress at least a foot high. With her bulk of more than two hundred pounds, it did make her look odd, "like an upside-down butter churn," as Nelly commented. Washy regarded her with amazement, cheeks growing redder and redder. Just in time Martha checked the imminent explosion of laughter by diverting his attention to Lucy's latest offspring, a lively, black-eyed, black-haired little boy who also bore the name of George Washington.

Poor lovable, good-natured Lucy! The new style was not her cup of tea, yet it was lucky for her that hoopskirts had long gone out of vogue. Martha herself rather favored the new, high headdresses. They made her look taller and less squatty. Though she would never affect the extreme, as some women did, piling their hair at least a foot, then topping it with another foot of lace, ruchings, ribbons, feathers, even vegetables, little windmills, bells, or a ship in full sail! Her favorite headdress was what was called a "Queen's Nightcap," a lovely crown of gauze and lace ruffled in two layers, which circled her white hair like a halo. She was to wear it in a portrait painted of her by Edward Savage.

It should have been a satisfying life. Martha played her new role to perfection. All her life, it seemed, she had been preparing for it, developing the necessary skills, patience, poise, tact, social ease, courtesy, kindliness. Yet she was soon writing Fanny in the mood of one who would always consider this life as "First Lady" her "lost days":

"Mrs. Sims will give you a better account of the fashions than I can. I live a very dull life here, and know nothing of what passes in the town. I never go to any public place—indeed, I am more like a State prisoner than anything else. There are certain bounds set for me which

I must not depart from, and as I cannot do what I like, I am obstinate and stay at home a great deal."

George echoed these sentiments when he wrote: "I can truly say I had rather be at Mount Vernon with a friend or two about me, than to be attended at the seat of government by the officers of State and the representatives of every power in Europe."

He was coping with many problems, one of which was combining republican simplicity with what he considered proper official dignity.

"I walk on untrodden ground," he confided. "There is scarcely an action the motive of which may not be subjected to a double interpretation. There is scarcely any part of my conduct which may not hereafter be drawn into precedent."

He soon found that he could not satisfy everybody. Some criticized his walking on the streets like an ordinary citizen, even complained because his levees and dinners were too simple. Staid New Englanders read of his stables with a dozen horses, his chariot drawn by six cream-colored steeds, his servants in livery, and many, like one writer, feared the "old General" was being "taken over by the great." One Boston paper countered that it was not his fault, that "our beloved President stands unmoved in the vortex of folly and dissipation which the city of New York represents."

Abigail Adams stoutly protested these slurs against New York and the President, claiming that there were six elaborate dinners in Boston to every one in New York.

It was during a dinner in August when the cheerful Baron von Steuben was a guest that a letter arrived which quelled all festivity. Mary Washington had died. George had felt on his last visit that he would never see her again. Though he ordered black cockades, sword knots, and arm ribbons for all the men in his house and suspended levees for a week, he did not go into "deep mourning." Martha knew that, although he found her death "awful and affecting," he had never felt a warm love for his mother. Surprisingly Martha herself felt a sense of genuine loss, born not of affection but of appreciation for the qualities of the sometimes obdurate and difficult old lady. She realized suddenly that it was his mother who had endowed her son with some of his finest attributes—physical strength and endurance, perseverance, punctuality, a love of the land, indomitable courage in the face of baffling difficulties.

More than ever now in this life of new challenges he needed both courage and perseverance. But as that first year crept forward, some of the most formidable initial tasks had been completed. In spite of the embarrassing delays of Congress in passing necessary legislation, the new government was finally organized.

"At last!" he exclaimed in relief to Martha on July 27. "Today I was able to sign the bill for the establishment of a Department of Foreign Affairs!" and on August 7 he did the same for a Department of War. It was August 28 before debate over a Treasury Department and its function had been concluded. Salaries for the President and Vice President and pay for members of Congress had been a mooted issue. Though George had recommended that he receive no pay except for bare expenses, his allotment had finally been fixed at twenty-five thousand dollars, to include expenses. He continued to act on the principle that he was receiving his expenses only, for these were heavy and would consume nearly, if not all, of the full amount. Federal courts were set up without the opposition he had expected.

He was even more relieved when the Federalist majority of Congress proved determined to approve no amendments which would change the structure of the Constitution. He heartily approved the first ten amendments, the Bill of Rights so necessary to George Mason, which were formulated and sent to the states for ratification.

Now one of his most vexatious tasks was the appointment of chief officials. He must not show favoritism, yet there were certain friends and old acquaintances whose abilities he knew and trusted. He must not show partiality to any one state or section. As Secretary of War he chose Henry Knox, who had held the same position under the Continental Congress; as Secretary of Treasury the young but cannily able Alexander Hamilton. Thomas Jefferson, presently minister to France, would become Secretary of State. Edmund Randolph, thirty-six, former governor of Virginia and an ardent supporter of the Constitution, would be Attorney General. Judges of the Supreme Court, five of them, some of the best lawyers in the country, with John Jay as Chief Justice, would make up that body.

Congress adjourned on September 29 to meet again on the first Monday in January.

"Now," thought Martha hopefully, "there will surely be time for a few days, at least, at Mount Vernon."

"Now," said George almost apologetically, probably aware that he was pricking her bubble of hope, "it's time I took that trip through New England that I have been long planning. I'm sure you've heard us discuss all the reasons why I should go."

She had heard and recognized the need. It would help him explore, as he put it, "the temper and disposition of the inhabitants toward the new government." He was the symbol of that government as well as of their struggle for freedom. A visit would strengthen their support of the Constitution.

"Yes," she said, stifling her disappointment. And such a trip, she reminded herself, getting him away from pressures, might restore him to full health. Not, however, like the fresh air and broad green vistas of Mount Vernon!

"I'd like you to go with me," he urged with a touch of wistfulness.

It was a temptation, for she dreaded another long separation. But she resisted. The children needed her, and their schooling should not be interrupted. Though she would have taken them without a qualm to Mount Vernon, a jaunt through distant country, with possible hazards, unfamiliar foods, strange inns or homes, was dismaying. She did not even consider leaving them in competent care. And in her modesty it did not occur to her that her cheerful, affable, comely yet unassuming person would be a political asset.

She saw him off on October 15 with Tobias Lear, another secretary, William Jackson, and six servants. The twenty-nine days of his journey seemed longer than any period since she had come to New York, longer even than some of his previous year-long absences. More and more she was feeling confined by the rigid rules of decorum which controlled her every action. Mercy Warren was disappointed that she had not accompanied George on the trip. Martha wrote Mercy, by dictation as she often did these days, so that her letters would not reveal her lapses in spelling:

"Though the General's feelings and my own were perfectly in unison with respect to our predilection for private life, yet I cannot blame him for acting according to his ideas of duty in obeying the voice of his country. The consciousness of having attempted to do all the good in his power, and the pleasure of finding his fellow citizens so well satisfied with the disinterestedness of his conduct, will doubtless be some compensation for the great sacrifice which I know he has made. With respect to myself, I sometimes think the arrangement is not quite as it ought to have been; that I, who had much rather be at home, should occupy a place with which a great many younger and gayer women would be prodigiously pleased . . . I know too much of the vanity of human affairs to expect felicity from the splendid scenes of public life. I am still determined to be cheerful and to be happy in whatever situation I may be; for I have also learned from experience that the greater part of our happiness or misery depends upon our dispositions, and not upon our circumstances."

There were pleasant features in their life. At least Sundays were their own. They attended church in the morning at St. Paul's, and Martha often went also in the afternoon with the children while George sat in the library and wrote his innumerable letters. In the evening he would read to them, a sermon or some other devotional material, and close the day by reading scripture to her in their apartment. And they enjoyed pleasures together on other days. Sometimes they went to the theater, which was one of George's favorite diversions, seeing plays like *The Clandestine Marriage* and *The School for Scandal*, and Sheridan's opera *The Duenna*. The director at John Street Theater had composed special music called "The President's March," which was always played when they entered their box. They developed some warm friendships, with the Schuylers, the Hamiltons, the Jays, the Knoxes, the John Adamses, the Rufus Kings, and others. Martha often gave parties for the children on Saturday afternoons, complete with games and dancing and Fraunces's fabulous cakes and ices.

On many fine days they would ride out together in the new coach which arrived from England in December, a really splendid equipage, its body and wheels cream-colored with gold moldings, so comfortably fitted with iron springs that one could hardly feel the jolts. Always people gathered along the way to watch them pass, their coming heralded, it seemed, by magic. Martha reveled in these rides. They were a temporary release from the prison of prescribed decorum and protocol. No need of worrying lest one congressman's wife received more attention than another, or that Mrs. Adams was not seated in her proper place at her right hand! She could smile and nod and wave at all with impartial freedom, feel herself a part of this beautiful commixture of human life that was America.

She could not fully know what her presence meant to the man who had so reluctantly assumed such herculean responsibility, or how, after all the years of playing a loyal, subordinate role, she had suddenly become a distinct and important personality. During the war she had been noticed, of course, commended for her service, and she had made a few friends, but her public image had been vague, shadowy, with little substance apart from the Commander in Chief. Now she sprang into clear identity, an invaluable complement to what might have been his limitations. Qualities commendable in a general—austerity, sternness, brevity of speech, even at times a hot temper—could in a President be termed stiffness, pride, coldness, unapproachability, stubbornness. She imbued the scene with ease and warmth. At her formal dinners conversation sparkled. He seemed less preoccupied, more sympathetic, occasionally even humorous. In fact, she helped him down from his hero-pedestal and revealed him as a human being. Not only for being the President's wife but for herself she was more and more acknowledged as "First Lady."

19

Seventeen eighty-nine. Year of profound change, painful sacrifice, but of some satisfying achievement. Martha was not sorry to see it end. The new year came in gloriously fair and balmy as in May. It was the mildest winter in generations. Farmers and gardeners were cultivating their land in January. Portent of a happier era to come? Perhaps. After all, George had promised that he would keep the Presidency only until the government was well established and the country securely unified.

It was the custom in New York to pay social visits on New Year's Day. Between one and three in the afternoon many people came to the house, the Vice President, cabinet ministers, the Governor of New York, foreigners of distinction, members of Congress, in fact, "all the respectable citizens." That evening Martha held a reception for three hours. Never before had there been such a huge attendance at one of her levees. It was so warm that the ladies appeared in summer dresses. The evening was delightful, with a full moon as a bonus. Fraunces served tea, coffee, plain and plum cakes. The house bulged with guests.

In fact, the house on Cherry Street with its low ceilings and cramped spaces had been from the beginning unfit for the demands of a President's household. When the French minister, the Count de Moustier, left the Macomb house on lower Broadway, George made arrangements for its rental, and they moved there on his birthday, February 22, 1790. It was much larger, four stories instead of three, an inviting balcony off the drawing room, and from the rear windows a beautiful view of the Hudson and Jersey shores. Its popular name, the "Mansion House," was descriptive of its superior advantages. Fitted with improvements, a new stable, green carpets, better lighting, it was an ideal official domicile. Twenty-seven persons could be seated at the dinner table, and of course the inimitable Fraunces was equally at home in this far more demanding setting for his faultless cuisine.

Nearly faultless, that is. At least once he delivered a creation which, in Lafayette's lingo, could only be called a *faux pas*. A dessert appeared at a formal dinner most delectable to the eye but, to Martha's horror when she tasted it, full of rancid cream. She saw Mrs. Robert Morris, who was at George's right, make a face and whisper to him. Politely he changed her plate. What to do? Calmly Martha kept on eating her portion as if she had noticed nothing wrong, and many of the other guests followed her example. Let the fastidious Mrs. Morris think ill of her if she chose, that she was either greedy of sweets or insensitive to taste. Martha would not for the world have embarrassed "Black Sam" by making an issue of his mistake.

Speaking of embarrassments! Rancid cream was nothing beside the occurrence at one of her Friday levees soon after they moved into the Broadway house. One of the most fashionably dressed guests, a Miss McIvers, appeared in a headdress so monstrously tall that as she stood beneath one of the chandeliers, its topping of ostrich feathers caught fire from the glowing candles. Fortunately Major Jackson, George's secretary, rushed gallantly to the rescue, extinguishing the flames of the burning plumes between his gloved hands.

At last George was feeling more comfortable in his new post. The Senate had confirmed his appointments of his cabinet. Thomas Jefferson, who had arrived from his duties in France to become Secretary of State, was proving a wise adviser in foreign affairs. Stirred by the uprising of the French people, George treasured a gift sent him by Lafayette which occupied a place of honor in the new house, the key to the Bastille, sent as a symbol of the new freedom hopefully coming to France. It had been forwarded from London through Thomas Paine, who wrote: "That the principles of America opened the Bastille is not to be doubted, therefore the key comes to the right place."

Martha was glad to note also that George looked more relaxed, that he smiled more frequently, even burst into occasional laughter. And she knew one reason why. His teeth. He had begun losing his own at age twenty-two. Perhaps it was the false ones he had since acquired, two solid blocks of ivory, hand carved to fit the mouth and held in place with springs, obviously loose and uncomfortable, which had given him such a severe expression. Recently he had found a new dentist here in New York, Dr. Greenwood, an expert in fashioning artificial teeth. Taking a cast with beeswax, he had carved upper and lower plates from a hippopotamus tusk, working human teeth into the lower set, fixing them permanently with gold pivots. At least they were more comfortable, and his smiles were far less rigid and restrained. A pity that artist Houdon could not have seen him like this when he was seeking a characteristic pose!

Their private life also became more relaxed that winter. Every evening except Friday, when Martha held her levees, they spent alone with the children and, usually, Tobias Lear. Either he or George would read aloud from an entertaining book. Martha would retire at nine, when George would go to the library and write for an hour before retiring. Always both of them rose at daybreak, George to go again to his library until it was time for breakfast. During these relaxed evening hours Martha could almost imagine they were back at Mount Vernon.

With the coming of spring she began to feel fairly contented in the new setting. Cherry blossoms were as creamy pink and lilacs as heavenly mauve in New York as at Mount Vernon. Then came another threat of tragedy. It was a Sunday in May when George developed such a bad cold that he stayed home from church. The next day he had a high fever. Since Tobias Lear was away on his honeymoon, having married his boyhood sweetheart, Polly Long, in April, Major Jackson took charge of the office and arranged for medical attendance. Several doctors were called, Dr. Samuel Bard, Dr. John Charlton, and Dr. Charles McKnight, but their combined treatments effected no improvement. It was decided that he had a serious form of pneumonia. The household was in a state of panic. Once more straw was laid in the streets outside and ropes put across to prevent the passing of noisy traffic. And again Martha was with him day and night.

"He seemed less concerned himself as to the result," she was to write Mercy Warren later, "than perhaps any other person in the United States."

An eminent surgeon from Philadelphia, Dr. John Jones, was summoned. Though it was attempted to keep the news secret, it was soon known all over the country that the President was dangerously ill and that his death was likely. Scarcely less worried than Martha was Abigail Adams, who believed that no one else, not even her brilliant John, could cope with the complicated, unfinished tasks faced by the new government—trouble in Georgia over negotiations with Indian tribes, the argument over the site of a permanent capital for the new nation, jealousy of the southern agricultural states toward the industrial prosperity of New England, controversy over the state debts—and she was appalled at the thought of having to step into Martha's shoes.

Six days passed, for Martha each one of them an eon. The end seemed near. One caller found "every eye full of tears" and the President's life despaired of. Then about four o'clock in the afternoon came the miracle. The patient broke into a heavy sweat. The crisis was passed. The next day it was hoped he was out of danger. Four days later it was certain. For Martha it was like the joy of resurrection. As she wrote Mercy Warren in June, she was restored to her "ordinary state of tranquility and usually good flow of spirits." But she was not so happily confident as she sounded. Two illnesses so nearly fatal within a year? Suppose there should be a third! He was finding it hard to follow the doctors' orders, do less work and take more exercise. If only Congress would finish their business and they could go to Mount Vernon for a vacation!

But Congress was wrangling over two issues. One was the permanent location of the nation's capital. Hamilton and other New Yorkers wanted it in New York. Robert Morris, of course, favored Philadelphia. Jefferson and other Virginians wanted it on the Potomac. But even more bitterly divisive was the problem of debts incurred by the different states during the war. Should the new federal government be responsible for them? Yes, said Hamilton and others who believed in a strong federal government. No! thundered Jefferson and others, especially southerners who were firmly committed to preserving states' rights. The battle was hot right in George's own cabinet. This worried Martha, but George did not seem perturbed. Difference of opinion, he explained, was essential in a democracy. It preserved the delicate balance between anarchy and monarchy. In fact, such balance was the genius of their Constitution.

Still, he seemed relieved and of course secretly pleased when the issues were finally settled, apparently by compromise, the south agreeing to the assumption of state debts in return for promise of locating the Federal City on the Potomac. Philadelphia, it was agreed, would be its site until 1800, then it would be settled permanently near Georgetown. George had not sought to influence the decision of Congress as to the site of the capital. If any member voted for the Potomac site because he felt it was the President's wish, it was not because he had been asked to do so. And if Hamilton and Jefferson had played a part in the compromise, they had acted as individuals, not as officials. George had held rigidly to his conviction that the President must make no attempt to influence Congress.

Another move, this time to Philadelphia! Only six months in the Mansion House on Broadway! Martha sighed. She had become fairly contented here in New York. In fact, she had written Mercy Warren in June: "I contrive to be as happy here as I could be at any place except Mount Vernon. In truth, I should be very ungrateful if I did not acknowledge that everything has been done which politeness, hospitality or friendship could suggest to make my situation as satisfactory and agreeable as possible." But she was used to moving. And Philadelphia, where she had so many friends, would be an improvement over New York, which, in spite of its color and bustle, its familiar church services, thriving shops and pleasant homes and drives, had its drawbacks— unpaved, ill-lighted streets, mud and refuse, roaming swine, its water hawkers, its night carriers bearing away sewage to the river. Not that any city would be much better in these respects! Only in the peaceful countryside could one find cleanliness, quiet, tranquility.

They were to vacate the house before leaving for vacation at Mount Vernon. George was tired of the publicity attending his every movement.

"This time," he proposed gleefully, "we will steal a march on them. No one will know we've gone."

On the morning of August 30 they were ready. The servants had left before dawn with instructions to have the carriages and luggage over the ferry at Paulus Hook by sunrise. The family assembled by candlelight, Martha, George, the children, the secretaries. George was delighted that for once he had outwitted the populace. Suddenly an artillery band blared outside the windows. From every direction people began appearing. Among them were Governor Clinton and his suite, state officers, municipal authorities, clergy, members of the Society of the Cincinnati. George threw up his hands in resignation. "Well, well, they have found us out. Let them have their way."

Martha smiled to herself as she followed him down the steps and through the cheering throng. She knew that in spite of his longing for privacy he took pleasure in such evidences of the people's love. The crowd escorted them to the landing at Whitehall, where the beautiful barge which had brought them into New York was waiting. They were saluted by thirteen discharges of cannon and the huzzas of a tremendous multitude. Governor Clinton, Chief Justice John Jay, General Knox, Colonel Hamilton, and the Mayor of New York accompanied them in the barge to Paulus Hook, where they entered their English coach drawn by six horses.

They stopped in Philadelphia long enough to receive more plaudits, bells rung, a *feu-de-joie*, crowds and troops of Light Horse, as elaborate a welcome as if the President had been visiting the city for the first time. There would have been more dinners and garden parties, but Martha fell ill and remained in bed at their lodgings while George inspected the house they were to live in and gave minute directions to Lear for necessary improvements.

It was the sumptuous house where Robert Morris had lived when the Washingtons had visited him, where Martha had stayed several times. The Morrises had willingly moved next door in order to make their house available to the President. The state legislature had appropriated a fine building on South State Street, but George had refused it, unwilling to live in a house hired and furnished at public expense. Moreover, knowing that Philadelphians still desired their city to be the permanent capital and he personally desired it to be farther south, he did not want to give them the advantage that providing a Presidential mansion would afford.

The Morris house in Market Street was too small for his large household and would need alterations, an addition for servants, enlarged stables, offices for secretaries. Even with these it would be small and inconvenient compared with the Broadway house, requiring the President's business to be transacted in a third-floor room. A pity, thought Martha, to endure all this moving about and remodeling and pother when there was lovely Mount Vernon lying nearly empty, convenient in every way and designed to create the quiet and comfortable life they both so much desired! The very thought of Mount Vernon was so invigorating that she was able to leave with George on September 6, and they arrived home on the eleventh after an absence of sixteen months.

Two whole months at home! Martha savored them like drops of rare wine in a nearly drained goblet. No knowing how long the treasured memories would need to last! She saw the dogwood trees on the east lawn turn a bright orange-red, the locusts robe themselves in sunlight yellow. She watched the children romp on the bowling green, chase each other up and down the north and south lanes, jump up and down over the ha! ha!, the sunken wall which kept the cattle off the lawns yet kept clear the full view to the river. Let them enjoy their freedom while they could. The streets of Philadelphia, even its gardens, would be poor places to play. She reveled in the nearness of family, exclaimed how Betsy and Patty had grown, saw their faces light when she brought out her gifts, lockets for the girls, toys for Fanny's children, little bells for the new baby, a soft wool shawl for Nelly. But it could not last. The goblet was soon drained dry.

They left as planned on November 22, even though incessant rains had made the roads almost impassable, to say nothing of worse difficulties. Dunn, the driver, proved to be either drunk or incapable, and once nearly turned them over. Finally an Irishman, John Fagan, took the reins, consigning Dunn to the baggage wagon, which he upset twice. These misfortunes, added to the condition of the roads, made the journey almost intolerable. But they arrived at last, after five days, and went directly to the new house at 190 High Street. Though the remodeling was not yet complete, they found it habitable.

Martha settled into her new quarters with her usual adaptability. There was an adequate dining room, about thirty feet long, with a new bow window overlooking a pleasant garden. She was given the whole second floor, with a drawing room and a private study, besides the bedrooms. There had been changes in the household. Humphreys, who had gone as a diplomat to Europe, was greatly missed, but Martha's nephew Bartholomew Dandridge was one of the new secretaries, and Lear's sprightly new wife Polly soon helped assuage Martha's homesickness for her beloved Fanny.

She lamented the loss of the fabulous Fraunces, who had retired to the management of his New York tavern, but now the chief cook Hercules came into his own. Though technically an underling to the new steward Hyde, "Uncle Harkless," as he was called, a giant of ebony hue, reigned supreme in his own domain. To Martha's delight he was a stickler for cleanliness. His kitchen even *smelled* clean. When preparing his Thursday state dinners, he might wear as many as a half dozen clean aprons, one after the other, and used myriad napkins. After the steward placed the dishes on the table, he would retire to reappear in what he considered faultless attire, black smallclothes, a blue cloth coat with velvet collar and shining metal buttons, silk stockings, a cocked hat, enormous silver buckles bedecking his equally enormous feet. Martha herself, in her new velvet gown purchased for her first Christmas reception, was scarcely as resplendent.

She was happier in Philadelphia than in New York, for she was surrounded by old friends, Morrises, Biddles, Powels, Chews, and she no longer felt like a prisoner. Life, too, was simpler because of the Quaker influence in the city. With George she attended occasional balls, as well as occupying a pew each Sunday in St. Peter's Church (happy reminder of the St. Peter's of her girlhood!). There were occasional theater parties at the Old Southwark theater, where at one of them they saw *The School for Scandal* from an east box reserved for their use. It had red draperies and cushioned seats, and the United States coat of arms was on the front. When they entered the theater there stood Mr. Wignall, the manager, in full dress, holding a silver candlestick with a lighted candle in each hand, to conduct them to their box while musicians played "The President's March," later to be known as "Hail, Columbia." Though such ceremony was scored by some as being undemocratic, George accepted it as deference, not to himself, but to the essential dignity of his office.

Such criticisms distressed Martha more than they did George. The idea of Thomas Jefferson hinting at "monarchical ceremony" when he himself had been acting and dressing like a European lord since his return from the French court! And of that Colonel Bland complaining that George's bow was "stiff and haughty"! Of the latter George had merely commented in a letter to Dr. Stuart: "That I have not been able to make bows to the taste of poor Colonel Bland (who, by the by, I believe, never saw one of them) is to be regretted, especially as they were indiscriminately bestowed and the best I was master of."

Martha was comforted by such observations as Benjamin Franklin's, who had bequeathed "my fine crabtree walking stick with a gold head curiously wrought in the form of the cap of liberty" to "my friend and the friend of Mankind, General Washington. If it were a sceptre, he has merited it and would become it."

If George was not worried by such superficial criticisms, he was more and more distressed by the differences of opinion (animosities?) developing among his own official advisers: Hamilton, who believed in a strong central government, Jefferson, who with other southerners like Edmund Randolph, held that, except for a few delegated powers, all major functions of government were reserved to the states. They also represented divisions within the populace. Some who had supported the Constitution were having misgivings. Parties were developing, calling themselves "Federalists" and "Anti-Federalists." While George attempted to steer an even course between the proponents of two differing views of government, he thought and acted by one simple principle: There must be a strong central government or the country would lose its freedom. It could not exist with powerful self-willed states jealous of each others' rights and insisting on their own sovereignty. It was a struggle that would not be settled in his lifetime. A hundred years later it would result in a civil war, proving that his fears were justified. Two hundred years later it would still be rearing its head.

Fortunately, Martha was only vaguely conscious of these rumblings of what would soon be future trouble. She entertained at her Friday evening levees, yielding sufficiently to Philadelphia social custom to permit them to close at ten instead of nine. She presided at the usual dinners for dignitaries. She enjoyed shopping in the Philadelphia stores, especially in Mr. Whiteside's drygoods shop, though she usually made more purchases for the family than for herself—a doll for Fanny's little Maria, painting supplies for Betsy and Patty, a watch for Fanny. "It is of the newest fashion. The chain is Mr. Lear's choosing, and such as Mrs. Adams, the Vice President's lady, and those in polite circles use." For herself no watch could ever take the place of that gift of Daniel's bearing her initials on its face.

"I send to dear Maria," she continued, "a piece of chene to make her a frock and a piece of muslin which I hope is long enough for an apron for you. In exchange for it I beg you will give me a worked muslin apron you have, like my gown that I made just before I left home, of worked muslin, as I wish to make a petticoat to my gown of the two aprons."

Social obligations, entertaining, yes. But far more important always was her involvement with her children. Nelly was a constant joy. At twelve she was already a beauty, her dusky loveliness reminding Martha more and more of her lost Patsy. But Washy, at ten, was altogether too much a repetition of his father at that age, lovable, lazy, hating the Academy where he was enrolled. And unfortunately Martha had not learned from previous mistakes. She was hopelessly indulgent, especially to Washy. It was well for her peace of mind that she did not read some comments of Tobias Lear in a letter to Humphreys, who was now minister to Portugal:

"Nelly and Washington have every advantage in point of instructors that this country can give them, and they certainly make good progress in those things which are taught them. But I apprehend the worst consequences particularly to the boy, from the unbounded indulgence of his grandmama. The ideas which are insinuated to him at home that he is born to such noble properties both in estate and otherwise . . . and the servile respect the servants are obliged to pay to him . . . He is on the way to ruin."

Nelly, subjected to the discipline of a day school where she studied reading, English literature, spelling, grammar, writing, arithmetic, French, geography, grumbling at the hours Grandmama required her to spend at embroidery, drawing, practicing at her harpsichord each day, would have scoffed at the idea that she was being spoiled. And, indeed, Martha seemed to compensate for her overindulgence of Washy by this far stricter regimen which she imposed on poor Nelly.

This unevenness of discipline was due perhaps to reminiscences of her own childhood, when an especially strict mother had deemed it her essential province to train her daughters in the necessary housewifely arts, while the education of her sons had been left entirely to tutors. Or perhaps it was just the love and pride of a doting grandmother who wished the beloved to excel in those skills which society deemed most important for a young girl. Both children were indulged with an excess of gifts and privileges, by George as well as Martha.

While dutifully and usually with enjoyment Martha was playing the role of "First Lady," she was as much concerned with the homely happenings at Mount Vernon as with the routine of Presidential life in Philadelphia. George's letters to George Augustine were full of her admonitions:

"Mrs. Washington requested the Gardener's wife to superintend the
care of the Spinners" . . . "Mrs. Washington desires that you will
order the Ashes to be taken care of, that there may be no want of
Soap" . . . "Mrs. Washington desires you will direct Old Toll to distil
a good deal of Rose and Mint Water & ca., and we wish to know
whether the Linnen for the People is all made up . . ."

People. George always called them his "people" or his "family,"
never his "slaves." The very word "slave" was repugnant to him.
Though he had been born into a world in which slavery was the accepted order of society, had inherited many slaves and acquired more
by birth and by purchase, his attitude toward the institution had under-
gone a profound change. Since the Revolution and the establishment
of the new nation he had determined never again to buy or sell a slave.
"I am principled against this kind of traffic in the human species," he
had written, "and to disperse the families I have an aversion." He had
become convinced that emancipation was the only solution. To fellow
Virginians he had expressed his feeling: "I wish from my soul that the
Legislature of this State would see the policy of a gradual abolition of
slavery." To Arthur Young, an English agriculturist, he once wrote:
"There is not a living being who wishes slavery abolished more than I
do. But there is only one proper and effectual mode by which it can be
accomplished, and that is by Legislative authority, and this, as far as my
suffrage will go, shall never be wanting."

Though it was George who saw that his "people" were not over-
worked, that they were taught skills, that careful records were kept of
their families, that they could travel and visit other plantations, plant
gardens and raise livestock to supplement their rations, it was Martha
who saw that they were properly fed, clothed, cared for when sick,
provided with gifts on special occasions, given extra care if aged or
infirm. Even here, far away and in a different life, she felt responsible
for them.

She could hardly bear to watch George leave on a long southern trip
after Congress closed in March of 1791, partly because he would be
gone for at least three long months, but also because he would be
stopping for a time at Mount Vernon. But she realized it was a necessary implementation of his purpose to visit all the states eventually in
order to weld them into a greater sense of unity. Also she rejoiced that
he seemed in better spirits than for many months. The session of

Congress had been a success. As Abigail Adams commented: "Our public affairs never looked more promising." After much wrangling a bill had been passed establishing a national bank. Excise legislation had provided necessary funds for running the government. Kentucky and Vermont had been admitted to the Union. Arrangements had been made for laying off the "Federal District" on the Potomac. Bills encouraging self-dependent American shipping had been passed. Yes, and opposition to the administration seemed to have died down. Even the Boston *Independent Chronicle,* long a critic, was praising the work of Congress and had words of commendation for the President.

George was looking forward eagerly to the trip, which would involve acquisition of land on the Potomac for the new Federal City, as well as visits to all the southern states. He had acquired a light chariot for the journey. Besides Major Jackson he was accompanied by a mounted footman and valet and his servant Paris, also mounted and leading a white charger for George's later use.

Three months. They were some of the longest Martha had ever spent. George had made every provision for her well-being, instructing Tobias Lear to see that she had all the money she required, adding, "and from time to time ask her if she does want, as she is not fond of applying." There were compensations for loneliness, and not only the grandchildren. Tobias and Polly Lear had a new baby named, not George Washington as one might expect, but Benjamin Lincoln Lear after the revolutionary hero of their native New Hampshire.

"Many express their surprise," wrote Lear, "that a son of mine born too in the family, should receive any other name than George Washington. But although I love and respect the great man who bears that name, yet I would not for the world do a thing that would savor of adulation toward him."

Possibly also the qualities displayed by little Wash did not encourage the creation of another George Washington growing up in the same house!

It seemed that she always became sick as soon as George went away, perhaps because while he was there she refused to yield to feelings of weakness. She relieved her homesickness for Mount Vernon by writing to Fanny.

"Your letter of the 29th of May," she wrote on June 5, "did not reach my hands till yesterday—I was then very sick having got cold by the change of weather;—or I would have got and sent by Hercules the sil and &—I will as soon as I am well enough to go out and make the best collection I can and send it by a safe hand. As to fine muslin I have never been able to find a yard of fine Jaconet muslin in this place. I send by Hercules some rufles for my little Boys boson which I beg you will make charlot hem—and ship them ready to sew on and send me six at a time as his old ruffles are worne to raggs—Hercules comes home to be ready for his master . . . I also send some East India sugar—it seems to be clean and while I was in hopes it would have arrived in time to preserve and dry cherreys—I have had let from the President from Savanna—and expect he will be with you by this day week . . ."

George returned home on July 6, and the children listened spell-bound to his exciting stories. Some of them made Martha shiver. After crossing Chesapeake Bay they had run into a tremendous thunder-storm. Their boat had run aground. Since they could not be rescued in the wind and darkness, they had spent the night on the vessel, fearful that the high waves would pound it to pieces. At dawn they had finally been rescued. But his news from Mount Vernon was even more dis-turbing. George Augustine was failing. It was the story of his beloved Lawrence all over again. Dr. Craik wanted George Augustine to go on another pilgrimage to the Berkeley Springs in the hope of giving him reprieve from the disease a while longer. During his absence George would let his nephew Bob Lewis take his place as manager at Mount Vernon.

In her distress Martha begrudged every moment which kept them from their summer holiday at home. How Fanny must be suffering, and she had said nothing about it in her letters! But George was immersed in affairs of state, worried over events taking place in France. The new government born of the Revolution seemed committed to increasing and indiscriminate violence. He was distressed to learn of the flight of Louis XVI and Marie Antoinette, their capture and return to Paris as virtual prisoners. How could Lafayette's efforts at democratic reform take place amid such violence?

Suddenly George himself was sick again, another bout with a carbun-cle similar to his previous attack, only not so severe. Then in the middle of August, Wash came down with measles, and prospects of Mount Vernon retreated even further. "Spoiling him again," she could see people like Tobias Lear thinking when she ordered the servants to take the boy ices and cold drinks every hour and she herself scarcely left his bedside. But she could not help it. And fortunately George understood.

"Mrs. Washington is bound up in the boy," he told Lear with an indulgent smile. "Any rigidity used towards him would perhaps be productive of grievous effects on her."

It was August 29 when Martha was able at last to write Fanny that they were coming. She was to make ready for a large company. They could stay no longer than October 17 because Congress would be meeting on October 24. "Make Nathan clean his kitchen and all in it," she directed. "Will bring work for Charlot. Dear little Wash is well enough now to go to school."

Already Martha was counting the years (just one and a half), the months (eighteen of them), almost the days, when George's term of public service would be ended, when instead of this little reprieve in the summer they would be leaving for home to stay the rest of their lives.

20

It was 1792. Only one more full year, thought Martha as Oney laced her stays tight, arranged her several petticoats, slipped over her head the new dress for the New Year's reception. It was a brocade, pink with scattered scarlet roses, more elaborate than she usually wore, but in the prevailing style, which favored bright colors and contrasts. She knew that she would look dowdy and dull beside the slender, shimmering Mrs. William Bingham, queen of Philadelphia society, who had traveled to Paris, London, the Hague and now lived in a palace with a white marble staircase.

The months could not pass swiftly enough. George also, she knew, was looking forward with anticipation to retirement. On his birthday, February 22, he was sixty years old. There was much celebration. The household awoke that morning to the sound of a cannon salute and the ringing of bells. They kept chiming all day. That night the whole town, it seemed, was illuminated. Candles and oil lamps lighted every window. In spite of the festivities George seemed unusually depressed. Finally Martha, worried, asked him what was the matter.

He was suddenly feeling old, he admitted. He was afraid his memory, never too good, might be getting unreliable. Suppose he was unconsciously revealing a mental decline. And he feared his hearing was becoming impaired.

"Huh!" scoffed Wash, who managed to overhear most interesting conversations. "He can hear me if I tiptoe past the door when he's entertaining important visitors!"

Martha did her scoffing silently. It was not age that laid the burden of fear and doubt on those obdurately straight shoulders. It was this job he had never wanted that was making him feel like an old man. Let him greet the dawn riding one of his favorite horses over his five farms instead of laboring over his desk by candlelight, and he would not be complaining of waning mentality and deafness! Just a few more months, and the weight of years would drop from him. There would be no more of these worrying problems—trouble with Indians on the frontier, insurrections, squabbles over paying state debts, tension in his cabinet, worst of all those scurrilous articles about him in some of the newspapers.

It was one day in May, when James Madison came to visit, that Martha felt the first premonition of disaster. Madison was one of George's most trusted advisers, and he had wanted to consult him, he told Martha, about when he should make his announcement of retirement. Perhaps Madison could even help him prepare a farewell address which could be delivered at the next session of Congress. They were closeted together all the morning, and at dinner, fortunately without other guests, they seemed still in a mood of serious deliberation. All Martha's attempts to introduce lighter topics were rebuffed by silence. Then suddenly the morsel of delectable Mount Vernon ham which she had just started to chew lost its tangy flavor.

"I must repeat," Madison was saying with his usual cool, dispassionate precision, "that your retirement would be a stunning surprise and shock to the people. And I fear it would be extremely detrimental to the country."

"Nonsense!" replied George. Obviously they were continuing an argument which had consumed most of the morning. "My return to private life is consistent with every public consideration. All these criticisms of my administration, this rise of party spirit—"

"All the more reason for you to continue," interrupted Madison crisply, his thin, narrow features honed into sharp obstinacy. "Two weak minorities, one bent on overthrowing the government, the other on creating a monarchy! Another four years would give such a tone and firmness to the government as would secure it from danger from either of these descriptions of enemies. Again I beg you, my dear Mr. President—"

Perhaps George saw the horror on Martha's face. Abruptly he put an end to the argument: "As I told you, sir, I want you to reflect on when and how my retirement can best be announced. Now this Mount Vernon ham, doesn't it inspire you also with a desire to return to our own Virginia? Have another portion, sir, I beg of you."

With steady fingers Martha transferred a generous slice from the silver platter to the visitor's plate. In spite of George's reassuring words, intended, she feared, for her, she found the rest of her dinner tasteless, if not bitter. He had made up his mind, yes, she was sure of that. He was determined to leave the office as soon as possible, as he had so often assured her. But she knew him better than he did himself. If enough people felt, as did Mr. Madison, that he was necessary for the welfare of the country . . . She knew she would not rest easy during all of the next nine months. Nine months, how fitting! They would be like an uneasy pregnancy, with constant doubt whether they would bring forth life or death.

Soon afterward, Congress having closed, George left with Lear on a hurried trip to Mount Vernon. They returned with both good news and bad. The crops were flourishing, and, as George wrote a friend in Ireland, "the country generally exhibited the face of plenty." But George Augustine was in far worse condition, spitting much blood, and the doctors felt he must take a complete rest. George was going to give his farm manager full responsibility for the estate, though it would mean closer supervision on his part. Martha was torn by conflicting emotions, grief for Fanny and her husband, but a guilty relief because George was more firmly determined on retirement. Already he was beginning to formulate his farewell address.

The first of July she wrote Fanny that they were leaving on the twelfth. "Have Frank clean the house from garret to cellar. Have the china looked over, the glasses all washed and clean. Wait until I come home to have the chairs stuffed. Put up the window curtains and the bed curtain."

Summer was a reprieve, at least from worry about a possible second term, but there were other worries. Fanny was worn out with nursing her invalid (dying?) husband, and she wept in Martha's arms. Her three living children—Maria only four—were in need of grandmotherly concern. George, while exulting in his new six-sided barn on the Dogue Run farm, was plagued with many problems. There had been a severe drought. His manager was not making the farms pay. Only George might be able to do that. The death of George Mason, though they had been long estranged because of the Constitution, had left a great void. And the bulging mailbag kept him writing letters before dawn and long into the night. Spain was stirring up trouble in the west. Strife between Hamilton and Jefferson was becoming more heated. An excise tax on whiskey was stirring up rebellion in Pennsylvania. And a paper called the *National Gazette* was making bitter attacks on the Administration.

"The free citizens of America," one writer averred, "will not suffer the *well-born* few to trample them under foot." These and other accusations were aimed at creating dissatisfaction and contributing to the overthrow of the Federalists.

Such barrages, George knew, were attacks on himself only indirectly, for he had signed into law the bills they were condemning. Other attacks were definitely personal, recurring accusations of his "monarchical practices." Since he believed he had carefully toed the line of republican conduct which he had set for himself, these attacks smarted. Angrily he refused the request of one Philadelphia tradesman who wanted to ape the British custom and put the Washington arms over his shop, boasting that he was "Silversmith to the President"! Such an affectation, he replied sternly, would be "very disagreeable." However, he could not resist the Virginia planter's favorite prerogative of sporting an impressive coach and four, preferably six, with handsome decorations, including his coat of arms on the door. If that was "monarchical display," let them make the most of it.

He did not tell Martha that many of the letters he received urged his acceptance of reelection. However, when Jefferson was visiting on October 1 on his way to Philadelphia from Monticello, she overheard a disturbing conversation. She despised eavesdroppers, but she was knitting in the little parlor before breakfast, and they had come from the study to take chairs on the porch outside the open window. Thinking they had already finished their serious conversation, she did not move.

They were talking of their mutual desire to retire from public service to their country estates. Good! For once George and his Secretary of State were in full agreement. Then suddenly her flying fingers halted.

George was saying that he was still in doubt about a second term, not that he was at all sure the country would want him! He had asked Tobias Lear to make inquiries about how people felt in the north, and it seemed to be the people's wish there that he remain in office. What did Jefferson think about feelings in the south?

Martha held her breath. "I believe," said Jefferson, "that you, sir, are the only man in the United States who possesses the confidence of the whole country. The public mind is no longer confident or serene, and that is from causes in which you are in no way concerned. Your continuance at the head of government is of supreme importance."

There was more talk, but Martha did not hear it. She continued knitting, though her fingers felt cold and stiff, her hands trembled, and she dropped a stitch without knowing it. So . . . it was decided. George might not know it yet, and he would probably keep dillydallying, but *she* knew. If Jefferson, the Anti-Federalist, whatever that was, the states' rights man, believed that George was needed to save the country . . . Oh, yes, of course he would do his duty, even if it killed him, and it very likely would. Words from her quiet hour that morning echoed in her mind, for she had been reading the story of Ruth. They were not new to her experience. She had been living them for a long time. "Whither thou goest, I will go."

When breakfast was announced she laid her knitting aside, rose, and proceeded to the small dining room, where she presided with her usual quiet, smiling courtesy.

"Do have some more of our good Virginia corn pone and honey, Mr. Jefferson. We won't be getting it like this in Philadelphia, and we'll be missing it for a long time."

Never had she so hated to leave Mount Vernon as on that day in early October when they started for the capital. Fanny was taking her children and sick husband to Eltham, where the winter would be milder than on the Potomac. She and Martha clung together, trying to control their tears. Both knew that George Augustine was unlikely to see Mount Vernon again.

For the first time the estate was left in the care of strangers, Whiting in charge of the farms, a housekeeper as the only mistress of the mansion. Martha knew that George was as concerned as she. He tried to reassure her: "Only five months, my dear. The new administration will take over in March."

She smiled back at him. She knew better.

Back in Philadelphia, Congress met on November 5, and George gave his annual message. A farewell address? No. It was a simple document dealing mostly with Indian affairs. Its most notable feature was the absence of any word about his wishes or intentions in regard to a second term. Martha could not help knowing that people were continuing to press him for a decision, many urging him to accept, others merely insisting that he should make his purpose known. On November 17 their mutual friend Elizabeth Powel was writing, regretting that he had not made a favorable decision and announced it in his message. Still he was silent. So was Martha. Patiently she waited.

Finally he could put off discussing his problem with her no longer. "What should I do?" he asked one evening after the children had gone to bed, the secretaries had left, and they were alone in their upstairs apartment. While she had been quietly knitting he had been walking the floor like a man in torment. "You know what I want and what I promised both you and myself. But"—he made a gesture of despair—"you have no idea—you don't know—what people are saying! They're besieging me—from all sides—"

Martha laid aside her knitting. There was no coldness in her fingers now, no trembling of her hands. She had long ago faced the challenge of this moment and won her battle. "Yes," she said quietly, "I do know. I understand just what a struggle you are having."

His relief was like a suddenly opened petcock, loosing the flood of pent-up emotions. She must know how distasteful the idea was to him, for the distress it would cause her as well as himself. He hadn't wanted a first term as President, to say nothing of a second! Surely he had made enough sacrifice for his country already, twelve years of his life! Suppose he did agree, after so long making it plain that he would not seek office again. Might not people say that he had become so corrupted by power that he could not bear to relinquish it? They had maligned him in plenty of other ways! It was hard to believe that, as so many people seemed to think, he was so important to the Union that he should continue. Surely there were plenty of other leaders far wiser and more fitted for the job! And yet—they seemed so sure!

Finally the flood ebbed, and he stood looking down at her, looking very much like Washy when the mercurial ten-year-old labored over the problem of what activity to tackle next.

"What should I do?" he repeated in desperation, then again, "What should I—what should *we* do?"

Martha took up her knitting, and the needles began clicking. "You—we—will do the right thing, of course, at least what you believe is the right thing, as you always do."

He frowned. "But—what *is* the right thing? How can I know?"

She looked up at him, smiling, her needles never missing a stitch. "I think you know already," she said confidently. "If you don't now, you will when the time comes."

Suddenly he was on his knees beside her. He took one of her small plump hands in his and raised it to his lips. "No wonder they call you the 'First Lady,' " he said almost with reverence, "and not just because you're the wife of the President."

After he had returned briskly to his letter writing, she sat for a long time, hands idle, eyes unseeing, thoughts focused inward with sudden clarity of vision. *First Lady.* What a name to have to live up to! She was just beginning to realize what it should mean. No honor, certainly, nothing to be proud of, to arouse other women's envy. She had thought at first it was enough to be just a good wife to a man burdened with problems quite apart from a woman's proper functions, a competent housekeeper, a gracious and affable hostess; to protect him as much as possible from unnecessary stresses; to encourage and calm and soothe and relieve him of minor duties and be ready at the end of the day with his slippers and milk toast and cup of tea. Enough perhaps for the First Lady of the General. Not anymore. For you were not just the President's wife. You were wedded to a nation, *people*—millions of them—for better for worse, *their* better, if necessary *your* worse. Their good must come first. And, worst of all, you must be the first in a long succession of First Ladies. It wasn't just George who was setting precedents, as he called it. Horrible, challenging thought! You might be setting examples for the next hundred—two hundred years! She picked up her knitting, a warm stocking for Washy now that the weather had turned cold, and once more her fingers flew.

The rivalry in George's cabinet between Hamilton, the Federalist, and Jefferson, the so-called Democrat, was as bitter as ever. The only issue they seemed to agree on was their mutual conviction that he should accept a second term. Day after day he put off his answer. The states were preparing to name their electors, and his silence was taken as consent. On February 13, 1793, when the votes were counted, once more he received first place unanimously. John Adams was not so fortunate, receiving only seventy-seven votes to Governor Clinton's fifty. The matter was settled, as Martha had known long ago it would be. Months to count now? No, years. Four of them.

Seventeen ninety-three. Almost from its beginning there was family tragedy. Burwell Bassett fell from his horse and never recovered. His death was followed on February 5 by George Augustine's. Martha, too stricken with grief for poor Fanny to find words, let George express their mutual sorrow and desire to help.

"To you," he wrote on February 24, "who so well know the affectionate regard I had for our departed friend, it is unnecessary to describe the sorrow with which I was afflicted at the news of his death. The object of the present letter is to convey the warmest assurance of my love, friendship, and disposition to serve you. These also I profess to have in an eminent degree, for your Children." She must always consider Mount Vernon her home, he continued, and, though he did not state it in so many words, Martha knew that he would make himself responsible for the needs of her three children. How many were dependent on him now? Jack's two, Samuel's boys, now Fanny's three. Yet in spite of the expense and trouble, he never complained.

Dutifully, but with stiff lips and a heavy heart, Martha smiled as she greeted the crowds which came to celebrate George's sixty-first birthday on February 22. Every half hour during the day the bells of Christ Church rang in tribute. Looking back over the four years past there was much to be thankful for. The precarious welding into union of thirteen disparate states—fifteen now—had been accomplished with almost miraculous success. Prosperity had increased. Manufacturing, shipping, fisheries, and other industries were flourishing. The land was furnishing a healthy source of income. And, best of all, there had been peace with foreign nations.

Yet on his inauguration day, March 4, George had worries other than those relating to family and nation. News from abroad was terrifying. Europe seemed on the verge of conflagration. France and England were at odds. There was a new government in France headed by a rabid revolutionary, Danton, which was murdering royalists. The King had been imprisoned. And Lafayette, who, in spite of his democratic fervor and support of the Revolution, was considered by the extremists an aristocrat, was imprisoned in Austria. No one knew the fate of his family. George was as grief-stricken as he was alarmed. Martha's heart ached for him. His nephew George Augustine had been scarcely more dear to him than the gay and gallant Lafayette.

When he went briefly to Mount Vernon in March to arrange for George Augustine's burial, problems of state still pursued him. A letter from Hamilton brought dire news. France had declared war on England, Spain, and Holland. Marie Antoinette as well as King Louis had gone to the guillotine. Congress was in upheaval speculating on consequences of the war to the United States. Fearful of precipitate action by his Secretary of State, who was an outspoken partisan of France, George hastened to warn him.

"It behooves the Government of this country," he wrote Jefferson, "to use every means in its power to prevent the citizens from embroiling us with either England or France by endeavoring to maintain a strict neutrality." The next morning, early, he started for Philadelphia by the shortest route.

Martha greeted him anxiously, noting his utter weariness and intense disquiet. Oh, dear! She had so hoped this trip would give him needed rest, yet here were the stern lines back in his face, etched deeper than she had ever seen them.

The next months were so incredibly difficult that she felt they could not be real. She must be living in a bad dream. She had almost become used to the sharp little barbs of criticism which were cast at the President. Though she knew they hurt George more than he admitted, he had convinced her that they were not worth worrying about. No one could please everybody, and he was a passionate champion of the freedom of the press. It was one of the democratic bulwarks of the Constitution, he believed, necessary for the protection and education of the people, just as education itself was crucial for a republic where the popular will should be sovereign.

There had been more of these sharp barbs in recent months, a revival of the old charges of monarchical pomp and ceremony, jibes made at "those apparent trifles, birthday odes" and "the evil at its root . . . witness the Drawing Room!" "It appears," noted a writer in the *National Gazette*, "that a new order of citizens has been created, consisting only of the officers of the federal government. The privileges of this order consist in sharing exclusively in the profits of the 25,000 dollars a year allowed for the President's table, and in the honor of gazing upon him once a week at his levees."

But the criticisms directed against him now were more than barbs. They were barrages as deadly as she had heard at Cambridge, at Newburgh, at Valley Forge, only these were words, not guns. The whole country seemed to have gone mad. They had been united, it seemed, in wanting—needing—George to be their President again. Now many of them had turned against him. They had urged him, almost forced him into this second term against his will, and now they were crucifying him. And all because he was trying to keep his country out of war!

If she sometimes appeared to know and care little about political issues, it was because she understood fully the necessity for discretion. She never permitted political discussion among her guests or expressed an opinion on public questions except in private. Though some people often attempted to draw her out, she fenced them off adroitly. But not because she had no knowledge, no opinions! Her convictions were as strong as George's, and she often gave him advice. Better far to be considered ignorant or indifferent to government policy than to run the risk of disclosing delicate information which she had overheard or which had been given her in confidence! She had overheard enough, been told enough, to understand the situation.

Neutrality. It was a new word, and it had set the country on fire, multiplied a feud between two members of the President's cabinet into bitter strife between two powerful factions in the country. When George signed the "Proclamation of Neutrality" in April, there was instant divisive reaction. Sympathy for the French cause swept much of the country. It was fanned to white-hot heat by a new envoy from France named Edmond Genêt, who, disregarding all government supervision, went about the country inflaming emotions, even outfitting American ships to prey on British vessels. According to the treaty of 1778, he and others maintained, the United States was bound to aid France in her war against England, especially since the treaty with England of 1783 had never been fully observed, the British still keeping garrisons on the border posts, inciting Indians, seizing vessels carrying products of the French islands.

Even Martha, a novice in politics, had an answer to that spurious argument. The treaty with France had been made with the French King, and the new government had murdered him. Hamilton agreed.

He wanted to abrogate the treaty. Jefferson, who in spite of the brutal excesses of the new French government was still loyal to its revolutionary concept, stoutly maintained that treaties could not be broken. George was caught between the two factions and became a target of abuse for each one. He found the venomous attacks bewildering.

"I would not have believed," he admitted bitterly, "that while steering a steady course to preserve this country from the horrors of a desolating war, I should be accused of being the enemy of one nation and subject to the influence of another, and that too in such exaggerated and indecent terms as could scarcely be applied to a Nero."

From the beginning he had made clear his philosophy of the nation's role: "My tenets are few and simple . . . to be honest and just ourselves and to exact it from others; meddling as little as possible in their affairs where our own are not involved. If this maxim was generally adopted wars would cease . . . and our harvests be more abundant, peaceful and happy."

Especially was he wounded by the scurrilous attacks of Benjamin Franklin Bache in his *General Advertizer*, ridiculing the Proclamation as "a perfect nullity" and "a firebrand," which had turned a sacred treaty with France into a private pact with England. It was shocking and humiliating that this close relative of his loyal friend Franklin should have so turned against him. However, he endured the barrage with outward granite calmness in order to preserve the dignity of his office. Only Martha saw him when his guard was down, when in the privacy of their little parlor and bedroom he yielded to utter weariness and frustration. There was little she could do except feed him his nourishing toast and tea, make him comfortable, regale him with some amusing incident which would make him laugh, for she had a flair for telling stories. There was the one, for instance, about the quack mesmerizer who had come to Philadelphia declaring that he could cure all sorts of ailments, which had won her a reputation for witticism even with the sedate Vice President.

"They had got this quack into the President's house," Adams had written Abigail, "among some of the servants, and Mrs. Washington told me a story on Tuesday, before a number of gentlemen, so ineffably ridiculous that I dare not repeat it in writing. The venerable lady laughed as immoderately as all the rest of us did."

It was a hilarious incident involving Hercules, the cook, and several of the other servants. Lear had heard the story and repeated it to George and Martha. The kitchen help, it seemed, had brought the quack into the house in order to have some sport with "Uncle Hark-less," who had been complaining of rheumatism, hence, they felt, putting more work on them. This miracle worker, they told him, would cure his ailments, make him so strong he could lift a whole hog. Very well, he agreed, tongue in cheek, let him try. He'd be glad to pay his price, whatever it was. Though the mesmerizer, a small man, looked slightly alarmed at the sight of his huge black subject, he bravely embarked on his mumbo jumbo. Clever old Hercules pretended to let himself be hypnotized, groaning, rolling his eyes, making strange gestures, finally leaping up, shouting, "I's cured! Whar's dat hog? Let me at him! Oh, dar he is! He make fine dinnah!" Whereupon he seized the small quack, lifted him in his powerful arms, and bore him struggling and screaming to the open fire, holding him at arm's length over the blaze, until his assistants, thoroughly alarmed, rescued him and sent him away—without his pay.

"Needless to say," Martha finished with a chuckle, "he has not been heard from again."

She needed all her powers of rousing merriment during these torturing days.

Problems multiplied. The arrogant Genêt, it was learned, had armed a ship to take military aid to France! His patience taxed beyond endurance, George took action and met the French minister face to face. Though mad with his sense of power Genêt suddenly realized, in the face of the President's grim, cold dignity, that here was the actual government. It was the end of his brief triumph. At last the country saw him for what he was, and a demand was made for his recall. Slowly the fires he had kindled would subside.

"It is on great occasions only, and after time has been given for cool and deliberate reflection," George commented, "that the real voice of the people can be known."

That summer of 1793 had more shocks to deliver. Toward the end of July, Polly Lear came down with fever and within a week she was dead. Lear took his little son Lincoln home to his people in New Hampshire. Martha and George were almost as grieved as the bereft young husband. It was like losing three members of their own family.

Another shock to George was Jefferson's resignation as Secretary of

State, to take effect the first of September. Hamilton also was talking of resigning. Martha was more indignant than shocked. It was they who had helped persuade him to take a second term, and now they were deserting him! They could leave when the going got difficult; he could not.

Fate had not finished dealing its blows. Polly's death, it seemed, had been a forerunner of a plague of epidemic proportions. By August yellow fever was sweeping the city. Panic spread. People began frantically to leave. George did not fear for himself. When Hamilton fell sick and it was feared he might be in the first stages of the disease, George still invited the Secretary and his wife to dine at his house on September 6. It was discovered two days later that Hamilton did indeed have the disease but in a light form. George had planned to leave for Mount Vernon later in September, but when Martha refused to leave immediately without him, he changed his plans, and they left earlier than intended, on September 10. At last. For the first time in months, it seemed, they could breathe clean air again. The fields were green along the roads south. As one visitor to their beloved Potomac expressed it, everything seemed to "look smiling."

It was to Germantown, where the seat of government had moved, that in December they returned to find Philadelphia ravaged by the death of more than four thousand, among them Samuel Powel, one of their dearest friends. Hamilton had fully recovered. With the coming of frost and snow the last traces of the fever had vanished. The year of national peril and international tension, of personal calumny and family grief, more difficult than all the preceding four put together, was over. George's last act that year was typical. He made a gift "without ostentation or mention of my name" for the relief of the widows and orphans of the city.

Seventeen ninety-four. It began auspiciously with almost spring weather. When George's birthday, his sixty-second, was celebrated with the usual parades, jingling bells, artillery salutes, one could almost forget that magazines like Bache's were continuing to print articles of personal abuse, declaring that he was "inefficient," "treacherous," had "little passions," was "in search of personal incense." "If ever a nation was debauched by a man," it stated at one time, "the American nation has been debauched by Washington." In the evening Martha went with George to a birthday ball given in his honor by the City Dancing

Assembly. And earlier that same day George received the new French minister, Jean Antoine Fauchet, in his parlor. The heyday of the arrogant Genêt was ended, and by the end of March the danger of possible violence he had incited against Spanish dependencies in the west and in Florida was past.

"The new French minister seems to be a plain grave and good man," Martha wrote Fanny on March 2. "As far as we can judge from his looks and manners he is a very agreeable man."

Here, she felt with satisfaction, was one way she could make her contribution both to the Presidency and to the country. Foreign visitors of importance could be made to feel at home in her drawing room and at her dinner table. Even differences of opinion in Congress and the cabinet were sometimes peacefully resolved in the atmosphere of an informal tea or dinner.

Not that problems had diminished appreciably. British naval commanders had been told to seize neutral vessels in trade with the West Indies, and it looked as if England was trying to force the country out of its neutral position. But in April good news came. William Pitt's government had revoked the order to seize neutral vessels. Chief Justice Jay was sent to London on a mission of peace. The country became comparatively quiet.

Martha had other matters than politics to take up her attention. Her two older granddaughters were visiting her. Patty, now sixteen, had fallen in love with Thomas Peter, son of Judge Peter of Georgetown, a good friend of George's, and they were to be married the following year. Betsy was obviously envious, and Martha feared she might act too hastily in seeking marriage. She was delighted when this oldest granddaughter, who turned eighteen on August 21, wrote asking George for his picture. It was an opportune request, for when he sent it he gave her some affectionate advice about love and marriage:

"Do not then in your contemplation of the marriage state, look for perfect felicity before you consent to wed. Nor conceive, from the fine tales the Poets and lovers of old have told us, of the transports of mutual love, that heaven has taken its abode on earth . . . Love is a mighty pretty thing . . . but it is too dainty a thing to live upon *alone,* and ought not to be considered farther than as a necessary ingredient for that matrimonial happiness which results from a combination of causes; none of which are of greater importance than . . . good sense, good disposition, and the means of supporting you in the way you have been brought up . . ."

Martha smiled when he showed her the letter. Good, practical George! Had he used those tests when he was seeking a wife? Good sense, good disposition, even "means of support"? Yes, she supposed she had had them all. Would they have mattered to him one iota if he could have had Sally Fairfax? How silly to be asking such questions now after all these years of—yes, "matrimonial happiness," of which he had called love a necessary ingredient! Yet she knew the vision of Sally, slender, scintillating, provocative, that white flame which could kindle such passion, could never be quite banished from her memory.

George was about to leave on a trip west in September with the militia to dispel an uprising called the "Whiskey Rebellion," when the letter from Fanny arrived. She was living in their little house in Alexandria, not far from the site of the Federal City, where Tobias Lear intended to set up a new business. They had been seeing each other. Suppose they wanted to marry, two lonely people bereft in the same year, needing the care of another parent for their children? Would George and Martha approve?

Martha certainly would, and in George's absence she tried to express the gist of what would be his reaction in a letter: "The President has a very high opinion of, and friendship for Mr. Lear, and has not the least objection to your forming the connection, but no more than myself would not wish to influence your judgment either way, yours and the children's good being among the first wishes of my heart."

Western insurrection? European war? Overthrow of the extremist government in France? Martha found it hard to become alarmed or excited about such issues. Though she rejoiced with George in his proclamation signed on New Year's Day, 1795, designating a day for public thanksgiving that the "United States again enjoyed domestic tranquility," and presided with him that day over a repast of cakes and wine for members of Congress, her chief interest was the wedding of Patty about to take place in just five days. Nelly was going to Hope Park to act as her sister's bridesmaid, and her excitement permeated the house. She had a new dress, and Martha had promised her the loan of her famous watch with her initials circling the dial. Fifteen, she thought as she adjusted the billowing folds of blue silk embroidered with little pink flowers and tiny green leaves about the slender figure, just the age she had been when she was laced into her first tight stays and fitted into her first grown-up gown before her first Assembly in Williamsburg.

Eleanor Parke Custis—Nelly—was growing more and more beautiful. At present she was an entrancing and exasperating combination of childhood and womanhood. Just recently Martha had written Fanny: "I hope when Nelly has a little more gravitie she will be a good girl—at present—I fear she is half-crazy," or, as Nelly herself put it: "Harum scaram sans soucie." But already she was turning men's heads. One admirer, Benjamin Latrobe, would later write of her: "She has more perfection of form, of expression, of color, of softness and of firmness of mind than I have ever seen before or conceived consistent with mortality. She is everything that the chisel of Phidias aimed at but could not reach, and the soul beaming through her countenance and glowing in her smile is as superior to her face as mind is to matter."

At fifteen Nelly was just awaking to the glamor of romance. During the wedding festivities she wrote back a glowing account of a ball she had attended, where she had been surrounded by eager admirers, one of whom aroused lavish superlatives.

"Oh, dear!" worried Martha. "She sounds carried away. Suppose she does something foolish, like—like—"

"Yes," said George. He knew whom she meant. His nephew George Steptoe Washington had shocked them all by eloping with a fifteen-year-old girl. Though the marriage was proving a success, and the girl was the sister of one of their most admired friends, Dolley Madison, it had caused George much disgust and concern.

He was concerned now. If to the delicate Patsy he had been a loving and protective father, to the lovely, vivacious Nelly he was the doting and even more protective grandfather. In spite of his heavy burdens, he sat down and wrote her a letter epitomizing his beliefs about love and marriage in even greater detail than he had written Betsy:

"Men and women feel the same inclination to each other *now* that they have always done, and which they will continue to do until there is a new order of things. And you, as others have done, may find perhaps that the passions of your sex are easier raised than allayed . . . In the composition of the human frame there is a good deal of inflammable matter, however dormant it may lie for a time, and . . . when the torch is put to it, *that* which is *within* may burst into flame . . . Love is said to be an involuntary passion . . . that cannot be resisted. This is true in part only . . . When the heart is beginning to kindle and your heart growing warm, propound these questions to it. Who is this invader? For, be assured, a sensible woman can never be happy with a fool. What had been his walk in life? Is he a gambler, a spendthrift or drunkard? Is his fortune sufficient to maintain me in the manner I have been accustomed to live, and my sisters do live, and is he one to whom my friends can have no reasonable objection? If these interrogatories can be satisfactorily answered, there will remain but one more to be asked. That, however, is an important one. Have I sufficient ground to conclude that his affections are engaged by me? Without this, the heart of sensibility will struggle against a passion that is not reciprocated, delicacy, custom, or call it by what epithet you will, having precluded all advances on your part. The declaration, without the *most indirect invitation* of yours, must proceed from the man to render it permanent and valuable, and nothing short of good sense and an easy unaffected conduct can draw the line between prudery and coquetry . . ."

Martha nodded with satisfaction when she read this exhaustive credo. It was a perfect description of their own courtship and marriage. And, whatever his experience had been with the "inflammable matter," he had at least implied the necessity of the man's "affections" being engaged. Begone, ghost of Sally Fairfax!

George's excursions into the philosophy of romance were brief. With the arrival in March of the text of John Jay's treaty with Britain he was again plunged into a turmoil of opposition. Even he had to admit that the treaty accomplished little of the country's aim, to persuade the British to relinquish their forts on the frontier and to order their warships to stop seizing American merchant ships. Its final blow was in one article: England reserved the right to declare and seize, whenever she chose, all foodstuffs and provisions as contraband of war. And it did not even mention the flagrant practices of the British admiralty, searching ships and impressing their seamen! The Anti-Federalists exploded in anger. Attacks were not only in words, on platforms and in the press. In June when Alexander Hamilton tried to speak in favor of the treaty, he was actually stoned.

At least, to Martha's relief, there was escape in July to Mount Vernon, George traveling alone in his double-rigged phaeton, the others following in a coach and four, with two mounted servants and George's saddle horse in the rear. It was a hot and disagreeable six days' journey, and one of the horses took sick and died. But George visibly brightened as problems were left further and further behind. Not that his troubles had ended when they arrived! Each post brought letters to be answered. There was difficulty among the commissioners at the Federal City. Heavy rains kept him from making the rounds of his farms. Then suddenly he was called back to Philadelphia.

"Oh, dear!" Martha lamented. "You will miss Fanny's wedding."

He did indeed, for he could not postpone his trip, and he was gone a month. It was September when he returned, as tired and discouraged as she had ever seen him. He had signed the treaty, though not really approving it. Better, he had felt, to ratify it than to leave matters unsettled. He had only a month to inspect his fields, arrange for the winter work with his new manager, Pearce, and visit with the neighbors. They were still at Mount Vernon when a letter came which gave him grave personal concern. It informed him that his namesake, George Washington Lafayette, son of his friend the Marquis, had arrived in Boston and wanted to come to Philadelphia to place himself in the President's care. The children were delighted, for they vaguely remembered the gay Marquis and had been reared on stories of his virtues and misfortunes.

"Will he live with us?" asked Nelly, tossing her brown curls in anticipation.

"Jolly!" enthused Wash. What fun to have another George Washington something, only a year older than himself, as a companion!

George was in a quandary. A reception of the French youth in his own household would be fodder for political criticism. Hostile newspapers would be sure to connect his apparent support of France with wrong reasons. Unhappily he penned a letter to Boston asking a friendly senator to sponsor the boy temporarily and enter him in Harvard College, impressing on him that he would have him come as soon as possible.

Back in Philadelphia, George and others tried to keep from Martha news of the deluge of abuse from Anti-Federalists which followed his signing of the treaty. But she had good ears—she heard the whispers— and good eyes—papers came to her attention.

"The President," wrote Bache in the *Aurora,* was "a malediction on departed virtue, whose false ambition has carried the nation to the precipice of destruction." Another journalist called him "Saint Washington," a man distinguished only by "the seclusion of a monk and the supercilious distance of a tyrant."

How, wondered Martha as she agonized for him, could he seem so impervious to all these slanders, like a rock unmoved by a tempest? Only when someone accused him of spending more of state funds than the twenty-five thousand dollars a year Congress had insisted on allotting him as President, did he prepare a scathing reply, never stating, however, that on taking office he had requested that he receive no pay whatever!

During the days before George's sixty-fourth birthday Bache let loose another volley. Previous celebrations of this event, he scoffed, had been so extravagant that it was no wonder the President behaved "with all the insolence of an Emperor of Rome." But the celebration of the day was proof of the continued love of the majority. At one minute past midnight bells pealed; there were more bells and a cannon salute to greet the dawn. Crowds came to the house. Cannon sounded again at noon, and the Pennsylvania legislature arrived in a body. Chimes rang through the afternoon. There was a gala supper, then a grand ball with decorations of transparencies and paintings, attended by more than five hundred. One congressman described the festivities: "The ladies were elegantly dressed in white and waving plumes on their heads . . . The President and Mrs. Washington mixed with the company and conversed sociably with everyone." There were other celebrations throughout the country. He was still almost universally admired and loved. Martha could almost forget the slurs and innuendos. But, looking at him, she shook her head in dismay. He looked *old*. As one traveler who saw him that day recorded: "He seems considerably older than his years. The innumerable vexations he has met with have very sensibly impaired the vigor of his constitution and given him an aged appearance."

But at last it was 1796. Once more Martha began to count years— only a little more than one—months, days. The future looked brighter. The Senate, after long and acrimonious debate, accepted the treaty with Britain. Another treaty with Spain gave the country free use of the Mississippi River. As one official expressed it, "Since the treaty, we see nothing but blue sky."

Martha had other concerns now than politics. In February, Betsy—who now wished to be called Eliza—had announced her engagement to Mr. Thomas Law. George did not approve of the match. Mr. Law was thirty-nine, Eliza only twenty. He was a wealthy Englishman with three Asiatic sons, whose mother was supposed to have died in India. But the Stuarts had given their consent, and Eliza was headstrong. She was married on March 21. If this could be considered a happy event, sadness was soon to follow, for on March 30 news came of Fanny's death after a short but severe illness. She had been only twenty-nine, and this second happy marriage had lasted only eight months.

Martha was devastated. She had loved Fanny like a daughter. Though she signed her name with George's in his letter of condolence to Lear, its stilted expression of resignation aroused rebellion. *Why?* Fanny had been so young, so happy! "It is our duty to submit . . ." She did not feel like submitting. "She is no more, but she must be happy, because her virtue has a claim to it." How could there be happiness with those little children left motherless? For the first time in her life Martha did not find comfort in her quiet hour. No psalms of praise now! She turned unerringly to other passages: "My God, my God . . . why hast thou forsaken me?" . . . "Out of the deep have I called unto thee, O Lord . . ."

But life had to go on. Young Lafayette and his tutor, a Monsieur Frestel, were with them that summer at Mount Vernon, and there were many other guests, as usual. Though still in deep mourning, Martha went through the normal motions of housekeeping, visiting, entertaining guests, including Mr. Latrobe, the new architect for the Federal City, and rejoiced that George seemed rejuvenated by life on the plantation. Already he was immersed in details, checking with Pearce on the orders he had been sending in such minute exactness every week—repairs to the north end of the house, new venetian blinds, painted green, to protect the west windows, the gleaming white paint on the pillars of the piazza, the new Windsor chairs which he had shipped from Philadelphia, damage to crops caused by a wet winter and spring droughts. But he was soon called back to Philadelphia. Only seven months now, thought Martha. When he left on August 17, to be gone until late in September, she had the satisfaction of knowing that they might be separated for the last time. And when next he left for Mount

Vernon, God willing, it would be not as President Washington but as George Washington, Potomac farmer.

She breathed a sigh of relief when she learned that on September 19 his "Farewell Address" had been published—the remarkable document which was to outline his credo for the country for future generations: inseparable union, the indispensability of religion and morality, a program of public education, a rule of conduct in regard to foreign nations (to have with them as little *political* connection as possible).

"The nation which indulges toward another an habitual hatred, or an habitual fondness, is in some degree a slave. It is a slave to its animosity or to its affection, either of which is sufficient to lead it astray from its duty and its interest."

Six months . . . five months. It was October 31 when they arrived back in Philadelphia. Electors were chosen by the states on the fourth of November. On the last week of the month Martha entertained the King of the Cherokees, with many of their chiefs and their wives, marking an end to the uneasy relationships between them and the government. As proof of the President's "esteem and friendship" each of the chiefs was presented with a dress coat, a rifle, a saddle and bridle, and they pledged peace to one another.

On December 7 George gave his last address to Congress, with the largest assembly of citizens which had ever attended such a gathering. Martha sat in a place of honor in the gallery. Never had she been prouder of him. If there could be compensation for these "lost years" in public life, this was it. It was a speech of triumph and encouragement. He told of many recent government successes—assurance of peace with the Indians, evacuation of posts in the Northwest so long occupied by the British, a new pact with Spain. He recommended boards of agriculture, support of manufactures, and, as he had done for many years, he made a plea for a national university. He ended with a sort of valedictory:

"The situation in which I now stand for the last time . . . recalls the period when the Administration of the present form of Government commenced; and I cannot omit the occasion to congratulate you and my Country on the success of the experiment; nor to repeat my fervent supplications to the Supreme Ruler of the Universe, and Sovereign Arbiter of Nations, that . . . . the virtue and happiness of the

People may be preserved, and that the Government, which they have instituted for the protection of their liberties, may be perpetual."

Three months. It was one of the worst winters in memory, with excessive cold, heavy snows and rains. Already they were living in spirit at Mount Vernon rather than Philadelphia. Were they getting rain there also, to break the disastrous drought? Martha's worries were no longer for political crises, but for the children. Wash did not seem to be studying at Princeton. Would Nelly miss this exciting life in Philadelphia, her singing lessons, debating societies, lectures on chemistry, astronomy, electricity, and such? What an accomplished, level-headed woman Nelly, at seventeen, was turning out to be! Certainly no longer the half-crazy harum-scarum she had once called her!

It was 1797. Only two months. They went to church on New Year's Day. A few days later they went over to Germantown to visit Gilbert Stuart, who had made such a fine portrait of George, perhaps the best that had ever been painted by any artist. He had made one of Martha, too, though that did not interest her so much. There was more abuse in the newspapers. Its worst feature was an open letter to George written by Thomas Paine, the noted democratic author whose best-selling treatises, *Common Sense* and *Rights of Man*, had contributed so much to the people's passion for freedom and independence. He had been one of George's firmest supporters. Now, having been imprisoned in France, he blamed the President for not somehow effecting his release. His letter was violent, vituperative.

"As to you, sir, treacherous in private friendship . . . and a hypocrite in public life, the world will be puzzled to decide whether you have abandoned good principles or whether you ever had any." It was a diatribe, Martha knew, which hurt him more than all the tirades of smaller men like Bache, for he and Paine had been brothers in democratic fervor and revolutionary zeal.

It was February. Only one month. It was settled, to George's satisfaction, that John Adams had been elected President, defeating the Anti-Federalist Jefferson by only three votes. There was a tremendous celebration for George's sixty-fifth birthday—the last the nation would ever celebrate? Schools were closed, cannon fired, the militia paraded, flags flown. Bright colors flew on ships in the harbor. One person remarked that "even Democrats forgot for a moment their enmity and seemed to join heartily in the festivity." Callers came to the house in multitudes, congressmen, the Governor and Pennsylvania legislature in a body, the Society of the Cincinnati. In the evening, which was clear and fine, George and Martha went to an "elegant entertainment" at Ricketts' Amphitheatre, where there was a supper and dancing with some twelve hundred persons present. "Mrs. Washington was moved even to tears," one person wrote, "with the mingled emotions of gratitude for such strong proofs of public regard and the new prospect of the uninterrupted enjoyment of domestic life. I never saw the President look better," he added, "or in finer spirits, but his emotions were too powerful to be concealed. He could sometimes scarcely speak."

People, it seemed, could not do enough to show their love and esteem. When they attended the theater on February 27, the place was crowded, a view of the President and the First Lady proving a far greater attraction than the performance on the stage. The next day, Tuesday, February 28, at George's last formal levee, there was no room for all the guests. It was the same at Martha's final "drawing room" on the evening of March 3. On March 2 George had written his farewell to the rector, wardens, and vestrymen of Christ Church and of St. Peter's and acknowledged addresses of other denominations.

"As the curtain of my political life is about to drop," he wrote Wash, "I am a great deal hurried in the closing scenes of it."

On the afternoon of March 3 he entertained at dinner a large company "to take my leave of the President elect, of the foreign characters, the heads of departments, &ca." At first it was a gay gathering, but at the end the cheerful mood vanished. After the tablecloth was removed, George filled his wineglass and, smiling at his guests, said, "Ladies and gentlemen, this is the last time I shall drink your health as a public man. I do it with sincerity, and wishing you all possible happiness." All gaiety had ended. Most of the guests were weeping, Martha also, but for her they were a mixture of sad and happy tears.

At last it was here. No more years, months, even days to count. Near noon on Saturday, March 4, George walked alone to Congress Hall. He even looked like a private citizen in his suit of black, military hat with black cockade, hair neatly powdered. He was greeted with tremendous applause as he entered. John Adams, on the other hand, following just behind, had assumed more elaborate garb than usual, a pearl-colored broadcloth suit, a sword, and a cockade. After a moment of comparative silence George rose and with great dignity introduced Adams, finishing by reading his own brief farewell. Adams was sworn into office by Chief Justice Oliver Ellsworth. At the end the new President covered his face with his hands, his wrist ruffles becoming wet with tears. There were sobs from the assembly.

"A solemn scene it was indeed," Adams wrote his wife of the inauguration, "and it was made affecting to me by the presence of the General, whose countenance was as serene and unclouded as the day. He seemed to me to enjoy a triumph over me. Methought I heard him say, 'Ay! I am fairly out and you fairly in! See which one of us will be happiest!' "

George and Martha did not leave at once. There were calls to pay, packing to be done, furnishings to be disposed of. Some were set aside for sale. Much had already gone to Mount Vernon. They chose a pair of lamps for Mrs. Powel, wine coolers for members of the cabinet, the drawing room lusterware for Mrs. Morris.

When Mrs. Oliver Wolcott, wife of one of the officials, called to take leave, Martha asked if she would like a memoir of her husband.

"Oh, yes," the guest replied. "I should like a lock of his hair."

With a happy smile Martha instantly cut a large lock from George's head, adding to it one from her own.

She should have felt grief at leaving these good friends, but she did not. If they wanted to see her again, they could come to Mount Vernon. She had caught a severe cold during the festivities, but she would not hear of postponing their departure. They left Philadelphia on March 16 amid a welter of crowds and confusion. Tobias Lear, who had been with them, remained behind to finish the packing and get ninety-seven boxes and fourteen trunkloads off by the sloop *Salem*. George Washington Lafayette and his tutor traveled with them, but not Wash, who was still in school. With all the preparation there were still things forgotten. The first night at Chester, George wrote back to Lear.

"Thus far we have arrived safe, but found it disagreeable cold." He begged Lear to be careful of the looking glasses and gave him other commissions, adding at the end on a facetious note: "P. S. On one side I am called upon to remember the parrot, on the other to remember the dog. For my own part, I would not pine much if both were forgot."

Nothing, not even cold and snow, could make the journey really disagreeable. They stopped in the new Federal City to dine with Eliza and her husband, then stayed overnight with Patty and Mr. Peter in Georgetown, admiring Patty's little daughter, Eleanor, a saucy, charming tot just learning to walk. Then at last . . . home.

They were over, sixteen years which had seemed like expulsion from paradise, given willingly if not gladly to a cause dearer than happiness, even than life itself. Eight of them in the wintry gloom of war, eight more in the heat and glare of public service. Cold, devastating winters, mercilessly hot and searing summers. But now it was spring. Buds were swelling, leaves unfolding. Already tulips and daffodils were in bloom. It was the time and place for new life, new beginnings, their own Garden of Eden. The years of exile were past. Twice Duty had driven them away from their beloved paradise. Now, miraculously, they were returning.

As George and Martha rode through the west gate and up the drive, her eyes lifted to the weathervane on the cupola. Never had it looked so white and shining against the blue of the sky, or seemed such a glorious welcoming symbol, that dove of peace.

21

How could there be such joy in the simplest things—the opening of scarlet bells on the flowering horse chestnut or the crimson flash of a cardinal; the whirring of spinning wheels and the sound of the plantation bell signaling the end of a working day; the smell of hot steaming suds in the washhouse, or the fragrance of a honey-scented locust cluster; the feeling of warm earth on your fingers as you loosened the soil about the mint and parsley and fennel in the kitchen garden! It was like having been surfeited with rich, cloying pastries and then tasting the good, satisfying flavor of corn pone.

"I cannot tell you, my dear friend," Martha wrote Lucy Knox, "how much I enjoy home after having been deprived of one so long, for our dwelling in New York and Philadelphia was not home, only a sojourning. The General and I feel like children just released from school or from a hard taskmaster, and we believe that nothing can tempt us to leave the sacred roof-tree again, except on private business or pleasure. We are so penurious with our enjoyment that we are loath to share it with any one but dear friends, yet almost every day some stranger claims a portion of it, and we cannot refuse . . .

"Our furniture and other things sent to us from Philadelphia arrived safely; our plate we brought with us in the carriage. How many dear friends I have left behind! They fill my memory with sweet thoughts. Shall I ever see them again? Not likely, unless they shall come to me here, for the twilight is gathering around our lives. I am again fairly settled down to the pleasant duties of an old-fashioned Virginia house-keeper, steady as a clock, busy as a bee, and cheerful as a cricket."

George too was exulting in the return to more humdrum pursuits.

"To make and sell a little flour," he wrote his friend Oliver Wolcott on May 15, "to repair houses going fast to ruin, to build one for the security of my papers of a public nature, and to amuse myself with Agricultural and rural pursuits, will constitute employment for the years I have to remain on this terrestrial Globe . . . If I could now and then meet friends I esteem, it would fill the measure, but if this ever happens, it must be under my own vine and fig-tree, as I do not think it probable that I shall go beyond twenty miles from them."

The word "under" was figurative, for there was no lounging in their shade. He plunged immediately into such repairs and rebuilding that he was soon writing to another friend: "In a word, I am already surrounded by joiners, masons, and painters, and such is my anxiety to be out of their hands that I have scarcely a room to put a friend in, or to sit in myself, without the music of hammers and the odoriferous scent of paint.

"I begin my diurnal course with the sun," he continued. "If my hirelings are not in their places by that time, I send them messages of sorrow for their indisposition; having put these wheels in motion, I examine the state of things further; the more they are probed the deeper I find the wounds which my buildings have sustained by an absence and neglect of eight years; by the time I have accomplished these matters, breakfast (a little after 7 o'clock, about the time, I presume that you are taking leave of Mrs. McHenry) is ready; this being over, I mount my horse and ride around my farms, which employs me until it is time to dress for dinner . . . The usual time of sitting at the table, a walk, and tea bring me within the dawn of candlelight; previous to which, if not prevented by company, I resolve that as soon as the glimmering taper supplies the place of the great luminary I will retire to my writing table and acknowledge the letters I have received . . . Having given you the history of a day, it will serve for a year, and I am persuaded that you will not require a second edition of it."

There were necessary repairs on the barns, the overseers' houses, the slave quarters, fences. The marble chimneypiece in the parlor had to be replaced, a new one installed in the small dining room. The work seemed endless, but there would be plenty of time to do it. He wrote a gay letter to their friend Mrs. Powel telling her that he had agreed with the powers that be not to quit the world at least until 1800. There was not plenty of money, however. As usual, he was land poor and distressingly short of cash. He had been obliged to sell no less than fifty thousand dollars' worth of his precious western lands to defray the huge expenses of the Presidency, and now more lands must be sold to bring the estate into a semblance of decency.

The goods packed in Philadelphia by Tobias Lear arrived, together with Lear, on the last day of March—97 boxes, 14 trunks, 43 casks, 13 packages, 3 hampers, and other items. Martha enjoyed unpacking, arranging the fine furniture, silver, china, glassware accumulated in Philadelphia. She was feeling stronger now, the serious cold contracted before leaving the city yielding at last to the combined therapy of springtime and home.

There was the new carpeting for the blue parlor, to harmonize with the side wall panels, ceiling, and stair-skirting of delicate French gray, almost a robin's-egg blue. There was the beautiful new harpsichord which George had imported for Nelly from London. Lear had packed it well. There was not a mark on its smooth, satiny mahogany surface. Martha ran a finger along one of its inlaid borders. She had it placed in the "Little Parlor," facing the door into the hall, so guests seated in the room could see the face of the performer. Nelly was not so pleased with its arrival, for it meant long hours more of practice. Though she no longer wept during the enforced sessions, she would rather be out riding over the farms with George Washington Lafayette or visiting friends in Alexandria.

There were portraits to be hung—the one by John Trumbull of George beside his horse, the one painted by Gilbert Stuart in 1795, and the one she liked best of the whole family, by Edward Savage, finished just a year ago in 1796. Martha was wearing her black lace scarf with a white fichu and a cap, fashionably high but not towering like some women's monstrosities. George's favorite servant Billy was standing in the background. Poor Billy, he was getting old, had injured both knees in a fall, yet he had managed to give token service all the time they had been in the Presidency. How young the children looked, for Savage had sketched it back in 1789, Washy looking almost like a girl with his collar opened wide and a ruffle at his neck, Nelly in her dotted muslin gown with its wide sash.

Martha sighed these days at the thought of young Wash, now a student at Princeton. A letter in May from the college president, the Reverend Samuel Smith, bore a distressing similarity to some penned long ago by the harassed Boucher. It reported misconduct as well as negligence in studies. There ensued a long correspondence between George and Dr. Smith, between George and Wash, in which George deplored his grandson's "almost unconquerable disposition to indolence in everything that did not tend to his amusement," and Wash confessed humbly that he had "shockingly abused" George's goodness and was now the "sincere penitent," hoping to restore peace of mind to his "dearest sir." Repentance was effective temporarily, and the crisis passed, though George continued to be concerned over Wash's studies. "I do not hear you mention anything of Geography or mathematics." Oh, yes, Wash was "now engaged in geography and in English grammar too." George sent him money to come home for summer vacation, desiring that he not travel by water (because of accidents) or by Philadelphia (because of yellow fever).

If George had expected, or even hoped, that his peaceful retreat under his own vine and fig tree would be invaded by only relatives and friends, he was sadly disappointed. Once more visitors came in droves, to discuss politics, to get his advice on decisions of national import, to examine his innovations in farming, like his rotation of crops, his six-sided barn, his threshing machine, to simply look at this most famous man in the country, eat his food, satisfy their unbounded curiosity. Many, like Samuel Chase of Maryland or Noah Webster, were most welcome guests, but all were received with genuine hospitality. Most stayed to dinner, some overnight or longer. Many, like Elkanah Watson, an adventurer who shared George's dream of western expansion, were surprised by the excess of courtesy.

"The first evening I spent under the wing of Washington's hospitality," Watson wrote, "we sat a full hour at table by ourselves, without the least interruption. After the family had retired, I was extremely oppressed by a severe cold and excessive coughing. He pressed me to use some remedies, but I declined. As usual after retiring my coughing increased. When some time had elapsed, the door of my room was gently opened, and on drawing my bed curtains, to my utter astonishment I beheld Washington himself standing at my bedside, with a bowl of hot tea in his hand. I was mortified and disturbed beyond expression.

This little incident occurring in common life would not have been noticed; but as a trait of the benevolent and private virtue of Washington, deserves to be recorded."

Both George and Martha received guests graciously but without ceremony. If they were in working clothes, they made no apology. Once, when he was home on vacation Wash met a stranger inquiring for the General.

"You will meet, sir," he told him, "with an old gentleman riding alone, in plain drab clothes, a broad-brimmed white hat, a hickory switch in his hand, and carrying an umbrella with a long staff, which is attached to his saddlebow—that person, sir, is General Washington."

The visitor smiled. "Thank ye, thank ye, young gentleman. I think, if I fall in with the General, I shall be apt to know him." And he should. He had fought beside him in the army.

Guests! They kept coming. Foreigners. A Danish merchant, Englishmen bent on the liquidation of claims of British creditors under Jay's treaty; the Viscount d'Orléans from France; Mr. Gahn, a Swedish merchant; a man from Bremen and one from Hamburg; one from British Guiana; Mr. Julian Niemcewitz, a Polish gentleman, who recorded his experience in a diary and called Martha "one of the most delightful persons one can meet. Good, sweet, and exceedingly pleasant, she likes to talk and talks well of old times." And of Nelly he indulged in superlatives. "She was one of those celestial beings so rarely produced by nature, sometimes dreamed of by poets and painters, which one cannot see without a feeling of ecstasy."

On July 31, early in the morning before any guests could arrive, with Nelly and Lafayette and his tutor on a visit to Hope Park, George wrote in a note to Lear: "I am alone at *present*, and shall be glad to see you this evening. Unless someone pops in, unexpectedly—Mrs. Washington and myself will do what I believe has not been done within the last twenty years by us—that is to set down to dinner by ourselves." His diary did not record whether this happened or not.

Entertainment was becoming such a burden that George decided he must have someone to assist him with such duties. He would have liked Humphreys, whom he had always thought of as a "companion in my latter days," but Humphreys had married and wanted a home of his own. George thought now of his nephew, Lawrence Lewis, Betty's son. To his and Martha's sorrow, Betty had died suddenly the previous year after a severe attack of pneumonia. Having this favorite nephew here would be a real consolation.

"Whenever it is convenient to you to make this place your home," he wrote, "I shall be glad to see you at it . . . As both your aunt and I are in the decline of life and regular in our habits, especially in our hours of rising and going to bed, I require some person to ease me of the trouble of entertaining company, particularly of nights. In taking these duties, which hospitality obliges one to bestow on company, it would render me a very acceptable service."

Lawrence arrived before the end of summer. Unmarried at age thirty, he was affable, handsome, efficient, and became not only a useful assistant to George but also a happy addition to the youth of the household, Nelly, young Lafayette, the Laws and Peters and their children, who often visited, and Wash, when he returned in the fall. It was almost like having a son of his own, thought Martha, watching George and Lawrence together, for he was a Washington in all but name, the image of his mother.

George had been worried, too, over Martha's weariness from so much responsibility. She would persist in going about all her supervising tasks even when ill. Though there were always two persons, a man and a woman, in the kitchen and other servants in the house, they required direction. He advertised for a competent housekeeper at a wage of $150 a year.

In October there were changes. On the twelfth, George Washington Lafayette and his tutor Félix Frestel left for Georgetown, to take a stage to New York, where they would embark for France. George went with the boy as far as the Federal City, gave him three hundred dollars for the voyage, and sent with him an affectionate letter to his father. Rumors had come of the Marquis's liberation, and, though George feared that he was acting hastily, for France was in greater turmoil than ever, young Lafayette had determined to go at once, hoping for reunion with his father, mother, and sisters. Hamilton was to arrange for his care in New York and his passage to France. Both he and his tutor were greatly missed at Mount Vernon, for they had endeared themselves to all.

But Wash had arrived from college in time to compensate for their absence, presenting new problems, however, for he had no intention of returning to Princeton. George was angered, grieved, frustrated. As

Wash was to confess in later life, his grandfather shed tears when reprimanding him.

"Perhaps," urged Martha hopefully, "he could have a tutor and stay at home. Or after the vacation he could go to another school, where he might do better. After all, he's only a boy, just sixteen."

George compromised by giving him a set of strict rules for conduct while at home, demanding many hours of study, prompt attendance at meals, and limited freedom for sports and other recreation. Doubtless the most irksome was a rule to which he himself set a meticulous example: "Rise early, that by habit it may become familiar, agreeable, healthy, and profitable. It may for a while be irksome to do this, but that will wear off, and the practice will produce a rich harvest forever thereafter whether in public or private walks of life."

Martha was finding to her dismay that they had not escaped the maelstrom of political turmoil after all. The world with all its problems was invading George's precious sanctuary under his vine and fig tree. Not only was he still revered as a national hero, but eight years as the first President had endowed him with knowledge and authority of leadership which far exceeded that of the less popular John Adams. He was besieged by letters, by visitors asking his counsel. And the country was in crisis. Federalists and Anti-Federalists (who now called themselves Republicans) were in mounting conflict with each other. Europe was in turmoil, and the American government was embroiled in the quarrel between France and England. It was, as Jefferson defined it, the "fruit of the British treaty" which Jay had effected. The two political parties were increasingly taking positions in opposition to each other as the "British Party" or the "French Party." French ships were making depredations on American shipping. Because of the neutral position of the American government the French Directory treated the American minister there with such rudeness that the nation was aroused. Though George tried to keep clear of participation, he could not fail to be concerned, and people were constantly appealing to him for advice.

"If our citizens would advocate their own cause instead of that of any other nation under the sun," he wrote, "if instead of being Frenchmen or Englishmen in politics, they would be Americans," he had no doubt that "the wisdom, temper, and firmness of the government would dispel the threatening clouds and that all would end without the shedding of blood."

George was embarrassed when the citizens of Philadelphia insisted on celebrating his sixty-sixth birthday with a banquet in Concert Hall. It had been one thing to attend a ball on February 12 in Alexandria, which still observed the old calendar, according to which his birthday, the eleventh, would have fallen on a Sunday. But it was quite another to have the erstwhile President honored in the capital city. He could well imagine the feelings of the emotional and sensitive John Adams, forced to play a secondary role to one who was now but a private citizen!

Yes, thought Martha shrewdly, and the present First Lady would feel the slight even more keenly. She was right. In fact, she could picture the reaction of the brilliant, friendly, but frankly ambitious Abigail without seeing the resentful words that poured from her pen: "These Philadelphians . . . They are about to celebrate, not the Birth day of the First Majestrate of the union as such, but of General Washington's Birth day, and have had the politeness to send invitations to the President, Lady and family to attend it . . ." President Adams refused the invitation, thereby arousing uncomplimentary comparisons between the two men.

"There never was perhaps a greater contrast between two characters than between those of the present President and his predecessor," wrote James Madison. "The one cool, considerate and cautious, the other headlong and kindled into flame by every spark that lights on his passions; . . . the former Chief Magistrate pursuing peace everywhere with sincerity . . . the latter taking as much pains to get into war, as the former took to keep out of it . . ."

Though George followed all these developments with deep concern and was involved in endless correspondence about them, to Martha they seemed as far removed as that distant and fabulous Paris where many of them were taking place. The problem of what to do about Wash seemed far more important than indignities to ambassadors, even to the seizing of American ships. Tutors were obviously not the solution. They did not afford the necessary discipline or direction. Finally, after consultation with his stepfather, arrangements were made to enter him at St. John's College in Annapolis, and Dr. Stuart took him there in March. Martha breathed a sigh of relief. The crisis had passed . . . temporarily, and George was writing that "Grandpapa receives much pleasure to find that you are agreeably fixed, disposed to prosecute your studies with zeal and alacrity." A month later, however, Wash was displeasing them both by reporting a rumor that Charles Carroll, Jr., was courting his sister Nelly and giving his warm approval to the match. Their Nelly thinking of marriage! Young Carroll had indeed paid a visit to Mount Vernon recently, but that he had come on purpose to court Nelly—impossible! George promptly sent off a stern admonition to his grandson to pay more attention to his studies than to gossip and to maintain strict silence about any rumors he might have heard.

Martha was enjoying renewed health that winter and spring, partly because of the arrival in December of Mrs. Forbes, a competent housekeeper secured through George's nephew Bushrod, who had become a successful lawyer practicing in Richmond and did much of George's legal work. There was time to enjoy more leisurely activities—gardening, taking little trips with Nelly to Hope Park, sitting on the piazza with her knitting and watching the sailboats and barges go up and down the river, even the more laborious task of writing letters. In one, penned to Elizabeth Powel, she gave vent to a bit of humor:

"I am now, by desire of the General, to add a few words on his behalf, which he desired may be expressed in the terms following, that is, to say—that disparing of hearing what may be said of him, if he should really go off in an apopletic fit or any other fit (for he thinks all fits that issue in death are worse than a love fit or a fit of laughter, and many other kinds he could name) he is glad to hear before hand what will be said of him on that occation; conceiving that nothing extra will happen between this and then, to make a change in his character—for better or for worse—and besides he has entered into an engagement with Mr. Morris and several other Gentlemen not to quitt the theatre of this world before the year 1800 . . . At present there seems to be no danger of giving them the slip, as neither his health nor his spirits were ever in greater flow, notwithstanding, he adds, he is descending and has almost reached the bottom of the hill, or in other words, the shades below."

As months passed Martha knew that George was coming to be more and more concerned about foreign diplomacy. A delegation of three men sent to Paris by President Adams in an attempt to negotiate difficulties received only rebuffs, plus demand for a loan (in reality a gift, or bribe), to which Charles Cotesworth Pinckney, leader of the delegation, was said to have responded hotly, "Millions for defense, but not one cent for tribute!" When the result of the negotiations reached Congress, both Federalists and Republicans united in a policy of preparation for the war which the French government seemed determined to precipitate.

London and Paris! To Martha they still seemed far removed from problems of daily life—housecleaning, summer clothes for the servants, the smoking of hams, a new dress for Nelly. But in May, England moved almost as near as the ruins of Belvoir on the next point of land, when George shared with her a letter he had written to Sally Fairfax. It had been twenty-five years since she and George William had moved to England. For ten years she had been a widow, still living, they supposed, in Bath, and in poor health.

"During this period," George began, "so many important events have occurred, and such changes in men and things have taken place, as the compass of a letter would give you but an inadequate idea of. None of which events, however, nor all of them together, have been able to eradicate from my mind the recollection of those happy moments, the happiest of my life, which I have enjoyed in your company."

The happiest of my life. Martha felt only a momentary qualm at the words, a breath of sadness long since forgotten. He wrote briefly about the French menace, longer about his two pet enterprises, the Federal City and the opening of navigation to western lands. "In a word, if this country can steer clear of European politics . . . and be wise and temperate in its government, it bids fair to be one of the greatest and happiest nations in the world."

The next day Martha also wrote a letter to Sally, assuring her warmly of her friendship and telling her more personal news. They sent the two letters to England by Bryan Fairfax, who was going to claim the title of Lord Fairfax that Sally had once coveted for her husband.

Mercifully Martha knew little of the correspondence which had been going on between George and James McHenry, the Secretary of War, and others. The prospect of war with France still seemed to her remote and unreal. Just a few years ago France had been their ally and England their enemy. Now it seemed to be just the opposite, for France was fighting England, and they seemed to be England's ally. It didn't make sense. Then one evening in July, McHenry arrived with a letter from the President. George could not keep its implications from her any longer.

"You mean," she was horrified, "he wants you to be Commander in Chief of all the armies—*again?*"

"Not the way it was before," he assured her. "I would make it plain that I shouldn't be called into the field unless circumstances demanded it. And of course," he tried to look hopeful, "there probably won't be any war, after all."

She tried to smile back at him. "Of course." She could see that he was just as distressed as she was. The deep lines were back in his face, the lips compressed, the blue eyes darkened to steel. Martha sighed. He had looked just so on the night before his men had secretly seized Dorchester Heights.

"I hope you know—I wouldn't do this, Patsy, if I didn't consider it my duty, and that there's only one thing I love better than our life here together—"

"Yes," said Martha calmly, "I know. Your—*our* country."

He showed her the long letter he wrote President Adams in reply to the appointment:

"When I retired to the walks of private life, I had no idea that any event would occur that could induce me to leave them. That the pain I should feel, if it be my fate to do so, can easily be expressed. Yet if this Country should actually be invaded, or such manifestations of a design to do so, as cannot be mistaken, I should be ready to render every Service in my power to repel it."

So . . . was it to start all over again? Couldn't his country leave him in peace even now? Already he was gone from her, from this life he loved, closeted with McHenry, choosing men to serve with him, Hamilton, of course, Knox, Harry Lee. How he would miss Nathanael Greene! In spite of the July heat, the very word *war* made her shiver. More guns, more bloodshed, more death? But perhaps, as George said, there might be no war. Surely that tyrant Talleyrand, who sounded as bad as King George, would have enough to do fighting the British without sending soldiers away across the ocean! Perhaps . . . She wished she had time to go to her room, sit quietly, and think. But there was no time now to think or worry, with guests pouring into the house and twenty-eight people besides the family for dinner!

The news spread like wildfire. Or perhaps she had been one of the last to hear. A letter soon came from Wash congratulating his grandfather on the appointment. It was a jubilant letter: "Let an admiring world again behold a Cincinnatus springing up from rural retirement to the conquest of nations, and the future historian in erasing so great a name insert that of the Father of his Country."

Father of his Country! George smiled in derision. He wasn't sure he liked the epithet. Back in 1776 it had been applied in London to King George III, and, though the words had previously been used to describe the patriot Peyton Randolph, first President of the Continental Congress, they still carried the taint of connection with the royal image. Besides, George knew he did not deserve them.

Fortunately, to Martha's relief, he could fulfill the duties of the new office at home, though with such an increased burden of correspondence that he fell ill with persistent fever. Dr. Craik was summoned and administered "Jesuit's bark." Convalescence was slow, and George lost at least twenty pounds. But the arrival of Tobias Lear as his secretary somewhat eased his double burden of farmer-commander—triple, in fact, for he was intimately involved with the completion of the Federal City, to become the center of government in two years. Early in the project he had bought four lots at various points in the city, not for speculation but to prove his own impartial interest in its future. By late September he had recovered sufficiently to spend two days there in order to settle on a location for two dwelling houses.

It was November when he was finally called to Philadelphia to hold a conference with his new Major Generals for the recruitment and organization of the provisional army. Martha saw him leave with a mixture of anxiety and relief. He would be gone for four or five weeks. But already four months had passed, and still there was no further indication that France had any intention of extending its war on the sea to the American mainland. Perhaps it was all a false alarm. And when news came of the President's Annual Address to Congress in December, there was more encouragement, for it was a message of peace, of harmony between nations.

Martha could hardly wait for George's return to apprise him of a new, exciting development, something she had expected for a long time and had hinted to him. Now she was sure. Nelly and Lawrence Lewis were in love. He had scarcely entered the house on December 19 when a starry-eyed Nelly broke the news. "Grandfather!" she announced breathlessly, "I want to be married. Please say you approve—please!"

He affected surprise and bewilderment. "And who may the fortunate aspirant be? Don't tell me, child, let me guess. There have been so many anxious and attentive swains. Charles Carroll, George Washington Craik—" He named a half dozen, all of whom had presumably been aspirants for her hand.

"Oh, Grandpapa, surely you know!" She flushed prettily. "How could it be anyone but your own nephew Lawrence? Surely you must have noticed—"

George did approve, heartily. It probably did not occur to him that Lawrence Lewis, looking so much like his mother, who was almost the image of himself, was as near the masculine ideal as his adoring adopted granddaughter could have found. Martha felt a keen delight in his pleasure. Lawrence was his favorite nephew, as dear as a son could have been. And he could not have loved a daughter more than Nelly. It was a bit of atonement after all these years, thought Martha, for not having given him children of his own. They wanted to be married soon. In late January, George rode to Alexandria to become Nelly's legal guardian so he could authorize a license for her marriage.

Life at Mount Vernon continued as usual, with the war, if there was to be one, causing little change in the routine. Guests arrived and left, among them a young Englishman, Joshua Brookes, who chronicled his impressions in detail. Received by Tobias Lear and served with wine, he and his two companions found the entertainment dull until Nelly appeared, beautiful in sprigged muslin, held in at the waist by a blue silk cord, her hair hanging about her neck in ringlets. Though somewhat shy, she "made judicious remarks and conversed with propriety."

When George appeared from his ride about the farms, wearing his greatcoat and cocked hat, muddy boots, blue overalls, read the letter of introduction and asked his guests to be seated, the young Englishman found him reserved and stiff. But when Martha came in a gown of "mazareen blue satin," her gray hair combed back straight beneath a loose cap, the atmosphere changed, became pleasant, free, and easy.

"Mrs. Washington and Miss Custis pleased me most," wrote the guest, "especially the former." Invited to dinner, the guests found George much less austere. He became "pleasant, free and sociable." They enjoyed the meal, served by three servants in liveries of white trimmed with crimson and lace, and consisting of a leg of pork at the head of the table where Martha sat, a roast goose in front of Lear at the foot, also two kinds of beef, and mutton chops. Dessert was tarts and cheese, served with port and madeira. George, always the perfect host, saw them on their horses as they went away, as Brookes recorded, "much pleased." It was a typical example of the hospitality being constantly dispensed to strangers as well as friends.

As usual, there were two birthday celebrations for George in that year of 1799. The first on February 11 at Alexandria was replete with ceremonials, marching men, a sham battle, an elegant supper and ball, one of the most brilliant affairs Gadsby's Tavern had ever seen. To Martha's surprise George, usually embarrassed and irked by such adulation, seemed to take peculiar pleasure in these tributes from friends and neighbors.

"They were honoring me," he confessed, "not as Commander in Chief or as a onetime President, but as a Potomac farmer, one of themselves."

His real birthday, February 22, 1799, his sixty-seventh, was even more enjoyable, for Nelly had chosen it for her wedding day. Though it started with cold wind and rain, the weather cleared before guests began to arrive. Nelly wanted him to wear his uniform. They had hoped his new one would be ready, splendid with gold embroidery, but the tailor had not finished it, so he wore his old Continental buff and blue, fortunately still a good fit, and his plain black-ribbon cockade. The magnificent white plumes which General Pinckney had brought him from Paris he gave to the lovely bride. For this was her day, not his. Today he was not even an honorable Potomac squire, simply Grandpapa.

With his usual simplistic brevity he recorded in his diary: "The Revd. Mr. Davis and Mr. George Calvert came to dinner, and Miss Custis was married about candlelight to Mr. Lawrence Lewis."

Martha saw them off on their honeymoon to Lawrence's married sister's in the mountains, then on to Berkeley Springs. The extra work and excitement had been too much, and she succumbed to one of her severe illnesses. But by the time they returned she was almost well again and rejoiced in their news that in November she would become a great-grandmother.

She could not help feeling a slight unease—superstition? premonition?—when, soon after the wedding, George talked of making a new will. Silly, of course, and George, always sensitive to her emotions, gently derided her fear. He had never felt in better health and expected to live for many years. And the danger of war seemed more and more remote. Talleyrand was suffering setbacks in Europe. The President had sent another delegation seeking peace with France. And surely she wanted the new wedded couple to be secured for the future, preferably close to Mount Vernon. How about bequeathing them the Dogue Run Farm along with the mill, about two thousand acres with a fine site on Gray's Hill for a new house?

All that spring and well into the summer he pondered. It was July before he was ready. He dipped his pen, took a sheet of his best paper, with its watermark of a draped figure of the goddess of agriculture seated on a plow, holding in one hand a staff surmounted with the Liberty Cap, in the other a flowering twig, and began to write: "In the name of God amen, I, George Washington of Mount Vernon—citizen of the United States,—and lately President of the same, do make, ordain and declare this Instrument . . ."

When he finished there were over twenty-eight pages in his swift, clear script. Martha, of course, was to have the whole estate as long as she lived, except such parts as were otherwise designated. At her death all his slaves were to be freed, the infirm and incompetent to be fed and clothed by his heirs. His servant would be given immediate freedom if he wished it. He had long had a guilty conscience about possessing human beings, but his obligation for the welfare of his "people" had always been a controlling factor in his actions. After Martha's death there would be no one to make sure of their well-being. They must have their freedom.

Education. Always it had been one of his chief concerns, perhaps because he had had so little of it himself. He had educated not only many relatives but also the children of friends, when he could ill afford it. Especially had he supported the work of Phillips Academy, in Andover, Massachusetts, and had helped send nine Washingtons there. How pleased and humbled he had been when, back in 1788, he had been chosen a chancellor of William and Mary College! In his Farewell Address he had pleaded for a national university, saying, "It is substantially true that virtue or morality is a necessary spring of popular government . . . Promote, then, as an object of primary importance, institutions for the general diffusion of knowledge. In proportion as the structure of government gives force to public opinion, it is essential that public opinion should be enlightened." Now he designated fifty shares of his Potomac Company stock for the support of such a university, together with other bequests to certain free schools.

There were provisions made for all his nephews and nieces, to Tobias Lear and other friends, as well as many minor bequests, such as Franklin's gold-headed crab-tree cane to his only surviving brother, Charles.

And what of Mount Vernon itself? As she read this section at his request Martha suppressed a swift feeling of hurt. His best-loved possession was not to go to Wash or to Lawrence and Nelly but to his nephew Bushrod! And yet—why not? Bushrod was steady, competent, already appointed by Adams as a Justice of the Supreme Court. And— he was a Washington. Wash, still somewhat of a problem, had a large inheritance from his father, a big tract of land overlooking Alexandria, and George was setting aside for him a big contiguous estate. He had been wise, as always. And, please God, it would be many years before the document would be needed. Every man, even one in the best of health, should make his will. Still, she felt that vague unease, not exactly fear, but—could it be premonition?

Yet George himself must have had a bit of the same unease, at least unconsciously, for in September, when she was recovering from another severe illness, she wrote about a queer incident to one of her relatives in New Kent:

"At midsummer the General had a dream so deeply impressed on his mind that he could not shake it off for several days. He dreamed that he and I were sitting in the summer-house, conversing upon the happy life we had spent and looking forward to many more years on the earth, when suddenly there was a great light all around us, and then an almost invisible figure of a sweet angel stood by my side and whispered in my ear. I suddenly turned pale and then began to vanish from his sight and he was left alone. I had just risen from the bed when he awoke and told me his dream, saying, 'You know a contrary result indicated by dreams may be expected, I may soon be leaving *you.*' I tried to drive from his mind the sadness that had taken possession of it, by laughing at the absurdity of being disturbed by an idle dream, which, at the worst, indicated that I would *not* be taken from him, but I could not, and it was not until after dinner that he recovered any cheerfulness. I found in the library, a few days afterwards, some scraps of paper which showed that he had been writing a Will, and had copied it. When I was so very sick, lately, I thought of this dream, and concluded my time had come and that I should be taken first."

Never had there been a more glorious autumn. Recovering from the severe attack of ague which had brought Dr. Craik on numerous visits to give heavy doses of "Jesuit's bark" (quinine), Martha felt resurrected to new life. With restored energy and zeal she tackled the usual fall tasks. The kitchens were fragrant with the scents of bubbling apple butter, grape, quince, and currant jellies. In the Greenhouse loft, flowers and herbs were hung up to dry and seeds spread for next year's plantings. Wheels were thrumming and looms creaking with preparations for winter garments. Gardens and lawns and trees were golden with the warm glow of Indian summer. And, best of all, Nelly and Lawrence were back at the Mansion, happy in the prospect of building their home nearby instead of on Lawrence's inherited land over in Frederick County. This last year of the century, Martha felt, was moving to its end with a promise of well-earned peace after storm.

True, the autumn was not free from misfortune. George's brother Charles died in September. "I was the *first*, and am now the *last*, of my father's children by the second marriage, who remain," George wrote, adding, "When I shall be called upon to follow them, is known only to the giver of life." In November, returning from Sunday service in his pew at Christ Church, Alexandria, with Lawrence and Wash, he was thrown violently from his horse, but rose unhurt, able to walk as briskly as his companions until they overtook their frightened horses, which had sped away in the confusion. Truly, thought Martha, remembering the prophecy of the old Indian chief, he seemed to lead a charmed life.

The last week in November the house was all preparation and expectancy. A midwife had been installed. Nelly's mother, with her two older daughters, Mrs. Law and Mrs. Peter, were there. Doctor Craik, who had been making frequent visits, was summoned early on the morning of the twenty-seventh. That forenoon Nelly was delivered of a daughter. Holding her first great-grandchild, Frances Parke Lewis—another Fanny!—Martha felt that surely this year so fast approaching its end could yield no happening of greater moment than this living promise of a new year, a new century, cradled in her arms. She was wrong.

Even birth could not stem the flow of guests or the busy routine of the household. The very next day the Carringtons arrived. Edward Carrington had served in the war and had been Washington's witness in the struggle for ratification in Virginia. They were kindred spirits. Eliza Carrington declared her visit "charmingly spent," whether in Nelly's room watching the new baby, "the delight of the grandmama," or in Martha's chamber. In fact, she painted a word picture of her hostess in this haven of contentment:

"Let us repair to the old Lady's room which is precisely in the style of our good old Aunts—that is to say, nicely fixed for all sorts of work. On one side sits the chambermaid with her knitting; on the other a little colored pet learning to sew. An old decent woman is there with her table and shears cutting out the negroes' winter clothes, while the good lady directs them all, incessantly knitting herself. She points out to me several pairs of nice colored stockings and gloves she had just finished, and presents me with a pair half done, which she begs I will finish and wear for her sake. It is wonderful, after a life spent as these good people have spent theirs, to see them, in retirement, assume those domestic habits that prevail in our country."

December. The last month of the year, the decade, the century. It began propitiously, with fine weather and congenial guests. The Bryan Fairfaxes, who had returned from England, dined at Mount Vernon on the second, and the following Sunday, the seventh, George and Martha rode over to Mount Eagle to dine with them. On the ninth they said good-bye to Lawrence's brother Howell and his wife, who had been visiting for ten days, and also to Lawrence and Wash, who were setting out for New Kent on a business trip. It was a beautiful, frosty morning, and George's enjoyment of his world was at a high peak.

"He had taken his usual ride," one of his nephews observed later, "and the clear healthy flush on his cheek and his sprightly manner brought the remark from both of us that we had never seen the General look so well. I have sometimes thought him the handsomest man I ever saw; and when in lively mood, so full of pleasantry, so agreeable to all with whom he associated, that I could hardly realize that he was the same Washington whose dignity awed all who approached him."

There was rain on the eleventh but unseasonable warmth, so the guests who came for dinner that day could return home without staying overnight. But when George went out on the porch before retiring that night, he came back reporting that there was a large circle around the moon. Another storm, thought Martha, wondering if it would be rain or snow.

They rose early as usual on the twelfth, George to pen a letter to Alexander Hamilton, Martha to take an early-morning peep at the cradle before starting the household routine. Nelly was still confined to her bed with a slight fever after the birth of her child. By ten George was in the saddle for his usual ride over the farms. The circle had indeed portended storm: first snow, then hail, finally a cold, steady rain which had turned once more to snow before his ride was ended. When he returned he had been in the saddle over five hours. Tobias Lear, bringing him some letters to be signed and franked, noticed that snow still clung to his clothes and that his hair and neck were wet.

"You had better change, sir," he suggested anxiously, "before going in to dinner. It's not good to sit in wet clothing."

"No, no, I'm late, kept them waiting. My greatcoat kept me perfectly dry." Though he usually changed before dinner, punctuality was higher on his list of rules than formality of dress.

Friday, the thirteenth, it was still snowing heavily, and, nursing a sore throat, George forewent his usual ride, but when it cleared in the afternoon, in spite of Martha's remonstrance, he went out for an hour, tramping through the snow marking trees to be cut to improve the grounds between the house and the river. Though he was hoarse that night, he read to Lear and Martha from the recently arrived gazettes. Martha withdrew to go upstairs and visit with Nelly before going to bed.

"You'd better take something for that cold," Lear advised when they said good night.

"Nonsense!" scoffed George. "You know I never take anything for a cold. Let it go as it came."

Martha woke suddenly between two and three, realizing that George was shaking with ague and breathing with difficulty. "You're ill!" she exclaimed in alarm. But when she wanted to get up and call the servants, he forbade it, fearful that she herself might contract one of her dangerous colds. She lay in agony, listening to his heavy breathing yet unwilling to defy his insistence. It seemed that dawn would never come on this dark December morning. With sunrise, after seven, the housemaid Caroline came to light the fire.

"Call Tobias Lear," Martha directed, "immediately. He must send for the doctor."

Lear sent his own servant posthaste for Dr. Craik. So hoarse that his words were almost unintelligible, George directed that his overseer Rawlins be brought from Union Farm to come and bleed him, since it would be a long time before the doctor could arrive.

Dressing hurriedly, fingers numbed with cold and anxiety, Martha went to prepare a mixture of molasses, vinegar, and butter in the hope that it would relieve his throat, but he could not swallow it. Each attempt brought on a spasm, seeming to make him almost suffocate.

Rawlins arrived. "Don't be afraid," George told him huskily, noting his reluctance, then, when the incision was made, "The opening is not large enough."

Watching the blood flow copiously, Martha wondered how such loss could possibly help rather than hurt, and at her insistence Lear tried to stop the bleeding, but George only requested, "More!" The bloodletting did not help, nor did sal volatile, applied externally to his throat.

He wanted to get up and, dressed by his servant Christopher, he sat by the fire for some time, still getting no relief. It was nine o'clock before Dr. Craik arrived.

"Inflammatory quinsy," he diagnosed, and applied a blister of cantharides to the throat, hoping to draw the inflammation to the surface. A second bleeding was performed. George managed to inhale from a steaming kettle of vinegar and water, but leaning back to allow a mixture of sage tea and vinegar to run down his throat, he once more nearly suffocated.

More remedies. Another bleeding. Still no change. He could not swallow. Another doctor, Elisha Dick, was called. Remembering a previous suggestion by Dr. Craik that in case of serious illness at the estate, Dr. Gustavus Richard Brown of Port Tobacco be called, Martha sent the groom Cyrus to bring him also. More bleedings. More medicines. When it was observed that the patient could swallow a little, a dose of calomel and tartar emetic was given. No change.

The afternoon wore on, each minute seeming an agonizing hour. Martha stood at the foot of the bed, her hand clasping one of the slender posts so tightly that it turned numb, its knuckles whitened, her face as pale as the hangings of white dimity, until Tobias Lear led her away, unwilling, resisting, and made her lie down in one of the guest rooms. But she was back again almost immediately. She could see as his gray-blue eyes met hers that he was glad for her return, and after that no one could have persuaded her to leave again. Lear also stayed constantly beside him, trying repeatedly to raise him and turn him into a more comfortable position. Though the lips scarcely spoke a word, the eyes still expressed gratitude, to Lear, to Christopher, to Martha. When he realized that his servant had been standing all the time, George motioned him to sit down. At about four-thirty in the afternoon he gestured to Martha to come to his side.

"Bring—the two wills," he mouthed huskily. "Downstairs—desk—"

The knowledge came to her then. This was not like his other illnesses. It was that terrible dream come to life. Always before, his incomparable strength had been the victor. Somehow, no matter how formidable the odds, he had won. Not this time. With the knowledge came, first, hot, helpless rebellion, then a cold calmness, hopeless but strong, as ice has hard substance and strength. She went downstairs, seated herself in the rounded leather-covered chair whose curving arms seemed to reach out to enfold her, opened the little drawer in the high mahogany desk which held the two documents, and took them upstairs. "Burn this," he told her, choosing one of them. She went and placed it on the fire. It was the one, she knew, written back in 1775 before he had left for Cambridge. She took the other and placed it in her closet. Then she returned to her post at the foot of the bed.

The day wore on. The candles were lighted. Martha heard George speaking to the doctors, his voice low and strained. "I feel myself going. I thank you for your attention. You had better not take any more trouble about me, but let me go off quietly. I cannot last long."

She did not weep. It was Dr. Craik, sitting by the fire, who displayed more outward grief. They had been through much together, he and his patient, from the time of the campaign in Great Meadows and Fort Necessity, all through the Revolution and since. It was he who had told of the strange prophecy of the Indian Chief and had seen it as strangely fulfilled. Now, though close to the fire, his stout thickset body was shaking as if with cold. His broad shoulders, always heretofore perfectly erect, were stooped as if with age.

"I, who was bred among scenes of human calamity," he was to write later, "and had so often witnessed death in its direct and most awful terms, believed that its terrors were too familiar to my eyes to shake my fortitude; but when I saw this great man die it seemed to me as if the bonds of my nature were rent and the pillars of my country's happiness had fallen to the ground."

Still the doctors kept trying, producing blisters on the legs, applying soft poultices to the throat. The patient cooperated dutifully with all their efforts. Duty. Self-discipline. They were as controlling in this as in all other crises of his life, whether as planter, as Commander in Chief, as President.

At ten that night he seemed to be breathing more easily. Lear was holding his hand, Dr. Craik still sitting by the fire, Martha still standing at the foot of the bed. Suddenly there was a change. Lear called Dr. Craik, who rushed to the bedside. George's hand dropped from Lear's, who took it again and lifted it to his breast. James Craik laid gentle fingers over the patient's eyes. There was a long silence, broken only by Martha's voice.

"Is he gone?" she asked, firmly, calmly. Then, as Lear made an agonized gesture of assent, she said simply, " 'Tis well. All is now over." Then she added, "I shall soon follow him."

22

Life . . . death. So inextricably bound together! The crib with its canopy of lace and its blanketed morsel of new life; the bed with its curtains of white ribbed cotton dimity and its emptiness. Martha knew she could never sleep in it again. Her clothes and other personal possessions would be carried up to the third-floor south bedroom, which she intended to make her own. This room where they had slept, dressed, planned, communicated intimately, as only husband and wife can do, would be closed. While she lived, no one would occupy it again.

Probably some considered her unfeeling because she could not weep. Even in Nelly's room, with their arms about each other, she was unable to yield to the merciful release of tears. She felt only the same rigid coldness, a blessing because of all the duties she must attend to. Weeping was a luxury she could not afford.

Early Sunday morning, the fifteenth, she gave Lear directions for having the coffin made in Alexandria, and he made the necessary measurements of the body, still as tall and straight as in youth, the shoulders just as broad. Messages were dispatched by the servant Caesar to Lawrence and Wash in New Kent, letters sent to the President, Colonel Hamilton, other officials and friends, relatives. The Stuarts, Laws, and Peters arrived. Martha was busy with the endless details of entertainment. On Monday the family vault was opened and made ready. It was not to be sealed with brick as formerly, she ordered. A door should be made, for "it will soon be necessary to open it again." Strangely enough, just five days before his death, George had pointed out to one of his nephews the spot where he wished a new vault to be built at the foot of what was called the "Vineyard Enclosure."

"First of all, I shall make this change," he had observed with cheerful good humor, "for after all I may require it before the rest."

Mourning clothes must be provided for the family, overseers, and servants, refreshment for all the many guests who would come for the funeral on the eighteenth. Forty pounds of cake, Martha decided, would be enough, with punch. Though George had made the "express desire" in his will that his interment should be "in a private manner, without parade or funeral oration," it was impossible to observe his wishes as she would have liked. Public officials, Masons from Alexandria, military groups, relatives, neighbors, friends—it was inevitable that there should be crowds, yes, even a parade of sorts.

Martha sat upstairs with Nelly and the baby, silent, dry-eyed, listening, reflecting, holding in her hand the lock of hair which Tobias Lear had cut before the still figure was placed within the folds of lace lining the box of dark mahogany. She had said her final farewells down in the New Room when the casket was still in front of the lovely ornate mantel, before it was taken to the porch that morning. Already the past was beginning to possess more reality than the present. The minute guns firing their salutes from the schooner anchored on the river were but echoes of thunders heard long ago at Cambridge, Newburgh, Valley Forge. The roll of muted drums was a sound which had awakened her out of troubled sleep more times than she could count. And, though she could picture the procession moving slowly from the porch south toward the river—guard, infantry, cavalry, saddled horse without its rider, pallbearers, family, delegates of the Masonic Order, Alexandrian officials, overseers, servants—it was merged in her mind with so many other processions, parades, marches, crowds acclaiming, troops returning home in victory, tattered soldiers in retreat, that it was all nothing but a blur. Only one thing was clear in this medley of past and present: Never before had there been the horse without its rider.

It was over at last. The guns had ended their tribute; the drums and bands were silenced. The guests had left. Still Martha could not weep. But Lear was only partly right when he observed that "she bore the afflicting stroke with a pious resignation which showed that her hopes were placed beyond this life." She was merely stunned, not resigned.

And she had not even begun to think about the future, whether in this world or hereafter. There was only today, to be lived through and its tasks performed . . . then tomorrow . . .

As soon as the news reached Philadelphia, on the very day of the funeral, letters were sent by express messenger from President and Mrs. Adams. It was when Martha was reading them, especially the one from Abigail, with whom she had shared so many unique, often bitter experiences of her "lost days," that the ice within her suddenly melted, and she wept. Though they were not long, it took her two full hours to read them. Then she sat down and wrote the first of her responses to the myriad letters, tributes, memorial addresses, official resolutions, condolences of a country suddenly immersed in grief.

"Accept the thanks of a heart oppressed with sorrow but grateful for your friendly sympathizing letter. May you long very long enjoy the happiness you now possess and never know affliction like mine."

It was not only America that grieved. France, in spite of the recent conflict which had led to the brink of war, mourned as if the loss had been her own. "Washington is dead," said Bonaparte, now the head of the French state. "His memory will ever be dear to the French people." He announced the death to his army, ordered black crape to be suspended from all the flags and standards in the French service for ten days.

England, which had once been Washington's enemy, was equally lavish in both grief and praise. In Bath, Sally Fairfax, now lonely and arthritic, was doubtless reading in the city's *Chronicle:* "When all that elevates and all that adorns human nature are found concentrated in one character, the loss of such a man cannot be considered as a *local* misfortune but as a general *calamity* . . . not confined to a *hemisphere* only but extending to a *world.*"

Did she feel a nostalgic yearning, perhaps, regret, or merely a stirring of pride, knowing that she had once been his youthful ideal of womanhood? Did she take out and read again the three letters, two now yellowed with age, one which had come so recently? ". . . those happy moments, the happiest of my life, which I have enjoyed in your company . . ."

In America, of course, the eulogies of press, pulpit, poets, official pronouncements and resolutions, memorials, letters, were all-pervasive and extravagant. Even Bache, the journalist who had sullied George's

Presidency with such opprobrium, was prophesying that "his name will spread with liberty from age to age."

The reply to one letter Martha found almost impossible to write. Congress, in session at the time of George's death, had decreed a public funeral where his friend Harry Lee would give the oration, first enunciating the famous words, "first in war, first in peace, first in the hearts of his countrymen." But Congress had also resolved that a marble monument should be erected in the new capital to commemorate the great military and civil events of his life, and they now requested that the family permit his remains to be deposited under the monument. No! Martha felt cold dismay. Couldn't they leave him alone even now, in this place he had loved so much, where he had expressed a wish to be laid? Must the nation own him even in death? And how could she bear to lose the small comfort of having him near? She spent her morning quiet hour now close to the little dormer window of her new room, where she could look down over the lawns toward the vault. She had chosen this south room purposely instead of the other third-floor bedroom, which had a fireplace, because here she could feel a little closer to this symbol of his nearness.

But . . . she sighed. Even more than his beloved Mount Vernon he had loved his country. He had never really belonged to this tiny part of it . . . or to her. She wrote her reply, submitting it to Lear for correction of her spelling, as George had done often in recent years, then painstakingly rewrote it.

"Mount Vernon, December 31st, 1799. Sir: While I feel with keenest anguish the late Disposition OF Divine Providence, I cannot be insensible to the mournful tributes of respect and veneration which are paid to the memory of my dear deceased Husband—and as his best services and most anxious wishes were always devoted to the welfare and happiness of his country—to know that they were truly appreciated and gratefully remembered affords no inconsiderable consolation.

"Taught by the great example which I have so long before me never to oppose my private wishes to the public will—I must consent to the request made by Congress—which you have had the goodness to transmit to me—and in doing this I need not—I cannot say what a sacrifice of individual feeling I make to a sense of public duty.

"With grateful acknowledgment and unfeigned thanks for the personal respect and evidences of condolence expressed by Congress, and your self. I remain, very respectfully, sir, Your most obedient and humble servant, Martha Washington."

A pity she could not know that it would be nearly fifty years before the ground would be broken for such a monument, eighty-five before it would be completed, and that long before that time she would be lying beside him, not to be moved, in the new vault he had wanted built at the foot of the Vineyard Enclosure.

Lawrence had returned from New Kent to take over the management of the farms. Though he had already begun to build his own house on Gray's Hill, he and Nelly assured Martha that they would remain at Mount Vernon as long as they were needed. Wash also returned, sobered and anxious to prove his worthiness of the trust George had placed in him, designating him as one of his executors as soon as he should be twenty-one. The household returned to as near a normal state as possible, but like a ship devoid of its rudder or a watch which has lost its mainspring.

Martha spent no time idling or grieving. She was as busy as ever, busier, for there were duties George had attended to which she felt could not be trusted to overseers or servants—seeing that poorer neighbors had all the fish they needed when the seines were drawn and that the extra shad and herring were properly stored in kegs in the salt house; that the fires in the smokehouse were banked well to slowly cure the huge shanks of hams and bacon; that the gardener was planting all the necessary herbs in the kitchen garden and that George's favorite imported plants in the Greenhouse were not neglected. And of course there were the constant visitors to receive and entertain, President and Mrs. Adams, Governor Trumbull, foreign dignitaries, lords, ladies, barons, neighbors, relatives, strangers. Always she was ready for them, no matter who they were or what hour of the day, kindly, hospitable, serene, simply but tastefully dressed, trim, well groomed, tidy.

"In her dress, though plain," grandson George Washington Parke Custis was to note in his *Recollections*, "she was so scrupulously neat, that ladies have often wondered how Mrs. Washington could wear a gown for a week, go through her kitchen and laundries, and all the varieties of places in the routine of domestic management, and yet the gown retained its snow-like whiteness, unsullied by even a single speck."

Though now all the snowy whiteness was in caps, cuffs, kerchiefs, the blacks of mourning gowns were just as faultlessly correct and neat.

Morning, noon, and night she gave guests the same hospitable welcome, as the Reverend Manasseh Cutler, arriving one morning with six other unexpected men, could and did testify:

"We were received in the most polite and cordial manner, and handsomely entertained . . . When our coaches entered the yard, a number of servants immediately attended, and when we had all stepped out of our Carriages, a servant conducted us to Madam Washington's room, where we were received in a very cordial and obliging manner . . . Mrs. Washington appears much older than when I saw her last at Philadelphia, but her countenance very little wrinkled and remarkably fair for a person of her years . . . She regretted that we had not arrived sooner, for she always breakfasted at seven, but our breakfast would be ready in a few minutes. In a short time she rose, and desired us to walk into another room, where a table was elegantly spread with ham, cold corn beef, cold fowl, red herring and cold mutton, the dishes ornamented with sprigs of parsley and other vegetables from the garden.

"At the head of the table was the tea and coffee equipage, where she seated herself, and sent the tea and coffee to the company. We were all Federalists, which evidently gave her particular pleasure. Her remarks were frequently pointed and sometimes very sarcastic, on the new order of things, and the present administration. She spoke of the General with great affection, and observed that, though she had many favors and mercies, for which she desired to bless God, she felt as if she was become a stranger among her friends, and could welcome the time when she should be called to follow her deceased friend."

Favors and mercies, yes, and she enjoyed them, rejoiced with Nelly and Lawrence in the birth of their second little girl, Angela, and the building of their lovely new home not far away, to be called Woodlawn; in Wash's plans to build himself a house on property he had inherited on the Potomac, across the river from the new Federal City, which he was going to call Arlington, after old John Custis's home on the eastern shore of the Bay. She was heartened by his growing maturity, amused by his agility in avoiding matrimonial involvement.

Days passed, months, years, two of them since she had entered this half-life which was more existence than real living. It was 1802, and she was seventy years old. She was beginning to feel tired now when her day's work was not nearly finished. The two flights of stairs leading to her little garret room seemed to have become steeper and longer.

Suddenly she knew there were two things she must do. It was March, and everywhere the buds were swelling. The willows were turning gold. She wished she could get out in the garden and dig, feel warm earth against her fingers. Much more to her taste than sitting at her little desk, picking up her quill, and writing, slowly, painfully, trying to decide!

"In the name of God, Amen." That was the way such things must be started. Now what?

"I, Martha Washington, of Mount Vernon, in the county of Fairfax, being of sound mind . . ." Others would have to put it into proper words, so it would be legal. Now all she must do was think what must be done with all the multiplicity of *things*. Money to her nieces, of course. The silver plate and many other objects to Wash, the Cincinnati tea and table china, pictures, the new bedstead made in Philadelphia, books, all except her large Bible and her Book of Common Prayer. Other things to her granddaughters, especially to Nelly, looking glasses, chairs, marble table, plated ware, linen, all for her new house. Money for the education of her sisters' and brothers' children. George's will had already provided for the freeing of all their slaves as soon as she was gone.

It was done, put into proper form and signed in the presence of four witnesses, two of whom were Lawrence Lewis and her granddaughter Martha Peter, on March 4, 1802.

The other task? It would require no witnesses. In fact, there must be none, for someone might object. She chose a time when Lawrence and Nelly were at the new house, Tobias Lear in the library busy at his tremendous job of sorting and classifying all of George's official papers. A fire was burning in the little parlor. She could be alone. One by one she took them, the letters she and George had written to each other through the years, and laid them on the fire, watching them, like the events and thoughts and emotions they chronicled, blaze up, then sink into forgetfulness. It was not paper that she saw there burning, flaring for a moment into vivid, bold relief, then shriveling into ash to rejoin things long since gone. It was all the years of their life together, laid reverently on the altar of memory.

An altar, she thought, was for sacrifice, an offering made possible through searing pain. So many of the letters were such—from Cambridge, from Morristown, from Valley Forge! There had been almost a smell of gunpowder, of danger, of death on them, yet how eagerly she had read them, hoping for the summons that would take her with him into all that uncertainty and struggle! Yes, even the few from New York and Philadelphia and Mount Vernon during those seemingly endless "lost days" of the Presidency had carried with them the pain of sacrifice. Now they became just another burnt offering, symbols of the sixteen long years that they had both given for freedom and love of country.

But an altar was for thanksgiving also. This one giving her permission to come to Cambridge in the dead of winter—what joy and excitement it had brought! How swiftly she had rushed to make ready! And these telling of hope and victory, from Trenton and Princeton and Yorktown . . . if only the latter had not told also of Jack lying sick—dying! But, as she had long ago learned and accepted, life and death were closely intermingled.

A hearth was an altar, too, this one, warm and glowing with so many memories. She lingered long over letters they had written to each other from Mount Vernon, telling of little things that did not concern the world, only themselves—trees budding, fish running, a good crop of wheat, the number of hams in the smokehouse, new trees being planted. Slowly she fed them into the blaze. Now and then a phrase, a paragraph boldly limned against the flames would rouse another stab of memory before slipping into the past. She had read them all during past days, had kept out only two to once more reread, hidden away in an inner drawer of her little writing desk, the ones telling of his new duties as Commander in Chief, when he had first used the words "My Dearest." What conflicting emotions they had aroused! But that had been the pattern of her life—joy and pain, sacrifice, thanksgiving, the warmth and contentment of home. Looking back, she saw that it was good.

There! It was done. Nothing but ashes of the past remained. She could not know the frustration, the anguish this act of burning would cause in the next hundred, two hundred years, and she would not have cared. The papers in the library must be preserved, of course, for they belonged to the rest of the world. But these were their own, nobody else's business. They belonged only to themselves.

It was May, most beautiful of all months at Mount Vernon. The apple trees would be in bloom and the lilacs. The gardens would be a riot of spring color. A pity to be laid up with an attack of the old bilious fever when she longed to be out of doors! But at least it was warm enough for the window to be open, and Nelly had brought a bouquet of fragrant lilacs up to her third-floor room.

"You shouldn't be bothering with me," she told her anxiously. "I know you're anxious to be on with your packing. And—please, child, don't feel you have to postpone moving as you planned, now that the new house is nearly ready. You know these attacks of mine don't last very long."

But this one was different. She could tell by the look on Dr. Craik's face, which always seemed to be there, hovering over her, day after day, every time she opened her eyes; by the other faces, so many of them, gathered about, looking so anxious; by the tiptoeings and hushed whispers. Poor Dr. Craik, trying so hard with all his bleedings and blisterings and little doses of calomel and "Jesuit's bark" and all the rest! She wished she could make them all understand that in spite of the raging heat in her body she was happy and at peace. As long as she could she talked cheerfully, giving them encouragement and advice, speaking to them of the blessings of Christian faith and divine promises.

How long had she been lying like this—waiting? "Seventeen days," she heard someone say. Could it have been that long—or that short? It seemed like just a day—or forever.

Things began to look vague, objects to blur, but the faces were still there, familiar, so dearly loved. No . . . one was missing. Good. George must be away on a trip somewhere. He worried so when she was sick. How many times she had tried to keep going during one of these attacks until he was away, then gone thankfully to bed! She must manage somehow to be up and about when he returned.

Someone lifted her head and shoulders. Wash? No, it couldn't be. Little Wash was her baby. This was a man, gentle, as strong almost as George. The taste of bread was in her mouth, a goblet of wine pressed to her lips. She must be in a church, to be receiving the Sacrament. But where? In St. Peter's? No, that had been long ago, in New Kent. Pohick Church? No. It was good Dr. Davis looking down at her, so it must be Christ Church, Alexandria . . . No, it was not a church, after all. She was here in her own garret bedroom, and there was the window. She wished she could get up once more and look down across the lawn where George . . . But the window looked dark. It must be night, for the candles were lighted. There would be nothing to see from the window. And, anyway, George wasn't there. He had gone away somewhere—but to what place? She couldn't remember the name. There were so many places. Cambridge? Something called a Valley— Valley . . . It didn't matter. All that mattered was that he had written asking her to come. He wanted her. She must hurry, so much to do to get ready, food to pack, clothes . . .

"Nelly," she said suddenly, clearly, and there Nelly was beside her, tearful for some reason, she couldn't imagine why.

"Yes, Grandmama?"

She struggled to lift her head from the pillows. "My white gown, Nelly dear—the one I've been saving—remember? Bring it here, please —I'll be needing it—for this journey—"

"Yes, dear Grandmama. Don't worry. You shall have it. I understand."

There! She drew a long sigh and sank back contentedly against the pillows. The chariot was packed. Everything was ready. It would be a long way, through country where she had never been. But George would be waiting for her. It was time to go.

"It's just midnight," someone said softly.

"Yes," said another. "And now it's Sunday, her day of rest."

"Died, at Mount Vernon," reported the Washington *Federalist*, "on Saturday evening, the 22nd ultimo, widow of the late illustrious General George Washington. To those amiable and Christian virtues, which adorn the female character, she added dignity of manners, superiority of understanding, a mind intelligent and elevated. The silence of respectful grief is our best eulogy."

PARTIAL LIST OF SOURCES

Andrews, Marietta Minnigerode. *George Washington's Country*. New York: E. P. Dutton and Co., 1930

Bellamy, Francis Rufus. *The Private Life of George Washington*. New York: Thomas Y. Crowell Co., 1951

Boller, Paul F., Jr. *George Washington and Religion*. Dallas, Texas: Southern Methodist University Press, 1963

Booth, Sally Smith. *The Women of '76*. New York: Hastings House, 1973

Bourne, Miriam Anne. *First Family: George Washington and His Intimate Relations*. New York: W. W. Norton and Co., 1982

Bowen, Catherine Drinker. *John Adams and the American Revolution*. Boston: Little, Brown and Co. An Atlantic Monthly Press Book, 1950

Busch, Noel F. *Winter Quarters: George Washington and the Continental Army at Valley Forge*. New York: Liveright, 1974

Cary, Wilson Miles. *Sally Cary*. New York: The De Vinne Press, 1916

Conkling, Margaret C. *Memoirs of the Mother and Wife of Washington*. Auburn, Derby, Miller and Co., 1851

Corbin, John. *The Unknown Washington*. New York: Charles Scribner's Sons, 1930

Cunliffe, Marcus. *George Washington: Man and Monument*. Boston: Little, Brown and Co., 1958

Custis, George Washington Parke. *Recollections and Private Memoirs of Washington. By his Adopted Son*. Philadelphia: William Flint, 1859

Custis, Nelly. Fictitious Diary, 1789–1799

Desmond, Alice Curtis. *Martha Washington: Our First Lady*. New York: Dodd, Mead and Co., 1942

Dutton, Joan Parry. *Plants of Colonial Williamsburg*. Williamsburg, Va.: The Colonial Williamsburg Foundation, 1979

Earle, Alice Morse. *Child Life in Colonial Days*. Norwood, Mass.: The Macmillan Co., 1899

———. *Costume of Colonial Times*. New York: Charles Scribner's Sons, 1894

———. *Two Centuries of Costume in America*. New York: The Macmillan Co., 1903

————. *Home Life in Colonial Days*. New York: The Macmillan Co., 1931

Fay, Bernard. *George Washington: Republican Aristocrat*. Boston and New York: Houghton Mifflin Co., 1931

Fede, Helen Maggs. *Washington Furniture at Mount Vernon*. Mount Vernon, Va.: Mount Vernon Ladies' Association, 1956

Forbes, Esther. *Paul Revere and the World He Lived In*. Boston: Houghton Mifflin Co., 1942

Ford, Paul Leicester. *Washington and the Theatre*. New York: Benjamin Blom, 1899. Reissued, 1967

Freeman, Douglas Southall. *George Washington: A Biography*. Seven volumes. New York: Charles Scribner's Sons, 1948–

Goettel, Elinor. *America's Wars—Why?* Chapter I, "The American Revolution." New York: Julian Messner, 1972

Headley, Hon. J. T. *The Illustrated Life of Washington. Together with an Interesting Account of Mount Vernon as It Is*. New York: G. F. Bill, 1859

Heusser, Albert H. *In the Footsteps of Washington*. Paterson, N.J.: Privately published at 334–446 Godwin Street, 1921

Hughes, Rupert. *George Washington: The Human Being and the Hero, 1732–1762*. New York: William Morrow and Co., 1926

Knollenburg, Bernhard. *George Washington, the Virginia Period*. Durham, N.C.: Duke University Press, 1964

Lear, Tobias. *Letters and Recollections of George Washington. Being Letters to Tobias Lear and Others Between 1790 and 1799*. Garden City, N.Y.: Doubleday, Doran and Co., Inc., 1932

Lewis, Nelly Custis. *Housekeeping Book*. Mount Vernon, Va.: Mount Vernon Ladies' Association.

Lossing, Benson J. *Martha Washington*. New York: J. C. Buttre, 1864

————. *Mary and Martha: The Mother and the Wife of George Washington*. New York: Harper and Brothers, 1886

————. *The Home of Washington, or Mount Vernon and Its Associations*. New York: Virtue and Yorston, 1871

Maxims of Washington, Political, Social, Moral, and Religious. Compiled and arranged by John Frederick Schroeder, D.D. Mount Vernon, Va.: Mount Vernon Ladies' Association, 1974

McClellan, Elizabeth. *Historic Dress in America, 1607–1800*. Philadelphia: George W. Jacobs and Co., 1904

Moore, Charles. *The Family Life of George Washington*. Boston and New York: Houghton Mifflin Co., 1926

Mount Vernon, An Illustrated Handbook. Mount Vernon, Va.: Mount Vernon Ladies' Association, 1974

Mount Vernon Ladies' Association of the Union. *Annual Reports*, 1966–1980. Mount Vernon, Va.: Mount Vernon Ladies' Association

Niles, Blair. *Martha's Husband: An Informal Portrait of George Washington.* New York: McGraw-Hill Book Co., 1951

Nordham, George W. *George Washington's Women: Mary, Martha, Sally, and 146 Others.* Philadelphia and Ardmore, Pa.: Dorrance and Co., 1977

Padovar, Saul K. *The Washington Papers.* New York: Harper and Brothers, 1955

Pryor, Mrs. Roger A. *The Mother of Washington and Her Times.* New York: The Macmillan Co., 1903

Sawyer, Joseph Dillaway. *Washington.* New York: The Macmillan Co., 1927

Schmit, Patricia Brady, ed. *Nelly Custis Lewis' Housekeeping Book.* New Orleans, La.: The Historic New Orleans Collection, 1982

Sears, Louis Martin. *George Washington.* New York: Thomas Y. Crowell, 1932

Somerville, Mollie. *Washington Walked Here: Alexandria on the Potomac.* Washington, D.C.: National Society of the Daughters of the American Revolution, 1970, 1981

Sparks, Jared. *The Life of George Washington.* Boston: Ferdinand Andrews, 1839

Special News Releases. Relating to the Life and Times of George Washington. Prepared and issued by the U.S. George Washington Bicentennial Commission, 1932

Stephenson, Nathaniel, and Dunn, Waldo Hilary. *George Washington.* New York, London: Oxford University Press, 1940

Stetson, Charles W. *Washington and His Neighbors.* Richmond, Va.: Garrett and Massie, Inc., 1956

Steward, Austin. *Twenty-two Years a Slave and Forty Years a Freeman.* Menlo Park, Calif.: Addison-Wesley Publishing Co., 1969

Tebbel, John. *George Washington's America.* New York: E. P. Dutton and Co., 1954

Thane, Elswyth. *Washington's Lady.* New York: Dodd, Mead and Co., 1954, 1959, 1960

————. *Potomac Squire.* Mount Vernon, Va.: Mount Vernon Ladies' Association, 1963

Thayer, William Roscoe. *George Washington.* Boston: Houghton Mifflin Co., 1922

Virginia: A Guide to the Old Dominion. Compiled by workers of the Writers' Projects Administration in the State of Virginia. American Guide Series. New York: Oxford University Press, 1940

Warwick, Edward; Pitz, Henry C.; Wyckoff, Alexander. *Early American Dress: The Colonial and Revolutionary Period.* New York: Benjamin Blom, 1965

Weems, Mason L. *The Life of Washington*. Edited by Marcus Cunliffe. Cambridge, Mass.: The Belknap Press of Harvard University Press, 1962

Wharton, Anne Hollingsworth. *Martha Washington*. New York: Charles Scribner's Sons, 1897

Williamsburg, Virginia: A Brief Study in Photographs. Williamsburg, Va.: Colonial Williamsburg, Inc., 1940

Wilson, Woodrow. *George Washington*. New York: Harper and Brothers, 1896, 1924

Wilstach, Paul. *Mount Vernon: Washington's Home and the Nation's Shrine*. Garden City, N.Y.: Doubleday and Page and Co., 1925

Wish, Harvey. *Slavery in the South*. New York: The Noonday Press, a division of Farrar, Straus and Co., 1964

Woodward, W. E. *George Washington: The Image and the Man*. New York: Liveright Publishing Corp., 1946

―――. *Tom Paine: America's Godfather*. New York: E. P. Dutton and Co., 1945

Young, Joanne (text), and Lewis, Jr., Taylor (photos). *Washington's Mount Vernon*. Mount Vernon, Va.: Mount Vernon Ladies' Association, 1980

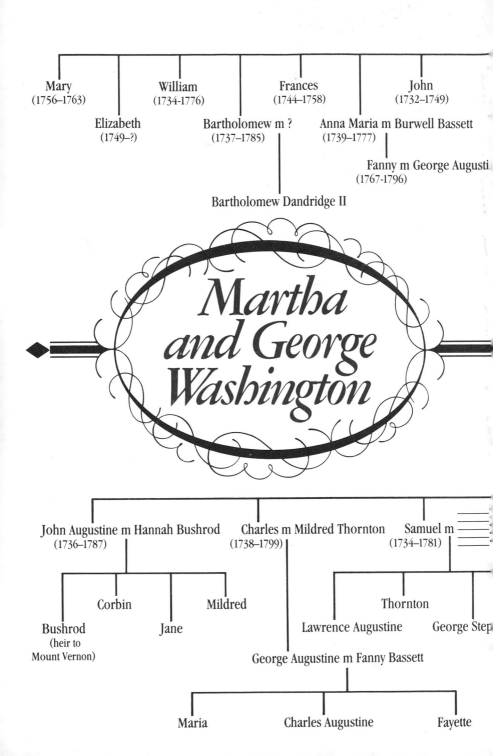

Mary
(1756–1763)

Elizabeth
(1749–?)

William
(1734-1776)

Bartholomew m ?
(1737–1785)

Frances
(1744–1758)

Anna Maria m Burwell Bassett
(1739–1777)

John
(1732–1749)

Fanny m George Augusti
(1767-1796)

Bartholomew Dandridge II

Martha and George Washington

John Augustine m Hannah Bushrod
(1736–1787)

Charles m Mildred Thornton
(1738–1799)

Samuel m

Bushrod
(heir to
Mount Vernon)

Corbin

Jane

Mildred

Thornton

Lawrence Augustine

George Step

George Augustine m Fanny Bassett

Maria

Charles Augustine

Fayette